Praise for
An Unlasting [Home]

"So fresh and unsettling that it will ench[ant] [...]
page and linger for days after reading. . . . [...] . . . . Its
epic family saga style echoes that of Hala Alyan's *Salt Houses* and
The Arsonists' City, Ayad Akhtar's *Homeland Elegies,* and Min Jin Lee's
Pachinko."

—*Los Angeles Review of Books*

"Deeply enchanting, at times suspenseful, and always engaging,
An Unlasting Home is filled with tales of women's lives and their
intersection with the often volatile and unpredictable currents
of nations, war, and political history. Mai Al-Nakib's storyteller's
voice is fresh and original—her book grabbed me from the out-
set and kept me entranced to the last page."

—Diana Abu-Jaber, author of *Fencing with the King* and *Crescent*

"*An Unlasting Home* is an unforgettable story of people making
choices for love, family, freedom, and identity against the tidal
forces of history in the Arab region. Shimmering with poetic
prose and as pressingly real as the white heat of August in Baghdad, this poignant debut will keep you in its thrall."

—Juhea Kim, author of *Beasts of a Little Land*

"A spellbinding family history unfolds as a Kuwaiti woman goes
on trial for blasphemy in a world gone mad. Deftly written and
structurally brilliant, *An Unlasting Home* is a lasting novel that
splits open time and leaps across continents. Mai Al-Nakib cre-
ates the sort of characters we carry forward into our hearts and
lives. I absolutely loved this book."

—A. Manette Ansay, *New York Times*
bestselling author of *Blue Water*

an
unlasting
home

an unlasting home

a novel

Mai Al-Nakib

MARINER BOOKS
New York   Boston

HarperCollins books may be purchased for educational, business, or sales promotional use. For information, please email the Special Markets Department at SPsales@harpercollins.com.

A hardcover edition of this book was published in 2022 by Mariner Books, an imprint of HarperCollins Publishers.

FIRST MARINER BOOKS PAPERBACK EDITION PUBLISHED 2023.

Designed by Jen Overstreet

Library of Congress Cataloging-in-Publication Data

Names: Al-Nakib, Mai, 1970- author.
Title: An unlasting home : a novel / Mai Al-Nakib.
Description: New York : Mariner Books, 2022.
Identifiers: LCCN 2021045384 (print) | LCCN 2021045385 (ebook) | ISBN 9780063135093 (hardcover) | ISBN 9780063135109 (trade paperback) | ISBN 9780063135116 (ebook)
Subjects: LCSH: Women, Arab—Fiction. | Families—Fiction. | LCGFT: Fiction.
Classification: LCC PS3601.L28 U55 2022 (print) | LCC PS3601.L28 (ebook) | DDC 813/.6—dc23
LC record available at https://lccn.loc.gov/2021045384
LC ebook record available at https://lccn.loc.gov/2021045385

ISBN 978-0-06-313510-9

23 24 25 26 27 LBC 5 4 3 2 1

For the women who made me

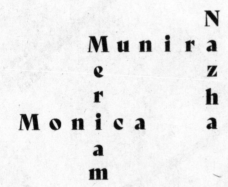

Munira
Nazha
Meriam
Monica

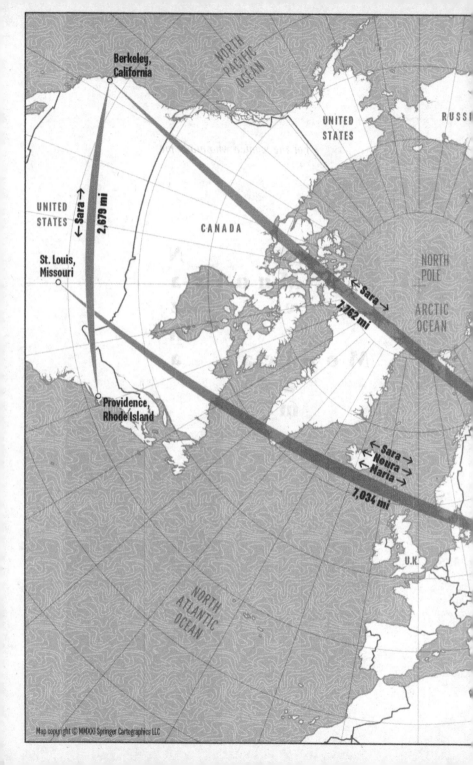

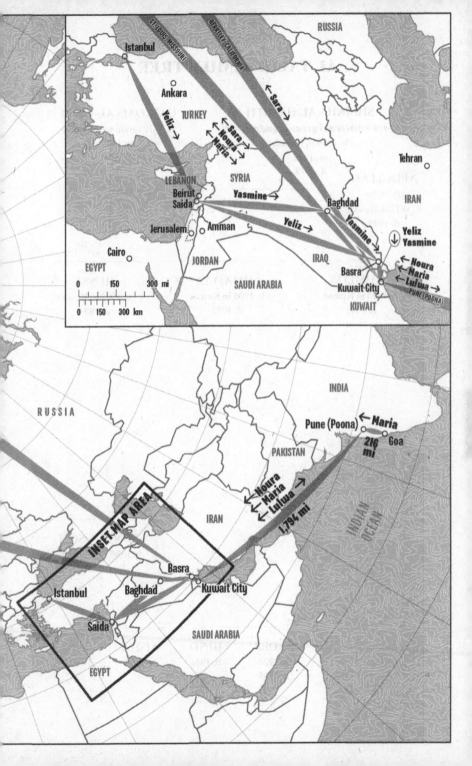

AL-TALIB FAMILY TREE

SHEIKHA AL-HAMITH
[Sara's maternal great-grandmother]
b. 1889 in Kuwait
m. 1902
d. 1979

QAIS QAIS AL-TALIB
b. 1875 unknown location
m. 1902
d. 1928

ABDULLAH
[her brother]
b. 1872 in Kuwait
d. 1899

AHMED
b. 1903 in Kuwait
d. 1992

SUMAIYYA
b. 1905 in Kuwait
d. 1993

HUSSA
b. 1907 in Kuwait
d. 1994

SON
b. 1895

SON
b. 1897

BADER
b. 1926
d. 1967

HIND
b. 1936

AISHA
b. 1938

DANA
b. 1944

LULWA QAIS AL-TALIB
[Sara's maternal grandmother]
b. 1909 in Kuwait
m. 1924 to **Mubarak Al-Mustafa**
d. 1995

AL-MUSTAFA FAMILY TREE

ZAINEB AL-FATEH
b. 1879 in Kuwait
m. 1894
d. 1955

KHALIFA KHALID AL-MUSTAFA
b. 1869 in Kuwait
m. 1894
d. 1936

SON
b. 1900

MUBARAK KHALIFA AL-MUSTAFA
[Sara's maternal grandfather]
b. 1907 in Poona, India
m. 1924 to **Lulwa Al-Talib**
d. 1978

HAYYA
b. 1908 in Poona, India
m. 1932
d. 1973

NOURA MUBARAK AL-MUSTAFA
[Sara's mother]
b. 1945 in Poona, India
m. 1968 to **Tarek Al-Ameed**
d. 2001

MARZOUK
b. 1947

MAZEN
b. 1949

SULEIMAN FAMILY TREE

YELIZ ELMAS
[Sara's paternal great-grandmother]
b. 1898 in Istanbul, Turkey
m. 1915
d. 1989

HUSSEIN SULEIMAN
b. 1893 in Saida, Lebanon
m. 1915
d. 1933

HASSAN
[his brother]
b. 1890 in Saida, Lebanon
d. 1933

HIKMET BEY
[her father's cousin]
b. 1871
disappears c. 1928

DR. SHERIF
[his friend in Iraq]
b. 1888

YASMINE HUSSEIN SULEIMAN
[Sara's paternal grandmother]
b. 1916 in Saida, Lebanon
m. 1935 to **Marwan Al-Ameed**
d. 2010

YOUSEF
b. 1917 in Saida, Lebanon
m. 1957
d. 1997

MALIK
b. 1936

SELMA
b. 1937

HISHAM
b. 1938
m. 1970 to Clara
d. 1991

AL-AMEED FAMILY TREE

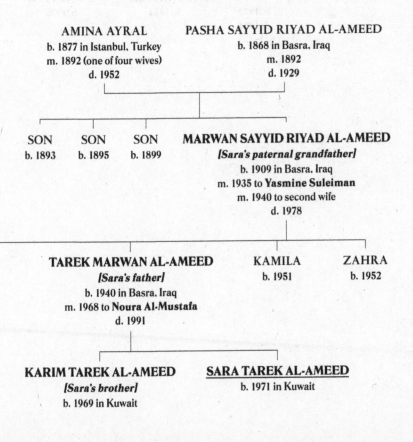

AMINA AYRAL
b. 1877 in Istanbul, Turkey
m. 1892 (one of four wives)
d. 1952

PASHA SAYYID RIYAD AL-AMEED
b. 1868 in Basra, Iraq
m. 1892
d. 1929

SON
b. 1893

SON
b. 1895

SON
b. 1899

MARWAN SAYYID RIYAD AL-AMEED
[Sara's paternal grandfather]
b. 1909 in Basra, Iraq
m. 1935 to **Yasmine Suleiman**
m. 1940 to second wife
d. 1978

TAREK MARWAN AL-AMEED
[Sara's father]
b. 1940 in Basra, Iraq
m. 1968 to **Noura Al-Mustafa**
d. 1991

KAMILA
b. 1951

ZAHRA
b. 1952

KARIM TAREK AL-AMEED
[Sara's brother]
b. 1969 in Kuwait

SARA TAREK AL-AMEED
b. 1971 in Kuwait

D'SOUZA-TORRES FAMILY TREE

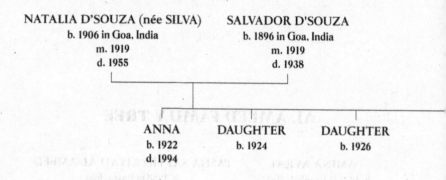

NATALIA D'SOUZA (née SILVA)
b. 1906 in Goa, India
m. 1919
d. 1955

SALVADOR D'SOUZA
b. 1896 in Goa, India
m. 1919
d. 1938

ANNA
b. 1922
d. 1994

DAUGHTER
b. 1924

DAUGHTER
b. 1926

MARIA TORRES (née D'SOUZA)

[Sara's ayah]
b. 1930 in Goa, India
m. 1948 to **Lazarus Torres**
d. 2013

b. 1921 in Poona, India
d. 1965

SALVADOR
b. 1950 in Goa, India
m. 1978 to Lucilla
d. 1995

Lazarus
b. 1980 in
Kuwait

CHRISTINA
b. 1955 in Goa, India
m. 1978 to Anthony

Natalia
b. 1980 in
Kuwait

JOSEFINA
b. 1960 in Goa, India
m. 1982 to John

Maria
b. 1986 in
Kuwait

And yet they are in us, these people long since passed away, as a disposition, as a load weighing on our destinies, as a murmur in the blood and as a gesture that rises up out of the depths of time.

—RILKE

I

S

Lulwa

r

Yasmine

Sara

I open my eyes to a bloodred sky. I submitted my grades a few days ago; now I have three months to think and write. Karl comes in July. I visit Karim in August. But today, under the indifferent rust of a desert storm, it's just Maria and me.

Still in my pajamas, I skip down the stairs to the kitchen. Its walnut cabinets and Formica counters are worn, nearly thirty-six years in use, but the ochre fridge and stove gleam under Maria's care. Maria stands guard over the warming milk, daring it to froth over. She cracks three cardamom pods with her teeth, as she always does, and tosses them into the pan.

"Gross, Maria!" I tease, as I always do.

She spins around and cackles at me, reaches out as if to pull my hair. I wrap my arms around the back of her shoulders and kiss her on the cheek. I may be forty-one, but my days in the Surra house with Maria make me feel ten.

After breakfast, Maria chats on the phone with one of her daughters, and I go up to my parents' bedroom. I sit at my father's desk, which faces the long window looking out on a garden wall pink with bougainvillea. At this desk my father wrote articles for prestigious medical journals, keeping himself current with the literature. I've changed nothing here. Not the enormous four-poster bed that never quite fit the seventies vibe of the house. Not the avocado-green walls that remind me of hospitals. Not the shelves stuffed with decades of *The New England Journal of Medicine* and my mother's copies of Fanon and Arendt. I write at my father's desk late into evening, but I spend every night in my childhood bed.

Around noon I smell cumin and coriander. Maria is making something special. This will upset Aasif, who will ask whether his food isn't good enough that Maria must cook also? I'll reassure him, as usual: "Your food is famous all over Kuwait. One little plate of bhajia won't change that. It makes Maria feel useful. You can understand, no?" Aasif will snort, but the swollen vein on his forehead will deflate. Maria will cross her eyes at me behind his back, and calm will return to the kitchen.

I head downstairs for lunch, and Lola the cat follows. She's more Maria's than mine, but she enjoys the warmth of my lap. As soon as she sees me, Maria announces, "Josie's getting a raise!"

"At last!"

"She had to wait. Kuwaitis first."

"I know. It's not fair. I'm so happy for Josie. You're a good mother, Maria."

She smiles, but I catch the fleeting wince. I hold my breath, and it passes.

I finish off her samosas. We drink our tea with extra sugar, then Maria heads to her room to nap. I go back up to my father's desk, this time with an idea to write an essay on what teaching philosophy at the primary level in Kuwaiti public schools might achieve. In the thirteen years prior to their arrival at university, the capacity of young people to think is liquidated. They take everything literally. Supplementing the religious curriculum with an early introduction to philosophy could, I will argue, change that.

About an hour into my work, the doorbell rings. I'm surprised. We aren't used to afternoon intrusions.

Aasif, groggy from his nap, knocks on my open door a few minutes later. "Two police outside, Sara."

I slip on my flip-flops and grab a shirt to wear over my tank top. The public municipality probably needs me to move my car so that it can dig up the sidewalk for new water or sewage pipes.

Outside, the sky is still red. Two men stand a few steps below the front gate. "Duktora Sara Tarek Al-Ameed?" one of them asks.

I nod and smile reflexively. "That's me."

"You're under arrest for blasphemy. Please go inside and get what you need for a few nights in jail. We'll wait." My face must convey a total lack of comprehension because he repeats what he's said more slowly: "You are under arrest for blasphemy by order of the recent amendment to Article 111 of the Penal Code of the State of Kuwait. Please put a few things into a clear plastic bag and come with us."

I consider anyone I might know with some connection to the police, someone who would pull a stunt like this. "You must be kidding!" I say after a minute or two. "Who put you up to this?" I can think of no one.

"Duktora, this is no joke. Go inside, please, prepare your belongings, and come back out." He sounds impatient this time.

Suddenly I feel detached, floating upward. My pulse is not

racing. My breathing remains steady. Aasif fidgets behind me, slamming me back to earth. "Aasif, say nothing to Maria. Tell her I had to go to Bahrain to meet someone for work, that I'll be back tomorrow or in a few days."

"I will." His eyes reflect the fear I cannot feel.

"Please make sure she eats. And change Lola's litter? Maria can't manage."

He nods.

"Don't forget Bebe Mitu."

"I won't. Don't worry, Sara."

I rush to my room, stuff a few things into a Ziploc, and call a colleague whose father is a civil rights lawyer.

"Hanan, there are two policemen outside saying I'm being arrested for blasphemy. I don't understand what they're talking about."

She groans. "It's the new law."

"What law?" I haven't paid attention to any laws, new or old. Unlike my mother, I'm not politically inclined. My palms start to sweat. "What do I do? Do I go with them?"

"Go with them, but don't say anything. Take your phone with you, and text your location when you get there. If you can't, it's okay. We'll find you."

Muhannad Al-Baatin, Hanan's father, my new lawyer, is standing in front of the building—a black-brick monstrosity in the middle of Kuwait City—when the police pull up. He is tall and wide as an elephant. Mine is not the first blasphemy case, it seems, so he knows where to find me. I'm in the habit of flipping through the daily papers, so how I missed this development, I'm not sure. But if I'm honest, I've kept myself removed for so long, my ignorance is no great mystery.

Mr. Al-Baatin booms instructions at me as the gray officers, diminished in the face of my lawyer's presence, lead me up the stairs and through the glass doors. "Don't answer any questions! A student recorded one of your lectures. A member of parliament has raised a case. Sara, pay attention to what I'm saying! Not a word, do you hear me?" I have a hard time following any of it, but I hold on to his last words: "You'll be out tomorrow morning."

The small, filthy cell in the women's section of the building is beautiful in its way, covered with words in many languages. Arabic, Urdu, Tagalog, Malayalam, French, Hindi, English. The three walls, the low ceiling, the floor, even the toilet—every inch of space etched with words. Messages from one woman to another or to someone far away.

I try to recollect the faces of all the students I taught during the spring semester. Three all-girls classes, twenty students per class, sixty students total. I think of them sitting in the circle I make them arrange themselves into so that we can discuss things more equally. It doesn't quite work the way it did at Berkeley, but I persist, hoping the circle will make them brave. My accuser had to be in my eight-o'clock Intro to Phil class. A freshman offended to learn not everyone believes the same truth. I go around the circle in my mind, trying to pinpoint faces, to remember names. The girls in their hijab and niqab blend together. It's bigoted of me to think so, but they're hard to tell apart. I can't single anyone out.

I give up on my class and turn to the walls of the cell. Poems, laments, prayers to God, cries for mothers. *Please, Ma, save me.* I feel cradled by thousands of writing hands, their fear blending with mine, outsiders in a closed country. They were here before me. How many were deported home? I have nowhere to be deported to. And yet, their words of longing lull me, allowing me to drift into pockets of sleep.

Mr. Al-Baatin comes to collect me the next morning. I sign some sort of pledge and am released on my own recognizance. He drives me home and stays for tea. The dainty love seat gives off dust the instant he sits on it; the formal sala has been neglected for months.

"A recording was made by one of your students," Mr. Al-Baatin tells me. "On the recording you were heard stating that God is dead. The student handed the recording to the most conservative member of parliament. The Salafi MP, on behalf of the student, has lodged a complaint against you. The public prosecution has filed a case. You are being accused of blasphemy under the new law designating it a capital crime." He pauses. "Thankfully the law has provisions. You may be allowed to retract before the trial even begins. But *if* you are found guilty—and I assure you, that would be a highly improbable outcome—execution is not guaranteed." My blood freezes. "Even if all appeals are overturned, you should be allowed to retract your 'blasphemous statement' before the final judge and that could influence the punishment." He makes little curly signs in the air with his forefingers for scare quotes. Derrida made the sign for scare quotes exactly the same way in a lecture he gave at Berkeley. Derrida and Berkeley are deserts apart from Mr. Al-Baatin and Kuwait, but unexpectedly in this gesture they aren't.

I focus on Mr. Al-Baatin's statements. I don't like the sound of the words *should* and *could*.

"In that case, the sentence would likely be commuted to five years in prison and a ten-thousand-dinar fine."

I don't like the sound of the word *likely*.

He pauses again, an elephant with its eyes shut. "In the meantime, as the case proceeds—and these cases can go on for years—you are not permitted to leave the country. You are free to work, and you will be paid. Apart from travel, you can do whatever you please." Mr. Al-Baatin winks at me incongruously. I stare back in shock as he continues. "Within the bounds of the law."

I have been living with this accusation for seven days. A week like a lifetime.

Maria doesn't know. It'll kill her, with her heart of stents and scars. I tell Aasif and beg him not to share the news. Aasif, a man of integrity, will remain chup chaap. He closes his eyes and tilts his chin upward, hides the newspapers from Maria, my face plastered on the front pages.

Unable to sleep, I've been holding vigil with Bebe Mitu beside his cage on the landing of the stairs. Bebe Mitu—Mama Lulwa's African gray parrot—keeps a trace of my grandmother alive. She brought Bebe Mitu back from India almost sixty years ago. Mama Lulwa never wanted to return to Kuwait, but she didn't have a choice. Nobody made me come back, and now I couldn't leave if I wanted to. So here I am—unlikely caretaker of an ancient parrot, accidental collector of fading traces—stuck in place.

Lulwa

One August morning in 1924, Lulwa woke to the chirps of thirsty sparrows and warblers lined along the low parapet surrounding the sateh. Lulwa, her brother, and two sisters, like most of the townsfolk of old Kuwait, slept on the flat roof of their mudbrick home during the summer months to catch the sea breeze.

Lulwa rolled her bedding, tied it with a pink ribbon that had slipped out of the basket of a visiting seamstress. She tiptoed over her brother and sisters. The heat would wake them soon enough. She hoisted the bedroll on her hipbone and hauled it down the narrow stairs leading to the central courtyard.

Her mother, Sheikha, had completed her fajer prayers but remained seated on her threadbare mat in a corner of the liwan. She often sat this way after morning prayers, still as sea stone. Lulwa wrapped her thin arms around her mother's waist, inhaling yesterday's trace of dihin 'oud.

Sheikha stiffened. "You're too old for all this, Lulwa."

Lulwa tightened her grip. She was a few weeks into fifteen, slender but strong.

Sheikha felt like she was being punished for the news she was about to break. At thirteen, she herself had been forced to marry a twenty-seven-year-old stranger. Sheikha's father accepted the proposal because he had mistaken the pompous, bisht-wearing Qais Qais Al-Talib for a successful merchant. The man was not known in Kuwait Town, but Sheikha's father could not afford to reject the generous dowry he offered. The amount promised to buy him and his sons out of debt. Neither Sheikha nor her father ever saw a paisa of that promised dowry.

Growing up, Sheikha rarely saw her father and brothers. Nine months of the year, they were out at sea, on the boums and baghlas of wealthy merchants, trading along the eastern coast of Africa or the western coast of India. Even during the three months of monsoon, when Sheikha's father and brothers were back in Kuwait, they were out pearling. At the end of a summer combing oyster beds, the divers would return to shore, legs scored with cuts, ribs visible for wives and children to count. Like most of the divers and sailors of Kuwait, Sheikha's father was poor, in debt all his life, relying on advances from his nokhada to sustain his family.

Sheikha was the youngest of four. Her eldest brother, Abdullah, was her favorite. In the few days he was back from sea, he whittled small dhows out of wood for his little sister to play with. He carved intricate figures of boys and girls, Salukis and hamour. She watched his fingers as he worked, captivated by his descriptions of the leopards of Zanzibar, the monkeys of India, and how the color of the sea could switch from the palest streak of blue to swathes of black in an instant. He described the great bellied sail, a swan swooping through silvered water. Sheikha would close her eyes and imagine the fantastical colors and animals her brother described, the sounds of chattering monkeys and whittling wood one and the same.

Abdullah's body looked like the teakwood of the ships he sailed from the bustling port of Kuwait Town, prized timber collected along the Malabar Coast. He was sleek and golden brown, every inch of him taut and strong as a wire. His skin showed early signs of the leather it would have become after a decade more of sun and sea.

It was a foolish accident, the kind that made even seasoned sailors shake their heads. Like his father and so many men of Kuwait, Abdullah was a diver. He could stay underwater longer than most, a full two minutes, and he had a special knack for bringing up more oysters than the other divers every time. He was a favorite among the crew, his rich baritone leading them as they sang the bahri together. His water-soaked eyes would twinkle as he teased the younger divers, urging them on with promises of wealth.

Everyone believed he was setting another record. Abdullah's hauler did not feel the weak tug or notice the ropes dancing like yellow snakes in azure blue. The rope of the net basket had looped around his neck, and the weight of the oysters, thumping against his spine, choked him to death.

The delicate purple rings around her brother's neck were the first thing Sheikha noticed as the sailors carried his body over the threshold and placed it in the middle of the courtyard. She would always remember how careful they had been with Abdullah. Her mother's long wail filled the lanes of the fireej and brought the neighborhood women to their door to help ease in another the pain known to them all. Sheikha forgot most of what happened after that, but she never forgot what it felt like to love a man and lose him.

Abdullah drowned in 1899, when Sheikha was ten and he was twenty-seven, her husband's age when they married. She had hoped there would be some magic in the coincidence of numbers. There wasn't. Sheikha's husband, Qais, had the eccentric proclivities of the wealthy minus the wealth. He kept an owl in the house and spoke to it in undecipherable code. He placed a circle of stones around their mattress every night before sleep and refused to let Sheikha off once the stones were in position, not to comfort her bawling babies, not to relieve herself. Qais stopped speaking to anyone but the owl after five o'clock in the evening. Twice a week, he would shake his adolescent wife awake at precisely three in the morning, hold down her head so she could scarcely breathe, and rip from her what he believed was owed him.

By the time she was twenty, Sheikha had given birth to her fourth and final baby. A few months later, early one dawn after Qais had rolled off her torn body, something inside her had bled out in garnet clots. She thought she might die, but she didn't, and afterward she could no longer become pregnant. That, at least, was a relief. Qais and his ways had come between Sheikha and her babies. She could feel nothing for them, despair over her own fate smothering any shred of tenderness. The three eldest had absorbed her rejection and kept to themselves, like wounded foxes in the desert. But Lulwa was different. No matter how hard

Sheikha pushed the child away, Lulwa came back, trying to force her into the shape of a mother she could never be.

Sheikha's heart did not budge in response to her daughter's arms around her that morning. She was going to sell Lulwa off to the son of a rich merchant, a merchant who, unlike Qais Qais Al-Talib, was known throughout Kuwait and far beyond. Qais had no interest in the children, so Sheikha could do as she pleased. The merchant's wife had come to ask for her daughter's hand a few days ago. Sheikha couldn't understand why this family that could choose any of the suitable daughters of rich merchant families like their own would choose Lulwa. But the woman was adamant, and her insistence had made Sheikha bold.

"I will accept your proposal on one condition. Your family must pay me one thousand rupees. This amount will be in addition to any muqaddam you choose to pay the girl."

The woman frowned.

"And neither my husband nor my daughter can know of this," Sheikha added.

The woman sniffed the air around her in what Sheikha believed to be scorn, but she did not refuse.

"Go prepare our tea and bring it here, Lulwa. I have something to tell you." Lulwa was used to her mother's stern commands, her father's frosty indifference.

Lulwa drew water from the cistern at the center of the courtyard. During the dry summer months, the cistern was filled with fresh water purchased from the local kandari. Lulwa heated the water along with a few teaspoons of tea leaves in a tin kettle on a charcoal duwah kept in a room off the courtyard. Once the tea had boiled for five minutes, she poured the brew into two istikans and sat at her mother's feet.

"In one week's time, you will marry the youngest son of Khalifa Al-Mustafa. You are a lucky young woman. Who knows why they've chosen you, but they have, and we're in no position to question. They don't want a big fuss. A small ceremony with the mullah and you're off."

Sheikha's voice was a jagged shell, but Lulwa let out a shriek of delight. She knew exactly who Khalifa Al-Mustafa's youngest son was. His name was Mubarak. He was the boy who would linger in the dhow yard at the water's edge with boys much less wealthy than himself. Lulwa had seen her brother, Ahmed, talking to him as she and her sisters washed their calico dresses on the nig'a, the stone breakwaters. Ahmed had waved at them, and they had waved back, giggling because it was not entirely proper. They were astonished to see the boy with their brother lift his hand to wave at them too, and this time they turned away. It was one thing for their brother to wave at them in public, quite another for a stranger to follow suit. But the unknown boy could not have missed them pinching each other under their thobes or the small smiles curling the edges of their heart-shaped mouths.

That night on the sateh, the sisters probed Ahmed for details.

"What's his name?" Sumaiyya, the oldest, asked.

"What does he do?" Hussa, the middle one, cut in.

"Is he married?" Lulwa added before Ahmed had had a chance to answer the other two.

"Mubárak Khalifa Al-Mustafa. He lives in India. And no, he's not married." Mubarak and his parents were in town for the month of August to visit family. His father's trade was based in India, and that was where they spent most of the year. He was studying something called English literature at Aligarh Muslim University. Lulwa repeated the word in her head. *Aligarh . . . Aligarh.* It sounded like a prayer for rain.

After Mubarak's first wave, every time the girls went down to the beach to wash soiled clothes, he would be there, and he would wave at them even if their brother was not around. Lulwa began to wave back. A small flick of the wrist at first, her arm at her side, an almost imperceptible flap of a moth's wing. Then, with her elbow at a right angle, a stiff back and forth. And finally, one auspicious morning, her arm raised above her head, a wave for all to see.

In the hours after midnight, the day after Lulwa's open wave, Mubarak wrote on his father's newly whitewashed wall:

*THE THREE DAUGHTERS OF QAIS QAIS
AL-TALIB ARE MADAMAAT!*

He chose that word, an Arabicization of *madam,* because he thought no one would understand it. He was not likening the Al-Talib sisters to port town bebes. Madams were lively creatures full of light. A madam was what he wanted to marry, not a girl covered in black, incapable of embracing the world beyond her sheltered fort.

Mubarak was too young to consider how his words might tarnish the girls' reputations. Luckily, his father, Khalifa, stepping out for a walk in the hours before the August sun took over, saw the defacement of his otherwise pristine wall before anyone else in town had the chance. Khalifa marched straight to Mubarak's room, knowing this reckless whimsy could only be his youngest son's, like his insistence on English literature, his wandering through jungles, his frequent commingling with those beneath his class. Mubarak was fast asleep when his father burst through his bedroom door, shouting, "It must have been you who wrote it!"

Mubarak sat straight up and was instantly alert, ready to declare what he had been rehearsing for days. "Yes, Yuba, I wrote it. And I mean to marry the youngest one. Lulwa will be my madam."

His father put his hands on his son's shoulders and shook him. "These girls are not the daughters of merchants, ya Mubarak! Their family has no connection to India. How do you know she will leave her family?" Khalifa Al-Mustafa was one of the most successful merchants in Kuwait. He owned a fleet of ships ranging from a massive old baghla, one of the last to sail from Kuwait, to more boums, sambouks, and jalbouts than anyone could count. Like most wealthy Kuwaiti merchants, he owned vast date plantations in Basra, which supplied the primary cargo that enabled the rest of his trade down the east and west coasts of the Indian Ocean. Also, like his father before him, Khalifa had been exceptionally lucky at pearling. The Al-Mustafa oyster harvests always brought in the most coveted pearls. One of the reasons the family had settled in India was to expand their already formidable trade interests to include jewels.

Mubarak thought about Lulwa's wave and said, "She'll come." And she did.

Everyone in town could see it was that rare thing. The two of them, fifteen and seventeen, held hands as they walked along the twilit shore. Sumaiyya, Hussa, and Ahmed formed a ring around their sister and her young man. They were making plans, conspiring to move to India with them, away from their parents. When they were younger, the neighbors would remark over the happy band of siblings, so unlike their dour parents. To survive their mother and father, the four of them had had to stick tight. Letting Lulwa go was tolerable only because they knew Mubarak could be trusted. "I have three older brothers and one younger sister," Mubarak proclaimed. "Once they set eyes on Lulu, they'll all want their share of the lovely Al-Talib madamaat and"—he turned to give Ahmed a sharp salute—"our fair sir!"

Mubarak's mother, Zaineb, visited their home every day before the milcheh with bolts of hand-printed silks and seamstresses in her wake. She draped Lulwa's neck with an intricate pearl necklace, loaded her wrists with heavy gold bracelets studded with rubies. When she learned that Lulwa's ears hadn't been pierced, she paid the neighborhood kandari to deliver a small block of ice, numbed the girl's lobes, and expertly pushed through a needle she had sterilized with the flame of a candle. She fitted Lulwa's ears with tiny gold hoops decorated with turquoise beads, promising that as soon as her ears healed, she would have dangling earrings to match the ornaments around her neck and wrists.

Zaineb's ease with Lulwa—her hands on parts of Lulwa's body, her wiping of bloody earlobes, her tight embrace of the girl upon entering or leaving the house—unnerved Sheikha. She could not comprehend how this woman, a stranger to her daughter, could touch her, chirp with her over some shared observation, gather her into her arms like she belonged to her. Zaineb strode into Sheikha's humble home like she owned it, brought with her the optimism Sheikha's children had always suspected existed. Sheikha watched her daughter wrap her skinny arms around Zaineb's waist as she had done to her only days earlier. Unlike Sheikha, Zaineb did not stiffen. Zaineb hugged the girl back.

Sheikha had felt jealousy before. She remembered at eight seeing her mother rub her brother Abdullah's sore legs and feeling her own legs turn to ice. The jealousy she felt now was similar. It was directed not toward Zaineb, but toward her own daughter. Her legs froze as she watched her girl laughing with the woman. Her jealousy thickened as she thought about Lulwa in the boy's arms, his young body carved and lithe. She pictured Lulwa's hands on Mubarak's chest and abdomen. She imagined them on their first night, fumbling for that novel fulfillment. Lulwa laughed with glee in the middle of the courtyard, surrounded by a pouf of gold-threaded silks and pearls like the ones Abdullah had died in the process of collecting. Sheikha resented her daughter, and she hated Mubarak, this boy with a starred future.

The siblings were convinced they would be together again soon, so seeing Lulwa off to India on the Al-Mustafa family's baghla did not feel like goodbye, more like the start of an adventure. They presented their sister with small gifts, talismans from the place she was leaving behind: a bottle of shells, a piece of cerulean sea glass, the tiniest pearl. Lulwa promised to send them wondrous things from India, objects none of them could imagine: peacock feathers, inlaid rosewood boxes, ivory combs.

As the ship prepared to embark, the family lined up along the shore for a final glimpse of their departing girl. The siblings waved at each other. The three were too far down to see Lulwa's runnel of tears. Mubarak clasped her hand in his, squeezing it tight. She squeezed back, grateful for this boy, not yet a man, on whom she knew she could depend. What neither of them noticed in the hurly-burly of heaved oars and pulled ropes were Sheikha's slow-burning eyes.

Yasmine

Majid told Yasmine he loved her a week after her father died, in April 1933. "I will love you," he whispered, "forever." They stepped barefoot into a stream in the Saida hills, the air ringing with bulbul. Yasmine's mother was grief-stricken enough to allow her daughter to go on a picnic with a group of youngsters, boys included. It was not far from home, and Yousef would be there to guard his sister's honor. But Yousef, distracted by pretty girls, neglected his fraternal duty. Majid promised Yasmine he would marry her as soon as she graduated from high school in a month and a half. She swelled with pride and forgot her dead father. She was sixteen.

Hussein Suleiman's heart attack had come without warning. He was forty years old. Unlike other fathers in the conservative city of old Saida, Hussein had insisted his daughter enroll in the Sidon Girls' School, established by American missionaries in 1862. He was not irreligious, but he believed in reason and saw no contradiction between praying five times a day and educating his only daughter in the ways of the West.

By the time Yasmine started attending the Sidon Girls'

School, the curriculum had shifted from home economics and childcare to academic subjects, and the language of instruction had switched from Arabic to English. The villagers chafed at these changes, but nothing bothered them more than the Christianity that would no doubt rub off on Hussein's daughter. Each villager had his or her own vivid account of how the daughter of one relative or another boarding at SGS had converted to the dreaded faith. "That could be your daughter, Hussein! English first, then the Bible, and then, overnight, Jesus Christ her Lord and Savior!"

As the trusted friend and secretary of Hikmet Bey, kaimakam of the Ottoman Empire in Saida, Jaffa, and Baqubah, Hussein Suleiman was often far from home. But when his neighbors managed to catch hold of him to share their avalanche of conversion stories, he would smile and shake his head. Hussein was aware that cases of conversion from Islam to Christianity were far rarer than conversions in the other direction. His daughter had been well-instructed in the Quran by her mother, his Turkish wife, Yeliz, daughter of Hikmet Bey's cousin. Hussein felt secure in the hold of their faith.

That afternoon at the picnic, after his proposal, Majid asked Yasmine what she wanted him to be. "I want you to be an architect," she replied without hesitation. What she knew of architecture came from her exposure to Roman ruins and crumbling Crusader castles dotting the landscape. She had listened to her teachers tell tales of brave Crusaders spreading the gospel in her homeland hundreds of years ago, just as the missionaries were continuing to do. What stirred Yasmine was not the bravery of those God-fearing soldiers, but the romance of the castles they had left behind, from the Sea Castle to the Castle of Saint Louis. She imagined herself the occupant of a castle, a secure turret all her own.

"I have to go home," Yasmine said, after she told Majid what she wanted him to become. "I have to study. I have to think about my essay."

"Your exams, your essay competition, two months from now they won't count for anything. Don't you understand, Yasmine? I'll take care of you. After the wedding we'll move to Beirut, study together at university. You can major in Arabic literature," he said, "and write to your heart's content."

She stuck her fingers in her ears, blocking his extravagant promises. "I have to go home."

Yasmine spent the last month before graduation studying for her final exams and preparing for the nationwide essay competition. If she won the competition, she would receive a scholarship to the American University of Beirut, which Majid attended. Majid didn't need a scholarship. His family was rich. If her father hadn't died, Yasmine might not have had to fret over money. But it turned out that her father had been in enough debt to leave nothing behind for her education.

Yasmine did not doubt Majid's proposal, but she kept it to herself. She continued to study for her final exams like they were her only way out. Yasmine had always been a star student. She had learned Arabic by reciting the Quran to her mother at an age when most children were still struggling to speak. It had come easily to Yasmine, much easier than it ever had to her poor mother, forced to live in a language not her own.

Yeliz had been taught Arabic by a tutor in Istanbul, a wrinkled Syrian woman who allowed the young girl to light her rolled cigarettes. This ill-advised ritual had left Yeliz with a lifelong predilection for tobacco, a fondness she indulged until the end of her days. In addition to Arabic, Yeliz also had been taught to play oud by a talented musician who visited the family home three times a week. He taught music to the children of those with aspirations to wealth, families more regular with tuition payments than the ancestrally rich. Yeliz's Arabic instruction and oud lessons made her feel like a courtesan in a sultan's palace. She wasn't sure what her parents were preparing her for.

She found out one cloudy afternoon in 1915. Gray skies threatened to pour down a river. Swallows, usually filling the skies with dance, had vanished. The children of the house were on edge; they knew their mother would shortly order them to scamper through the rooms with clay pots, placing them to catch leaks from loose wooden window frames. But on this rain-threatened afternoon, Yeliz's mother was unperturbed. She had ordered Yeliz to dress smart for esteemed guests, not to put on the worn dress she normally did for catching leaks and drips. Hikmet Bey was coming.

Hikmet Bey was only a few years older than his cousin, Yeliz's father, but he was, as Yeliz's mother constantly reminded her husband, far more accomplished and ambitious. Hikmet Bey was well-placed in the behemoth Ottoman administration. To Yeliz's parents, his position appeared grand, and given the turbulence of the last few decades, it seemed miraculous to them that Hikmet Bey not only had managed to cheat death, but, even more awe-inspiring, had maintained a respectable position despite revolutions, coups, and wars. They weren't sure what it was that his responsibilities entailed. They knew it had something to do with the management of Arabs. Now their empire was involved in a war whose outcome was unknown. In the gamble of political intrigue, Hikmet Bey had squeaked through in one piece. On account of this alone, Yeliz's parents were impressed.

Hikmet Bey arrived on time, a handsome young man at his side. The stranger had light gray eyes, out of keeping with his dark hair. He was awkward and angular. The bey—who donned a red fez and waxed his imposing black moustache upward like one of the Three Pashas—summoned Yeliz. He informed her that she would be traveling with him to Saida, and upon their arrival, she would marry this fine young man. Yeliz, who had been staring at the tiled floor until the bey spoke, looked up at him in disbelief, then glanced over at her parents. They did not appear surprised. Yeliz felt both betrayed and hotly thrilled. Her parents had their hands full with her six younger siblings. Yeliz was seventeen and ready to leave home. She would never see her family again.

Yeliz had taught her daughter, Yasmine, to be as self-sufficient as was possible for a girl in Lebanon in the early decades of the twentieth century. As it turned out, the shy gray-eyed man she was forced to marry wanted the same things for their daughter. He had been a good man, kind and hardworking. He wrote remarkable letters to Yeliz when he was away, thick with descriptions of glassy deserts, gruff nomads, sparkling constellations in the night sky. Now he was dead, and his older brother Hassan was ordering

his foreigner sister-in-law to remain in the house, refusing to allow her to take her children and return to Istanbul. She resented
her brother-in-law's order, but she wasn't sure she wanted to leave
in any case. After eighteen years away, Istanbul was no longer
home.

Yeliz was a skilled seamstress and could earn what was necessary for her family to live on as well as to send her son to college.
But she recognized that it was her daughter, not her son, who
deserved to go. School had always been a struggle for Yousef.
He had a roving eye, beguiled by all things shiny and pretty. It
would not be acceptable for her to send Yasmine to university
over Yousef, but Yeliz predicted her son would fail, wasting her
hard-earned savings. She hoped Yasmine would marry a man not
in debt, who would take care of her and make her happy. It was for
this that she had allowed Yasmine to go on that picnic. She held
her breath for her daughter, for herself.

For three weeks Yasmine concentrated only on her studies. Years
later, she thought her unswerving commitment might have been
her way of mourning her father. Her mother kept her prying uncle away, and Yousef stayed out of the house most of the day, giving Yasmine the quiet she needed.

She had been judged the best student of Arabic composition
of all the girls in her graduating class, and now she would be competing against the other top female fourth-year secondary students in Lebanon. The topic for the next stage in the competition
had been given to her the day after the first results: *What do you want
to do after you graduate and why?* Most of the girls Yasmine knew—and,
she was certain, all the girls in all the schools across Lebanon who

hadn't won—wanted to be housewives. She planted the bottoms of her feet against the cold mosaic tiles of her bedroom floor and remembered the cool water between her toes a few weeks earlier. Majid's proposal. She wanted that with him, maybe. A wife, a mother, a string of children like amber beads. But she wanted more than that, too.

She won best in the region.

There would be no advance notice of theme for the final essay. She would be competing with five other girls. The principal of her school informed her that SGS would happily welcome her back: "If you win the scholarship to AUB, Yasmine, we'll hire you here once you complete your degree. You can be our new Arabic teacher." It was this she wanted, maybe. The very thing she had written about in the second essay. To write and to teach and to be, above all, independent, beholden to no one's debts nor death.

While she waited for the date of the last essay, she passed her finals. She was valedictorian of her class. She wrote her speech, which bloomed with predictable enthusiasms. Her uncle Hassan, when he heard about Yasmine's upcoming public speech, had shouted, "No daughter of mine will speak onstage, head uncovered." Yasmine had shouted back, "I'm not your daughter," which had earned her a slap. Her own father had never raised a hand against her.

Her mother promised Yasmine she would give her speech and would walk onstage to collect her diploma. Yeliz would divert her brother-in-law's attention with a lie about someone ready to pay back money owed. "Your fat, greedy uncle won't put two and two together." The man had always been jealous of his brother, gray-eyed Hussein, friend of beys, husband of the exotic Yeliz.

As Yasmine sat waiting in the echoing hall for the final essay question, she thought about the five other candidates scattered in halls like this one all across Lebanon. What made them special? She felt herself to be special. It was her cleverness, her ability to be decisive. But it was also her creamy skin and rosy cheeks and the physical effect she had on strangers. She was not especially tall, but she was shaped like an Egyptian film star. Her straight black hair swung down her back. Her rare gray eyes, like her father's, were haunting. She was arrogant sometimes, she knew. This was a flaw she worked on, tried to hide.

She could feel the rough wood of the chair against the backs of her knees, and she thought about what her father's death was going to mean for her mother, for herself, and for her wayward brother. The proctor walked into the large hall where her graduation would be held the following week. She tore open the brown envelope, placed the sheet with the question on it facedown on Yasmine's desk, handed her ten sheets of foolscap paper and a sharp pencil. Yasmine had one hour to complete the essay.

She won best in Lebanon.

She was the only girl in her graduating class that year to walk up onstage three times: first, to pick up her award for best Arabic essay written by a girl in Lebanon; next, to make her speech as class valedictorian; and, lastly, to collect her high school diploma. The diploma was made of leather with her name embossed in gold and, under it, the year, *1933*. It would always be Yasmine's most prized possession.

Yasmine's mother and Yousef were in the second row. Majid and his parents were there too, for his sister Ihsan, also in Yasmine's graduating class. After the ceremony, Ihsan pulled Yasmine by the hand to meet her mother. Madame Majida wore emerald drop earrings and a cream chiffon dress with a matching cape. Her hair was pulled back in a devastating chignon. Ihsan smiled knowingly at her mother. "Mama, this is Yasmine."

Yasmine could sense Majid hovering behind her. Yasmine beamed at Madame Majida, curtsied, and came forward to kiss her. Madame Majida glared down at Yasmine with the hazel eyes of a lizard. She did not bend to receive Yasmine's kiss, did not nod in acknowledgment or say a word. Yasmine was humiliated in front of her friends, who knew about Majid; in front of Ihsan; and in front of Majid, the boy who had proposed to her but who had failed to mention his mother. Yasmine spun around to look for him, still confident in his devotion. He wasn't there. Her nostrils flared, and her fingertips tingled. She turned back to face his mother, bit down on her lower lip, tasted blood, and said, "Madame Majida, it's a pleasure to meet you. Congratulations on Ihsan's graduation."

Madame Majida blinked her reptilian eyes in haughty acknowledgment or cold disregard. Yasmine thrust out her chin. Saying goodbye to no one, she made her way to the exit, face on fire.

Yasmine would remember that day two ways: with pride and with fury. She marched home against the wind, her hair funneling like a tornado. She burst into the house and slammed the door behind her. Her mother, who had arrived only moments earlier, screamed. Yasmine, feet planted, hands on hips, announced: "I have a plan."

Two days before her father died, Yasmine had secretly applied for a teaching job in Baghdad. A notice in a local paper was advertising for qualified female teachers from Palestine, Syria, and Lebanon to teach primary- and secondary-school girls in Iraq. Yasmine wasn't sure what had made her send in an application. There had been no hint of her father's impending death. She was busy preparing for her exams, confident of their outcome and her likely acceptance at AUB. She had no credentials to speak of, only the promise of a diploma from SGS in a couple of months' time. She had had no sensible reason to apply for that teaching position. She did it because her acceptance would be another accomplishment to add to a collection that would come to mean so little, much sooner than she would have believed.

Yasmine had heard back from the school in Baghdad a few days before her graduation that the job was hers if she wanted it. Yasmine knew she could not set foot in Beirut now, not after the scene with Madame Majida. She would not be marrying Majid, and she could not imagine attending AUB while he was there, too. She would forfeit her newly won scholarship, would burn every bridge, leave everyone behind, exactly as her mother had been forced to do. But no one was forcing Yasmine. She would show them what she was made of, and they would all live to regret it. She didn't see it as running away, tail between her legs. She saw it as a triumphant leave-taking, karama intact, the departure of a princess soon to be a queen. Someone else would build her castle.

It was unthinkable for any young girl in Saida to travel alone beyond the borders of Lebanon, as inconceivable as a girl choosing her own husband. "I've decided to go to Iraq to teach Arabic literature to primary-school students," Yasmine informed her mother. "I will live in a boardinghouse for women. Don't try to stop me."

Yeliz wouldn't have bothered, recognizing her own stubbornness in Yasmine's steely gaze. And Yasmine's uncle—who would have killed her before letting her go, who had stolen even the tiniest crumb of inheritance left to them—that man died of a convenient stroke before he heard of Yasmine's plan. His family blamed Yeliz's evil eye.

As Yasmine prepared for her departure, she learned that Madame Majida had whisked Ihsan and Majid off to Europe the day after graduation. Surrounded by the splendor of Europe, Majid would no doubt forget Yasmine, forget their imagined life together. Yasmine gritted her teeth and continued to pack.

She left Lebanon at the end of August on a bus—NAIRN EASTERN TRANSPORT CO. painted on the side—with a group of young women from Beirut, accepted to teach at various schools dotted across Iraq. She rested the side of her head against the hot glass and sighed. How wrong she had been in that final essay: *What makes you happy and why?* She had been judged correct. She had won. But she was wrong. The dusty road opened before her, and twelve hours later, somewhere between Baqubah and Baghdad, Yasmine turned seventeen, alone and without ceremony.

Sara

Eight days since my arrest and Aasif still hides the papers, although by the fifth day my face no longer makes the front pages. The choking fear from that night in jail has dissipated, replaced by numbness and an intermittent vertigo. I sit at my father's desk, books and papers everywhere, and try to write. It looks as if nothing has changed, but something has, and I don't know what to do about it.

The name of the girl who made the recording has not been disclosed to Mr. Al-Baatin. "The court wants to protect her identity because she's not yet twenty-one," he explains over the phone. "I've submitted a request for her name to be released to me on condition of preserving her privacy. I believe it will be approved in a week or two." Knowing her name won't make any difference to me or the case. She's interchangeable, one of many. This battalion of girls, my students, following in the footsteps of their conservative parents and their religious teachers, are closing in. In the rare moments I can bring myself to think about her, the unknown girl, I'm filled with a rage so annihilating, I throw up. *She started it,* I want to scream. *Her.*

Mom used to instruct Karim and me: *If someone hits you, hit them back.* Not exactly the lesson in playground ethics we were being taught at the American School of Kuwait, but there would be no turning the other cheek for Noura's kids. We were to stand up for ourselves. In one breath she would bring up South Africa and Palestine and Malcolm X, giving us lessons in global inequality and the function of power. Karim and I would roll our eyes behind her back. *Write it down, you two,* she would say, ignoring us. *I want you to remember you got it from me.*

Karim and I understood as teenagers, maybe even earlier, that Kuwait wasn't for us. Things weren't bad then. Looking back on it, we came of age in golden times. But with the unsullied vision of youth, we just knew. My brother cut ties with a severity I couldn't muster. When Mom died, eleven and a half years ago, I faltered. I came back.

As a kid I believed that in the ways that counted, I was American. When my mother told the story of how we might have stayed in the States if it weren't for my uncle's call in the middle of the night, my teeth would twinge with regret. When she recounted how she had boarded a plane from St. Louis, where my father was completing his residency, a few weeks before my delivery—defying my father, fooling the airlines—because she wanted me to be born in the same country as my brother, I would thump my hands against my head. Everything could have been different. I could have been whole instead of split down the middle.

Nine months out of the year, Karim and I attended a school that was as American as any in the U.S. American teachers, American curriculum, mostly American kids. We celebrated Halloween and Christmas and Easter. We played baseball and basketball. We spoke English all the time, loathed Arabic and religion class. We watched American TV shows and coveted American food.

Summer months we spent in Orange County, California, in a three-bedroom condo with a view of a man-made lake. Dad would join us for one month in August, unable to leave his patients in Kuwait any longer than that. In California, nobody cared where we were from. Hardly anyone had ever heard of Kuwait. When "near Iraq" drew blank stares, my mother started naming states. "Illinois. We're from Kuwait, Illinois." Or, "Kuwait, Florida. You should visit, but avoid hurricane season." No one challenged her. My mother decried American ignorance of global geography, but I was elated. For three months we could be from Kuwait, Illinois, as American as funnel cakes and corn dogs.

I would weep on the plane from California to Kuwait, anticipating the seismic shift that would rock me. At Mama Lulwa's Thursday lunches, Karim and I were made fun of by our maternal cousins for speaking Arabic with an accent. Our aunts and uncles would tsk-tsk our parents for not pushing us into Kuwaiti society. Meanwhile we would steal away to our dead grandfather's study, inhaling the odor of stale pipe tobacco, scanning Baba Mubarak's meticulously arranged bookshelves. We would sit on one of his teak benches, breathlessly dissecting the impossible story our cousins repeated about how Mama Lulwa had been kidnapped by her own mother. Or we would read together in silence, ignoring the commotion behind the door.

The weather outside has been dusty since my arrest, varied shades of red and orange and beige. It's stifling and gives me an excuse to stay indoors. Sometimes I think the dust in Kuwait addles our brains, clouding perception and choking hope. Lola has been keeping her distance, curling up on a warm patch of carpet rather than on my lap. My lack of movement must seem odd to her. When I head down for lunch, she follows, but not too closely. Bebe Mitu, in contrast, squawks and calls all morning. Sometimes it's Mama Lulwa's voice I hear, other times Baba Mubarak's, or my mother's. This afternoon it's my own voice he uses to ask, "What's on the agenda, Sara? What's on the agenda?"

"I made ghee chapatis today to go with Aasif's potatoes and peas," Maria confesses. "He can't be upset with me for that." She laughs as I tear off an edge of chapati and stuff it into my mouth. "I'm going to spend one extra night at Josie's this weekend. We're going to celebrate her promotion. I'll leave tomorrow afternoon. You'll be okay?"

The chapati stops in my throat. It's almost the weekend already. I had forgotten Maria would be going to her daughter's. Her family might know something. That they haven't mentioned anything to her over the phone already is a small miracle. I can't let her find out that way. I have to tell her myself immediately, but instead I reply, "I'll be okay. I'll do some work. I'll swim. Do you have anything planned in this stinking weather?"

"Dust! Dust! It should be raining during monsoon season." Even after decades in Kuwait, monsoon season to Maria still means rain. "Will you go to the bookstore?"

"Maybe. I don't know. Not many customers anymore."

"Sad, nah? Your poor maa put everything into it."

She had, and now there was almost nothing left to show for it. Before my arrest, I would spend a few hours every evening at

Curiosity Bookshop, cocooned by my mother's shelves of books. Since the accusation, I haven't opened the shop at all. I doubt anyone will stop by, mainly because most of my remaining customers have gone for the summer, but also, I think, for fear. My case is scary; people will want to keep away from the bookshop and me.

"You rest now, Sara. Stop writing all the time. Nap, and tonight we'll watch Jerry Lewis."

I let out a slow breath. I believe I'm protecting her by not telling her, but there's more to it than that.

I have my first appointment with Mr. Al-Baatin since the day of my release at around six in the evening. (I tell Maria he's a colleague from work.) He has promised to visit once a week to keep me updated. He'll call if there's anything urgent, and I'm to call him any time of day or night if I start to lose my nerve. When he arrives he makes his way to the love seat again like it belongs to him. I make a wager with myself: if the love seat survives Mr. Al-Baatin, I will survive this case.

There isn't much to report. Various petitions, including one to dismiss my case altogether, have been filed and are in process. Mr. Al-Baatin has been trying to get the travel ban lifted, but there haven't been any developments on that front. If I'm allowed to travel, will I try to flee? I'm not sure. I suspect the judge or prosecutor or whoever lifts such bans will assume yes. I'm certain, despite Mr. Al-Baatin's optimism, it won't be revoked.

He leans back, and the seat creaks. "I knew your mother. She was a troublemaker like you. Smuggling Salman Rushdie in a suitcase. *The Satanic Verses*, no less." He chortles, his hands resting neatly on his rolling belly.

The way he puts it makes me smile. I remember Mom purchasing twenty copies of *The Satanic Verses* on one of her visits to California after Kuwait's liberation from Iraq, but I don't remember her getting into trouble over it. I was used to her smuggling in copies of controversial books for Curiosity Bookshop. Customs was more focused on confiscating booze than banned books; I'm surprised she got caught. "What happened?"

"She signed a notarized *Declaration and Undertaking* stating that she wouldn't import contraband material into the country again, and it was over."

"Was she upset?"

"Livid. She went on and on about the stupidity of being prosecuted for bringing words into the country, of being imprisoned for our thoughts. She mentioned Orwell, I believe."

I imagine she would have.

There are three copies of *The Satanic Verses* left in her bookshop, locked in a hidden box. None of my mother's customers ask for Rushdie anymore.

"You'll recant your blasphemy," Mr. Al-Baatin says, "and we'll put this to rest like your mother did."

"And if they don't accept my retraction?"

"We'll challenge the law in Constitutional Court."

I've spent the last decade avoiding political life around me, trying to ignore the rising tide of extremism. I thought of it as a pendulum: conservative today, liberal tomorrow. I kept my head down, did my job, and hoped for the best. I abdicated responsibility, unlike my mother.

————————

My mother opened Curiosity Bookshop in September 1978. It was a small foreign-language bookstore, and Karim and I spent hours after school there when we were little. Mom would let us pull the big picture books off the shelves, and we'd take them under her desk and turn the pages carefully, trying not to smudge them.

Years after the invasion, I remember my mother's complaints from across the ocean during our weekly phone calls. At the time I listened with one ear, but it sticks with you, a mother's laments. She complained about the National Museum still being closed. "It's a mark of our national failure. We have failed to rebecome a nation despite the extinguished oil fires and tar-smoothed streets. Our culture dies an unhappy death and attention turns to phony calls to prayer. The unholy stench of it." My mother spoke as if she were making a case in the National Assembly. To an undeserving audience of one, she unfurled the splendor of her intelligence, the misfortune of her stolen ambition.

I remember her trying to explain the problems she was facing with Curiosity Bookshop, linking it to the new parliament. I didn't understand what she was talking about, but I let her sound off as I washed my dishes thousands of miles away. "They're making it harder and harder for me to order books. Do you know when all of this started, Sara? Way before the invasion. When we were drinking our dry martinis at the Gazelle Club in the seventies, the Muslim Brotherhood was taking over our government schools and university. Now they won't let me order the books I want."

"What does that have to do with parliament?" I asked.

"Conservative today means Islamist, not monarchist. Those students the Egyptian Brotherhood teachers got their paws on?

They *are* the new parliament. Well, them and the Salafis. It makes me sick."

I didn't really understand my mother's criticism then, but I get it now. I kept Curiosity Bookshop open after Mom died, despite Karim's discouragement, because I convinced myself that it was her only legacy. Shut down the bookstore, kill my mother a second time. But I'm beginning to question whether my mother would have persevered and why, for all these years, I've embalmed myself in her stubborn persistence, fighting a fight that isn't mine.

Mr. Al-Baatin's visit leaves me apprehensive. Nobody from the prosecution has unearthed the fact that I own a foreign-language bookstore. They might. I imagine it would add bulk to the case against me, more evidence that I'm corrupting our community with filth from the West.

My case is debated in the newspapers. The few on the side of freedom of speech deplore the changes to Kuwait. An accusation of blasphemy in this day and age is a farce, they write, a barbaric allegation that signals the decline of civilization. But these nostalgic, often poetic editorials are shunted to the back of the papers. The voice of the majority, unified and strong, dominates the front pages. Those on the side of conviction warn of the corruption of youth, the dissolution of 'adaat-u-taqaleed, our precious customs and traditions. They warn of the punishment that awaits those who strike against God and his prophet, those like me who spread ideas contrary to the practices and beliefs of Islam, the one true religion. Their headlines are bold and dramatic, incontrovertible to the already convinced. In all this I remain invisible as a ghost. The intellectuals writing on my behalf do not seek me out. No journalists come for interviews. Not that I could speak to them. Mr. Al-Baatin forbids it.

I decide to take a bath to clear my thoughts. I slip my head under the scalding water. I hear small pops and clicks from the pipes and imagine I'm swimming in the wide-open sea. It's only June, but already there is no cool water in the pipes, the metal tanks on the roof absorbing the heat of the sun all day. The water is so hot, my pulse hammers and I start to sweat. I push my toes against the tub, raising myself out of the still-steaming water. I'm suddenly shivering as though naked in a snowdrift, and I'm so scared, I want my mother.

Lulwa

The journey to India was without incident, waters tranquil, skies clear, crew obedient and in fine spirits. It was the type of journey any prudent nokhada of a dhow would wish for, especially sailing earlier than the mid-November mawsim. But for Lulwa and Mubarak, every bright blue day marked a shortening of their honeymoon. They prayed for gales to impede their steady pace.

The family's old baghla, *Amwaj Al-Salam,* was one of the last of these capacious vessels built in Kuwait. For this journey, the nokhada had loaded it with over five thousand packages of dates from the Basra plantations before returning to Kuwait to collect the family. Although these days the baghla was used primarily to transport the Al-Mustafa family between Kuwait and India, no opportunity to shift cargo on any of the family's vessels was squandered. Once the family disembarked in Bombay, the baghla would be loaded with cotton textiles, then sail to the east coast of Africa to discharge the dates and cloth. The ship might make two or even three runs across the water during the mawsim before heading back up to Kuwait, maybe with some members of the family on board again.

For the month it took to sail from Kuwait to Bombay, the newlyweds existed in ethereal mist. They skipped meals, preferring to remain alone together in their little cabin under the poop deck. In that confined, steaming space, they learned to undress in front of each other. At first, Lulwa insisted Mubarak turn away as she peeled off her outer layers, leaving on her white muslin petticoat. Within a few days, Lulwa's petticoat came off too, and Mubarak was not asked to look away. Under his gaze Lulwa felt, for the first time in her young life, safe.

When all on board were asleep, Lulwa and Mubarak ventured out of their nest. They sat at the stern of the ship, feet dangling over the edge, mapping their future. Mubarak promised a home surrounded by banyan trees. A parrot that would speak to Lulu in Mubarak's voice. A houseboat in Kashmir. A glittering beach in Goa. A dance hall in Bombay. Snow in Shimla. Kuwait fast turned into a pinprick on a fading horizon.

On one of those velvet nights, the moon overhead as big as a sun, Mubarak told Lulwa that in a month's time he would have to return to Aligarh Muslim University in Uttar Pradesh. She would remain in Poona, in the largest of the bungalows on his parents' property. He would visit as often as he could.

"Don't be scared, Lulu. I promise you'll be happy in Poona. There are gardens with fruits in the shape of stars. Markets with spices, copper bowls, pottery, a traveling cinema. And before you know it, I'll be back for a visit."

Lulwa marveled at the phosphorescent wake below. She looked up at the stars, close enough to touch. Sights that belonged in fairy tales. "I'm not scared." She pinched Mubarak's arm and whispered, "I'm excited!"

They tarried only once along their journey, on a jewel of an island. The nokhada reported that this uninhabited island could not be located on any map because nobody who stepped foot on it wanted it discovered. The sailors lowered the 'owd, the largest lateen sail, and anchored the ship. The family climbed down the Jacob's ladder into the longboat, and the sailors rowed them to a beach of glinting white diamonds. The water was aqua glass. Tamarisk trees lined the shore, providing sufficient shade for a picnic. The island rang with the haunting call of birds unique to it.

It was after the uncommon birds of this unnamed dot in the sea that the nokhada had commissioned the ship's carpenter to carve *Amwaj Al-Salam*'s wind vane. The carpenter carved partly from memory and partly from imagination because although the birds rose up and down from the trees in colorful, undulating belts, it was not easy to single one out. He had carved the wind vane from teak and had collected a marvel of feathers caught on the lower branches of the island trees to attach to the tail of the wooden bird. The slightest breath of air through the feathers would shift the wind vane, and the nokhada would be alerted immediately.

The nokhada and his mu'allim could read coast and sea with the knowledge of decades of sailing. They interpreted the curves of shores, natural and man-made landmarks, swirling currents, winds, and reefs, but also, when necessary, fish and birds. Fish revealed the nature of the seafloor, birds the advent of storms and proximity to land.

Five days after leaving the island, *Amwaj Al-Salam* sailed into the teeming Sassoon Docks in South Bombay. Lulwa leaned against the low rail of the ship and gazed down. Before the mawsim and after, when ships returned home, Kuwait's waterfront heaved with action. But Lulwa had never before seen a spectacle like the throng of bodies and boats at the Sassoon Docks. Unlike Kuwait and other ports along the coasts, these wet docks were not reliant on the tides to berth ships. Lulwa stepped gingerly onto a gangplank, then directly on land. No ladders to scamper down, no longboats rowed to shore.

"The Sassoons are friends of ours," Mubarak offered, sensing his young bride's trepidation. "Well, friends of my parents anyway. They have a mansion in Poona."

"What are the Sassoons?"

"Who, not what."

"*Who* are the Sassoons?"

"Owners of these docks and much more. Great merchants from Baghdad."

"Arabs?"

"Baghdadi Jews. They've been here almost one hundred years. Longer than our family."

Lulwa looked around, trying to piece together the connection between Iraq and this tumult before her, between her husband's family, who had been in India for many years, and the who-not-what Sassoons, who had been here even longer. The shift from fresh wind and billowing sails to this rat-tat noise and clinging humidity was overwhelming. Sinewy men in lungis, directed by the ship's nokhada and sailors, loaded the Al-Mustafas' trunks onto rickshaws. After paying their respects to Khalifa and Mubarak, the nokhada and sailors disappeared into the baghla to continue their journey.

The family spent a few nights at the Taj, where a room cost

more than the sailors earned in nine months. Mubarak showed Lulwa the sights, although the hotel itself, with its electricity, ceiling fans, elevators, and view of the almost completed Gateway, was enough to keep Lulwa enthralled. Zaineb introduced her daughter-in-law to the Bombay aunties, who were instantly charmed. Once they had all recovered their land legs, they booked passage on a train from Victoria Terminus to Poona.

To Lulwa, the family property in Poona seemed enormous. A chalk white colonial mansion with wide verandas, generous windows, French doors, and two floors. The property was just south of the Mula Mutha River on Koregaon Road, between the British cantonment and the old city. It was an area rapidly expanding with the mansions of princes and wealthy merchants, Parsi, Muslim, and Hindu alike. The Al-Mustafas' home was set in the middle of lush, tended gardens. A few quaint bungalows and small huts were scattered around the periphery of the property for family guests, as well as for the small army of cooks, house boys, maids, and gardeners it took to run the household. East of the tended gardens, as Mubarak had promised, was a jungle so thick the air beneath the canopy of trees was sapphire blue.

Lulwa kept her head bowed as Mubarak introduced her to everyone—siblings, friends, servants. She was new to shaking hands, but so many handshakes ensued in the span of an hour that she felt herself to be an expert in the bizarre practice by the end of it. When the line of well-wishers ended, a young woman in a glorious pink sari, her lustrous brown hair twisted up in a stylish bun, stepped forward. She looked familiar. Lulwa stretched out her hand and was taken aback when the young woman pulled her in by the shoulders to kiss her on both cheeks.

"Mabrook, habibti Lulwa! I'm Hayya, Mubarak's sister."

Lulwa recognized Mubarak's kind eyes in the young woman's face and immediately felt at ease. "Forgive me, Hayya! I didn't know. I'm so happy to meet you! Mubarak hasn't stopped talking about you."

"Mama Zaineb has had nothing but good to say about you, and I know my brother wouldn't marry any but the most remarkable girl. He's hard to please, you know."

Lulwa, not used to compliments, blushed.

Hayya took Lulwa's hands in hers. "I'm your third sister, Lulwa. Welcome home."

On the first evening of Mubarak's return to university, Hayya brought Lulwa a plate of gulab jamun to ease her sister-in-law's sadness. The next morning, she and Zaineb whisked Lulu off to Sadar Bazaar to pick out bolts of velvet and gossamer silk for new curtains and bedcovers. They wanted to distract her during the weeks without her husband, but Lulwa didn't need distracting. Her life had become wondrous, and she didn't want to miss an instant of it.

In the spring of Lulwa's first year in India, Mubarak's father, Khalifa, brought her three siblings down to Poona for a surprise visit. Since Khalifa, Zaineb, and their eldest sons would be sailing back to Kuwait in a month's time, the Al-Talibs would have convenient passage back. Mubarak, and so Lulwa as well, would be staying behind in Poona that summer to see to the business while the rest of the family was away. Khalifa hoped this visit from Ahmed, Sumaiyya, and Hussa would help ease Lulwa's first experience of summer as an unending wall of rain.

As she watched her siblings debark the boum, Lulwa realized just how much she had missed them. Seeing them in this place she already thought of as home made her want to hold them close and never let go. Her excited squeals pierced the air, causing hundreds of birds with acid-green and rose feathers to shoot out of nearby trees. Her siblings looked up at the feathery fireworks, then down at their sister, who, in nine short months, had transformed into something equally striking. Lulwa was no longer a child. The siblings paused together before stepping onto the gangway, suddenly shy, but Lulwa's happy shrieks and frantically waving arms reminded them that the luminous young woman eagerly greeting them was still their little sister. Soon the four were an octopus of limbs. Mubarak, back from Uttar Pradesh for a visit, stood to one side with Hayya, glad to welcome Lulu's siblings to India.

The month of their visit sped by. Mubarak had hoped that at least a few of the Al-Mustafas would fall in love with the Al-Talibs, but it was not to be. His three older brothers were absent most of the time, and Ahmed teased Hayya the way he did his own sisters. Mubarak took the siblings to potters' workshops in the winding lanes of Kumbharwada; to nondescript teahouses that served paan in Kasba Peth; to the graceful, timber-framed Peshwa wadas in Shaniwar Peth, with their freshwater wells supplied by a centuries-old aqueduct and central courtyards that reminded the Al-Talibs of home.

On one of their last mornings in Poona, Ahmed, Sumaiyya, and Hussa linked arms with Lulwa and went for a walk under the lapis canopy of trees. Lulwa had sensed the weight of something hanging over them during the course of their visit. She had asked them about it, but until this point they had shaken their heads in denial.

The four sat together in a circle on downy moss. Ahmed spoke first. "Sheikha has lost whatever semblance of sanity she had before you left." Among themselves, the three older siblings called their mother Sheikha, never Mama or Mama Sheikha, the way Lulwa did.

"She hardly speaks to us directly anymore," Sumaiyya continued. "If she wants to say something, she makes hazy statements we're supposed to understand. *The kitchen can't breathe* means it's time to clean the wind tunnels. *Dirt is a sin* means one of us should sweep and water down the courtyard."

"She wanders through the house, uninterested in chores or cooking or anything but the heavy box she hides in a hole under her bedding and thinks none of us knows about. There's a stash of money inside. We have no idea where she got it. But what troubles us most"—Hussa's voice fell—"is what she says about you."

Lulwa sat with her legs splayed in the shape of an M, the way she had since she was a child. It was the shape of the trade route down one coastal leg to Zanzibar in the east, down another coastal leg to Java in the west, with the Indian peninsula dipping between the two. Baba Khalifa had traced the M for her on an old map hanging in his study in the early days of her arrival in Poona. Her siblings had always said it looked like an uncomfortable way to sit. None of them could do it. Their mother could.

"She keeps repeating that it was a mistake to allow you to marry Mubarak, that he's a good-for-nothing loafer. She says she'll steal you back and force you to marry someone else, someone like our father." Ahmed picked at the moss beneath his feet as he spoke.

Lulwa was aware of her siblings' discomfort. Still, she threw back her head and laughed up into the trees. "Let her try." Lulwa was not afraid of her mother. Maybe her siblings had deflected the brunt of Sheikha's wrath away from her growing up, or maybe she saw something in her mother the others did not. Whatever the reason, with an ocean between them, Lulwa could not take her siblings' fears seriously.

They wanted to warn Mubarak and Hayya about Sheikha, but Lulwa forbade them. She would not poison Poona with her mother's madness. Despite their misgivings, her siblings honored her wishes. They left India as they had come, their family secret intact.

At the end of that summer, Mubarak was informed by his father that he would have to abandon his studies to help salvage what they could of their business in India. Mubarak's three brothers would be away most of the year, trying to reinvigorate flagging trade. Khalifa's key contacts along the littoral were dying. These relationships had relied on decades of shared meals, exchanged gifts, and strategic favors in times of famine or war, as much as they had on waraqas, or paper contracts. Khalifa had a reputation for being a fair trader, which had made him a wealthy man.

But these days his sons had taken his place, just as the sons of the elders of the littoral towns had taken the places of their fathers. These sons of fathers who had been friends were not friends, and neither side had the patience to cultivate the slow-growing, long-lasting relationships of the past. Khalifa, who now remained in Poona most of the year, keeping books with the help of an accountant and managing the family jewelry boutiques, was bewildered by the changes.

But something far more disastrous than the deaths of village elders and tribal leaders was stoking the profit decline and potential total failure of Khalifa Al-Mustafa & Sons Trading Co. Ltd. The culprit would bring down not only Khalifa's jewelry business but the entire economy of Kuwait. In Japan, about a decade earlier, Mikimoto Kokichi had discovered a way to culture pearls. Rumors of these imitation pearls had spread like cholera up and down the Gulf. Many had not wanted to believe the rumor, mocking claims that even the most experienced brokers would not be able to tell the difference between a manufactured pearl and a pearl grown from a speck of sand in the heart of an Arabian mollusk. Khalifa had listened with one ear, skeptical but still nervous. By 1925, there was no denying it. Cultured pearls had made their way to market, and prices were beginning to decline. A cultured pearl contained the same opalescence of a natural pearl. The pleasing weight of a string of marble-size orbs in the cup of a hand was the same for cultured pearls as it was for natural ones. To their own dismay, not even the most seasoned pearlers could tell the difference.

It pained Khalifa to inform Mubarak that he would not be returning to Aligarh to complete his final year. Khalifa had always indulged his son's studiousness. Unlike his father and brothers, Mubarak was not transported by the rise and fall of sails or trade. Mubarak was different. Reading under the hush of trees. Sitting at a desk, pen in hand, scribbling away. Throwing himself into friendships with boys Khalifa believed he had no business be-friending, the sons of blacksmiths and shrimpers, rice pickers and street sweepers. Still, he was pleased with his son's commitment, his innate openness. Much as he hated to cut short his son's education, Khalifa needed Mubarak close, to escort him across India, to help negotiate the transition from pearls to emeralds, rubies, sapphires, diamonds, whatever was necessary to preserve their way of life.

Mubarak took the news easier than Khalifa had predicted, in large part, he believed, because of Lulwa. He was grateful his daughter-in-law would cushion the stall of at least some of his son's ambitions. Little did Khalifa know that Lulwa was equally grateful to him. She was pregnant and as happy as Gulf oysters, lately safer in their shells, that her husband would no longer be far away.

Yasmine

"Are you Yasmine?"

"Are you Dr. Sherif?"

"Welcome to Baghdad!" The man peered into Yasmine's face, seeking out someone familiar, then planted a friendly kiss on each cheek.

A few days earlier, Yasmine would have been struck by this physical contact with an unknown man in the street. But the short trip from Saida to Baghdad had changed her. She had seen alien landscapes scorched by heat and dust and poverty. She had encountered men along the way—not boys like Majid, but men with frightening hawk eyes she guarded against as she relieved herself behind prickly bushes.

After all that, to be embraced by this Dr. Sherif, stranger or not, was a relief that sparked tears Yasmine fought to hold back. Glancing up at him as he led her down Al-Rashid Street in the direction of his home, she thought he looked something like her baba.

In the first few hours of her journey east, Yasmine had sobbed for her father with an abandon that had frightened the girls on the bus. Every once in a while, the foreign driver would glance at her, at first with sympathy, then with irritation. But Yasmine was inconsolable. She registered the finality of her father's absence in a way she hadn't before. Her father's death had been eclipsed by exams and essays and, shamefully, by the incident with Madame Majida.

Those final weeks at home, she now realized, she had behaved like a petulant child, barking at Yousef, indifferent to Yeliz's gentle efforts to salve her pain. Yeliz had brushed her daughter's hair, something she hadn't done in years, braiding it into neat loops secured with light blue ribbons. She fed Yasmine expensive eggs each morning, provided milk so fresh it was still warm. Every evening she took down her oud and sang to her daughter Turkish lullabies she had sung to Hussein in the early days of their marriage. Yeliz's voice would catch at words Yasmine didn't understand.

On that Nairn bus, Yasmine was overwhelmed by a slashing sense that she had committed a grave injustice against her parents. How much had it cost Yeliz to purchase those ribbons and eggs and milk? How much had it hurt her mother to sing songs she had learned from her own mother, a woman Yeliz would never see again? Songs that reminded Yeliz of her early days with the man who had been her husband before he was Yasmine's father? In the shadow of her father's eternal disappearance, what did Majid's mother matter? While her father was alive, she had not appreciated the things he had made possible for her in a society not made for girls.

But it was not too late. Through her tears Yasmine vowed to make good on the sacrifices her parents had made for her.

The moment Yeliz learned of Yasmine's plan to teach in Iraq, she had written to her husband's friend Dr. Sherif. Yeliz had not met Dr. Sherif, but from Hussein's affectionate accounts of the man, she felt like she knew him. Most importantly, she knew she could trust him.

According to her husband, Dr. Sherif diagnosed patients with the precision of a scalpel, reading their symptoms the way he did symbols in poems. Because Dr. Sherif read many poems, he was an excellent diagnostician. Once Dr. Sherif diagnosed his patients, he would not only treat their illnesses, he would soothe their souls with literature.

Hussein was only twenty-one in 1914 when he first met Dr. Sherif, on the first of many trips to Baghdad with Hikmet Bey. Every Thursday evening, Dr. Sherif opened his doors to local writers and poets. Young Hussein was an unpublished poet. His pieces were short and precise, sometimes no more than three lines. Hussein shared his poems with the bey, but he had no desire to expose them to others.

Hikmet Bey saw himself as a patron of the arts, though he lacked the means to fund any artists or writers. He encouraged his young secretary to write poetry in his free time and to mix with notable intellectuals in Lebanon. But Hussein was a shy man, and his lack of formal education made him reluctant to join the literary and cultural circles of his home country. What Hikmet Bey suspected was that Hussein's lack of exposure to the great Arabic literary tradition was precisely what had allowed him to forge his unique poetic path.

Although Hikmet Bey could make no headway with Hussein in Lebanon, in Baghdad he insisted that Hussein join him on his visits to Dr. Sherif's Thursday salon. He urged the young poet to share his secret writing with this potentially sympathetic group. Hussein, stuffing his doubts into his lower intestines, agreed to try.

The response to Hussein's first reading was not what a reluctant poet would hope for. He recited three short lines without much feeling. A few of that evening's visitors clapped politely, while others looked around, eyes narrowed, suspecting their legs were being pulled. Dr. Sherif himself was intrigued. Over pacheh and lamb quzi, prepared with care by Dr. Sherif's mother and sister in honor of the visiting bey, the doctor soon discovered that he and the Lebanese poet shared the same interests and hopes.

Their friendship cemented over two decades, through the changing shape of Arabic literature and Arab borders. Through the births of Hussein's two children and Dr. Sherif's unfortunate divorce. Through the decline of empires and the mysterious disappearance of their old friend the bey in the late 1920s, his conflicting loyalties finally catching up with him. Dr. Sherif and Hussein had often joked that only death or dominoes could end their friendship. Death, as it turned out, did it in.

The news of Hussein's death had reached Dr. Sherif by accident. A patient, also a regular at the Thursday salons—still going strong twenty years later—stopped by to offer his condolences. "Haven't you heard the news, ya Duktor? Hussein the Lebanese had a heart attack, Allah yarhama. There was a brief mention in one of the Saida newspapers. It happened a few weeks ago. 'The secretary of the vanished Bey of Saida,' it said. That would be Hussein, would it not?"

Indeed, Dr. Sherif had agreed, shaking his head, it could only be him.

Dr. Sherif had thought immediately of his dear friend's widow and children, had wanted to help them, but didn't know how. Then the letter from Yeliz had come, announcing Yasmine's arrival in Baghdad. Yasmine's teaching post was in a neighborhood on the outskirts of Baghdad, and she would reside in a nearby boardinghouse for women. But Yeliz asked Dr. Sherif if her daughter could stay with his family at weekends and during short holidays, and whether he would be willing to protect her girl.

It seemed like only yesterday that Hussein had proudly proclaimed to Dr. Sherif that his daughter loved to read and write, just like her baba. When she reached school age, he had shared some apprehension over her missionary education, which Dr. Sherif had swiftly dismissed. Hussein had spent long evenings with Dr. Sherif musing over his daughter's future, and Dr. Sherif had come to think of Yasmine as the daughter he never had. The girl seemed as formidable as her mother.

Dr. Sherif wrote back to Yeliz, promising he would treat Yasmine as his own. He would not let his old friend down.

Yasmine was a natural teacher. She wouldn't ever again be as happy as she was that year and a half she taught sixth-grade girls how to use their language to write essays. As her students learned to mold Arabic into the shape of their whims, Yasmine used it to write long letters to her mother, full of descriptions of the village school and her weekends at Dr. Sherif's in the center of Baghdad. Through those letters, Yasmine learned to make Iraq her home.

The local women, mothers of the girls she taught, had tattooed chins, covered their faces, smoked irgileh, and cackled rowdy comments across the alleyway about outsiders in their midst. "Here she comes, ladies! Swaying what God gave her. Our swan of the Tigris! How long do you think before one of our own lays claim to those pillows? The ones up front as well as that plush one in back that rolls like sambouks on the Shatt?"

Yasmine was insulted by their vulgarity. But over time she determined that their rough manners belied their unassailable devotion to their daughters. They didn't want the grimness of their own lives to shadow the lives of their girls. Here she was, this Yasmine from Lebanon, to show them it could be done. They teased her as she made her way to the school, but they handed over their daughters with faith in their hearts.

At Dr. Sherif's Thursday salon, Yasmine tried to picture her once-young father among the poets and writers, determined, maybe even slightly ambitious, despite his shyness. She wrote to Yeliz about encountering urbane men with more money than they knew what to do with. Between lines she hoped her mother would know to excavate, she contemplated what it might be like to marry one of these well-to-do pashas, never again to worry about money.

A wave of persistent suitors eager to acquire the young beauty from Lebanon approached Dr. Sherif, Yasmine's unofficial male guardian, asking for her hand in marriage. Yasmine felt herself pulled in two directions: on the one hand, independence; on the other, the draw of eligible men.

Yeliz had informed Yasmine in a letter that Majid had come to her door late one chilly night in December, four months after Yasmine's departure, tears flowing from his eyes like a natural disaster. "I want her back," he had sobbed to a half-asleep Yeliz. "I want her back! Please tell her to come back!"

Yeliz passed along the message. Yasmine's feelings toward Majid had almost completely dried up, the memory of her lost father stuffed into the spaces where her love for the boy had once been. But there remained a hairline fracture of something left for him. In part it was this that prevented her from saying yes to the doctor or lawyer or journalist or politician who begged for the privilege to make her his wife. But another part of why Yasmine refused the proposals that came as fast as fleas was because she wasn't ready to leave chance behind for a life as tight as a stone wall. Nothing was final yet. Not Majid, not teaching, not writing, not her future. Maybe she would enroll at university after all, fulfilling the goal she had let go for pride.

Dr. Sherif was proud of Yasmine, pleased that the young woman held herself in such high regard. He wanted Yasmine to be free, even if it meant her life would be modest and unglamorous, a village teacher at first, ultimately moving to a city school, a writer of essays or novels or poems, like her father. He saw in Yasmine the future of Arab women—independent, fearless, shaping their lives as they desired, not into shapes determined by mullahs or kings.

Sara

Mama Yasmine taught Arabic for only a year and a half of her life, but it was, she always claimed, her true calling. I'm not sure if teaching is my true calling. I may lose my job over this case, even if I'm not found guilty. Parents won't want their children registered in the classes of a *blasphemer*. Our department will be pressured to let me go. This should be the least of my concerns, but I've been thinking about it all morning. How it will feel to no longer be a university professor.

It's Thursday. Maria goes to Josie's early this afternoon. I have a few hours to figure out how to tell her.

In the fall of 2002, my first semester teaching at Kuwait University, the depressing, prisonlike campus was coated in black. Nearly all the women wore black hijab, black abayas, or black niqab. The men wore white dishdashas with red-and-white-checkered ghutras. As far as I remembered, thick red-and-white-checkered ghutras were worn only in winter. In the sauna of September, ghutras should have been white. Black, white, and red made no sense to me.

One morning, climbing three flights of stairs to my class, I heard an agitated "Duktora! Duktora!" It took me a second to realize I was the one being addressed. I wasn't used to being called doctor. My father had been a doctor. I was a professor of philosophy.

I turned to a bearded man in a short dishdasha, clearly a sharia professor.

"Duktora, hishmitich!"

"Excuse me?"

"Hishmitich! Hishmitich!"

I couldn't understand why this man, a complete stranger, was barking about my decency. And then I realized: *my skirt.* Apparently my honor, or lack of it, resided in the knee-length hemline of my skirt. I felt violated. "Why are you looking up my skirt? And why is your dishdasha so short?"

He spun around and stomped off. I was shaking with fury as I made my way to my classroom, a sea of black fabric. I doubted I would find sympathy in those covered bodies and hooded heads. I was convinced that if I shared what had just happened with them, the young women would have sided with the bearded man.

I made an appointment with the chair of my department. I would file a sexual harassment complaint. It was my second week at Kuwait University.

I was fifteen minutes early, but Nancy, the chairman's Egyptian secretary and one of the few women in the department not wearing hijab, led me to his office. The chairman himself was a short man, also Egyptian, with a sparse, unsuccessful comb-over. His Coke-bottle glasses made his eyes appear squeezed. He stood up halfway as Nancy shut the door behind her, and indicated for me to take a seat in the black pleather chair in front of his desk. "Duktora?"

"Please, call me Sara. I don't understand the need for this formality among colleagues."

"Duktora, you've returned from America after many years?"

He and I both knew that was true. It was a question as superfluous as the incessant *duktors* and *duktoras* everyone loved to toss around. I didn't answer.

"Things have changed." He was silent for so long, I thought he might be done. "This sharia professor, if you complain about him, he will humiliate you."

"What could he possibly do to humiliate me?" There was nothing this professor had on me. I wasn't afraid of him.

"He will drag your name in the gutter, the newspapers."

"This is what it's come to? Slander in the newspapers?" Allowing these small-minded morons to grab power through blackmail was not my idea of acceptable. "Let him."

"It affects us all, Duktora. It's difficult enough to get students to major in philosophy these days. It's haram now, don't you know?" He puffed out his cheeks, looking fed up. "May I?" He held a cigarette between his yellowed fingertips.

"Please."

He pulled out a heavy silver lighter from his desk drawer, lit his cigarette, then drew on it slowly, using the pause to consider his next words. "I've been here a long time, Duktora. Things have become"—he took another lazy drag—"complicated." Then, after one more interminable interlude, he concluded with: "Watch where you walk, Duktora. Not just here. Everywhere."

I promised to take the matter of the sharia professor no further and left his office with a blown-up sense of self-righteousness. Back into the swarm of black, white, and red all over, like some silly riddle from elementary school.

One thing I was wrong about in those early days was my women students. Whether or not I could see their faces, they were not unsympathetic. They were not judging me the way I was judging them. They wanted an education, just like the young girls Mama Yasmine taught in Iraq. And if they wanted an education, I was going to give it to them.

These girls are raised so differently than I was. They are forbidden to drive, are forced to wear black, not by law but by family dictate, more powerful than any law. Many of them are the first women in their families to go to university. Some of their mothers are illiterate. It took me a while to figure out how this could be. Mama Yasmine had won a scholarship to AUB. My mother and her friends had attended university, as had all of my generation. But these girls in black and boys in white and red are the daughters and sons of recently naturalized Bedouin. They do not share Kuwait's maritime past, and they missed out on the boom years of Kuwait's early statehood. Theirs is a new majority—conservative, traditional, with a sheen of religiosity—and it is not silent. Their fathers dominate parliament. One of them is taking me to court.

Out of every twenty, there's always one. This semester, the one of twenty—I can't remember her name, but of course it must be her—was especially clever. When I discussed the power of the masculine gaze, its threat to female agency, she had raised her hand, even though I had informed the class at the beginning of the semester that there was no need for that. I motioned for her to go ahead.

"*We* have the power of the gaze."

"Who's *we*?"

"Munaqabas."

"How so?"

"We look out, but you can't look in."

She was right. I couldn't see her. I still can't.

"Do you think you're invisible?" I asked.

"Yes. We are invisible."

"I see you." I remember smiling at her. "I see your niqab. It tells me something about you. It makes me assume certain things, even if they aren't true."

"What things?"

"That you might be wearing that niqab because someone made you. That the reason you wear it, even if no one made you, is because of the power of the male gaze. It's so powerful it renders you invisible. Or attempts to anyway. What do you think?"

I remember some of the other girls agreeing with me, but I don't remember whether she did. Maybe after that exchange she decided to start recording my lectures. She might have a vast collection of incriminating audio evidence. Mr. Al-Baatin mentioned that the death of God was on the recording, so I figure it must be Nietzsche. But I remember the Spinoza discussions being worse:

"Did God prohibit Adam from eating the apple because it was bad or because it was wrong?"

My students don't respond.

"What was wrong with the apple?"

"It was evil," someone mumbles.

"How do you know that? What if it was just poisonous? What happens when you eat poison?"

"You die."

"Is that good or bad?"

"Bad."

"Is it wrong to eat a poison apple, or is it bad to eat a poison apple?"

Silence.

"If someone wants to eat a poisoned apple, knowing the poison might kill him, I say let him. It'll be bad for him because his life will come to an end. But it isn't necessarily wrong. God wanted Adam to live, so he advised him not to eat the apple because it was bad for him, not because it was wrong for him to do so. That's been the great misreading of God. It wasn't a command. It was a suggestion."

Maybe after I say all that, I wink at her.

I go on to explain that ethics is about doing good because it adds to life, rather than doing bad, which takes away from it. "If you do something because you think it's right, you're doing it because you're banking on a reward in the afterlife or even in this one. If you don't do something because you think it's wrong, again, you're avoiding it not for some intrinsic reason but to dodge judgment. Ethics requires thought, assessment, joy. Morality demands obedience. It's sad and depleting."

Her complaint against me is fueled by morality, not ethics. She believes in right and wrong, in divine judgment and heavenly reward. She is no Spinozist.

The smell of Maria's dhal drifts up from the kitchen. Time for lunch. I have to stop obsessing over my student and Kuwait University. I'm going to tell Maria.

Lola tiptoes ahead of me. Today is the first clear day we've had since my arrest, a sky so blue it shimmers. Mom's outdoor flowers—kept alive by Aasif—grow as gladly as if they were in a Viennese garden. The clarity of the sky reminds me of winter, of riding bikes as a kid with Karim and the guys, practicing our wheelies and skids.

Back then Surra was an unceasing construction site, houses popping up to the left and right of Ali bin Abi Talib Street, which ran between Damascus and Maghreb Streets. I was one of the boys, refusing to wear anything other than ripped jeans and Karim's hand-me-down baseball shirts. After riding all afternoon, I would come home to Maria. "What have you done, Saru? Crazy boys! What's happened to your knees?" I had the ugliest knees, scabby, bloody, ashy with dust. "You must take care, Saru, or you'll end up with the knees of an elephant! I'll give you a bath tonight, then we'll rub them with coconut oil." At eight I was taking baths by myself most nights. But on the days when I came home cut up or plain exhausted, Maria bathed me, sitting me down in the same tub I still use, scrubbing my hair with the full strength of her arms.

I want to curl up in bed with the covers over my head and think about us in winter under a crystalline sky, oblivious of the shit that would pile on us in decades to come. To feel again Maria's reassuring arms cushioning childhood hurts. It's me who should be protecting her, not burdening her with this hideous revelation. I want to ostrich my way through the day, through the next few months. I think I may have ostriched my way through the last eleven years. It's become second nature.

Maria ladles dhal I know I'm not going to eat into a bowl. I take a sip of water and wait for her to sit down.

"Maria, something has happened I need to tell you about, but I don't want you to worry."

She looks alarmed. A bad start. "What is it, Saru beti?"

I take a breath. "You know these religious monkeys in parliament, always causing garbar? Well, they're saying that I said something against Allah."

Maria's eyes widen. She's no stranger to the changes in Kuwait since after the invasion. She's witnessed them firsthand, longer than I have. "What do you mean, *against Allah*?"

"At university, they're saying I taught my students something against God, and they want to take me to court."

"Oh, Jesus." She puts her hand on her heart.

"Maria, this is nothing, really nothing. I have a lawyer. He knew Mom. He promises it's going to be okay."

"He knew your maa?"

"Yes. He's good. He says it'll be fine." This is not exactly true, but it's what Maria needs to hear.

"What will happen, Saru beti?"

I hesitate. There is no benefit in sharing all possible scenarios with Maria, and yet, selfishly, I want to so that she can carry some of the fear for me. "If I'm found guilty, there's a small chance, a very small chance, I will hang." I circle my hand around my neck, and it feels oddly soothing.

Maria gasps, and I immediately regret the gesture. I get up to hug her. "It's not going to happen, Maria. I promise." I have no right to make such a promise, but I've caused enough harm already. "I had to tell you in case your daughters say something."

She whispers, "How would my daughters know?"

It feels like a slipup. "It was in the papers."

Maria cries out. She crosses herself and pulls her rosary from her pocket. She starts to pray, frantically worrying her beads. I sit down on the floor beside her chair and put my head in her lap. She puts one hand on my head, and I sob like I did as a child. I release a week's worth of despair.

"It's okay, beti. It's okay. Let it out." I've heard these words from Maria more times than I can count. Hearing them again reminds me of everything I've lost, and it feels like I'm losing it all again. I'm dizzy and I want to keep my head in her lap forever, but I force myself to rise.

"Maria, it's going to be fine. It's just a matter of waiting. We have to be patient. When will Josie come get you?"

"I'm not going anywhere." Her tone, the one I know so well, recovers its authority. Maria gets off her chair and stands beside me, shoulder to shoulder.

"You have to go! Josie's promotion."

"Have you told Karim yet? When is he coming?"

"Not yet," I say. "I will." My brother hasn't returned to Kuwait in over a decade; I don't know if this will be enough to bring him back.

"You tell that boy to come futta-fut."

I miss my brother. I want him to come. Karim and I see each other in California every summer, somewhere in Europe for a couple of weeks in January. A few days after my arrest, I made up an excuse about being pressured to teach summer session, telling him I couldn't make it to California this year. He didn't offer to visit me instead.

Maria calls Josefina and tells her she can't come. I imagine Josie will be disappointed, rightfully resentful. I think about all the times Maria has put my brother and me ahead of her own children, whether by choice or force of circumstance. It upsets me, but I can't convince her to change her mind. I walk her to her bed for her afternoon nap and kiss her on the forehead. Maria closes her eyes and is snoring fitfully within seconds.

I yawn as I make my way past Bebe Mitu's cage. I haven't been sleeping well. I remember none of my dreams, but I wake up in the middle of the night drenched in sweat. By the time I shove aside my soaked pillow and resettle on a dry one, I'm wide awake. I try to put myself back to sleep by counting backward from eight, a trick Mama Yasmine learned from her own grandmother and passed down to me.

Mama Yasmine was so proud of my degrees. "You get it from me too, you know. Not just your mother," she'd say. I'm glad she's not here to see what my degrees have brought me. By the time she died, Mama Yasmine had already seen too much.

Eight, seven, six, five, four, three, two, one. Mama Yasmine counted down from half a million to twenty thousand Marsh Arabs, stripped of the environment they had cultivated for five thousand years. "One crazy man decides to drain primeval marshes as punishment, and nobody stops him," she would rail against Saddam Hussein. With depleted marshes vanish reed warblers and marbled ducks, maybe the sacred ibis and snakebirds. With them go fish and foxes and otters and rats. Vanished rats are worth counting, too.

I count down from eight the ones who are gone: my father, Uncle Hisham, Mama Lulwa, Nabil, my mother, Mama Yasmine. My brother—not dead but not here with me. I arrive at one and hold my breath. If I'm lucky, by then I'm back to sleep.

Lulwa

The first six months of pregnancy were not difficult for Lulwa despite her birdlike build. She carried the weight of her belly with ease as she wandered through now-familiar jungles. She knew that the flutters she felt inside her would settle into her first son.

When Mubarak returned from trips with his father, he retreated with Lulwa into their bedroom for days. The French doors that opened onto the veranda were covered with herb-green velvet curtains that kept the outside out. Sometimes they would part them a sliver to let in the pale evening light. Mubarak whispered to Lulwa on the island of their bed that he hoped the flutters would coalesce into the shape of a baby girl. "With thick lashes and twinkling eyes. The kind of laugh that makes others laugh along."

Lulwa would laugh just that sort of laugh and say, "It's a boy, Mubarak. How many times do I have to tell you. My Bader, slice of the moon."

Mubarak tried to help his father redirect their business, to forestall what looked like its inevitable failure. Lulwa flew through her sixth month of pregnancy into her seventh with wings on her back. Mubarak put his nose to Lulu's protruding belly button and inhaled his baby's smell. He closed his eyes and pictured his son running barefoot through moss, chasing after his mother. Falling into contented sleep, Mubarak heard his boy's laughter chiming through trees, sending birds flocking into a crepuscular sky.

Lulwa mailed a flood of letters home to her siblings detailing the day-to-day changes she was experiencing. She was sixteen and didn't know what to assume. Everything felt right. *Nausea in the morning and then a swooshing hunger for chapatis,* observed one letter to her family. *Thicker hair and nails like claws!* exclaimed another. She was so busy dashing off letters to her siblings, she failed to notice that by the fifth month, few responses came back. She didn't mind. She missed her sisters and brother, but her pregnancy filled the hole of their absence.

Yet sometimes, alone at night, her ears muffled by the din of nocturnal insects, Lulwa yearned for her mother. She knew Sheikha would not caress her forehead or murmur calming prayers over her swelling belly. Lulwa did not want Sheikha for the impossible. She wanted Sheikha because it was Sheikha who made Lulwa a daughter, and being a daughter was not something Lulwa was ready to let go.

The reason the letters from Sumaiyya, Hussa, and Ahmed were decreasing was not because they weren't writing to their pregnant little sister, asking questions, offering reassurances, promising eternal love to their nephew. (They believed Lulu when she said her firstborn would be a boy.)

"Do you think Khalti Zaineb and Hayya are looking after her?" Hussa asked, dipping a nib into a jar of ink Ahmed had refilled at the British colonial office where he worked. *Office* was an exaggeration. It was a room where, once a week, a staff of two—Ahmed and his friend Saad—cranked out an English-language bulletin written by an officer for the British in the country. *Bulletin* was even more of an exaggeration. It was a one-page memo detailing the comings and goings of colonial personnel.

"Naturally," Ahmed retorted. "Khalti Zaineb must be doing a better job than Mainooneh Sheikha ever would." On an envelope for the letter Hussa was writing to their sister, he stuck a carmine King George V India postage stamp, *KUWAIT* overprinted on the king's profiled shoulder. All three siblings referred to their sister's mother-in-law respectfully as *Khalti* and to their own mother as *Mainooneh*. Crazy like the bougainvillea that climbed the walls of merchant family homes. Crazy like the shimaal winds that kicked up sandstorms in June, devouring ships tarrying at sea.

Had the Al-Talib troupe thought to search the contents of their mother's hidden box, they would have found most of their letters to Lulwa and Lulwa's to them. Sheikha had learned of Lulwa's pregnancy when a young boy from the fireej had delivered a letter directly, instead of waiting for Ahmed to visit the post office. The gesture was meant as a kindness. Sheikha ordered the boy to read the letter to her. He jumbled most of the words together, but *pregnancy* and *five months* were clear.

That girl of hers was going to have everything she never would. The thick burden of sad regrets and unnatural jealousies, unwieldy as wet rope, choked her. Sheikha's eyes rolled back in their sockets. Sweat poured from her forehead, dripped off her cheeks to the dusty ground and onto the toes of the barefoot boy. Then she gathered herself. "Listen here, little man. A word of this to anyone, and I will murder you in your sleep. At the start of each week, you will collect any piece of mail addressed to or from this family and bring it to me, as you've done today. I will pay you. You will tell no one. Do you understand?"

The boy nodded, then turned and ran as fast as his wet feet could go.

Lulwa was growing accustomed to small triangular pokes and oval prods, tiny impressions of elbows and feet under the surface of her abdomen. "Do you think his bones are flexible or hard?" she would ask Mubarak when he was home from his trips.

"As flexible as chickens' wings."

"Can he open his eyes? Do his lids have lashes?"

"I doubt he can open his eyes, but if his lashes are like yours, they must be growing already."

"Does he dream?"

"Sometimes he dreams of swimming in puddles. Sometimes he dreams of colors. Red like your blood, blue like your veins. Sometimes he dreams the same dreams as you. Other times, your thoughts."

Lulwa would pace her breathing and think happy thoughts about birds on a secret island. Bader would flip-flop in response.

One early morning in March, at the start of her eighth month, Lulwa bolted awake to a metal poker stabbing her lower back. She howled, and one of the maids ran to get Zaineb. Lulwa could not feel Bader moving. Without thinking, she called for her mother. "Help me, Mama Sheikha! Please don't leave me, ya Yumma!"

And then Zaineb was beside her, wiping her forehead with a clean towel. A British midwife who lived nearby rushed to the bungalow. The delivery was not easy. As it turned out, Bader had lashes and nails and ten fingers and toes. He was smaller than he should have been, but his lungs, the midwife assured them, pinching his thigh for a yowl, were strong.

Bader slept beside his mother in the drawer of a giant teak chest pulled open so that it was level with her side of the bed. Lulwa lined the drawer with cotton and soft linens, making a cozy nest. The white bassinet Zaineb had ordered for the newborn collected dust in a corner. It would have swallowed him up.

Mubarak traveled less during the first year of Bader's life, drawn to his wife and child with a magnetic pull. He cradled Bader when he whimpered awake, hungry or mystified by the stark light of day. He cooed to hear his son coo back. Mubarak exploded with a pride nothing, not even failing fortunes, could dampen.

By the time Bader turned one, Mubarak was forced back into a life of excessive travel with his father, patching together temporary solutions to problems soon to be exacerbated by a global economic depression. On top of the catastrophe of cultured pearls, an embargo imposed by Ibn Saud on Kuwait in 1923 was biting into the overland trade of merchant families like the Al-Mustafas. Mubarak's more frequent absences during Bader's second year forced Lulwa to fully register her siblings' missing letters. A few letters arrived sporadically, but these were confusing, containing bits of information missing key elements. One letter, arriving in April 1927, mentioned that Sumaiyya had found a home with a small courtyard and that Ahmed was the only one left in the house. How could unmarried Sumaiyya be living in a home with a small courtyard? What had happened to Hussa? Another letter mentioned that Ahmed's foot was healing. Healing from what? Lulwa fretted about Ahmed's foot, imagining it gangrenous or even amputated.

Bader kept Lulwa afloat. Everything was a marvel to her son, and Lulwa marveled along with him. His pudgy fingers would reach out to touch the crest of a mynah without fear of its snapping orange beak. He jumped up and down the first time he spotted the black-and-white mosaic wings of butterflies hovering around lime-laden trees. When he glimpsed stars glinting in a moonless sky, he squealed, "Mama, dhekko, chotta, chotta buttee!" Lulwa looked, seeing stars for the little lights they were. Flies swatted off the custard flesh of sitaphal were addressed by her son as *tiny birdies*. Bader's miniatured perspective distracted his mother, one star, one bird at a time.

In early August, in the midst of the interminable monsoon season of 1928, Lulwa and Bader were in the study when a letter was brought to her on a silver tray by a young maid new to the household. The letter was from Sheikha. Lulwa's body tensed. Her mother had never before sent a letter.

Lulwa sat at her secretary desk and, with rigid fingers, tore open the envelope and tried to decipher the sloppy handwriting.

> *Daughter Lulwa,*
> *Your brother Ahmed is dying. Come home before it's too late.*

Lulwa pushed back her chair, legs scraping the hand-painted tiles. Bader looked up from his set of wooden blocks, startled by the harsh sound.

Lulwa crashed to the ground. The young maid who had

delivered the letter ran back in, unsure what to do. Bader began to cry. The maid picked him up and ran to the main house to fetch Zaineb. Zaineb raced to the cottage to find her daughter-in-law moaning like the end was near. She pulled the scrunched-up letter from Lulwa's fist and gasped, then drew her daughter-in-law's limp body into her lap and caressed her hair. "Ya Lulu, take a breath! How could we not have heard?"

"The letters stopped coming. The letters! I should have paid attention. Not Ahmed! He hasn't seen Bader yet. Why didn't I insist they come? I'm leaving right now!" *Before it's too late.* Her mother's words echoed.

Zaineb scrambled to piece together their options. "Bader will stay here. We'll arrange passage for you as soon as Khalifa and Mubarak return."

"No! Bader comes with me. He must meet his uncle, his only uncle on his mother's side." Lulwa sobbed into Zaineb's lap.

"We'll fix it, Lulu. Don't worry."

It took over a month to organize Lulwa's trip to Kuwait. Meanwhile the Al-Mustafa family could discover nothing about the ailing Ahmed Al-Talib. The Al-Talibs, a poor family, would not have been known to the merchant elite journeying between Kuwait and India, bringing back news primarily of their own privileged circle. But also it was impossible to push against the southwestern monsoon winds and the strong shimaal that gusted across Kuwait during the summer months, making information even harder to come by. That year the shimaal blew for over ninety days, destroying an already precarious pearling season.

It wasn't until mid-September that Lulwa boarded a boum heading to Kuwait, Bader clasped in her arms. This boum would be captained by the Al-Mustafas' best nokhada, known for his ability to sail against winds. The captain warned that passage would be rocky and dangerous. Lulwa did not balk. Mubarak, putting his faith in the experienced nokhada, promised to follow soon, three weeks at most, weather permitting. As Mubarak gazed up at Lulwa on the ship—her eyes dry, no tears left to shed, their son in her arms—he had no idea they would not return to India for seven years.

Yasmine

By late August 1934, Yasmine had experienced unimaginable versions of Iraq's heat. Dusty heat erupting out of the desert at the end of April, cutting short the splendor of spring. The magnified heat of a July sun burning a hole through her paper skin. The white heat of August obliterating the divide between land and sky. Still, the heat on the night Yasmine first spotted Marwan was different.

That day had stunned everyone, even those accustomed to the relentless furnace of Baghdad summers. Early morning had been infernal but inert. "Like it's waiting for some catastrophe," Yasmine had overheard Dr. Sherif's sister Sula saying to her mother, Asya, behind a cupped hand, not wanting to tempt stray jinn. Yasmine would never forget Sula's words. As an angry sun rose into a blanched sky, the blinding shimmer kept people indoors. Shop fronts remained shuttered. Coffeehouses kept their chairs flipped on tables, figuring no customers would pass through their doors. Even the birds remained grounded.

Dr. Sherif considered canceling that Thursday night's gathering. Asya and Sula, not wanting to spend any part of the sweltering afternoon in the kitchen, hoped he would. But Yasmine, visiting the family for the weekend, as she had done all year, didn't want to miss a single one of the literary meetings she so eagerly anticipated. "Please don't cancel, Dr. Sherif," she pleaded, glancing at the two women who had become surrogate mother and aunt to her. Their eyes narrowed, but she caught their exchange of smiles and knew they wouldn't really be upset. "Your guests will come. A little heat won't stop them."

"This heat isn't little, ya Yasmine. It feels like we're treading shorbat 'adas. And you know writers and poets steam up even more than ordinary people. There won't be any air left to breathe!"

"Maybe it will keep away the regulars. Maybe only the valiant will show up tonight. Maybe, Dr. Sherif, we'll hear something extraordinary." She rolled the last word like an actress in the films they went to see at Cinema Al-Hamra.

Maybe, Dr. Sherif thought to himself, the girl was right. He decided not to cancel. He would live to regret his decision.

Yasmine's prediction that only the determined would show up proved correct. The room was not heaving as it normally was, and there were a few new faces. One intrepid visitor was Marwan. This was his first visit to Dr. Sherif's, but Dr. Sherif knew who he was, his identity given away by his impeccable linen suit and his easy Basrawi lilt. This was one of the many sons of the Pasha of Basra.

He was hard to ignore. He stood tall with a straight posture, his chin slanted slightly to the left. His thick hair was long in front, slicked back with a pomade ineffective by late afternoon. Much of his nervous energy was spent pushing hair off his fore-head. As he took a seat to the right of Dr. Sherif, Yasmine paid special attention to the bobcat color of his eyes, in sharp contrast to his black hair. For a second the contrast reminded Yasmine of her father. But this man was nothing like the humble Hussein Suleiman. This man was as full of his station as the loathsome Madame Majida.

The past few months, Yasmine had started to leave a few sheets of paper on Dr. Sherif's desk, under his copy of Taha Hussein's *Al-Ayyam*. Her pieces were short, using language tighter and cleaner than the ambitious young writers who frequented Dr. Sherif's sa-lon. She wrote about her grandmother standing behind the front door of her home in Istanbul, waiting for the knock that signaled all men had exited so she could remove her veil and begin the day's chores. Even after the knock, Yeliz's mother would lean against the door, look up at the ceiling, and count backward. *Eight, seven, six, five, four, three, two, one.* Counting down against accidental sin. Yasmine wrote about the little island of Ziri in Saida. Grow-ing up she had seen it as nothing more than a stub of pompous rock and had refused to join in clandestine trips with her friends. But from afar, Ziri had become a kind of amulet, surfacing in-side her like a promise. Mostly she wrote about her new life in Baghdad, about the roaming vendors specializing in everything from knife-sharpening to wood-chopping; about the competing pigeon tamers who released their birds together at the same time of day so that the skies thronged with movement; about the mys-terious, susurrating sound of palms in the wind.

Yasmine didn't dare read her writing out loud during the

weekly salons, not that she was invited to do so. Dr. Sherif might have believed in her writing, but he feared her presence alone was a risk to her reputation. That night of the static heat, Yasmine sat in the rear, as usual, her hair and body wrapped in a black abaya. She listened to a tentative Marwan Pasha read his poem. He kept his eyes glued to the back of the room as he recited, looking straight through Yasmine like she was a side table or upholstered divan. It made Yasmine want to throw off the black covering.

After Marwan finished, Yasmine stood up abruptly, scraping the legs of her chair against the floor and drawing attention to herself. When the men saw who it was, they turned away, eager to focus on issues more urgent than an unruly young woman. Yasmine stomped to the kitchen, pulled off her abaya, and set to work helping Asya and Sula arrange the food.

"What did you think, Yasmine?" Sula asked. "Did you hear anything *extraordinary*?"

"Nothing special, really." She hesitated. "Maybe just the last one? Marwan Pasha's poem."

"Oooooooh . . . the Pasha of Basra's youngest and brightest. A real catch!"

"Ishht, Sula! Enough!" Asya's brusqueness was uncharacteristic. "That's nothing to joke about."

Sula looked away, struck by her mother's sharp tone.

"She didn't mean anything by it, Mama Asya," Yasmine comforted. "Did you, Khalla Sula?"

"The pasha's son is nothing to joke about," Asya repeated. "One wrong word caught by one stray ear, and who knows what could fall on our heads! British officers, kings, and pashas—that's nothing to do with us."

This conversation had the opposite effect on Yasmine than it was meant to. Marwan and his over-precious poem and indifferent yellow eyes seemed newly worth considering. As she made her way to the dining room with a platter of rice layered with onion hashu and roast lamb, Yasmine left off her abaya.

The men lingered in the main sala, and Yasmine could hear them discussing politics. They lamented the deficiencies of King Ghazi, only twenty-two, easily swayed by savvy men with clout. Not that his father, King Faisal I, had been without fault, but at least he had managed independence.

"It couldn't have been easy for him," ventured a young man in a wool suit incongruous with the fiery night. "Still, foisted on us by the British, like we couldn't have produced a man of our own!"

"The British, the British," an older man interrupted. "Their fingers in every pot, yes, yes. But let's be honest, it's also us. Tribal sheikhs on one side, ulema on the other, and effendis clamoring to rein them all in—no offense, ya Pasha."

Marwan looked up at the mention of the title. "I'm no pasha, ya sayyidi. That was my father."

"Your father, the Pasha of Basra," the younger man piped in again, mopping sweat off his forehead. "That's exactly the sort of man I was talking about. If only the British hadn't wiped him off the scene in the 1920s. Instead of some puppet-king, a man of the people!"

Yasmine noticed that the men spoke more openly in front of Marwan than she would have presumed given Mama Asya's outburst in the kitchen. She also noticed that the son of the pasha nodded politely but paid more attention to his fingernails.

The Pasha of Basra had been an ardent nationalist. He was not Western educated and lacked the smooth edges the British preferred. But he was fearless and shrewd, managing to keep himself in the good graces of the Ottomans as well as the local sheikhs. He trusted no one, and no one trusted him. He evaded assassination attempts from Baghdad and Istanbul, carrying out successful assassinations of his own when threatened. He taxed the rich plantation owners of Basra and distributed that income to the poor. The pasha understood that without the support of the landless peasants, a nation could not be secured.

He struggled for Iraqi independence from the Ottomans, and when authority shifted to the British after the war, he wrestled for independence from them. He was perceived as a wild card by the British, not sufficiently pliable or reliable. His penetrating black eyes, nothing like his son's, paralyzed his children and colonial agents alike with fear. The British tried to use the pasha to further their interests, but they realized that he couldn't be controlled and decided that his cleverness and charisma posed a threat.

One afternoon in April 1921, when Marwan was twelve, the pasha went to tea at the British Residency in Baghdad. After exiting the agent's house, no doubt full of dry British scones and tepid tea, he was arrested on a bridge over the Tigris and exiled to Ceylon, where he would spend the next four years, a threat to the British no more. The pasha was permitted to return to Basra only on the condition that he stay out of politics. He had left Iraq a noble lion and returned a shell of a man. Basrawis suspected he had been poisoned in Ceylon—arsenic, the rumor went. He was permitted by the British to seek treatment in Germany, but he died a week after his arrival there in July 1929. The British refused to authorize an autopsy, despite the family's request. His funeral was attended by dignitaries and nobles from across the Gulf and by date pickers and fishermen, the near-destitute whose lives he had tried to improve. His body, carried through Mahalat Al-Seef by the people of Basra and by his sons, was buried in Zubair.

It had been only five years since the pasha's death, but Yasmine knew nothing of Basra's recent history. What she did know was that she wanted this pasha's son to see her. As the men made their way down the hall to the dining room, Yasmine held herself in place, slowed her rapid intakes of breath by counting backward like her grandmother, pretended to straighten cutlery and smooth out the lace tablecloth.

Dr. Sherif and Marwan entered the dining room first. Yasmine looked up and smiled the smile Majid had wanted to marry. Dr. Sherif smiled back. But when Marwan made his way toward her, extending his hand to shake hers, Dr. Sherif asked nervously, "Yasmine, shouldn't you be with my mother and sister?"

"I'm helping them bring out the food, Dr. Sherif," Yasmine said, careful not to look at Marwan. "We have a few more dishes."

"Is this your daughter, Dr. Sherif?" Marwan asked. "It's an honor to meet you, Miss . . . ?"

"Yasmine," she whispered, still refusing to look at the pasha's son.

"Yasmine," he repeated, lowering his volume to match hers.

Yasmine turned away from the group of men and sauntered, unhurriedly, back to the kitchen.

Marwan was back the next day with a bunch of sweet-smelling razqi for Yasmine. And the day after that, and most of the following weekends, he returned. Week after week, more and more bunches of razqi. He would hand Yasmine the flowers, and they would exchange a few words about poetry.

Dr. Sherif couldn't understand Marwan's fixation. His persistence seemed to be something other than love. Acquisitive rather than passionate. But Dr. Sherif kept his opinion to himself. He put up with Marwan's visits, his flowers, the short exchanges between Yasmine and the young man because he believed the pasha's son would soon tire of her. He could have anyone—why would he settle for a fatherless girl from Saida? Also, Dr. Sherif suspected that to forbid Yasmine would be to make the forbidden irresistible. So he tried not to imagine Hussein's disappointment and made sure he was present during their brief chats, adopting the role of benevolent chaperone rather than domineering patriarch.

Marwan carried his sense of entitlement like a trophy, but Yasmine could detect his concealed vulnerabilities. This was a neglected, lonely man, keenly intelligent, who deserved to study literature at one of the esteemed universities—Oxford or Cambridge—but who had been prevented from doing so by the pasha. The pasha had had many wives and had paid only for the eldest son by each wife to study abroad. Marwan, a younger son, had studied law, which he hated, at the Syrian University in Damascus. He wrote poetry in his spare time and tended his mother's garden in Basra.

Yasmine was flattered by Marwan's attention and did not think to question why he pursued her. Since the debacle with Madame Majida, Yasmine had lost much of her vanity. It was an immoral trait, one the missionaries would disapprove of, but, Yasmine was now reminded, it felt splendid.

One afternoon, sixteen months after her arrival in Iraq, four months into Marwan's courtship, Yasmine received a letter from her mother. It made no mention of Yasmine's latest missive, crowded with descriptions of booksellers on Al-Mutanabbi Street and of quffas, round reed boats like bowls, floating back and forth across the Tigris. It mentioned, instead, that Yousef had stolen the last of the money Yeliz had stashed away in the chipped blue vase to spend on prostitutes and drink. Yousef had abandoned his studies, did not have a job, wandered the streets day and night. Yeliz ate nothing for five days, preferring to starve than to ask neighbors for help. On the sixth day, Yousef brought home some khubez from the local baker, crying his apologies into his mother's sharp ribs. This was not the first time. Yeliz needed her daughter's help.

Yasmine felt ashamed that her first instinct was not to save her mother; it was to protect her own desires. Then she remembered her vow on the bus.

Marwan proposed in front of Dr. Sherif, but without acknowledging the doctor's authority. Disturbed by Marwan's effrontery, Dr. Sherif cleared his throat to admonish him, pasha's son or not, just as Marwan turned his attention to the doctor. "I promise she will be my first and only," he said, blinking once with practiced deliberation.

It was a pointed promise given the number of wives his father had taken and Marwan's own elevated position. Dr. Sherif shook his head, unconvinced, but Yasmine chose to believe Marwan.

"I will marry you on three conditions," Yasmine answered. "My mother and brother must be permitted to live with us in Basra. I must be allowed to complete my academic term, then return to Lebanon before we marry to bring them back with us to Iraq."

Marwan bowed low, took Yasmine's right hand, and kissed it, to Dr. Sherif's dismay. "I accept your conditions. The women of my family will arrive the day after tomorrow to ask for your permission, Dr. Sherif."

After Marwan left, Dr. Sherif advised Yasmine not to accept. He warned that life in palaces was not what it seemed, and that wealth, like poverty, carried its own load of troubles. But Yasmine thought of her mother's hunger, her brother's likely ruin, and also, shamefully, how this news would make Madame Majida choke on her arrogance, and chose to ignore him.

"He has the soul of an artist, Dr. Sherif. Surely that will compensate for any faults."

Dr. Sherif wasn't convinced. With Asya's help, he secreted a note in a pocket of Yasmine's dressing gown, where he knew she would find it. It read: *No mistake is irreversible. My home will always be yours.* And with that, Dr. Sherif let Yasmine go.

Sara

The day after I break the news to her, Maria is calmer, which calms me. We keep to our routine—breakfast and lunch together, films at night, looking after Lola and Bebe Mitu. Sometimes Aasif joins us at the kitchen table, though he doesn't say much and doesn't eat a thing. It's like he's waiting for something to be resolved. The skies have been uncharacteristically blue for days. From inside an air-conditioned bubble, it's deceptively inviting, but I know better. Out there it's hot as embers.

Maria wanders around the house, pretending to dust. When I'm not down in the kitchen, I sit at my father's desk, pretending to work, or I swim obsessively in our indoor pool. The pool occupies the center of the house in audacious seventies style. Uncle Hisham designed our Surra house and his own next door. Aasif balances the pH of the water following the instructions my father gave him decades ago.

Dad taught Karim and me to swim in a St. Louis public pool in the dead of winter. Back in Kuwait we would spend every weekend at the Gazelle Club. We swam in the deep end of the sea-filled Olympic-size pool until our fingers shriveled. Beyond the pool was the beach, beyond the beach, water so clear we sometimes forgot we couldn't drink it.

At the Gazelle Club, a long jetty jutted out from the barrier that ran along the outer perimeter of the pool. Its concrete was mosaicked with broken stones that cut our feet, its steel girders threatening to skewer us if we weren't careful. Our parents tried to keep us away from the jetty, beckoning us back to the bowling alley or dance floor in the basement of the club. But under the spell of cocktails in the sun, they would often let it slide. Karim and I would hide together under that jetty all the time. We would hum, echoing the sound of waves amplified by the concrete cave. Our timbre would gradually harmonize with the water, and sometimes we felt like we were levitating. The only person to join us sometimes was Nabil, who, when the reverie went on too long for his taste, would raise and lower his eyebrows, making us laugh.

Days waft by like stray feathers. I check my archaic Filofax to confirm how many have passed since my arrest: thirteen . . . fourteen . . . fifteen. Aasif has made chicken mechbous and dakous for lunch today, my favorite. His food, always delicious, has ascended, in these last two weeks, to the sublime. *He's trying to save me with his cooking.* How conceited of me to think so, but that's what it feels like.

"My lawyer's going to visit today," I tell Maria. It's been a week since his last visit, six days since I broke the news to Maria.

She drops her utensils. "Why? Any news?" Aasif stops spooning rice onto her plate.

"No, no, nothing at all. Just his weekly visit. He'll be coming once a week until the trial."

Aasif sits down, his hands clasped on the table in front of him.

Maria reluctantly picks up her spoon and asks, "Have you told your brother?"

I hesitate. Why haven't I told my brother? "No. Not yet."

"What about that Karl of yours?"

Why haven't I told Karl? "No. I will. Both of them. Soon."

"Aré Sara, you and Karim." She sighs and rests her hand on her heart. "My Pungra and Pungri. That boy's big gray eyes like Mama Yasmine's. In St. Louis people would stop us in the street to gawk at him in his stroller. Your mother would mutter words in Arabic. *Evil eye,* she said. I would pray to Jesus to protect his soul. And then you were born and it was the two of you. Remember?"

I've heard our stories dozens of times. "I remember."

"He was a Jain. You would smash those disgusting cockroaches in the garden, and he would bury them in matchboxes. That boy." Maria passes her hand across her forehead. She misses him, and tangled up in her longing for my brother is her ache for her dead son. I understand Karim's principles, refusing to step foot in this country, but it's not right that he doesn't come for Maria. I don't bring this up with him because I know that despite the arresting color of his eyes, my brother has a hard time seeing gray.

I don't remember much about growing up in St. Louis. I was just short of five when we left in 1976, Karim two years older than me. There aren't many photos to jog my memory.

In St. Louis I remember napping on a Pepto-Bismol pink mat at school. On the corner of that mat my mother had written my name in black Sharpie. I remember learning how to write my name. *S . . . A . . . R . . . A spells SARA.* I went home upset that my name was only four letters long.

In St. Louis I remember balancing on the tops of gargantuan pumpkins at Eckert's Farm. I remember chasing Karim, who kept running off to hide behind ever larger pumpkins. Always, my brother, just out of sight.

I remember Mama Yasmine visiting St. Louis. I was afraid she had come to replace Maria, who was on holiday in India at the time. I refused to kiss her. I would pull the cushion out from under her chair at the dining table. I drank her water when she wasn't looking so that she lifted an empty glass to her lips. Only in Kuwait would I come to understand that Mama Yasmine was no threat to Maria at all.

In St. Louis I remember taking walks in our neighborhood with Maria. I have no memory of walks with Mom and Dad. I feel my hand in hers, my body against her hip when she carried me. At a playground near our house, I remember a black-and-white snake like a plastic toy poking its head out from under some rocks. I reach down to touch it, and Maria, who hears the rattle, jumps off the bench, scoops me up, and runs. Before we arrive home, she stops and says, "Saru beti, you mustn't tell Maa about the snake, okay, my darling?" I feel her heart pounding. She doesn't need to ask. I would never say a word against her.

A pink mat, pumpkins like houses, a resented grandmother, a snake—these constitute my memories of St. Louis. In truth, St. Louis only revealed itself to me later, against the backdrop of Kuwait. Snow in place of dust. Green in place of brown. River in place of sea. What I didn't know then was that St. Louis was where my mother left behind her dreams.

Aasif brings up tea and small cinnamon walnut samosas for Mr. Al-Baatin. I sense him hovering beyond the open double door of the living room. Maria decides she wants to meet Mr. Al-Baatin, so she sits beside me on the couch across from the love seat, and I introduce her. "Mr. Al-Baatin, this is Maria. She's been with our family since before I was born. She's worried about things. I've told her there's nothing to worry about, that my case is in good hands." I sound hopeful or slightly deluded, and I smile in a way I suspect is simpering.

For a second Mr. Al-Baatin looks uncomfortable, and my bones melt. That one second lays bare the uncertainty of my situation. Mr. Al-Baatin is a seasoned lawyer, but blasphemy cases are unprecedented in Kuwait. Executions are rare, and I know there has never been an execution for blasphemy, but, it suddenly hits me, mine will be one of the first cases to go on trial since blasphemy has been classified a capital offense. I begin to shiver. I hope Maria doesn't notice Mr. Al-Baatin's fleeting expression or my response.

Mr. Al-Baatin quickly reassumes his sanguine demeanor. "Your Sara will be fine. I'll make sure of it."

Maria doesn't look reassured, and I continue to shiver. Lola saunters into the living room and curls up at Mr. Al-Baatin's feet. He reaches down and scratches behind her ears like he's done it a thousand times. "Sara, the travel ban hasn't been lifted, but the petition hasn't been denied either, so I remain optimistic on that front."

I nod, afraid that if I try to speak, I'll cry. I think he notices.

"If you retract your words, it's highly likely your case will be dismissed in court. That's how these things usually go. As you know, I filed a request with the public prosecution for early dismissal on the condition of your retraction days after your arrest. We'll see what comes of that. Kuwait is not an Islamist state yet. The rule of law still applies." I curl my lip, and he chortles. "More or less."

And if I don't take back the words? Terrified as I am, this thought sneaks in. *What would it mean to stand firm?* I cough a few times. "Thank you, Mr. Al-Baatin. For everything."

He shakes his head like it's nothing, hesitates, and then asks, "Any plans for your brother to come?"

"I haven't told him, but I will. Soon."

Mr. Al-Baatin gives Lola one final pat and lifts himself off the love seat with more grace than his girth should allow. "See you next week?"

"Unless the travel ban is lifted, I'm not going anywhere." For his sake and Maria's, I grin with a confidence I feel not at all.

"Call him tonight, Sara," Maria commands as we watch Mr. Al-Baatin stride toward the gate. "Tonight."

I make no promises. The murkiness between Karim and me that started when we were teenagers has long since cleared. We love each other, but we live separate lives on separate continents. Geographical distance takes its toll on intimacy. This applies as much to my brother as it does to Karl, my Norwegian partner of a decade.

Growing up, Karim and I shared an effortless closeness despite the two years between us. Under the staircase of our Surra home, we would create miniature laboratories or bakeries or supermarkets together. Karim imagined a given trade, and I played whatever role he wanted me to. Maria would call and call, but we couldn't hear her, engrossed in our undercover distractions. She would get upset, not believing we couldn't hear her voice bouncing through the house. We would swear it was true, and it was.

Karim's friends were my friends. I had grown up with Faris, Daoud, and Nabil. They were over at our house every weekend. I tagged along when they went out bike riding, kicked a ball around, or went swimming at the Gazelle Club. At first they thought our closeness, Karim's and mine, was weird. They weren't that way with their own sisters. But Karim continued to include me, and eventually the weirdness went away.

Our mother wasn't clingy with us. She was, if anything, eager to see us exploring, figuring things out for ourselves. When the Fifth Ring Road was being built behind our house, she let us ramble in the ditches of what would become a major eight-lane divided highway. I was eight, Karim ten. Hundreds of Korean construction workers built that highway while we were at school. By the time the bus dropped us home again, they were gone. We changed out of our uniforms, gulped down lunch with our parents—the one meal we ate together—finished our homework, and dashed off to play World War I. We would spend all afternoon down in the empty ditches.

Karim and I would have dinner on a folding table in front of the TV. Maria sat with us, making sure we ate. She would eat later in the kitchen with Aasif, after she put us to bed. Our parents would usually go out for dinner, but even if they were home, Karim and I would not eat with them. Lunchtime was for kids, dinnertime for grown-ups. We didn't mind. We had Maria. Before bed, Maria told us stories about Pungra and Pungri, the naughtiest monkeys in the jungle. "Nothing like the two of you," she would cluck as she kissed the tops of our heads and blessed our sleep.

I would sneak into my brother's room most nights after bedtime. Dad would find us huddled under the blanket in Karim's bed reading comics, which Mom didn't allow but which Dad bought for us anyway. He would take away the flashlight and comics, but he let me stay with Karim. I would fall asleep curled against my brother's back.

The last time my brother flew to Kuwait was for Mom's 'azza. He had made it known unequivocally: "I'm never returning to this hellhole again." I don't want to be the one to pull him back here. I'll postpone the call another day or two.

Lulwa

Lulwa spent four weeks at sea imagining her brother's wasting body, the gangrenous spread from foot to calf to thigh. She pushed back against her mind's urge to turn her brother into a corpse. She relied on her son to reel her in. The smallness of Bader's shoulders as he hunched over the crabs and shrimp sailors tossed on deck, his gleeful squeals as the creatures scampered across the slats to avoid the cook's pot.

Sailing into the bay of Kuwait, Lulwa held her breath. It was late in the season, and most of the larger ships were gone. But the harbor thronged with smaller sambouks and jalbouts from Basra, shuttling water, dates, rice, soap. The shoreline was unceasing movement. The sailors on Lulwa's boum sang, their rhythmic drumming announcing their triumphant arrival. Those onshore responded with their own songs and drums, a relieved welcome home.

Lulwa and Bader and their belongings were rapidly transferred to the boum's longboat, and the sailors rowed the two lone passengers to shore. Lulwa wasn't surprised to find the seafront empty of familiar faces. She pictured her sisters at their brother's side, wiping his febrile skin, coaxing each phlegm-soaked breath. What did surprise Lulwa was the sharp twist in her gut as she viewed the mud buildings of Kuwait Town. She recalled the smell of sun on crisp laundry and bemoaned how thoroughly India had nudged Kuwait out of her heart.

With Bader on her hip and two young boys lugging her trunk for a few paise, Lulwa navigated the complex warren of alleyways through her old fireej. A number of homes, made of coral stone and mud, had collapsed during one of the annual torrential storms. Though some of the wider alleys seemed slightly off-kilter, the narrow lanes she had routinely followed home from childhood chores and jaunts led her back again.

Lulwa pushed on the old door of the family house, not surprised to find it bolted. The sudden longing she felt to step through the entrance once again caught her off guard. She put Bader down and pounded hard against the thick teak door. The two boys carrying her trunk fought back smirks.

It took five long minutes for the door to heave open. Lulwa lifted Bader over the raised threshold, then carefully stepped over it herself. Sheikha emerged like a wraith, nothing but transparent skin casing brittle bone. Her eyes darted left to right, resting on neither Lulwa nor Bader for more than a split second.

Her mother's frail appearance shocked Lulwa; she was thin as a marsh reed. Lulwa felt an unaccustomed guilt, and she reached out to pull her mother close. "Mama Sheikha! How is he?"

Sheikha shuddered and pushed her daughter away. "He's dying, as I said." Lulwa had forgotten the desiccated insect rasp of her mother's voice.

"Where is he? Where are my sisters?"

"Your sisters, pfeh." Sheikha dry-spit into the air. "Your sisters are nowhere. And that brother of yours, equally useless."

Lulwa shook her head in disbelief. "Stop it, Mama Sheikha! I can't believe my sisters would leave him." She began to make her way to her brother's room. The house was exactly as she remembered.

"Where do you think you're going?" her mother called after her. "Ahmed isn't here. He's in Basra, drinking and misbehaving with boys. Shaming the family, abandoning his home."

Lulwa stopped dead, then fell to her knees, her head spinning. Ahmed was not dying? Ahmed was alive and in Basra? She leaned against one of the corridor pillars. Ahmed was misbehaving with boys? "His foot?" she managed to mumble.

"There's nothing wrong with that boy's foot! He's using it as we speak to tramp around Basra with his rich pasha friends, spending money that isn't his as his father dies."

Bader petted his mother's forehead, wiping away sweat collecting at her temples. Lulwa's thoughts flew from the deception in her mother's letter to her frantic journey home. She landed on the last thing her mother had said. "My father is dying?"

"Yes."

"Where are my sisters?"

"They've refused to step foot in this house since marrying those two good-for-nothing brothers, not a paisa to their name. No wedding, no dowry, no shabka, nothing. Stupid girls. For love, pfeh!"

For escape, more like, thought Lulwa. She stood back up slowly and took her whining son in hand. She walked past Sheikha and made her way to the room once occupied by her and her sisters. It smelled of dust, but she could detect a hint of the rosewater they used to sprinkle on their clean clothes. The walls, gray and etched with hairline cracks, hadn't been whitewashed in years. As far back as she could remember, Ahmed had taken on that task every spring, with Sumaiyya, Hussa, and Lulwa surrounding his ladder, keen to help with fresh rags and buckets of lime. The neglect of the walls tugged at a forgotten instinct in Lulwa. When she had departed to India at fifteen, she had left behind unfinished things.

The trunk was too heavy for Lulwa to lift on her own, so she opened it in the center of the courtyard where the two boys had left it and carried her belongings into the room piece by piece. She put Bader down for his nap and then went in to see her unconscious father. Growing up she had not understood what a father could be, what Khalifa was to Mubarak, what Mubarak was becoming to Bader. To Lulwa, a father had been silence and stones, preferring an owl to his own children, raging violence against her mother in the night. It would have been natural to fear him, to hate him as thoroughly as her brother and sisters did, but Lulwa had felt mostly pity.

Now here he was dying, this brutal, undeserving man, and again an unfamiliar guilt needled her. A version of what she was going to do began to take shape as Sheikha circled the bed.

Lulwa pulled out the worn letter from her brassiere. "You wrote that my brother was dying, not my father."

Sheikha ignored the accusation. "The boy I paid to write the letter must have made a mistake. Father, brother, makes no difference to the stupid child! If your brother wasn't such an imbecile, this wouldn't have happened. But he's never around, and I'm left to pay good money to donkeys to write a few lines on paper."

Those lines had made all the difference to Lulwa, and Sheikha knew it. She licked her dry lips and slipped out of the room, leaving her daughter alone with her father.

News spread that Lulwa was back in Kuwait at bayt Sheikha—everyone thought of the house as Sheikha's—and soon Sumaiyya and Hussa were beating the door with their fists as their sister had done a few hours earlier.

Sheikha stood obstinately behind the bolted door. "You will not come into this house, you filthy hussies! The dishonor you've brought upon your dying father and me."

"Mama Sheikha, let them in! What's the matter with you? They're your daughters, here to see their father. Here to see my son and me!" Lulwa tried to reach past her mother to unbolt the door for her sisters, but Sheikha shoved her away with the full strength of her sinewy arms and planted herself in front of the door, her arms and legs out like an X.

Lulwa had always felt her mother's fury smoldering just under the surface, but now, maybe because Qais was unconscious, no longer a threat, it seemed unchained and wild. Lulwa was shaken. "This is a disgrace, Mama Sheikha," she said. Sheikha puffed out her cheeks and did not budge.

Lulwa ran up to the sateh, open to the street below and to the sky. She called down to her sisters, her tears spilling on their heads like spring rain. They assured her Ahmed was fine, in Basra for a few days to visit his friend, the son of the pasha. They also informed her that it was Sheikha who had refused to let her daughters back in the house if they married their penniless sailors.

"Leave her house this instant, Lulu!" Sumaiyya ordered. "Bring Bader and come with us."

"I have to stay. I have to help her with Qais." Not even Lulwa called her father by anything other than his first name.

Her sisters returned every day to beg and cajole. And soon Ahmed—back from Basra, healthy and happy, sharing a room with his friend Saad—joined them. Days and weeks of useless persuasion ensued. Lulwa tended her father, who was unconscious most of the time, his eyes flickering open only when she forced drops of water through his parched lips. Lulwa wiped away urine, sweat, drool, pus—odious fluids of a dying body.

"Let him rot," her mother hissed, her words singed with the pent-up anger of a lifetime. Sheikha stormed through the room like Hmarat Al-Gayleh, the banshee who snatched stray children wandering the firjan on scorching summer afternoons.

But Lulwa understood that if she allowed Qais to rot, she could not live with the self she would become. Not even her vicious father deserved to die alone on a festering mattress.

Qais died in late December 1928, Lulwa's second month back in Kuwait. Legally the house now belonged to Ahmed, Qais's only son. Despite his mother's interdiction, Ahmed had to be permitted access.

The first thing Ahmed did when he stepped inside was hold his sister in his arms and whisper, "Leave this place. Mubarak has written."

But Lulwa furrowed her brow, an expression she had learned from her mother, and said, "She's hidden the key."

Ahmed washed his dead father with care but without emotion and swathed him in three sheets of white muslin in preparation for burial in the Salhiya magbara. The door was wide open—the first time since Lulwa's arrival, the last time for Qais Qais Al-Talib. Lulwa led her son up to the sateh, her mother's *good riddance* ringing in her ears. She clasped Bader to her chest and pointed at the sparrows and Arabian warblers along the parapet, her old friends. That night, her father's owl flew away, never to return.

The morning after their father's burial, Ahmed stood in the lane pleading with his sister to leave the house. "She can't do anything to you!"

Lulwa whispered back to her brother, "She swears on her brother's grave that if I leave the house, she'll divorce me from Mubarak. That I'll never see him again, won't go back to India. She says she'll marry me off to the Al-Ziyad boy—the one with lazy eyes and peeling skin—and take Bader."

Sheikha had been spearing Lulwa with threats since her return. Divorce. Remarriage. Keeping the child. There were ways, she threatened, to divorce Lulwa from Mubarak without his consent. There were ways to force Lulwa to remarry. That would mean that Sheikha would get custody of Bader by religious mandate. But although her mother's triple threat was the excuse Lulwa gave to her brother, it was not the reason she stayed.

Lulwa had always been drawn to her mother's wounds, even as Sheikha shoved her away. In marrying Mubarak she had conveniently forgotten what she had known innately as a child: to be a daughter to her mother was irrevocable.

Mubarak arrived in Kuwait a week after Qais's death. Unfavorable conditions at sea and work had delayed his trip far longer than he had anticipated. He whacked the great door like an enemy, bellowing for Sheikha to open it before he took an ax to it. The neighbors rushed to their rooftops, preparing for a showdown, itching for Sheikha's comeuppance. Lulwa called down to her husband from the sateh, leaning right over so that he could see her full face. "Mubarak," she called, "I'm not coming. Not yet. My mother needs me."

"Lulu, this makes no sense! *I* need you. You've done your duty, more than anyone could ask of you. Come down! Let's leave this place."

"Bader will be at my sisters' house this afternoon. Be patient with me, Mubarak."

So Mubarak decided to be patient. He didn't know it would take seven years. When he was away from Lulwa, he was certain he could stand it no more. Back in her presence, her face peeking down at him from the roof in the lavender light of early evening, the force that had propelled him from India to Kuwait would ebb. No one—not his own family and not the Al-Talib siblings—could understand why Mubarak did nothing to get his wife and son back. He could go to the amir. He could hire lawyers in India. He could consult the British Agent in Kuwait. Sheikha was a woman alone. There were pressures prominent merchant families could impose. But Mubarak knew he had to trust his wife, so he did not insist on her return to Poona. He did not remove Bader from her care. He spoke to her from the narrow lane below her sateh.

On one occasion, she tossed down a crumpled scrap of paper. "Take this," she instructed. "Fix things for your father."

Mubarak visited Kuwait as often as he could, and he waited.

Lulwa's attachment to her mother was incomprehensible to those around her. As a baby, Lulwa was left to cry for hours on a dirt floor because Qais would not permit Sheikha to leave their stone-surrounded mattress after sundown. Hussa, only two years older than her sister, would cradle her like a doll. Qais beat Sheikha black and blue, and everyone knew it. Sheikha refused to leave Qais, though she could have. Neighbors would have sided with her, girl of the town, over him, seething, savage outsider. Lulwa's siblings blamed their mother for choosing her husband over them. Lulwa did not.

She had come to understand her mother's stubbornness as defiance. She could have left Qais, but she stayed—against reason or expectation—because it was her decision to make. She had gotten herself ensnared in the curvatures of regret. For Lulwa too, staying in the net of her mother's capture felt like defiance, but while Sheikha's stemmed from anguish, Lulwa's was born of hope.

At first, Lulwa's docility filled Sheikha with a flinty disdain. She had been counting on having her daughter's resistance to sharpen her talons on. And Mubarak, that scrawny husband of hers, who hadn't done a hard day's work in his life, she had wanted him to chop down the door. She had wanted a vulgar display for the neighbors. Sheikha had been anticipating a release for her gurgling bitterness, only a thimbleful of which had drained away with Qais's death. Her plotting over the years had kept jealousy at bay, had muffled her fury over the loss of her brother, her youth, the happiness fate had robbed from her and had awarded, so unfairly, to her daughter. She could not tolerate Lulwa's redefining of capture, the unspeakable love in her daughter's eyes.

Every morning, Lulwa served her mother tea, swept the courtyard as Bader's laughter filled the air, prepared lunch and dinner, which they ate together in silence. As she cooked and cleaned, Lulwa would chitchat with her mother as she would with her sisters. Sheikha rarely engaged her daughter verbally, but in time she started to respond with unconscious facial twitches and nearly invisible hand movements that Lulwa noted with quiet contentment. In the flow of days that made up years, Lulwa became the daughter she had always believed herself to be—without her mother's permission. And she understood at last, in her passage from daughter to mother, why it had felt so necessary.

Seven years of her daughter's relaxed certitude; of her grandson cheerful despite his grandmother's indifference; of Mubarak not causing the ruckus Sheikha had hoped for, chuckling under the sateh at something Lulwa had murmured to him from above. Lulwa, with her shiny hair and captivating demeanor, was no longer a girl. She was a woman—the kind Sheikha had not been allowed to become.

One evening, Sheikha left the old teak door open and locked herself in her room. Like any experienced nokhada, Lulwa read the signs. She packed her trunk and bundled her son in camel-hair blankets against the sharp desert air. It was January 1936, and Lulwa was ready for her life to begin again.

Yasmine

Yasmine sensed that the whirlwind precipitated by Marwan's proposal had rattled Dr. Sherif. She worried that the women from Basra who arrived to assess her eligibility had made him feel small. He had sighed audibly when they clasped the heavy gold necklace around her neck, a symbol of everything he couldn't offer his old friend's daughter, much as he may have wished to.

Yasmine had arrived in Baghdad one year after Iraq's independence, and in Dr. Sherif's mind, the two events were linked. He had wanted the independence of his country to mark the end of differences of class and creed. But Yasmine's sudden engagement to these Basrawis was an engagement to the past, not the future. And to boot, Marwan wanted to drive Yasmine through the desert unprotected. Dr. Sherif's hopes for his country deflated.

"I don't mean to dishonor your intentions, Marwan," he said. "But you must understand that this girl has been placed in my care by her mother. For her to travel alone in a car with you is most irregular. I'm sorry, I simply cannot allow it."

Marwan blinked his sedate blink, half earnest, half something undetermined. "I'm not a stranger, Dr. Sherif. I'm her fiancé. Her reputation means more to me than anyone."

Yasmine listened to the conversation between her fiancé and her guardian, and she wasn't sure whose side she was on. She had accepted Marwan's proposal, but she knew she would miss teaching and writing. As soon as the women of Marwan's family left Dr. Sherif's house, their approval of Yasmine billowing in the tails of their silk dresses, she had started to think that she might be giving up too much by going south with this pasha's son. But what was the alternative? Her mother's destitution.

Yasmine stepped out from behind the kitchen door, surprising both Dr. Sherif and her fiancé. "Dr. Sherif, I'm convinced my reputation won't be affected. And my mother won't hold you responsible. She couldn't stop me from coming to Iraq, and you can't stop me from going back to Saida. I won't forget what you and your family have done for me, but you must allow me to take this journey with Marwan Bey."

And he did, exactly as Yeliz had before him.

Marwan didn't want to rush the trip across the desert to Beirut. Ryan, the gruff Australian driver of the black Cadillac hired from the Nairn Eastern Transport Company, explained that they had to speed over packed sand to reduce the chance of getting bogged down or being waylaid by raiders. The Cadillac could have accommodated up to five passengers, but Marwan had gone to great expense to ensure that he and his fiancée would have the car to themselves. He ordered the driver to reduce his speed.

In the back seat, Marwan and Yasmine held hands for the first time. A few hours into the ride, he had convinced her to remove the black flap from her face. It was atypical, to say the least, for an Arab man to push a related woman to remove signs of modesty, and Yasmine worried what the foreign driver would think. She noticed him stealing glimpses in the rearview mirror every once in a while. He couldn't seem to help himself.

Marwan's thumb stroked Yasmine's fingers, one by one, back and forth. Two hours passed. Then the inside of her wrist. She thought she should ask him to stop, but she didn't want to. He inched closer to her. Their shoulders touched. He placed her left hand on his right leg and put his right arm around her. He squeezed her shoulder. Yasmine gasped and caught the driver's fleeting glance, which Marwan didn't notice.

Another hour passed. Yasmine's head rested on Marwan's chest, and she pretended to sleep. He discreetly touched as many parts of her as he could, and, despite herself, she began to enjoy her fiancé's way of laying claim to her body.

Yasmine allowed some excitement to mount over being the soon-to-be wife of the son of the Pasha of Basra. She imagined a grand palace with canals running through fertile land. She pictured thousands of date palms in opulent gardens resplendent with flowers. She saw herself surrounded by servants catering to her every whim, inconceivable varieties of meats and sweets. She saw herself hosting parties the likes of which she had only read about. In the circle of Marwan's arms in a car speeding through the desert, she allowed herself to envision a sensational life, herself as its magnanimous star.

They arrived in Saida faster than either would have wished. Yasmine dove into her mother's arms, nestling under her neck like a gosling. Yousef hid sheepishly behind Yeliz, but Yasmine hugged him tight. All was forgiven this time and every time when it came to her brother. Marwan kept to one side.

Yasmine soon turned to him with her arm outstretched, smiling brightly. "Mama Yeliz, Yousef, meet Marwan Bey. Marwan, my mother and brother."

Yeliz stepped back, her eyes narrowed to slits, and gave Marwan the once-over. She nodded at the tall man, not taking his extended hand. The formality of her greeting bordered on contempt.

Yousef, making up for his mother's reticence, grabbed his future brother-in-law's hand with both of his and pumped it up and down. "Welcome! Welcome to our humble home. Please sit down, please eat! My mother, I'm sure you'll agree, is the best cook in Saida. You must be starving—eat, eat! How long did it take to get from Baghdad to here? In a Cadillac, no less! Was it comfortable? How do you like Saida? What's Basra like? I just can't imagine!"

"You'll see for yourself," Marwan said, cracking a smile. "The comfort, the Cadillac, and Basra, too. I haven't been to Saida before, but I'm happy to be here. It's my honor to meet you both in person and to consider you family." He stared meaningfully at Yeliz.

Yeliz mumbled something that passed for thanks. Yousef's chatter and Yasmine's attentiveness kept the hour from turning awkward. Marwan offered to take Yousef with him to Beirut so that the women wouldn't have him under their feet as they closed up the house. Yeliz agreed. Marwan would return with Yousef and the car to collect them in two days.

Yeliz understood the reason for this sudden coupling. She sniffed out Marwan's wealth and power, and it made her sick with guilt.

Yeliz knew her daughter was selling herself for her. There was no choice. Aside from their house, they had nothing. Yeliz was doing what so many mothers and fathers before her on continents far and wide had done. As her own parents had done. She had ended up happy, hadn't she? Maybe Yasmine would as well.

By the time Yasmine arrived in Saida from Baghdad, Yeliz had already done most of the work in the house. She had taken out all the furniture to air under the noon sun. She had swept the tiled floors, sluiced down soapy water to rinse away any dust and insects that might have eluded the bristles. She fit her belongings and her son's into two trunks. This included her oud and the framed photos of her husband and parents that hung on the wall above the divan. It included her English porcelain tea set, given to her by her mother, and the embellished silver tray given to Hussein by Hikmet Bey on the occasion of their marriage. She didn't own much, but she left behind nothing of value. She knew, as she had known in Istanbul, that she would not return to this place again.

Yeliz felt no great attachment to Saida. The women of the village had never warmed to her—the Turk. Her husband was dead and buried. Her husband's family blamed her for Hussein's death, for her brother-in-law's, too. She would wait and see what this pasha's son could do.

Unlike her mother, Yasmine adored Saida. Saida was her childhood sanctuary. Place of adolescent fantasies, old friends, first love. It was where her father was buried.

Her friends had organized a gathering to see Yasmine off. Everyone came except for Ihsan, Majid's sister. Reem, whose house they had gathered at, explained in a hushed tone, "I asked her to come, Yasmine, and she really wanted to, but she thought you wouldn't want anything to do with her after what happened."

Yasmine stuck her nose in the air. "I would be happy to see Ihsan again. None of that other business matters anymore. I'm engaged." Yasmine had been hoping to see Ihsan, to share the details of her upcoming nuptials with the one person she knew would take it straight to Majid and, more importantly, to Majid's mother. Yasmine's oversensitive karama poked at her.

She was bombarded with questions from the twenty girls who had shown up. They asked about Iraq, her teaching, and, most of all, how she had managed to nab the son of a pasha.

"Did he fall to his knees at the sight of those sorcerous eyes, ya Yasmine?"

"Will you really be living in a palace in Basra?"

"Are you still going to teach?"

"Will you ever return to Lebanon?"

"Does he have any brothers?"

Her friends' open admiration made Yasmine feel more confident in her decision to marry Marwan. After all, any girl would want to marry a pasha's son. Why should she be any different?

That night, as Yeliz and Yasmine finished up their dinner of olives, lebneh, and khubez, they heard a faint knock at the door. Yeliz knew immediately who it was. She remembered an identically timid knock at the same time of night a little over a year earlier. She opened the door.

"Hello, Majid."

"Is she here?" He blinked anxiously, and his face was gaunter than she remembered.

"You know she is."

"Please let me see her."

Yeliz shut the door and turned to her daughter. "You should say goodbye."

"I don't want to," Yasmine muttered, balling her hands into fists that matched the tightness of her racing heart.

Yeliz opened the door enough to see Majid in the moonlight. "She doesn't want to see you, Majid. We leave for Iraq day after tomorrow. Make your peace with it."

The young man's lean face fell. "Please, Tante Yeliz, for the love of God and his prophet, let me see her. I only want to talk to her."

Yeliz turned to her daughter, who shook her head despondently and retreated to her bedroom.

"I'm sorry, Majid. I really am." As Yeliz shut the door, she saw his face contort again.

The next day, Yasmine returned to Reem's house. This time Ihsan was there. She begged Yasmine not to go through with the wedding, to give Majid a second chance. "What happened last time with my mother won't happen again. We promise."

"But does your mother promise?" Yasmine couldn't help asking.

"Majid will make sure she accepts you into our family. Please don't do this, Yasmine. He loves you. He wants to have a life with you." Ihsan was near tears.

Yasmine considered what she knew—Majid's mother would never welcome her—and what she didn't—a privileged life in Basra among people who might—and chose the latter. "I'm sorry,

Ihsan. My fiancé arrives by car early tomorrow morning to collect my family and me. We'll travel together to Basra, where I'll marry him."

That night, at the same time as the night before, Yasmine and Yeliz heard another light knock at the door. Yeliz got up to answer it, glancing at her daughter, who kept her eyes fixed on her fists.

"Hello, Majid."

"Will she see me?" This time he seemed determined, no hint of apprehension.

Yeliz looked over her shoulder. "Well?"

Yasmine carefully arranged her face into a mask of indifference. "I can't see him, Mama. It would be disloyal to Marwan. Surely you would agree."

"You will live to regret it if you don't," Yeliz warned.

Yasmine cast aside her doubts. "I won't do it." It was too late to reverse course no matter what she felt about Majid, no matter what her mother said. She was doing this for her mother and brother, for herself, too. The decision was final, in spite of love.

Yeliz opened the door again to the dejected boy. "I'm sorry, Majid, she won't see you."

"I didn't think so. Please give her this note. I hope she never forgets me."

Yeliz took the envelope he handed to her and said goodbye.

Majid's note was written neatly inside a card with a dried poppy glued to the front. Yasmine wondered if he had saved it from that day at the picnic. The words were simple enough never to forget:

REMEMBRANCE OF A SHATTERED LOVE

Yasmine put the card back in its envelope and tucked it in the cardboard sleeve where she kept her leather diploma and her award for writing the best essay in Lebanon.

Dr. Sherif was waiting outside the door of his house when the Cadillac arrived. He held open the car door for the woman who could only be Hussein's wife, extending his arm to help Yeliz out. He kissed her hand and cried without embarrassment as he looked at her. With her hand in his, Yeliz recovered something of her lost husband.

After dinner, Dr. Sherif led Yeliz into his study, where they could speak privately. He pulled out a chair, then walked around his desk to sit on the other side, facing her. He lowered his chin toward his chest and sighed. "This is all my fault. I should never have let him anywhere near her. I tried to dissuade her, believe me, Yeliz. But there was no changing her mind. I've let down Hussein, Allah yarhama."

"You haven't let down anyone. She's doing this for me. It was that letter I sent about her brother taking money. You've done so much, Dr. Sherif. This is her decision to make."

"She's getting herself into things she knows nothing about. Their family—"

"Their family will be as difficult as any other family," Yeliz interjected. "That we'll be together is the important thing."

But Dr. Sherif wasn't convinced. His heart broke for the girl's displaced dreams.

The dead pasha's nineteenth-century residence, not quite the Crusader castle Yasmine had anticipated, was impressive nonetheless. It was composed of a series of large buildings, most sharing walls. There was a home for each of the wives and for many of the sons. The residue of the estate's former glory could be discerned in its enclosed courtyards and brick arches chiseled with designs of interwoven ovals and scattered stars. Wooden shanasheel covered oriel windows, and colorful stained glass glowed under wooden lattices. Wide verandas overlooked capillary creeks and, along one side of the buildings, the Shatt Al-Arab. Yasmine had been right about the canals, date palms, and abundant gardens. She had not foreseen the tennis courts, the elaborate nightly dinner service, or the stylishly turned-out women of the clan.

Once, no doubt, the palace had been intimidating, putting dignitaries in their place, but it was on the decline. Known as the Robin Hood of South Iraq, the pasha had dispensed land and cash to those in need or to those he felt had earned it based on his own eccentric assessment of allegiance and service. Toward the end of his life—nationalist hopes quashed, betrayals internalized—the pasha spent most of his time alone, and his burden of regrets made it easy for sly men to convince him to part with ever larger parcels of land, ever more cash. Wiser to give to those in need, he thought, than to leave it to his children, blessed as they had been with every opportunity to succeed.

The pasha gave himself too much credit. His children were lost souls, separated from the warmth of their mothers at the age of twelve, removed to the pasha's residence to be raised by servants and slaves. This, the pasha believed, would turn them into warriors like their father. The sons spent mornings being tutored, afternoons doing homework, early evenings playing outdoors or trying to sneak into the women's quarters to hug their heart-struck mothers.

Marwan and Yasmine married a few days following their arrival in Basra, in March 1935. It was a discreet ceremony with a mullah officiating and Marwan's cousin and Yasmine's brother standing as witnesses. The women of the family ululated, and a sumptuous dinner was enjoyed by all. The Turkish and Circassian wives especially were happy to welcome Yeliz and Yasmine, two of their own.

Husband and wife walked hand in hand through the gardens, Marwan's pride and joy. He shyly pointed out his rare flowers and assorted plants collected from Iran and Syria, explained how he had managed to keep them alive despite relentless sandstorms and summer temperatures. They rowed reed boats through canals, serenaded by thousands of sparrows that filled the date palms, the scent of razqi perfuming the air. They sat on their veranda eating salted cucumber and sipping from ice-filled tumblers of arak, discussing Arabic literature late into the night. Marwan disclosed his paternal wounds to his wife, seeking compassion, which he received, hoping for a cure, which not even she could provide. The misery of a wretched boy weeping for his mother, only a few buildings away. The knowledge that he was unloved by the man who had made him. Yasmine shared some of her own injuries with her husband—her lost father, her family's poverty, the missed opportunity to advance her education—but she couldn't share Majid, the main one. Even so, as their secret hurts merged, they felt close, mutually salved.

Sara

This weekend, like the last, Maria refuses to visit her daughters. I want her to go relax, take her mind off my problem for a few days. She pretends she's unconcerned, teasing Aasif in the kitchen, talking back to Bebe Mitu, tempting me at lunch with her treats. She insists on coming with me to the neighborhood co-op to buy whatever is on Aasif's grocery list. I try to convince her she needs some time away from this—from me—but nothing I say changes her mind. She murmurs to Josie or Christina over the phone, "I can't leave Saru beti alone. She's in trouble."

I wonder how it must feel for Josie or Christina to hear their mother calling me *daughter*. Maria has been my second mother since the day I was born. Karim was only two months old when she arrived in Kuwait to work for my parents. It isn't fair that she's had to give up a lifetime with her own children to secure their care. My brother and I have been the guilty beneficiaries of her sacrifice. I doubt Karim loses sleep over it, but I'm ashamed. And yet, after that phone call, I stop nagging her to go. I'm grateful she chooses me. Her daughters have husbands and children to comfort them. I have never felt more alone in my life.

———

When we were kids, Karim and I would watch the three-hour Hindi film broadcast on KTV-1 every Friday afternoon with Mom. Maria would watch the same film at her children's apartment. Dad, the only one of us who couldn't speak a word of Hindi, would water his potted ficus, then take a long nap. The old lady in the film—there was always an old lady in the film—would remind me of Maria. And when that old buddi died, as she invariably did, my throat would constrict, and I would fret over Maria until she returned home from her day off.

I've stopped the paper deliveries, so I don't know whether interest in my case has waned. Between Mr. Al-Baatin's visits, I pretend everything is fine. I can't focus on writing, and I can't sleep, but I nap during the afternoon and swim twice a day. Aasif has been asking me questions about gardening, about which I know nothing, and I realize he's trying to lure me outside the house. He waters the plants at twilight. "Otherwise the water boils the roots or evaporates too quickly," he explains. "Your mother planted these roses the year I arrived. Never, I thought, would they survive a single summer. But here they are. They will outlive us all. See this?" He lifts the head of a small white flower, heavy with petals and a scent I can smell without bending down. "Your father's mother gave this one to memsahib. Razqi from her garden in Basra. It must be at least as old as your Bebe Mitu."

I bend forward and touch the tip of my nose to the white flower. Mama Yasmine's descriptions of the Basra palace gardens fill my head. When I came back to Kuwait after Mom died, I visited Mama Yasmine daily for chai al-dhaha—taking my mother's place in all things—listening again and again to her stories about herself, Mama Lulwa, and Mom.

I rise up and tuck my hair behind my ears. "Thanks, Aasif."

He doesn't need to ask what for.

The sun has set and it's dark out, but it's still hot enough for my face to drip with sweat. I always sweat from my face and head, never from my armpits. In court this might be read as an indication of guilt. I brush away the thought and decide against going for a swim, though the cool water would be a relief. Instead, I head for the shower, which will be boiling hot. I try to make it quick.

When I go downstairs, Maria is not in her usual place at the head of the kitchen table, cutting khubez into quarters, easing open the triangles for cheese and tomatoes. Her bathroom door is wide open, lights on, so I can see she's not in there either.

"Maria?"

No response.

"Maria?" My voice quivers.

I rush to her bedroom to find her sprawled on the floor beside her bed, eyes closed, her right hand resting on the left side of her chest. I don't know how long she's been down or if she's even alive. I call out her name, and she stirs slightly. She has a weak pulse, and her breathing is shallow. I yell for Aasif, who materializes out of thin air. "We have to get her to my car," I hear myself say.

Calling an ambulance won't work. Last time this happened, Maria almost died because of the time it took the ambulance to get here through the trap of cars that in Kuwait do not part for a siren and flashing lights the way the Red Sea parted for Moses.

Aasif and I carry her up the stairs, past Bebe Mitu's cloth-covered cage, past the pool I did not swim in today. We step out into the searing night. I don't feel her weight. We lay her down as gently as we can on the back seat of my car. The only thought in my head is *hospital*. Aasif climbs into the passenger seat and orders me to go.

I don't remember the traffic or the speed I was going. I glance down at my watch and realize it must have only taken fifteen minutes. I remember screaming, "Heart attack! Heart attack!" as I pulled into the emergency room driveway and jumped out of the car.

"You can't leave your car here!" someone yelled at me.

"She's having a heart attack!"

"Move your car! Ambulances behind!"

I watched as Maria was shifted onto a gurney. I instructed Aasif to tell the doctors she has heart problems. "She's having a heart attack," I repeated and repeated.

For the second time that night, Aasif ordered me to go.

I don't remember finding parking.

Back in the emergency room, I see Aasif standing to the side of one of the beds in the ward. The bed is surrounded by white coats doing violence to a body I know must be Maria's. They are fighting to keep her alive. I hear beeping. For the moment, she's still here.

"Are you her daughter?" one of the white coats asks me.

"Yes," I say automatically.

The doctor looks at me quizzically, then starts to explain, "She needs to go into surgery." I stare at him blankly as my ears clog up. I make out certain words through the muffle: *Massive heart attack. Chances slim. Open-heart. High risk.* Sound returns in a thunderous clap, and I cover my ears with my hands.

The doctor pushes past me and orders the other doctors and nurses to prepare the patient for surgery. I catch a glimpse of Maria as they wheel her away. She's unconscious. Her skin is putty. She seems already dead. This is not her first heart attack or her first surgery.

I chase after the gurney, but it's too late for me to kiss her or reassure her. Or to say goodbye. The doors slam shut, and she's gone.

The reek of Dettol in the waiting room burns my nostrils. Aasif is sitting beside me. I look down at my watch. It's been over half an hour since they wheeled her in. I have to call her daughters. I jump up, but immediately the room reels and my head goes black, so I slink back down on the chair, its tan plastic a personal affront. I rest my forehead on my knees and feel a rush of blood, take a few long, deliberate breaths, and attempt to stand again. Better this time. "I'm going to try to find out what's going on, Aasif. I'll be right back."

There's only one nurse at the nurse's station, and she looks busy. "I'm here about Maria," I try.

She shakes her head.

"The Indian woman they took in for heart surgery?"

"Is she your mother?" She pauses. "You're Indian?"

"She's my second mother. My ayah growing up. I'm Kuwaiti."

"Ah. You speak Hindi, no? I heard you speaking to the man."

"It was my first language."

It must seem unusual to this nurse—a woman from some-where in India, undoubtedly weighed down by dying patients, by the family she supports back home—that a Kuwaiti woman knows Hindi. To me it's as ordinary as a white summer sky. The switch from English to Hindi and back as automatic for me as it was for my mother. "Is she going to make it?" I ask.

"It will be some time before we know anything. Open-heart surgery. Many hours."

If she's lucky, the nurse must be thinking. Or maybe I'm the one thinking it. The longer it takes, I try to convince myself, the better her chances.

The nurse hands me Maria's Civil ID card, and I'm puzzled at first by how she got it, then realize Aasif must have given it to her. I return to the waiting room, update him, and urge him to take a taxi home. "You should rest, Aasif. I'll call her daughters. Maria's going to be fine." He doesn't believe me, I can tell, but he gets up to go anyway, knowing perhaps, as I know with every cell of my being, that losing Maria is something I must face alone.

Things turn on a dime. Things turn on a dime. I repeat the phrase like a prayer as I wait for word.

L u l w a

One morning in the early years of Lulwa's captivity, someone knocked on the thick door of Sheikha's house. Sheikha, expecting Mubarak, refused to answer, but Lulwa called down to her mother from the rooftop that it was a stranger. Sheikha opened the door a crack, and Lulwa raced down to hear. They were being asked to sell a meter of land along the back of their house, where they had a modest decheh. The government had a plan to widen the lane, and the small mud seat was in the way.

"You will be compensated for the sale," said the man, one of a cadre of recently appointed government employees.

"How much?" Sheikha inquired.

"A fair amount to be decided once you approve."

"Do you take me for a fool? I will not approve without a fixed price. Tell me the amount and I'll give you my decision."

"Between you and me, Um Ahmed, you don't have a choice. The municipality decides to do something, they do it."

"And if I refuse?"

"What will you do? Take them to court? On the one hand, the municipality. On the other, the ruler. Everyone raking in rupees.

Unless you have some connection to the ruler, there's not much you can do. If you have wasta, use it. Mark my words, people will be making money hand over fist!"

"I still refuse. Do what you will."

The man rolled his eyes, clearly believing Sheikha was making a mistake.

Nothing came of the stranger's visit. The back lane was not important enough to transform into a street yet. Sheikha forgot about the encounter. Lulwa did not. The Al-Mustafas, like all merchant families, had ties. In a note she flung down to Mubarak on his next visit, she wrote:

> Speak to the amir. Acquire land. Future speculation.

Mubarak worked with his brothers to save their family from ruin. Littoral trade remained brisk enough in those years, and Mubarak's brothers had proven themselves to be shrewder than even they had expected in their efforts to maintain their father's old networks of trust and obligation. That and selling a number of their dhows prevented the Al-Mustafa family from slipping too far down. Mubarak managed to expand the family's jewelry interests in India, deflecting the blow of cultured pearls. And thanks to Lulwa, Mubarak's father acquired extensive tracts of land in prime locations, securing their future.

In the first months of Lulwa and Bader's return, Mubarak would wake in a panic, convinced they were still caught in Sheikha's web. He would turn to find his wife by his side, breathing peacefully, and he would wander the hallway to Bader's room to find his son fast asleep, spread-eagled on his back. Mubarak's rapid heartbeats would slow as he shuffled back to his room.

Once Mubarak and his brothers had closed their land deals in Kuwait, Mubarak decided to remain in Poona, leaving the day-to-day running of the business to his brothers. Kuwait had left a sour taste in his mouth. Mubarak directed his attention to expanding his family with Lulwa and then, at long last, decided it was time to do what he had always wanted. He transferred his long-suspended credits to Fergusson College in Poona and completed his degree in English literature.

Lulwa settled back in Poona effortlessly. Mama Zaineb, worn down by years of worry over her family's future and recently bereft of her husband, Khalifa, gratefully accepted her daughter-in-law's offer to take over the responsibilities of the household. With Mubarak's sister, Hayya, married and living in Bombay, Lulwa was the only one left to do it. Before the seven-year interlude, the canopy of trees surrounding their property had absorbed Lulwa's childhood wounds. On her return, the tangle and pull of domesticity turned itself into another kind of balm, repairing recent damage. She had one healthy birth after another and, unlike her friends, suffered no miscarriages or early infant deaths. Mubarak's infatuation with his madam was undiminished. She sorted salaries for the household's considerable staff; planned weekly menus for children and adults; hosted tea parties for the society ladies and, with some initial hesitation, cocktail parties with their husbands, too. She selected the best lamb and chicken and made sure lentils and rice were properly destoned. Through the hubbub of raising children and administering household chores, Lulwa experienced life as a sheltering embrace.

After four difficult but healthy births—Bader first, followed ten years later by Hind, then Aisha, then Dana—Noura slipped out in May 1945 with an ease that brought grateful tears to her mother's eyes. A week after delivery, Lulwa was ready to welcome the Poona aunties to see the baby, as was custom. Noura was swaddled in ivory cloth that matched the color of the lace on the hood of her brother Bader's handed-down bassinet.

Angelina, Noura's ayah, bustled around the nursery, setting picture frames straight and checking for dust. The society ladies were coming to see the baby, but their eyes would flit left and right, taking in Lulwa's status and, by extension, Angelina's. That morning, Lulwa had instructed the servants to open all the windows to let in fresh air. Angelina wanted to close the nursery window against motes and spores landing on her spotless surfaces, but she hesitated. She didn't want to upset Lulwa memsahib. Anyway, the air was thickening, and the order would soon come to shut the windows and start the punkahs. For the moment, Angelina left the nursery window open and set off to retrieve a feather duster.

When Mubarak walked past the nursery on his way to his study, he didn't notice the missing baby at first. What stopped him in his tracks was the open window, the absent ayah, and the swaddling cloth on the floor. What he saw next was a small, brown, long-haired homunculus standing upright on the blade of the ceiling fan, holding his daughter upside down by the soles of her feet. Mubarak's gasp drew the monkey's attention downward, its eyes wide as lamps. They both remained frozen for minutes that felt like years.

The cackling orb of ladies tottered toward the nursery, Lulwa's crystal laughter leading them on. Mubarak heard their collective intake of breath as they took in the scene.

"Lulwa, please back away. Don't make a sound." Mubarak's voice was low and steady. "Bring me a bedsheet and bananas. Ladies, wait by the door. I'll need you in a minute."

The monkey eyed the humans below with mild interest. She rolled her eyes from the retreating circle of women to Mubarak to the feet in the palm of her hand. Mubarak inched under the fan, hoping to avoid the creature's detection as he positioned himself directly under his daughter's fragile head. He glanced up at Noura, her tiny balled fists almost close enough to touch. He could hear the animal's nails scratching as they caught in the wicker of the punkah.

The monkey shifted her gaze from Noura's feet to the window she had leapt through only moments before. She peered beyond the window-framed space toward the trees and cocked her neck in that direction. Then she let out a screech that nearly knocked Mubarak flat out, flipped Noura around, and cradled the unusually silent baby in her arms.

Lulwa tiptoed in with the sheet and bananas. She handed both to her husband without glancing up.

"Ladies," Mubarak directed in a low voice, "come form a circle around the fan. Easy does it. Hold the edges of the sheet tight as you can."

As the women did what he asked, Mubarak slid one foot in front of the other toward the open window, then held the bananas up high like a prize. The monkey jerked her head toward Mubarak, dropped Noura, grabbed the bananas, and bounded back into the clutch of trees. The circle of ladies caught the baby in the sheet, together releasing their held breath. Lulwa collapsed to the floor, and Mubarak rushed in to lift Noura, checking his baby's feet for scratches, her head for signs of injury. But she was perfect. Noura gazed into her father's eyes, emitting not even a whimper. Mubarak slid down beside his wife, their unhurt baby in his arms. The aunties left the couple alone, clucking to themselves that this could only be a portent of good things to come for the child.

Every evening, Mubarak allowed himself one glass of Scotch on ice and one pipe out on the veranda. He read through a random miscellany of newspaper clippings sent by friends in Uttar Pradesh, Delhi, Bombay, Calcutta. Twice a month he also received a packet of clippings from newspapers around the Arab region, mailed to him from Kuwait by his brother-in-law Ahmed. Mubarak pored over full-length articles and shorter, no less compelling snippets covering the day's most pressing political events, along with ephemeral human interest stories that had momentarily captured the attention of one or another of his mates. India's struggle against the British. Gandhi's incarceration in the Yerwada jail in 1932, not far from their home. Independence and the ensuing bloodbath of partition. The assassination of Bapu. These blended together with the suspected murder of a village elder and the mysterious disappearance of his pregnant, much younger wife. The dissolution of Palestine, to his mind the holiest of holy places, and the disastrous defeat of the Arabs, intersected with advice to the residents of Kuwait Town on how to deal with the oppressive increase in dust, stoked by the rise in construction. Indian success and Arab failure, murder and dust, fused through the flutter of clippings spread before him every evening. The tragedy of newly enforced borders, arbitrary and cruel, decimating farms and families with a casual indifference that baffled Mubarak. And there were the British, skulking in the shadows of Palestine, India, Egypt, Sudan, and—it dawned on Mubarak—Kuwait as well. Mubarak organized the clippings into neatly labeled, color-coded files, as if ordering them could provide some clue about the future.

Mubarak started to feel that, like the British, the Al-Mustafas had overstayed their welcome. India would always be their real home, the place where his children were born, where he and Lulu had created a life out of the childish love that began with graffiti on a whitewashed wall. But by the early 1950s, it was clear to Mubarak that his imminently oil-rich country was on the brink of its own independence. It was time to return to Kuwait, to accept a key position at the Kuwait Oil Company offered to him directly by the amir. He could not refuse.

This would not be a return for his children—not for six of the seven anyway. They knew nothing other than their Poona life of Anglican boarding schools, afternoon tea with cardamom milk, romping through what they thought of as *their* jungle. Kuwait to them would be a dusty town. He would point out the crystal sea and limitless desert, but he knew it would not feel like home to them.

One evening, sipping his drink on the veranda, Mubarak tried to gather the courage to tell Lulu. An hour later, no braver, he entered their bedroom to find his wife in bed staring up at the ceiling. It was rare to see Lulwa unoccupied. Like all the women of her generation and class, she relied heavily on ayahs and domestic help when it came to the children. But much of her time was still spent on the infinite particulars of child-rearing: manners at table, marks at school, rambunctiousness, mild illnesses. The house was impeccable, every surface gleaming, every light fixture sparkling, closets neatly ordered, kitchens and bathrooms relentlessly disinfected.

"We're going back to Kuwait," Lulwa said impassively.

He sat at the edge of the bed. "Yes, Lulu, we are. It's for the best. It's our time to go."

"It's a mistake."

"I know you think so, and it won't be easy on the children, but my brothers say it's full of opportunities. We have our house there. You'll make it as wonderful as you've made it here. We'll be together, Lulu. That's all that matters."

Lulwa was silent. The children. Leaving would break the spell, put them at risk. She thought about her mother and shuddered. She took Mubarak's hand in hers and kissed it because she didn't know what else to do. "So we go."

Mubarak was never convinced that leaving India was the right decision. Regret would scour his stomach over the years. But in August 1954, as he led his family up the gangway of his father's baghla, *Amwaj Al-Salam*, moored at the Sassoon Docks for the last time, Lulu on his arm, he had no doubt in his mind that departure was necessary.

At nine, Noura was unaware of her father's doubts or of her mother's conviction that this leave-taking would mark the end of tranquility. She had no idea that her twenty-eight-year-old brother, Bader, whose hand she clasped as hard as she could to avoid falling into the violet water below, had spent the early years of his life in this unknown place where the ship would be taking them. Her older sisters were crying. Her younger brothers, Marzouk and Mazen, were sobbing too in solidarity. Noura couldn't force out tears to match those of her siblings. In the curious heart of the girl who might have been lost to monkeys, an adventure was beginning. It was called Kuwait.

Yasmine

A year into her marriage, Yasmine found herself in a pregnancy of nausea, dizziness, vomiting, and simmering rage. Marwan would disappear for weeks at a time to Baghdad, Damascus, or Kuwait Town, where he had relatives and friends, and so Yeliz took over her daughter's care. Thrown off by the effects of her pregnancy, Yasmine couldn't tell when Marwan was away and when she was simply asleep.

Malik, a healthy baby boy, was born in late December 1936. Yasmine named him, aware that only two letters separated the name of her firstborn from the name of her first love. Marwan inhaled the infant's fig smell, happy for the chance to undo inherited trauma. Into his baby's shell ears, Marwan murmured promises of loyalty he would fail to keep.

Yasmine responded to the demands of newborn life with innate authority. She knew how to press Malik's mouth against her breast so that he would latch without struggle. She anticipated his hunger or his wet nappies before he could express discomfort. He became known among the women of the clan as the baby without tears. At first Yasmine didn't accept the women's eager offers to help, finding it physically painful to relinquish Malik. But then sleep would overcome her, and Yeliz—to Marwan's constant aggravation—would appear the minute her daughter's eyes shut, removing the baby from her bosom so that the girl could rest.

For Marwan the novelty of his son quickly wore off. The baby became yet another force splitting him from Yasmine, one even more powerful than Yeliz. For forty days he was not permitted to sleep with his wife. She needed to heal, Yeliz explained. Once those forty days were over, Marwan couldn't resist. Yasmine's young body recovered its elastic contours, and he couldn't tell that pregnancy had recently filled her. He wanted her with a hunger as urgent as Malik's for milk, but Yasmine's response to her husband's desire was less intuitive and far less immediate. If they were together and the baby cried, her nipples would leak, and Marwan would silently fume as she switched from wife to mother.

Yasmine was pregnant again in no time. Again, she was in bed for months fighting nausea and exhaustion, with a husband even more distant than before. If he happened to return while she was awake, she would beg him to spend time with Malik. He would promise, but Yeliz would report otherwise. Their daughter Selma was born in December 1937.

"Don't allow him to come near you for at least six months!" Yeliz warned Yasmine.

"But I miss him! Why is he always so far away?" Yasmine could not reconcile the Marwan of their first year in Basra with this remote specter floating in and out of their lives. On the rare occasion that he was present and genial toward her and the children,

Yasmine flew to him. She ignored Yeliz's warning, and within two months of her second birth, she was pregnant with her third. Hisham was born in November 1938.

Though Yasmine could see the futility of the pattern, she couldn't stop repeating it. Neither could Marwan. A leaden anger festered between them, and they found themselves caught in a downward spiral comparable to the one into which Europe was sucking the world. By the end of January 1940, Yasmine was pregnant again for the fourth time.

During her daughter's pregnancies, Yeliz shielded Yasmine from rumors of Marwan's indiscretions. The women of the palace tittered over the genetic makeup of their men. "They can't keep their privates private for long, not a single one of them. We married them. We birthed them. And here we are, all in the same boat." Together with Yeliz, the women protected Yasmine from the humiliation with which they were all acquainted. "Let her early flurry of pregnancies subside," they remarked, "before she's forced to confront her future."

But seven months into her fourth pregnancy, casual words exchanged between women in the garden over tea and tobacco drifted up to Yasmine. Something about another woman, another pregnancy, and Marwan in the middle of both. Yeliz found her daughter in a heap on the balcony of her bedroom. A doctor was summoned.

"Yasmine? Can you hear me? What day of the week is it, ya Yasmine?" He tapped her on both cheeks to no effect. He took out the instruments of his practice from a large black bag, probing and listening to significant organs. Yeliz stood beside the doctor as the palace women recited urgent prayers under their breath.

"She and the baby are in no immediate danger," the doctor reported at last. "She has suffered shock, but her heart rate and blood pressure are normal, and the baby is kicking. Make sure she eats, drinks plenty of water, and rests. Don't leave her alone. Call me if there's any change."

It took Yasmine a week to speak. "Is it true?" she croaked.

Yeliz knew not to lie. "Yes."

"Has he married her?"

"Yes."

"Since when?"

"Four months ago, after she was three months pregnant."

"They will be the same age."

"Yes."

Marwan hung back once he learned from his own mother that Yasmine had discovered the truth. He took up residence with his second wife, keeping her outside the family estate. Marwan considered this a declaration of fidelity to Yasmine; Yasmine was not equipped to decode his obscure gesture.

She delivered their third son, Tarek, in October 1940, a few weeks early. Marwan begged Yeliz to let him into the room. Yasmine permitted him to see his son, but she refused to see him herself.

Marwan's son from his second wife was born a few weeks later.

Yasmine couldn't bring herself to breastfeed her newborn. Her milk, sensing her disinclination, wouldn't come. The women located a wet nurse to breastfeed the baby and took turns holding him against their chests, reciting prayers over his head. They tried to compensate for his mother's heartache, his father's absence, but the baby would carry it inside him until the end.

Yasmine spent the next month moaning into her mother's lap. The month after that, she paced her room, still refusing to see Marwan, who called to her from under her balcony at night, pleading to allow him to explain.

Yeliz became her daughter's second skin. When Yeliz told Yasmine to eat, she ate. When Yeliz told her to drink, she drank. When Yeliz told her to hold her children in her arms, she did so. Sometimes Yeliz would neglect to remind her to breathe, and Yasmine's anger would choke her. In those strangled moments, Yasmine would think about Dr. Sherif's hidden note.

In early March 1941, almost six years to the day from her marriage to Marwan, twenty-four-year-old Yasmine boarded a BOAC Douglas DC-3 for the first time in her life and flew to Baghdad. A secret letter had been dispatched to Dr. Sherif, so he would be expecting her. Yasmine would remain in Baghdad for a month. After that, she would make a decision.

Dr. Sherif met her at the Baghdad airport. "Yasmine." He put his arms on her shoulders and kissed her on both cheeks. She didn't break in his arms, though she wanted to. She didn't break at his house, either, when Asya and Sula held her and recited short du'aa against the jinn responsible for devastating her marriage.

Dr. Sherif led her to his study. "Yasmine," he began, "I'm sorry for everything. Tell me how I can help."

"I'm leaving him, Dr. Sherif. I've come here to make a plan. *No mistake is irreversible*, remember? We still have our house in Saida."

Dr. Sherif wrung his hands. Her plan would compound, not reverse, the mistake. "How will you support four children alone?"

"My mother is a talented seamstress. I can teach, like I did before Marwan. I have my degree, my award. My school will hire me. I could tutor."

"Who will take care of your children while all this work is happening?"

"My mother can work from home."

"Yasmine, how many rooms does your house in Saida have?"

Yasmine shook her head vigorously. "Please, Dr. Sherif. Stop."

He walked around his desk and put his hand on her shoulder. This trouble couldn't be resolved that day. For the moment, they would eat his mother's food. Yasmine looked cadaverous.

Over the next two weeks, they had similar conversations. Dr. Sherif listened to Yasmine spell out her plan, then exposed obstacles she overlooked. Would Marwan agree to divorce? What about custody of the children? His was a powerful family. Even if sharia dictated that the children belonged to her until they reached the age of discernment, the courts might not stick to the letter of the law. And even if everything worked out exactly as she wanted it to, what would happen once the boys turned seven, the girl nine? Would she survive the separation if Marwan claimed them, as was his right?

Yasmine was adamant that by then Marwan would have forgotten all about his children. "All it took was nine months for him to forget about me!"

Neither Dr. Sherif nor Yasmine anticipated Marwan's arrival one night at the start of Yasmine's third week there. Yasmine was in the kitchen with Sula, preparing their evening meal, when there was a sharp knock at the door. She heard her husband's voice in the hall and dropped the soup ladle.

Dr. Sherif led Marwan to his study. Marwan accepted most of the blame for his behavior, but he also laid blame at the feet of his mother-in-law. Yasmine's loyalty was to her mother and brother first. This was insufferable to Marwan. "A husband," Marwan demanded, "must come first." Marwan was willing to attempt repairs if Yasmine was willing to shift Yeliz and Yousef outside the bounds of their marriage.

After two hours of discussion, the study door opened, and Dr. Sherif escorted Marwan down the hall to the front door, saying he would see him the next day. Then Dr. Sherif called for Yasmine.

"Six years ago I gave you advice you did not take. I will advise you again, and I pray you do what I say. For the sake of your children, Yasmine, go back to him. He regrets his behavior, will make amends. You loved him once, didn't you? *The soul of an artist,* you said. Stay with him for the sake of your children. Their life without a father in Saida, children of a divorced woman, would be tragic. Marwan has agreed to allow you to teach in Basra. Do you understand what this means? You'll be more independent. Teach, write, love your children. They'll have opportunities as Marwan's children they wouldn't otherwise. Live for them."

Yasmine listened to Dr. Sherif because she had not listened to him the first time. Reluctantly, she agreed to do what he advised. Dr. Sherif had said nothing to Yasmine about Marwan's complaint against Yeliz and Yousef, key to the whole calamity.

The next morning, Marwan came to collect his wife. Asya and Sula linked arms with Yasmine, laughing cheerfully to buoy her despite the dread in their souls. Dr. Sherif held her face in his hands. "Write to me, Yasmine. Every day if you like. I'll write back. I have a poem written by your father that I'll send to you. Keep your father alive, 'azizti Yasmine."

Back in Basra, Yasmine and Marwan quickly fell into their old ways. Yeliz and Yousef rarely left the couple alone, and Yasmine, unaware of the real cause behind Marwan's distance, kept them close. Marwan once again began to spend as much time away from the palace as he could.

Dr. Sherif had managed to write to the education office in Basra to secure Yasmine a teaching position in a girls' school. She took her diploma and award to the office. They held her documents for a few days in order to finalize procedures. When she returned to the office, they said they couldn't employ her since her husband had refused to sign a release. "You can't work in Basra without your husband's consent," they scolded.

Yasmine felt dread flare in her stomach. "Where are my diploma and award?" she asked.

"Your husband has them."

The diploma and award were not in the cardboard sleeve in the drawer where Yasmine normally stored them. Neither was Majid's card. She pulled out all four drawers, turned their contents onto the floor, and rifled through the pile of clothes. She didn't notice Marwan in the unlit room, sitting in a chair facing the window. His placid monotone interrupted her search.

"Those things you're looking for you will not see again. I burned them."

Yasmine jumped, flew around the wingback chair to stare

him down. "I'm leaving you. I'm taking my children and going to Saida. Divorce me, don't divorce me, I don't care. I want nothing more to do with you."

Marwan snickered. "And where do you think you'll live in Saida?"

"My father's house, obviously!"

"You mean the house that was in Yousef's name?" Yasmine froze. "Your drunk brother signed that property to me the first day we met. That old house was sold years ago. You have nothing, Yasmine. This is your home. I am your husband."

There was no recourse. Yasmine didn't ask Dr. Sherif for help again. Dr. Sherif—coups and riots in Baghdad hijacking his attention—neglected to write as regularly as he wanted to. Eventually Yasmine's letters would stop altogether, and the few anxious queries Dr. Sherif managed to pen were not answered. He never sent Yasmine the promised poem by her father. He forgot, overwhelmed by his nation's misfortunes, and she forgot to remind him, overwhelmed by her own.

Time tempered Yasmine's rage. If she was to prepare for the success of her children, she had to let bitterness go. She went to the cinema with friends, escaping into manufactured dreams. She got dressed up, painted her fingernails red, and enjoyed the admiration of strangers. She debated politics over arak and bridge. Yasmine's Lebanese accent all but disappeared, and the Basrawi inflection she developed during her twenty years in Iraq would persist, despite the next fifty she would spend in Kuwait.

Yasmine directed her energy toward her children, as Dr. Sherif had counseled. Her first four, plus two more girls, Kamila and Zahra, born over a decade after Tarek. Yasmine tutored her children after school and chose their careers. She pushed them to excel. A truce emerged between herself and Marwan. Yeliz and Yousef weren't forced out; Marwan didn't divorce his second wife.

As the youngest of the pasha's four sons by his wife Amina, Marwan hadn't inherited much property. In Basra his prospects were limited. Marwan was forty-five years old. His friends and relatives in Kuwait were encouraging him to claim citizenship and leave Iraq. Unlike his father, Marwan was no politician, but it didn't take a politician to realize that the instability of the present would not abate. He wanted nothing to do with it. Not pan-Arabism, not communism, not nationalism, not the British, not unions with Egypt, Syria, or Jordan. He wanted a simple life of plants and poetry. Kuwait might do.

Marwan bought two separate homes in Kuwait for his two separate families—six children on Yasmine's side, four on the other. He arranged for separate cars to drive the two wives and their sets of children, family members, and servants, even more cars for their belongings. Marwan drove himself with his thirteen-year-old son Tarek by his side. It was 1954, the end of August, and in the shimmer of mirages they passed along the way, Tarek made out the seven wonders of the world.

II

S

Noura

r

Maria

II

Sara

Aasif has gone home. I've tried calling Christina and Josefina dozens of times, but there's no answer. For them their mother is still alive and well at the Surra house, taking care of me, a forty-one-year-old baby. I tell myself that their not knowing will forestall anything bad happening, then feel appalled—a philosophy professor prone to magical thinking.

I get off the plastic chair to stretch my legs and wander to the nurse's station. It's empty. The nurse who spoke to me earlier ended her shift ages ago. The nurses must all be busy dashing between patients, checking vital signs, replacing IVs, noting changes in blue files at the feet of occupied beds.

My father wore down these corridors, cupping life and death in his hands. We knew Dad was a doctor, but we didn't understand the burden of that vocation or its effect on our mother. He refused to go private, forfeiting money for service. Even after the government prioritized care to Kuwaitis, my father continued to see patients in order of urgency, nationality be damned. He cared for the sick and fobbed off the spoiled, who nonetheless demanded to be seen by Dr. Tarek Al-Ameed, senior-most cardiologist in the country. "They insist they're having heart attacks when all they have is excess gas. *Pass gas,* I tell them. *Don't hold it in!* They eat too much, and then they hold in their farts because they don't want to have to redo their wudu' before prayer." Karim and I would giggle at our ordinarily discreet father discussing farts over lunch.

Dad would have turned seventy-three this October. I understood nothing of death at twenty, even less about what his loss meant to my mother. When Dad was killed, Mom was only five years older than I am now. By then my mother was already adrift: Karim and I gone; her interest in the bookstore waning; her belief in the human capacity to improve the world disappointed. Without my father, I'm not sure what anchored her to shore.

I catch the attention of a nurse as she exits a patient's room. "Maria Torres?" She shakes her head, not recognizing the name. "She's in surgery. Heart?"

"Give me a minute to check. I'll come to the waiting room after."

I try Christina and Josefina again. Nothing.

This is my fault. I should never have told her. I should have explained the situation to her daughters, asked them to say nothing. But I put myself before Maria, falling back on childish comforts that have long since faded. I came back to Kuwait to be with her, to take care of her, not to be taken care of. I came back for Curiosity Bookshop, not for atonement. I came back for Nabil—already gone.

"Madam?" The nurse puts her hand on my shoulder. "I'm sorry, my dear. So sorry."

———

Something happens to time in a crisis. The flux of temporality was the subject of my dissertation, but it still amazes me whenever I experience it directly. I phone Josie, and this time she picks up on the first ring. I break the news to her as calmly as I can, the sound of my own voice coming to me from a far distance. I volunteer to help with the bureaucracy and ask delicately whether they would prefer to bury their mother—I cannot say her name—in India or Kuwait. If they prefer India, I volunteer to pay the expenses.

Josie thanks me and says Kuwait. It would have to be Kuwait. Maria's family is here, most of their friends are, too. She spent decades in this country that wasn't hers to make a good life for her children. Josie says she'll tell Christina. I suddenly remember that it was the two of them who had first driven to the spot where my mother was hit, at Maria's anxious behest, because she was late home from her evening walk. And then the three of them drove together to this very hospital, only to find that my mother had died alone, her own children far away.

I promise to call tomorrow morning to update her about the paperwork. She says that she and Christina will arrange to have the funeral in the next couple of days.

I arrive home to Aasif waiting by the pool. I shake my head. He lifts his hands to the ceiling, to a God he believes in beyond that ceiling. He says a short prayer for Maria's soul, then asks me, "Do you want something to eat?"

"No thanks, Aasif. I'm going to bed." I leave it to him to switch off all the lights in the house and to lock the front door. With Maria gone, he'll have to start locking the door downstairs. I wonder if he'll think of it tonight. I collapse in bed with my clothes on, and for the first time in what feels like ages, I sleep the sleep of the dead.

My eyes blink open at four in the morning to bright sunlight slanting through my window. My mind feels white like a star or a blank page. Why didn't I draw the curtains last night? It takes a few seconds for things to recrystallize, and when they do, all I want is to return to the moment just before, when I first opened my eyes to the promise of a day with Maria still in it.

It takes all my energy to push myself onto my elbows, then inch my legs and feet across the bed and to the floor. Maria is dead, but my eyes are chalk dry. Then I remember the accusation against me and feel a glacier of guilt in my gut. Forgetting my case has come at the expense of Maria's life. I sink back down again.

Some minutes later, I force myself into the shower, scrubbing the stench of hospital disinfectant off my skin. It's 6:30 P.M. in San Francisco. I call Karim.

"Hey there, little sister."

"Hey." I can't temper the blow, so I blurt it out fast. "I have some upsetting news. Maria died last night. Heart attack."

"Oh, no!" I hear rattling as he puts down the phone, then I hear him sob. He gets back on a few minutes later. "Maria gone. This makes me so sad."

"Will you come for the funeral? It should be in a couple of days."

"Shit, Sara. I have a deadline."

I'm half-annoyed that even Maria's death is not enough to get him to return. The other half of me never wants him to come back here again. "It's okay. I'll be there. You can come after, pay your respects to her daughters? And, Karim, there's one other thing." If I don't tell him now, I may never. I begin explaining the 1961 Press and Publications Law—a vague law against fomenting hatred. I jump to the 2012 National Unity Law, more restrictive, more punishing. I sound like a lawyer rehearsing a defense or building an accusation. Karim doesn't interrupt, but I hear his breathing speed up.

"A few months ago, in April, the parliament passed an amendment to Article 111 of the Penal Code, which modified the National Unity Law. It made blasphemy a capital crime."

My brother stops breathing. "Sara, what's going on?"

I mumble, "I've been accused of blasphemy."

"*What?*" His voice explodes in my ear.

"I'm going on trial for blasphemy. My lawyer is doing things by the book and promises everything will work out if I retract my words. Worst case, I'll have to serve some time in prison or pay a fine. Maybe both. But I'm not going to die over this."

"I'll be on the next plane out."

"What about your deadline?"

"I'll sort it." He sounds wrecked.

"Look, Karim, let's wait until my next meeting with Mr. Al-Baatin. Finish up your project, then we'll see." I hear myself backtracking unconvincingly.

"I'm coming, Sara. I'm not going to let anything happen to you."

I don't know if Karim ever told Maria his secret. I suspect not. Maria lamented Karim's absence from Kuwait like it was a death, not like she understood it even a little. I never asked her because I didn't want to betray Karim. I was the keeper of my brother's secret long after anyone cared.

———————

It all started in California in 1983: the summer of Matt. Karim and I were in line for tickets at Edwards Cinema. Karim handed me the twenty-dollar bill Mom had given him. "Sara, you get the tickets."

"If I buy the tickets, he's going to ask how old I am," I protested. "We have a better chance if you do it." I was eleven; he was thirteen.

"No. You do it."

"Is it because you guys are going to see *Flashdance*, not *Return of the Jedi*?"

The two of us spun around, and there he was. Matt of the baby blue eyes and sunbaked skin. Matt, whose name we didn't know yet. He was older than us, but by how much, I couldn't tell. Karim and I were firmly on the kid side of the divide, and this guy, despite his shortness, seemed much more grown up.

"It's a great movie, you know, *Flashdance*. *Star Wars* is overrated." Matt's hair was dirty blond and shoulder length. He had a way of flicking it back without touching it, without any obvious movement of the head. "This is my third time. That last scene at the audition? *Totally* awesome. I'll get your tickets if you want. We can sit together."

I turned to Karim, willing him to refuse. He handed the stranger our twenty-dollar bill.

Matt, it turned out, was sixteen and spent most of his time in his parents' basement playing Atari. He didn't have many friends, and all he really seemed to do was listen to records, watch movies, and drive around in his beat-up yellow Volkswagen Rabbit. Matt wasn't a bad guy, but that summer I hated him. He was the first person to come between my brother and me, and I couldn't figure out why.

I became Karim's ready excuse. Sara wants to go to the mall. Sara wants to go to the beach. Sara wants to go to the movies. Mom would let us go out together unsupervised because she figured Karim was asserting his adolescent independence, and I suppose it was some relief to her that I wasn't being jettisoned in the process. If where we wanted to go was nearby, Karim and I would walk. If not, Mom would drop us off. After she drove away, Matt would arrive in his car. We would drive around for hours, listening to Missing Persons, not talking much.

I didn't mention Matt to Mom or Dad, and neither did Karim. The two of us didn't speak about Matt to each other, either, even when we were alone. Being with Karim and Matt that summer was nothing like being around Karim, Faris, Daoud, and Nabil back home. Karim's friends had become my friends, too. With Matt it was different. I was what made it possible for him to be with my brother, but I was also what kept them apart.

We would go over to Matt's house in Laguna Niguel when his parents weren't home. I'd hang out on the oversize brown couch in front of the TV in the living room with a bag of Doritos, watching reruns of *Gidget* and *The Brady Bunch*, while Karim went down to the basement with Matt. I was ordered not to follow unless I heard a car in the driveway, in which case I was supposed to run down and warn them. It didn't occur to me to ask why they would need to be warned.

I didn't hear a car in the driveway all summer, but on one of the final days of our vacation, I decided to sneak down to the basement anyway. I licked Dorito dust off my fingers and carefully turned the door handle. The stairs were carpeted and silent. It was dim, and it took a minute for my eyes to adjust.

The two of them were making out on the couch. Matt's right hand held the back of Karim's head. Karim's arms clasped Matt's lower back. My brother didn't look like a kid anymore, but I sure felt like one. I tiptoed up the stairs, hoping my brother hadn't seen me.

The phone rings and jolts me awake. It's Josie. The funeral is tomorrow.

Noura

The move from India to Kuwait had not been easy. Noura and Dana disliked the way sand could cling to every bodily crease. They would play outside their courtyard home in Shamiya, run along unpaved roads, and return at dusk with grayed knees and elbows. Their praying mantis of a grandmother squawked that they wouldn't find a husband if they allowed themselves to succumb to the weight of the desert.

Noura and Dana spoke broken Arabic with heavy accents. For five months they attended Abla Samira's Arabic language class with first graders at Zahra Elementary School for Girls in Jibla, folding their lengthening limbs under tiny desks. Though Noura was one year younger than Dana, the school decided it would be best not to separate the sisters. They were taught fifth-grade math, science, and all other subjects in Arabic, which meant that for the first few months, most of their lessons passed into oblivion.

At first, the girls at school disliked the sisters, the way children sometimes dislike what they envy or don't understand. They would surround them at recess and mock: "What's wrong with your Arabic, anyway? Have you landed from the moon?"

Noura and Dana, not understanding the questions, would remain silent, and their classmates would laugh, grabbing each other's hands and dancing around them in a tight circle. After about a week of this, the sisters decided to laugh along with their tormentors. They started asking their classmates for help with Arabic and poking fun at themselves for their linguistic blunders. Soon their classmates were asking them for help with their English homework, begging Noura and Dana to teach them how to say *I love you* in Hindi.

"Moobaaraak . . . Kaleefaa . . . Aal . . . Mustehfaa."

"Wrong again!" scolded Abla Samira, their young Arabic teacher from Palestine, who also tutored the sisters at home. "Listen to me: *Mu, Mu*barak, not *Moo*, not the sound of a cow! And your grandfather's name is *Kha*lifa. *Kha*, not *Ka*. And don't lengthen your vowels. Remember, girls, you're not Indian!"

Noura and Dana gulped down giggles. Abla Samira locked her gaze straight ahead and instructed the girls to repeat. Some days Abla Samira chittered along with them like a sparrow on a branch. Other days, like that day, she was all business, tapping on the desk with her metal ruler. Then the girls knew not to cross their pretty tutor. Without Abla Samira they would have been lost in their new country, their new language.

The reluctant sun was setting later now that it was the end of February. Earlier that afternoon, Mama Lulwa had asked their tutor whether she might prefer to conduct her lesson outside in the courtyard. Abla Samira thought it would be fine, but when the sun dipped under the horizon, a chilly wind kicked up. Dry air crept under skin differently here than it did in Poona. Noura couldn't understand how the fiery heat of last August could transform into this biting cold. She buttoned up her sweater as Abla Samira ordered the sisters to repeat their father's name once more.

Like all residents of Kuwait Town, Sheikha had been forced to sell her house so that the old firjan could be razed in preparation for the construction of the new capital. Inhabitants had to move to one of the recently developed suburbs. Thanks to the foresight of her son, Ahmed, she had purchased property in the residential area of Shuwaikh, not far from the old family home. Sheikha could view the sea from her sateh. Sometimes at dawn she would watch the rising sun turn the flat waters of the Gulf pink and think of her brother.

On the days Sheikha came to her daughter's house for chai al-dhaha, Lulwa would be waiting for her at the front door. Lulwa was the only one of Sheikha's children willing to see her, and the only child she wanted to see. Sheikha no longer sought to wreak havoc on her youngest's happy life. Her jealousy had transformed into a detached curiosity to see how long the girl's luck would last.

Lulwa's children hid when Sheikha visited, though the girls would spy on her from behind chiffon curtains. When instructed to do so by Lulwa, Noura, the more benevolent of the two, would volunteer a polite "Good morning, Mama Sheikha." Dana would place a begrudging kiss on each of Sheikha's cheeks.

Sheikha ignored them both. She allowed Lulwa to guide her by the elbow to the nearest divan. She seldom stayed for more than an hour and never for lunch, when the whole family, including her odious son-in-law, gathered to eat.

Mubarak had acquired the two-thousand-square-meter plot of land in Shamiya during the first land speculation boom, thanks to Lulwa's tossed note. It was not far from what would develop into the city center and retained some of the grace of the vanishing old town. He had planted trees around the perimeter that didn't need water to thrive, sidr and eucalyptus. When the time came to build their new home, the trees were thick and welcoming.

Mubarak had built a two-story home to accommodate his seven children, Lulwa and himself, and three domestic staff—Philomena, Inas, and Charlie the cook—who had accompanied the Al-Mustafa family from India. The home would not be as spacious as their grounds in Poona had been, but it would suffice. It followed the traditional style, courtyard at the center, sidr tree in the middle. But Mubarak's new home was made of durable concrete, not temperamental mudbrick, and there was a surrounding garden and a high wall circling the house, both of which would have been unthinkable before. In the old firjan, neighboring homes shared walls and satehs, smells and sounds. Neighbors needed each other more than they did privacy. Now the people of Kuwait, encouraged by the recent overspill of money, made unorthodox plans that included vast gardens, as well as two- or even three-story concrete homes. And they built walls around their properties, meters high, keeping neighbors out.

Despite the unfriendly wall between them, one of the first things Lulwa had done upon their arrival in August was to prepare a dish of sab-il-gefsheh to deliver next door. As she rapped on the iron gate, she took a covert inventory. Her neighbor's land was about half the size of her own, and it didn't have any well-rooted trees planted on it yet. The house was built in the traditional style, with a central courtyard, but it was only one story high.

A young African woman opened the gate. "Yes, ya sitti, how may I help you?"

"I'm your neighbor, Um Bader. I've brought sweets."

"Please come in!"

Lulwa stepped over the threshold into the liwan. The young woman took the plate from her and led her through carefully stacked porcelain dishes and metal pots, towers of books, and suitcases butterflied open. She looked embarrassed. "Excuse the clutter, sitti. We've only just arrived. Um Malik is trying to fit everything in." She lowered her voice slightly. "It's smaller than we're used to. I'm Naeema."

The place reminded Lulwa of her parents' old home in Jibla. The corridors and courtyard of her neighbor's home, like her own, were covered with kashi, the gray, black, and white terrazzo tiles that would soon become ubiquitous in Kuwait. The walls were whitewashed.

The lady of the house appeared under an archway dressed in a saffron derra'a. Lulwa's new neighbor was breathtaking. Milky skin, black hair fashionably cut and parted on the side, luminous gray eyes. The woman hurried over to Lulwa and kissed her on both cheeks. Another woman, older but equally graceful, followed close behind. "Ahlan-wa-sehlan, ya jarti. Please come into the sala and forgive the disorder. We arrived two weeks ago and haven't figured out how to sort ourselves. I'm Yasmine Suleiman, wife of Marwan Sayyid Riyad Al-Ameed, son of the Pasha of Basra. This is my mother, Yeliz Elmas, from Istanbul." Yeliz, vibrant at fifty-six, embraced Lulwa and led her to the sala, which contained one long divan, two wooden side tables, and not much else. Naeema brought istikans of tea, small plates and forks, and Lulwa's platter of warm sab-il-gefsheh.

What was supposed to be a cordial, half-hour visit stretched into a three-hour encounter between two women who detected in each other spines of steel. Over the disorienting next few weeks and months, Lulwa and Yasmine stole a few hours to themselves a couple of days a week, chatting over tea, helping each other come to terms with their unfamiliar lives in this unfamiliar country.

Lulwa, seven years older than Yasmine, sometimes felt sorry for her new friend. Yasmine's husband appeared to be a sullen, taciturn man who expressed limited affection to his wife and children. He was the opposite of Mubarak. He didn't have a job yet, so he moped around the garden or sat at a desk in his study off the main sala, where Yasmine and Lulwa would meet. He kept himself conspicuously apart during her visits, and they had never been formally introduced. He alternated one week with Yasmine and her children, the following week with his second family. Yasmine told Lulwa that she didn't know much about her husband's second family because she didn't want to. "Frankly, ya Lulu, it's nice to have some time to myself when he's gone."

Yasmine told Lulwa that Marwan felt alienated in Kuwait. As a lawyer, he could secure a job at one of the new government councils, but he purported to lack the energy to seek employment or to visit the diwaniyyas that would have helped him integrate more smoothly into society. His family was well-respected, with strong roots in Kuwait, but he couldn't shake off the inertia that held him back. He spent his days at his desk writing poetry no one would read.

One evening in October, sitting together on a bench in their courtyard, savoring the cooling weather, Lulwa casually mentioned to Mubarak something about Marwan's lack of employment.

"Marwan Al-Ameed . . . Al-Ameed. You know, I think your brother knows him."

"How?"

"Don't you remember? Ahmed would sometimes go visit the son of the Pasha of Basra. I seem to recall a Marwan."

Mubarak was right. Marwan and Ahmed had been friends. Lulwa remembered her mother's words about her brother spending time in Basra with men. She wondered if Marwan had been one of those men. Lulwa had never mentioned what her mother had said about Ahmed to her sisters, and it wouldn't have occurred to her to bring it up with her brother.

Lulwa went over to her neighbor's house the next morning, a Friday, even though it was not typical for her to visit on the holy day. "Yasmine, I have news. My brother, Ahmed, was friends with your husband." Yasmine's eyebrows rose. "Ahmed used to visit Basra in the late twenties. To flee my parents, really. They met at a coffeehouse."

"Marwan?" Yasmine called out hopefully. "Could you please join us?" Marwan, always elegant with his regal posture, walked into the sala. "Do you know who this is, Marwan?"

He bowed his head politely to Lulwa. "It's your new friend, our neighbor. Um Bader, a pleasure to meet you. I'm sorry I haven't introduced myself." Lulwa was surprised by his faultless manners; she hadn't bargained on that from everything Yasmine had told her about him or from what she had observed.

Yasmine interrupted before Lulwa could respond. "She's the sister of your old friend Ahmed. Ahmed Al-Talib!"

"Really?" Marwan smiled broadly, and his arms sprang up as if trying to grab the past on the wind.

It was the first time Lulwa had seen Marwan smile. "Ahmed is coming over for lunch today," Lulwa said. "We'd be honored if your family would join us. It'll be such a treat for Ahmed."

Noura loved it when her uncle Ahmed came to visit. They had grown up in Poona with a limitless supply of aunties and uncles, but none of them had been *blood*. She had been taught this distinction boarding at the Barnes School, when one of the older students had laughed at her announcement that her aunty Aruna had given her a can of boiled sweets for her birthday.

"No, silly," the girl had chided. "An *Aruna* couldn't possibly be the aunty of a *Noura*. Not a *blood* aunty anyway." When Noura had asked Mama Lulwa about it, her mother had explained that on her side, Noura had two blood aunties and one blood uncle, and that on her father's side, she had three blood uncles and one blood aunty. "But," Mama Lulwa had added, "your aunty Aruna was one of the circle of aunties who saved you from being raised by monkeys. That matters more than blood."

Now that Noura was in Kuwait, she was glad to see more of her blood aunties Sumaiyya and Hussa, though less of her aunty Hayya, who had remained in Bombay with her husband. But she especially loved Uncle Ahmed, who taught her how to play a Kuwaiti card game, kout-bu-siteh, and spoke to her in a clear Arabic she could understand. He told her stories about her father in the old dhow yard, how he had captured her mother Lulu's heart with an ingenious little wave. Normally Noura was the center of her uncle Ahmed's attention, but that day the tall man from next door was. Ahmed kissed the stranger on both cheeks and kept slapping him on the back and laughing.

The Al-Ameeds' first lunch at the Al-Mustafas' would be followed by many more. Ahmed and Marwan were able to rekindle their friendship, and Ahmed helped Marwan land a position on the Municipal Council. At the Al-Mustafas', Marwan recovered his long-dormant charm, and its residue adhered even after the Al-Ameeds went home. Though Yasmine's happiness was no longer contingent on her husband, it was still pleasing for her to experience Marwan again as he was before the children were born.

Maria

The youngest in a family of four daughters, Maria had assigned herself the task of caring for Bonita, leading her to graze, milking her, washing her down, polishing her bell before nightfall. Maria's three older sisters helped their mother, Natalia, clean their small, thatched roof hut at the edge of the village of Talaulim in Goa. They woke at dawn to carry fresh water from the well. They would sweep and lightly wet the dung floor each morning, and every evening they would light the cooking fire outside the hut. When the girls were old enough, they joined their mother at market to sell Bonita's milk. Maria, eight years old in 1938, was left behind with Bonita, her best friend.

Their father, Salvador, worked as a brickmaker from sunup till sundown and brought home just enough to keep the family from the brink. One hot afternoon at the end of the dry season, Salvador was removing bricks from the firing trench, ten at a time, stacking them neatly in the wheelbarrow at his side, when he suddenly dropped a set back into the trench. He stood straight as a poker and lifted his chin up in the air. The brickmaker in front of him, startled by the crash and break in the flow of work, peeked over his shoulder. There was Salvador, staring at the sky, his expression a puzzled grimace. He crashed to the ground, and the men rushed to his side.

In the time it took to carry his lean body through the narrow paths to his hut, Salvador was gone, his neck and cheeks splotched red from his exploded heart. And yet the news of his death arrived before he did, and Natalia and the girls were waiting in a semicircle outside their hut. Maria hung her arms around Bonita's neck.

The members of their close-knit village assisted the family, cleaning Salvador's body, praying over it, providing sustenance to those left behind. The brickmakers dug a hole, and Salvador was placed in it. A few hours later, a priest arrived to say a prayer over the mound.

The day after Salvador died, Natalia walked to Santana Church, a baroque landmark of the Portuguese rising out of verdant land like a lonely ghost. She prayed in the name of the Father, the Son, and the Holy Spirit for as much mercy as He saw fit to bestow. Without warning, Natalia was a young widow with four daughters to care for and no one to support them. Their only asset was the cow. Bonita would be slaughtered, sold as meat to well-paying Muslims to cover the family's debts and, if there was anything left, dowries for Natalia's daughters.

Natalia gently broke the news to Maria as she plaited her daughter's long black hair before bed. She tried to convince Maria that the cow would be sold to a family with a little girl, just like her, but Maria, tracing the thread of their lives, saw through the lie. Bonita was going to be killed. Maria insisted on going with her mother, and Natalia, unable to dissuade her, reluctantly agreed.

Maria spent that last night of Bonita's life murmuring words to her, scratching behind her ears. As Bonita slept, Maria polished her bell. She cried for her father, who had spent most of his life working, but who had always had a tender word for his daughters. And she cried for Bonita.

Natalia and Maria set out at dawn to Panjim with Bonita. It took them over two hours by foot to arrive at a square where animals were traded or sold to butchers. By then the air had thickened with humidity. Hens and sheep kicked up dust, men smoked bidis, and a food stall provided hungry peddlers with boje to eat and dhood-da-chi-chao to drink. A few women sat at mats selling hand-rolled bidis and, from under their saris, gold. This was not the main market. There were no covered stalls for spices, fruits, and vegetables here. No cooks or wives wandered through teeming passages, gathering supplies to prepare family meals. This was a hasty scramble of people desperate for cash, in possession of one thing or another to sell. Those on the other side of upcoming transactions sniffed out this desperation and vultured in to skim off easy profit.

Lazarus Torres had wandered into the square by accident. At seventeen, Lazarus wanted a job. This had not always been the case. Four years earlier he had left his home in Poona because he yearned to see more. Food, money, work—none had troubled his head on the night he bundled a change of clothing and a few paise and made for the open road without saying goodbye to his family. He was one of seven siblings. His mother and father worked and worked. He knew they needed him, but the pull through his organs was stronger than family duty. He wanted to see for himself the marvels described by travelers who came through Poona. Icy mountains and air so cold it burned to breathe. Jungles punctuated by the songs of strange birds, the scent of moss. The embrace of a blue ocean and the land of Arabs and Africans beyond. Languages foreign to his ears.

Lazarus relied on the goodwill of strangers to feed him and clothe him and transport him farther down the long road. A ripe mango or a palmful of rice, a worn lungi in Kerala, a warm cap in Kashmir. Carrying a memsahib's packages home for a few paise, loading a cart of palm fronds for a bit more. He managed to cover the longest distances at the back of a bullock cart transporting hay or wood, but on foot he saw more. People's decency, he realized, made itself known in their offhanded kindness and unasked-for generosity.

Several years after he left, he returned home for a visit. All was more or less the same. His parents still worked hard. A few of his siblings were married with babies of their own. His family was surprised to see him but laid no blame for his absence. One night his mother whispered in his ear that she was thankful he wasn't dead. A few weeks later, he couldn't fight the urge to leave again. But this time back on the road, his restlessness quickly dwindled.

By the time Lazarus arrived at the village of Panjim in Goa, he had decided that he wanted to learn a skill he could carry with him, to apprentice as a builder or potter, maybe as a coppersmith. This town appeared as friendly or as unfriendly as any other he had passed through.

It was little Maria, not her mother, who steered Bonita to the center of the square. It was Maria who, once the sale was complete, tugged at the animal's ear, leading her down a narrow lane, where she would be slaughtered by a Muslim in semi-secrecy to avoid the ire of the devout. Maria held the cow's head and looked into the animal's eyes. She smiled at Bonita, spoke to her soothingly. The Muslim—dressed in a crisp white shalwar kameez, confident in his skills—recited a brief prayer over the cow's head, his sharp knife concealed from the animal's view. Maria untied the bell from around the cow's neck and twisted the strap around her wrist. She never flinched, not as the blade sliced the cow's neck, not even as the animal bled onto her feet. She wiped the blood with the hem of her worn gingham dress, then walked away, not holding her mother's hand, the muted ring of the bell trailing her.

Lazarus was intrigued by the self-possessed child carrying the weight of the planet on her scrawny shoulders. "Are you all right, aai? Do you need help with anything?" Lazarus asked Natalia as she and Maria passed by.

"We're fine," Natalia said. She had a substantial roll of cash from the sale of the cow stuffed in her blouse under her sari and no wish to make conversation with a stranger. She grabbed Maria's hand and led her out of the cramped lane, through the square, toward home.

Lazarus followed them surreptitiously.

At the edge of their village, Natalia and Maria quickened their pace. Lazarus noticed men working in unison firing bricks. He let the mother and daughter go. It wasn't a large village. He would ask about them later.

Lazarus secured a position with the brickmakers, Salvador's erstwhile group. They told him about the abrupt death of their friend and that the widow was on her own with four daughters to provide for. The youngest of the daughters was the girl with the cow.

Lazarus found the widow and her daughters on one of his rambles about a month after his arrival in Talaulim. They sat in a circle on the rickety deck of their hut eating rice and dhal. Natalia looked up and noticed the young man in the tall grass across the way. Lazarus slinked back in the direction he had come from.

The following evening, around the same time, he was back. This time Natalia stood up and glared. Lazarus pretended not to see her and passed by the hut, looking straight ahead.

The third evening, he walked up to the cramped deck to speak to the mother directly. Natalia beat him to it.

"What do you want? Why are you coming here every night, every night? Leave us alone, you hear? My husband will come home from work any second."

"Aai, don't you remember me? I spoke to you when you sold your cow. I asked if you needed help."

At this Maria looked up. It had been over a month since Bonita's death, and she didn't remember the young man. She got up and went to stand beside her mother. Because she was standing on the deck and Lazarus was standing on the ground, they were almost level. She stared straight into his eyes, exactly as she had into Bonita's on that fateful morning. "What do you know about Bonita?"

"Bonita? Was that the name of your cow? You loved her very much."

"I did . . . I do. I'm never going to eat meat again because of Bonita."

"That's a good plan. Vegetables are plentiful and cheap."

Natalia glanced from Maria to the boy. "What is it that you want from us, young man?"

"My name is Lazarus Torres. I work with the brickmakers your husband worked with." Lazarus looked away from Maria and kept his eyes on the ground as he addressed Natalia.

"Did you know my husband?"

"No, aai. I was hired a few days after he died." Lazarus looked up at Natalia. "I'm sorry. I saw you with your daughter that day in the square, and I wanted to help you. I'm here without family. My people are in Poona."

"And what help do you think you can give us?"

Lazarus looked down at his feet again. "I can share some of my earnings," he mumbled without looking up.

None of this made any sense to Natalia and not much to Lazarus either. His wages, a pittance, were hardly enough to sustain him, and if he had any extra, he should have been putting it aside for his future or for his poor family in Poona, not promising to hand it over to these strangers.

"Go, will you, please?" Natalia shooed him away with both hands. "We don't need any help here."

But Lazarus came back at the end of his second month in the village with a good portion of his wages wrapped in brown paper. He handed the packet over to Natalia, bowing low. Natalia would not have accepted what he offered if she didn't feel herself to be at the edge of a great abyss over which her girls were strung. There was no place in her life for pride. She took the packet from his hand and blinked her appreciation.

Lazarus returned a week later with gifts for the daughters. Baked doll figurines he had molded with care from scrapped pieces of mud for the three older girls and a figure of a cow for Maria. Maria slept with the little cow clutched in her hand every night until it dissolved to dust.

Natalia began to warm toward Lazarus. He was a boy far from home. Soon he was having dinner with them nightly, bringing along whatever food he would have eaten alone on that evening to share with the five of them.

Over the next decade, Lazarus worked with bricks all day and spent his evenings with the women of the family he considered his own. The two middle daughters married and moved to remote villages to join their husbands' families. Bonita was replaced with a cat.

By the time Maria turned eighteen, she hadn't attended school or learned to read. She worked on other people's rice paddies and cashew farms with her mother and eldest sister, Anna. In the fading light of over three thousand evenings spent with Lazarus—a cat, a mother, and an older sister between them—Maria grew into him. There was no other choice for love.

They married in 1948, one year after India's independence. Maria, counting every paisa, refused even the most modest of weddings. Lazarus used the money instead to build a room at the side of Natalia's hut for himself and Maria to live in. Their first child was born in 1950. They named him Salvador, after Maria's father. Natalia stopped working so that she could care for the baby.

Lazarus continued to fire bricks, but during coconut harvests, he would also take the job of padekar. As a coconut plucker he learned how to launch himself up the trunk of a palm with the grace of a spider and the speed of a snake. Coconuts were harvested four times a year, and the extra income helped, though Maria worried about Lazarus dangling from fronds so high.

After the tragedy of her father's death, Maria had become a fearful young woman. It was only her unconditional and inherited faith in God that tempered those fears, allowing her to trust in small miracles. Her husband, one of those miracles, was, unlike her, an optimistic man. His early wanderings had instilled in him a feeling of contentment, a sense that he understood the goodness of life. Fear did not constrict his soul, and his ebullience was infectious. Over time, the family eased into it with growing confidence.

In 1955, Maria gave birth to their second child, Christina. A few months after Christina was born, her grandmother, Natalia, died in her sleep.

Sara

The funeral is at the Holy Family Cathedral in Jibla, not far from where Mama Lulwa grew up. I park in a sandlot behind the handsome sandstone church, and Aasif and I make our way to the entrance, scuffing our black shoes. I vaguely remember visiting the church with Maria one Christmas Eve for midnight mass. I must have been around nine or ten. I don't know why I accompanied Maria that cold night, but walking in this morning, the high marble walls and stained-glass windows seem part of a recurring, half-forgotten dream.

The church is packed. I know Maria had a life separate from the one we shared, but I'm still taken aback by this throng of unknown people. What I know is the smallest sliver. My Maria washed my hair, healed my scraped knees and elbows. She made sure I ate my dinner and that my uniform was neatly ironed for school. My Maria filled in the gaps left unintentionally by my parents. But Maria had also been mother to three of her own. She had determined to secure their futures, and she had.

Josie sprints down the aisle the minute she glimpses Aasif and me, and my tongue dries to sandpaper in my mouth. I look down, avoiding her eyes, but she embraces me tightly and bursts into tears, then leads us to the front to sit with family. Christina stands to hug me, and she too cries in my arms. They don't seem to blame me for their mother's death. Karim's absence feels like a fracture, and, not for the first time in the last three weeks, I wish he were here.

"I'm so sorry about everything that's happening to you, Sara," Josie whispers as soon as we're seated. At the mention of my case, the cathedral starts to spin. I lean forward and place my hands on my thighs to steady myself.

Before I can respond to Josie, the room falls silent. Six pall-bearers carry the coffin into the cathedral and place it in front of the altar. Maria's photo, surrounded by a wreath of flowers, is propped up on an easel to the right of the coffin. The coffin with Maria's body in it.

Maria was religious, so she would have appreciated the priest's prayers. I try to focus on his words. After mass, the body, Maria's body, is taken by ambulance to the Sulaibikhat cemetery, where my parents and grandparents also lie. I've never visited their graves because I don't believe in souls. But standing at Maria's open pit, something the priest said in church comes back to me: *They are with us though they are gone and until we follow them home.* I've made a horrible mistake; I should have kept my family company over the years.

Maria is buried in the Christian section. Not many people from the service have come, only family and special friends. The priest says another short prayer before Josie's and Christina's husbands and Aasif begin to shovel sand over the coffin. I wasn't allowed to attend my mother's burial or Mama Yasmine's because women aren't permitted to bury their loved ones in the version of Islam our family ostensibly belongs to. I've always thought that to have to wash a mother's body but not be allowed to bury her seems wrong. Or maybe it's a gift to be spared the vision of a mother buried in the ground for all eternity. I don't know. Karim was there to bury our mother, as were my uncles—Mom's two younger brothers—and so was Aasif. Mama Yasmine had her oldest son there, her grandsons, other male members of the family, and Aasif. Will my brother bury me? Aasif, no doubt, will.

Until this point, my eyes have been dry for Maria because I've been unable to register her absence as permanent. She's at her daughter's place. She's at church. She's anywhere and anything but dead. But standing at her gravesite, looking down at her resolute coffin, a layer of sand covering most of its surface, there can be no denying she's gone. Tears stream down, and sobs, finally, begin to wrack my body. I'm making a scene; I can't help myself. Aasif leads me away, a firm grip on my shoulder. As we go, I hear in my head a song my mother used to sing. *You are lost and gone forever, dreadful sorry, Clementine.* I leave Maria with her daughters, in the hands of a God she believed in, a God the state alleges I do not.

Mr. Al-Baatin visits at his regular time the day after Maria's funeral. Lola, anticipating his return, waits for him by the front door and follows him to the love seat like she would follow him into eternity. She tucks herself between his mammoth feet and purrs brazenly as he scratches behind her ears.

"I'm sorry for your loss, Sara. It was obvious she loved you very much."

I have no idea how Mr. Al-Baatin knows about Maria, but it doesn't surprise me. "Thank you."

"I have a name." Mr. Al-Baatin leans forward like he's about to share a juicy bit of gossip. The love seat creaks dangerously. "Wassmiya Al-Mutlaaq. She was, as you suspected, in your Introduction to Philosophy class last semester. She has one recording of you lecturing on her mobile phone and many other recordings on her computer. I've filed a request to prohibit the recordings on her computer from being admitted in court because of the possibility of tampering. I'm convinced it will be granted. But the recording on the phone will be allowed. It's the full lecture, Sara, but these are the lines that concern us." He pulls out a sheet of paper from his leather briefcase and starts reading like an erudite professor. "'The steady decline of belief in a Christian god should entail a commensurate decline in man's guilt consciousness. It also stands to reason—doesn't it?—that a complete and definitive victory of atheism might deliver mankind altogether from its feeling of being indebted to its beginnings, its *causa prima*. Atheism and a kind of "second innocence" go together.'"

"That's Nietzsche, not me. A direct quote from *The Genealogy of Morals*."

"I know, but that's not going to matter. The Arabic translation, which will be read in court, sounds even more damning." He rubs his cheeks hard with both of his hands. "There's more."

For the first time since the start of all this, I detect a strong note of doubt, maybe fear, in Mr. Al-Baatin's voice. My organs contract. I take a few deep breaths and wipe the sweat off my forehead. Mr. Al-Baatin doesn't seem to notice. He continues to read: "'The death of God signifies the birth of life and difference. The death of God signifies the end of idealisms and transcendent notions, which stifle life and prevent it from doing what it can. The Overreacher is the one capable of affirming life without guarantees, without false promises of heaven and threats of hell. The Overreacher does not need the crutch of religion or metaphysics to live. The explanations we come to accept as truth, whether Islam or whatever else, are the little lies we tell ourselves in order to live. But what kind of life? A life that denies life. A life without creativity, without action, without difference. A decadent life, squandered. Is that the life you want for yourselves?'"

I cover my face with my hands. "That's me, not Nietzsche."

"I know. Apparently the kids all yell out, 'No!,' which doesn't help matters."

"What does this mean?"

Aasif comes in with a tray of tea, and I know his appearance has nothing to do with the tea. I stop myself from looking at him because I need to keep it together. Mr. Al-Baatin takes a sip from an istikan too small for his potato fingers. "It doesn't change our defense in any way. We'll continue to argue that you were doing your job as a professor of philosophy at Kuwait University. Nietzsche is a world-recognized philosopher, and it's your job to teach his ideas. You're not advocating that students should believe his ideas, nor are you stating that you do. We'll make arguments about intellectual freedom and the sanctioned autonomy of the university."

"My tone on the recording will weaken your argument. It'll sound like I'm endorsing Nietzsche. I *do* endorse Nietzsche." There are professors who maintain a level of objectivity as they lecture, and more power to them. I'm not that kind of professor. "They'll hear it in my voice."

"That doesn't matter. What's going to matter are the arguments for the protection of ideas at Kuwait University and the protection of freedom of religion under Kuwait's constitution. We suspected all of this from the start. Now we know the specifics. Do you remember a Wassmiya Al-Mutlaaq?"

"Yes." That was her name, the girl who claimed the power of the gaze under the cover of her niqab. I don't know her particular life, but I can extrapolate from the lives of so many other girls like her I've encountered over the years. A big family, many brothers, a strict, religious father, a one-of-four mother. *The liquidation of thought* applies to her. Philosophy is against Islam, regardless of Ibn Sina and Ibn Rushd. So I, with my vulgar skirts and sacrilegious hair, am against Islam. "She attacks me because she's stuck. If she can't have it, no one can." Rage, swift and feral, combusts my guts.

"They're playing a game here and, unfortunately, you're caught in the middle. You'll retract and then it's done. If there are any hiccups, which there won't be, we'll take it to Constitutional Court, as I said from the start. For the country, it would be better, but we don't want to put you through that. This will be over before you know it."

For the first time, I see Mr. Al-Baatin as an older man, around seventy, as out of sync with the country he's from as I am, the legislation he's spent his career traversing shaking under his feet. Would it have been smarter to hire a religious lawyer? Someone well versed in the tricks and turns of the pervasive discourse? It's too late. In Mr. Al-Baatin we must trust.

"Sara, I have shitty news. I'm not going to be able to make it for at least a few weeks. We're at a crucial point in negotiating a major contract. If I leave, it's going to fall through."

I called Karim to tell him about Maria's funeral, but he opens with this update like he's been rehearsing it for hours. I don't say a thing. I don't have it in me to make him feel okay about not coming.

"I'm so sorry, Sara."

I hold my breath, prolonging my silent reproach.

"What did your lawyer say, little sister?" Guilt softens his question.

I release my breath, long and steady. "We know the name of the accuser. I remember her. But it doesn't change anything. Mr. Al-Baatin says this could take ages. Once we have a trial date, things will be clearer."

"What does Karl think?"

Karl. "He doesn't know."

"What are you waiting for, Sara? Why haven't you told him?" I hear his exasperation, but I can't answer his question, so I say nothing. "Here, Jonathan wants to talk to you."

"Sara, you okay?" I remember how Jonathan used to take pity on my perpetually cold hands, even on the balmiest night out on their veranda, patiently rubbing them until they warmed up. "I can't wrap my head around any of this."

His voice is so open it makes me sense my vulnerability in a way that feels risky. "I miss you, Jojo. Everything is . . . undecided."

"Tell Karl, Sara. He should be with you."

"I'll be fine," I say abruptly, wanting them both to stop nagging me about Karl and to come here themselves and save me.

"Karim's going to try to wrap things up quick as he can. We love you, Sara. Once this is over, you're getting the fuck out of there and moving in with us, you hear me?"

Jonathan says the words my brother does not. I can't speak because I'm crying and don't want him to know. "Love you guys" is all I manage before hanging up.

It's late, but I decide to swim anyway. I dive into the deep end and hear my father pleading with us not to jump into the pool. "No splashing! The chlorine will kill my plants!" I surface to a silence so complete it buzzes. Aasif is in his room, annexed to the side of the house with its own entrance, so there's no one in here but me.

The pool feels suddenly menacing, the cold water slimy against my skin. I can't swim to the ladder fast enough. I scramble out like some prehistoric water beast is chasing after me, but the darkness pouring through the glass wall of doors and windows facing me is equally frightening. I check that the door is locked. It is. I peer out to make sure the gate is shut. It is. I wrap myself with a thick towel, but that doesn't stop my teeth from chattering. I head to the bathroom for a hot shower, then to my room. I haven't locked my bedroom door in over a decade, but tonight, with Maria in the ground, I do. I close my eyes to sleep, and it is of my absent brother that I dream.

One day in November, after the summer of Matt, Karim didn't show up on our bus after school. One of the high schoolers informed me that my mother had picked him up earlier that day. He mumbled something about Karim being in a fight, but I couldn't get anything else out of him.

It made no sense. My brother had never been in a fight in his life. When I got home, Mom shared what she knew about it with Dad and me over lunch. Karim wasn't at the table. He had gone straight to his room when he and Mom arrived home. He was suspended for three days. Dad said something about boys being boys, but Mom didn't look convinced. I started shoveling rice into my mouth, swallowing down my nausea. If she caught my eye, she would know that I suspected something.

After lunch I burst into Karim's room. "What happened?"

He was angled on his bed like a cricket, staring at the wall. "I saw you, Sara," he said, ignoring my question. His voice was gravel from hours of silence or crying.

Karim didn't need to explain, and I didn't need to pretend I didn't know what he was talking about. I rubbed the ends of my hair between my fingers and looked down at the *Star Wars* bedspread our mother had bought for him that summer we were watching *Flashdance* with Matt.

"Sami called me a faggot in the changing room after PE. 'We know what you are, you Iraqi faggot. Do you know what happens to little faggots like you?'" Karim swept his hair off his forehead and kept his hand on his head like he was nursing a headache. "He pulled down my underwear, smashed my chest against the lockers, and started thrusting himself against me. I swung around and punched him in the jaw."

I couldn't put my brother's words together. "We're Iraqi?" I whispered.

"That's not the point." Karim sat up and glared at me. "The

point is, Sara, I'm a faggot." His eyes were two lit candles in a dark basement. "You know it."

I did know it. "So what?" It was a very Mom thing to say. *If someone hits you, hit them back. If you want to do something, do it. If someone doesn't like you, so what? Life goes on.*

"You don't understand."

He was right.

Karim put on the Violent Femmes, and we sat on his bed in silence for a good hour.

Noura

"**I** can't believe I'm turning sweet sixteen!" Noura tightened the straps of her new pointy bra, admiring her silhouette in the full-length mirror in the room she shared with Dana. She had coveted the bra since the start of term, and now, at the end of it, she had one at last.

One of their classmates had returned from Beirut that winter sporting one under her school uniform blouse. "Oui, Madame," Farida had replied to their French teacher, tossing back her bobbed hair and thrusting her sharp breasts skyward. That very afternoon, all the girls in class had rushed to the lingerie shop on Soor Street. All, that was, except Noura. Dana, in the same eleventh-grade class as her sister, was given permission to buy one. But Noura, still only fifteen, was not allowed. Noura had not dared to complain. Her mother was not overly strict, but the rules of society and propriety were observed. When Mama Lulwa said no, she meant it.

Baba Mubarak would return from work sometimes to find his youngest daughter perched like a parakeet at the edge of the teak bench in his study. The corner of his mouth would lift as Noura watched him remove files from his leather briefcase and organize them into neat stacks on his desk. He would listen as Noura recounted whatever injustice she felt her mother was responsible for. There was a fifty-fifty chance Baba Mubarak would side with his daughter, and if he did, Noura knew that Mama Lulwa could be persuaded. But a pointy bra was not something she could ask her baba for. She would have to wait until her sixteenth birthday.

A few months later, in May 1961, the moment had arrived. The most exciting things on Noura's mind were her new bra and the family's upcoming trip to Beirut. Kuwait was on the verge of independence. The sisters noted the raised flags and memorized the jaunty new anthem, and Noura made bold wishes for herself and for her country as she blew out the candles on her cake. The old town had evaporated, leaving hardly a trace of hundreds of years of community life shaped by weather and water. Attention turned from sea to streets, dhows to cars, souks to shops, wind tunnels to air conditioning. But what captivated the girls' attention was not Kuwait's emergence as a nation among nations or its meteoric transformation. The girls were enthralled by Omar Sharif, the man they desperately wanted to marry.

Noura turned left, then right, unable to get enough of herself in the mirror. "Would you wear this with a sari, Dana?" Banaras silk saris were often worn as eveningwear by young Kuwaiti women with ties to India. Noura's older sisters, Hind and Aisha, had both married in saris, and she and Dana had worn gold-embroidered saris to their weddings.

Dana, revising for finals on her bed, glanced up at Noura, a teeth-pocked pencil hanging out of her mouth like a cigarette. "I think it would work if the blouse is fitted correctly. Why? Are you planning to go to any weddings soon? Maybe mine and Omar's?"

"I was planning to wear it to my own wedding to Omar." Noura sucked in her flat stomach. "Don't you think Hisham and Tarek from next door look a little like him?"

"Like Omar Sharif? You must be joking."

"No, really. It's been a while since we've seen them, but the last time they were back from Vienna—about a year ago?—they were looking positively Sharify to me. Think *Sayyidat Al-Qasr*. The thick hair? The chin?"

"Please. Wait till we're in Beirut this summer, we'll be spoiled for choice."

The first few summers after their return, Mubarak took Lulwa and their four youngest children back to India. They spent a couple of weeks in Bombay, visiting his sister, Hayya, and her husband, then went on to Poona, to their old home on Koregaon Road. The children ran through the garden screeching with excitement, their cries circling up into the branches of their old banyan tree, but for Mubarak and Lulwa, the return was bittersweet.

At first, Mubarak, a keen admirer of Pandit Nehru, had been eager to witness the changes India was undergoing with independence. He buried himself for hours each day in *The Free Press Journal, Bombay Samachar, Dainik Jagran*. As the bright laughter of his children filtered through his old study, he diligently clipped articles he deemed relevant to his own country's future. Nehru on multiparty democracy. Nehru on secularism. Nehru on nonalignment. Nehru on education. Nehru on socialism and a mixed economy structure. Mubarak considered India to be the best model for Kuwait to follow. Like Nehru, he believed in socialism and the rights of the disenfranchised, that education was the key to everything else, and that women should have the same rights as men. He wanted his country to be nonaligned, not to waste its energy and resources on fickle political alliances with one great power or another.

His friends in Kuwait made fun of his constant mentions of India and Nehru the Great: "You look a little like him, ya Mubarak. Maybe he's your long-lost twin?" But when India stood with Egypt against Israel, Britain, and France in 1956 during the Suez Crisis, those same friends slapped Mubarak hard on the back, confirming to him that he had been right all along.

Mubarak would always believe India to be his true home, but it was a home he had left behind, a home that had never really belonged to him. His mother had died in her sleep in Bombay a few years before Kuwait's independence. She was buried beside his father in Badakabarastan cemetery. Mubarak's three older brothers and their families had relocated to Kuwait years before. Only his childless sister, Hayya, refused to leave, even after her husband's death in 1960. She did not want to leave the three souls behind.

Lulwa, like her husband, looked forward to the trips initially. To see Hayya again and all her beloved friends; to fall back under the spell of the home that had once protected her from harrowing ghosts; to step into habitual patterns that had shaped most of her adult life. But returns to departed places seldom fulfill expectations, as Lulwa soon discovered. She and the aunties laughed easily enough together over tea, but the kind of intimacy she now shared with Yasmine, she could no longer share with them. And their home, emptied of all the treasures collected over the years, felt foreign to her, like an anonymous rest house.

Her new city, her new home, her new garden, her new friends—Lulwa wanted to bask in these. After a few visits to India, Lulwa told Mubarak she didn't want to go back. Mubarak agreed. Hayya left Bombay and moved into the family property in Poona in 1962. None of her siblings would ever return.

Most of the work Mubarak did at the Kuwait Oil Company occurred behind a desk, writing letters and communiqués, putting his fluent English to work. He seldom had to venture out into the Ahmadi oil fields. Sometimes, though, for the sake of rigor, he would exit the air-conditioned offices into the fields of fire, mouth covered by a white ghutra to protect against choking dust, sulfuric fumes, and the unflinching circle of white sun overhead.

It was loud between the rigs, and Mubarak would shout himself hoarse to be heard by surveyors or engineers over the rhythmic clanking of the drills and the eerie whoosh of burned-off gas. Climbing up the rigs gave him vertigo. The crew teased him about pausing to steady himself on the way down the maze of iron ladders. Mubarak had become a middle-aged man.

He worked at KOC not because he needed to but because he was eager to contribute to the birth of his nation in some essential way. Oil—the liquid center of it—seemed apt. But literature remained his primary passion. The floor-to-ceiling shelves in his study off the courtyard groaned under the weight of three thousand books, and he ordered even more from the International Book Service, his favorite bookseller in Poona. Before discarding the packaging they came in, Mubarak would hold the brown wrapping to his nose and inhale the familiar smell of tea, sandalwood, damp earth, and naphthalene.

Like her baba, Noura loved books. Her passion began in the early days of their return as an antidote to homesickness. Not for Poona, but for English.

"Baba, why do I have to speak Arabic all the time?" she had asked him.

"We're in Kuwait, ya Noura. It's our language, and you have to learn it. How will you communicate if you don't know Arabic?"

"In English or Hindi."

"Not everyone here speaks English or Hindi."

"It makes me so tired, Baba." Fat tears collected at the corners of his ten-year-old's eyes.

Mubarak bent down, lifted her into his arms. "I'll tell you what. We can speak to each other in English, and your mother doesn't mind when you speak to her in Hindi. And whenever you want, I can give you books to read in English, so it doesn't feel this hard." He carried her to the shelf and pulled out *Alice's Adventures in Wonderland*.

From Barrie and Baum to Conan Doyle and Twain, Noura was hooked. She whipped through translations of Homer. Mubarak bought every Enid Blyton book he could find. He ordered the Hardy Boys and Nancy Drew, and, as she got older, gave her Austen and Shakespeare. Mubarak would recite Marc Antony's "Friends, Romans, countrymen," and Macbeth's "Tomorrow, and tomorrow, and tomorrow." But Noura's favorite, which, by twelve, she had memorized and would deliver standing on her father's desk, was: "O Romeo, Romeo! wherefore art thou Romeo? / Deny thy father and refuse thy name; / Or, if thou wilt not, be but sworn my love, / And I'll no longer be a Capulet."

"No daughter of mine will deny her father or refuse her name! And who is this Romeo? I'll kill him with my bare hands!" Mubarak would feign outrage, and Noura would jump off his desk and repeat the speech again, bouncing around his study.

After India, Mubarak and his family spent a few summers in London, and he would have preferred to continue going there. But by 1961, Beirut beckoned Lulwa and the girls, as it did many Kuwaitis, seduced by its cosmopolitan appeal. They stayed at the magnificently pink Saint George Hotel on Saint George Bay at Ain Mreisseh.

"'A thousand hearts are great within my bosom: / Advance our standards, set upon our foes,'" Noura cited in the spirit of fair Saint George.

"Stop it, Noura, for goodness' sake! Tidy up your bosom in that bikini and pipe down." Dana flipped her fringe and peeked over her Ray-Bans to see if any of the bronze gods lounging around them had noticed her sister. They had and were glancing over appreciatively.

Noura put down her Dr. Kildare romance and rolled onto her stomach. "Dana, do you think I'll marry a doctor?"

"I thought you wanted to marry Omar Sharif."

"You can have him if I can have Dr. Kildare." Noura counted eleven yachts anchored in the emerald sea before her. She watched water skiers practicing for the World Championship. Mount Sannine, a white chunk, peaked behind her.

"Why would you want to be with a doctor? A movie star, that's exciting! Or a prince or diplomat. I want to visit Buenos Aires and Venice, stay at fancy hotels, and fly first class!"

Noura was not seduced by the things Dana was. She had read *Madame Bovary*—secretly slipped off her father's shelf—and *Anna Karenina*—with her father's permission. She knew that wealthy, well-polished men did not always bring happiness to women and that riches and happiness were not the same. She suspected that a hardworking man, committed to an admirable profession, was preferable. The only point on which she was in total agreement with her sister was that the man, whoever he turned out to be, would have to be as handsome as Omar Sharif.

Noura and Dana spent their days dreaming by the pool; their parents socialized with friends from Kuwait on the round terrace of the hotel; and their two younger brothers got into mischief with boys their own age. From that summer on, Beirut was the destination of choice, and Mubarak alternated residence between the Saint George Hotel and the newly opened Phoenicia. Mubarak had hoped the new Kuwait would learn from India, but through the sixties, it instead turned to a radiant Beirut. A golden age was dawning in both cities, and Noura was part of it.

In 1966, on her twenty-first birthday, Noura's father bought her a hunter green Alfa Romeo Spider. After graduating from secondary school, Noura was recruited by her school to teach English. Mubarak had wanted Noura to attend the American University of Beirut, but she wasn't ready to leave home yet. She promised her father she would go to university someday, but for the moment she preferred to teach.

Noura's beauty was a declaration that filled any room she

entered. Many came to ask for her hand, but she refused them, not wanting to repeat Dana's mistake. Her sister had married the first rich merchant who had come her way, a nasty, selfish man. Mubarak, gratified by his monkey girl's restraint, had rewarded her with a convertible.

One year later, Noura, on the recommendation of her school principal, was selected by the national television station to host an evening program that covered local and regional cultural topics. *What's What?* would be a light show, Noura's face its main attraction. Noura, who hadn't sought out the job, thought it might be interesting to give it a try, and she figured that if her looks drew in audiences, her intelligence would keep them hooked. She became the talk of the town, and Lulwa was inundated with visits from mothers wanting to claim Noura for their sons. It was unconventional for a Kuwaiti girl from a family of high repute to be on public display, but it was not in Mubarak's nature to restrict the lives of his children. Although Lulwa furrowed her brow, Noura was allowed to continue.

That June, war rocked the region. Noura watched her father, head in hands, listen to Gamal Abdel Nasser's resignation speech with tears in his eyes. An influx of dazed Palestinians sought shelter in Kuwait with family and friends already established in the country. Noura wanted desperately to engage all of this on her Thursday night show, but no matter what she said to convince her producers, they refused. Noura began to see in the future not an open horizon, but limits she hadn't realized were there.

Maria

Maria read her mother's death as an omen that their lives would soon be overrun by the dangers she prayed to Jesus each night to keep at bay. Bonita's ghost, and her father's, haunted her, but Lazarus convinced his wife to believe in him.

Her elder sister, Anna, was beside herself. She trekked to Santana Church every day to pray for the souls of the lost. One evening, four months after Natalia's death, Anna was struck by a bullock cart on her walk back from church. Its sharp wheels ran over her right leg, mangling it below the knee. That she survived was a miracle.

After the accident, Anna stayed home to care for Maria's children, and Maria worked the fields. Caring for the children—five-year-old Salvador, Christina not yet one—brought Anna some relief. They loved the heavy wooden stump Anna wore attached to her knee. Salvador called it her horse and begged her to unstrap it so he could gallop through the field with it. To see him flying through tall grass on the apparatus cheered Anna. Once Salvador started school, little Christina took over, galloping as hard and fast as her older brother had. Like Salvador, Christina started out a sunny child, rarely crying and eager to please. The children's unaffected joy gave Anna the courage to go on.

Maria and Lazarus's third child, Josefina, was born in 1960. She was happy and healthy, exactly as Lazarus had promised. Lazarus continued to fire bricks and pick coconuts. Maria worked in the paddy fields. Together the parents made enough to pay for Salvador and Christina to attend school and, they hoped, would continue to earn enough to pay for Josefina when her time came. An education was what they wanted most for their children.

Fear, that battering thing, lingered in the undetected extra beats of Maria's heart, shading the gladness her husband's love inspired in her. Lazarus celebrated every day with wildflowers and crowed declarations of devotion to his wife. He made his children laugh by swinging them high over his head, telling them to imagine themselves as eagles in flight. He chased them through fields, mimicking a water buffalo on the attack, tumbling down with them when they fell, tickling them till they begged him to stop.

But fear still gnawed at Maria. Fear that she would lose this parcel of bliss provided by Jesus in His infinite kindness. Fear that the envy of villagers might creep through the cracks of her family's hut in the night. Fear for her children in a world of disease, starvation, and fatal accidents.

Maria kneeled down on her mat every night, her sandalwood rosary clicking in the dark. After twenty minutes, time enough for her to pray, Lazarus would kneel behind Maria on her mat and wrap his arms around her. "Enough for tonight, mhojea moga."

In Lazarus's arms, Maria would glide into untroubled sleep, fears quelled by the sound of her husband's lullabies, which Anna and the children, separated only by a bamboo wall, could also hear. They fell asleep to the trumpeting of dark-plumed coots, the friendly chatter of crickets, and Lazarus's songs. Only at night would Maria permit herself to bask in the generous glow of her husband's love.

Lazarus fell out of a palm tree during coconut season in 1965. His neck broke on contact. His body was deposited at the door of his hut by the other padekars, who swiftly withdrew from the unearthly wail of five-year-old Josefina and her aunt's horrified cry.

Salvador, fifteen, and Christina, ten, were at school when their father's body was delivered. Maria was in the rice paddies. By the time they returned home, Anna, with the help of neighbors, had already prepared Lazarus's body for burial. That night, the five of them slept in desolate silence, with no coots, crickets, or lullabies.

Maria could not afford to skip work the next day. She rushed to the fields right after Lazarus was in the ground. The two oldest children walked to school, staggered by their unexpressed agony. Anna cared for Josefina, who cried for her father the way the others could not.

Maria preserved their lives on the knife's edge by working without respite. Work prevented her from absorbing Lazarus's absence. She did not allow herself to cry. She was reserved with the children, cold with Anna.

But even with Anna rolling bidis at home, there was hardly enough to eat. One year later, it was clear that for Josefina to go to school, Christina or Salvador would have to be withdrawn.

This was not a compromise Maria was willing to make. Lazarus's hopes for their children were her last link to him.

There was one option left. They could move to Lazarus's village in Poona. Maria hoped Lazarus's family would provide them with space enough to unroll their mats, a bit of rice and dhal to coat their bellies. Only in this way could she afford to keep all three children in school.

Things went almost as planned. Lazarus's family took in their son's widow and his three children. They even accepted the widow's lame eldest sister. They allowed the five to live together in a cramped hut attached to their modest cluster. Lazarus's family was as poor as it had ever been, but they provided food when they could. They could not afford to help with the children's clothing or school. They too were hanging over the abyss by the tips of their callused fingers.

It was not possible for Maria to work the fields in Poona as she had done in Goa. Those marginally superior jobs were passed down through generations of poor families. Instead, with the help of Lazarus's mother, Maria managed to secure a coveted job rolling bidis in a bungalow. With Anna rolling bidis at home and Maria rolling bidis in the bungalow, which paid more, they managed to keep the girls in school. Salvador had refused to register for his final year. To his mother's dismay, he got a job at an automobile factory. Without his wages they would not have been able to make ends meet. Maria accepted her son's sacrifice with shame.

One early morning in August, three years into their move to Poona, rain fell to earth in fine lines. The overcast sky glimmered with wispy clouds not ordinarily associated with thunder and floods. On the short walk to the mudbrick bidi bungalow, Maria had thought that the gentle drizzle would hold steady, but she was mistaken. By afternoon, it poured down. The turbid light of the storm made it seem like the corridor of the bungalow was underwater. The storm produced a wall of noise, a roar that made it hard for Maria to steady her fingers enough to loop and knot the white thread around her bidis. She could not afford to lose a second. She had to roll as many as she could before five o'clock or the pittance she was paid would be cut.

Maria fretted over her girls' walk home from school, their leather slippers sticking in the mud, their light uniforms transparent with moisture. Josefina was nine, but thunder made her cry. Maria knew Christina would put her bony arm around her little sister, but Christina was a young fourteen, often more afraid of life than Josefina was. The world had not been merciful to her children. She thought about nineteen-year-old Salvador at the auto factory, the muggy heat generating a slick haze her boy would be forced to inhale.

Maria and the nineteen other women she worked with breathed in tobacco grime all day. They worked side by side on the dirt floor of a veranda-like corridor, with a low wall on one side open to the outdoors. Young boys inside the bungalow bundled twenty bidis together and wrapped them in colorful paper cones for transport. A large Bombay company sold the bidis in this and other villages. The women and boys had no contact with that company. They worked for the middleman of the bidi bungalow.

The women ranged in age from thirteen to sixty. They rolled bidis twelve hours a day, ten against one wall, ten along the other.

That day, like every other, was spent cutting small rectangles out of stacks of tendu leaves. Once they had more than a thousand rectangles each, at around eleven o'clock, they began the task of filling them with loose tobacco. Hunched over their baskets of tobacco, they rolled each bidi with care. The tedious process caused their fingers to cramp, their lower backs to throb, and their eyes to smart. Maria's three years of bidi rolling would leave her with a persistent cough. A common desperation bound the women together, all of them a bidi away from ruin. Often up to a hundred of the one thousand bidis each woman rolled daily would be deemed too slack for packaging, so the women tried to roll extra bidis so that their meager wages would not be docked.

By evening, the day's tempest had whipped the overseer into a frenzy. He marched down the corridor, stopping in front of each woman's pyramid of bidis. His pinched features betrayed a suppressed fury. Twenty bidis unacceptable here. Fifty too sloppy there. He grabbed neatly rolled bidis by the handful and smashed them to bits, destroying hours of agonizing work.

When he arrived in front of thirteen-year-old Gita's pile, Maria could feel the tension in the room snap tight. Gita, an orphan, was skeletal, her oversize insect eyes overwhelming her fragile face. She was severely asthmatic and spent her days battling the urge to cough. Her quantity never met the one-thousand-bidi mark. The other women tried to help when they could, sneaking tobacco sticks to her when the overseer wasn't looking. Maria had snuck bidis onto the girl's mound that morning. The overseer had noticed.

"So, what have you managed, young Gita?"

"Eight hundred bidis, I believe, sahib."

"Really? Eight hundred? Well done, Gita! Let's see. These seem a little different than the others, don't they?" His smirk stretched into a scimitar. He glared at Maria. "Who gave these to you?"

"Nobody, sahib, I rolled them myself."

"Who gave these to you, Gita? Don't lie to me."

"Nobody, sahib, I swear to God."

"Faithless girl," he hissed. "Don't bring God into your lies! I'm asking you one . . . last . . . time."

Gita didn't answer. Out of fear or loyalty, Maria wasn't sure.

The overseer kicked Gita's pile of bidis. He reached out and slapped the girl so hard on the cheek that she fell back and slammed her head against the wall. The women heard a crack. Gita slid down, leaving behind a red stain.

Maria rushed to the girl and pulled her into her arms.

"Just what do you think you're doing, you filthy, good-for-nothing kutri?" The overseer's voice boomed through the corridor, rising above the noise of the storm. "You dare to disobey my orders, helping others when you should be rolling your own? I know a hundred women who can take your place." He pulled Maria away from Gita by her hair. "Neither one of you will be paid a single rupee today or tomorrow."

"Please, sahib," Maria pleaded. "I can't survive a day without pay."

"You should have thought of that!"

"I'm begging you, sahib." Maria went down on her knees. The wind picked up, and horizontal rain sprayed in over the low wall.

The overseer pushed Maria to the ground. "Tuji aai chi! One more word out of you and you won't come back."

"I'm begging, sahib, please!"

He bent down, gazing into Maria's eyes like a lover or murderer. "Don't. Come. Back." He spat at her feet and thumped away.

Maria picked herself up. The women gathered around her and Gita, holding a piece of ripped sari against the girl's bleeding head. Gita still had her job. Maria no longer did. The women put their arms around Maria. On any other day, her fate might have been theirs.

Maria made her way to the family hut through the rain. Christina and Josefina were back from school, laughing at some private joke as they completed their homework, unaffected by the weather. Maria's worries about their slippers and thin uniforms had been for naught.

"Mai, you're home early," Christina noticed. Josefina rushed to her mother's arms.

"Did the thunder scare you, Josie?" Maria asked.

"No, Mai, Christina held my hand tight all the way back from school. I wasn't afraid."

"Good, shanuli. Go wash your hands for dinner."

Anna had fried some dried mackerel for them to share, an uncommon indulgence. It felt obscene to Maria, and she couldn't bring herself to eat even the tiniest morsel.

"Come, Mai," Salvador urged his mother, "try the skin, at least! It's delicious, Maxan." He smiled at his aunt.

Maria shook her head. She pushed away her tin plate and stood up. "I lost my job today." She tried to keep her voice steady. "Christina, you'll have to leave school. Josie needs a few more years. You'll have to help roll bidis at home with Anna and me so we can pay for Josie."

Salvador stood up, too. "I'll take a second job, Mai! Christina must go to school. Pai wanted it."

"Salvador, there's nothing more you can do. There are no more hours in the day for you to work. We eat because of you. We'll manage."

Christina remained silent, but Maria caught her shooting a forlorn look at Anna, whose right hand was clamped over her mouth. Their Anna maxan, who hobbled around on her wooden stump, always made things better. Not this time.

Everyone had stopped eating, so Maria collected the tin plates and took them outside to wash. The rain that had come down with such obstinacy all day had stopped. The night air was heavy with the smell of steaming mud.

The cautious equilibrium she had worked so hard to protect since Lazarus's death was lost. A kind deed for a girl one year younger than Christina meant that Maria was reduced to rolling bidis at home with Anna, earning less for the same work she had performed in the bungalow. It meant that Christina would have to forfeit school, rolling bidis at home with them. Her fourteen-year-old daughter rolling bidis. Her son breathing in noxious air. Her injured sister sitting for hours on a phantom leg that ached no less for its absence. With every bidi she rolled at home, Maria's rage mounted, coloring everything around her the red of Bonita's blood.

There were rumors in the village of a land across the ocean with jobs for the poor, money to feed, clothe, and educate children. Enough to build concrete houses with, not huts. A month after she lost her job, Maria decided to trek from the village up toward the river to Bund Garden, anxious to discover whether there was any truth to the stories. She wandered east down the main road along the Mula Mutha River, then strayed into side lanes, driven by a force beyond reason. She stopped in front of a home with white columns and a wide veranda the likes of which she had never seen before. The gate wasn't locked. An older woman in a gray silk dress too large for her stepped out of the great house and inched down the steps into the dusky garden. Her nest of fine white hair was only partially tamed by decorative combs.

The woman noticed Maria gazing through the gate. "May I help you?" She spoke Hindi with a slight accent.

Maria stepped back, startled to be addressed. She had wandered to these parts on instinct, hoping for an encounter with someone who might offer any opportunity. But it had all been a vague aspiration; confronted with reality, she wasn't sure what to do.

"Is there something you need?"

"No, memsahib. Sorry to disturb." Maria hesitated for a moment. "Memsahib, where are you from?"

"From right here," the woman responded with mild surprise. "Why do you ask?"

"In the village we've heard about jobs in a place across the ocean. I thought maybe it was your place."

Sixty-one-year-old Hayya Khalifa Al-Mustafa put on her glasses, hanging from a chain around her neck. She peered at the woman, thin as a bone, forehead creased with what could only be hardship. "Yes, I suppose you're right. My house staff tell me many from the villages have been leaving for my country, Kuwait, in Arabia. Do you know it?"

"No, memsahib. But I'm eager to go. I can cook, clean, look after children. I have three of my own."

"What's your name?"

"Maria Torres, memsahib."

"How old are you?"

"Thirty-nine."

"What do you do, Maria Torres?"

"Roll bidis, memsahib."

Hayya's glasses slid off her nose, as they often did. She let them, allowing the garden to blur. Lately things were blurring more and more for Hayya. Since she had moved back to Poona from Bombay seven years earlier, the obscuring fog seemed harder to fight. Poona was no longer the place it had been. The 1961 flood had transformed the surrounding landscape enough to disorient her when she ventured out. She was an aging Kuwaiti woman rattling around a large house with a few remaining household servants.

"Let me discuss it with my family. Come back in a week's time. I'll have an answer for you then."

"Thank you, memsahib. I will."

Maria strode home with a smooth pebble of hope in her belly, the first in four years.

Sara

I can't get out of bed. I hear Aasif outside my door, but I can't open it. I can't think about food. I drink water from the bathroom faucet. I can't think about the bookstore, about the cat or the parrot, about the empty house, the job that may no longer be mine. I certainly can't think about my case. I put my head under my pillow and sink into sleep, wake up gasping for air, fall into sleep again. In between I check my phone. I have missed calls from Karl. I haven't spoken to him in a week—atypical—so he must be concerned. I think Karim must have spoken to him, but even in my daze, I know it isn't true; that's not our way. I can't do anything but lie in this bed, my head under this pillow, thoughts blunted.

A few days into my hibernation, I see a missed call from Sana. I've missed a cascade of calls from her over the weeks, but this one, for whatever reason, I decide to return. Without giving myself a chance to change my mind, I tap her number.

"I've been worried sick," she says without a hello.

"Hi." I'm barely audible.

"What the fuck, Sara? Why didn't you tell me?" All I can think is, *About Maria?* But it can't be about Maria. "We're working on a petition to submit to the Kuwaiti government. Human rights groups are all over this. I can't believe this is happening in Kuwait. I can't believe this is happening to you!"

Sana works as a barrister in London. We've been friends since the first grade. Even as a child, Sana was irascible, often in trouble at school, but she always managed to talk her way out of serious consequences, heralding her success as a human rights advocate. If you happened to be under her wing when trouble arrived, you too were sure to be free.

"You think petitions will have an effect?" I ask. The West loves nothing more than a human rights atrocity or freedom of speech scandal to whip up condemnation of the Middle East. But well-intentioned letters delivered with indignation don't affect our sorts of governments.

"They might. Look, Sara, I'm coming. The kids are at camp. I have a few weeks off. Who's your lawyer?"

"Muhannad Al-Baatin. Have you heard of him?"

"Yes. He's still practicing?"

"He is."

"He has a solid reputation. Has a trial date been set?"

"No. It could be weeks or months or years. None of his requests have been responded to yet, so I'm banking on years."

"That's not what I hear. There's interest in this case, Sara. Your parliament wants to set a precedent, and you, a woman, a university professor, are perfect for that. Al-Baatin hasn't told you?"

My stomach heaves. "No. How do you know all this?"

"I have my ways. I've been calling you since I heard."

"I've been ignoring your calls."

"No shit."

"When do you think you'll come?" I sound desperate, but I don't care. I need Sana to remind me who I wanted to be.

"Soon as I can. A few weeks at most. We're getting you out of this."

I believe her. For the first time in weeks, I feel a prick of something good.

"Sana and Sara, just one letter between us. We're going to be friends forever," Sana had proclaimed in homeroom at the start of seventh grade.

I was twelve and battling my first period. When I told Mom about the drops of blood in my underwear, she handed me a pack of Kotex, explained how to fix the pad in place, and warned me to avoid tampons. I knew about periods from *Are You There God? It's Me, Margaret,* and the tampon business I would ask Sana about.

Karim, following his fight with Sami, seemed back to normal. The first few weeks after the fight, my mother watched her first-born with falcon eyes. She would urge him to go out with Faris, Daoud, and Nabil, who kept coming around, but Karim would shake his head and sulk in his room. I kept my brother company, listening to his music, sharing his silence.

My father registered Karim's drift away from the family as the natural order of things. He and his brother Hisham had spent most of their lives apart from their parents. "Let him go, Noura. He's a young man. He's not getting into any trouble. Why go looking for it?" My father's words calmed my mother, and then Karim started going out with his friends again, especially Nabil, and had no more issues at school. If he was slightly broodier than usual—well, that was not uncommon at his age.

That December, a bomb detonated in front of the American embassy. Our school, the one with the most Americans, was ordered to evacuate. Whenever we practiced fire drills, we marched confidently out to the sandlot adjacent to campus, where the buses lined up after school. This time, the real thing, administrators ran from room to room shouting about a bomb at the embassy, a bomb threat at our school, immediate evacuation. Teachers barked at us to *Go! Go! Go!* I ran across the bridge toward the high school, only to find Karim sprinting across the bridge in the opposite direction, looking for me.

In just over an hour, bomb after bomb shook the country. Bombs went off in the largest oil refinery, the desalination plant, the airport, the Raytheon compound, and the French embassy. The string of bombs caused less destruction than they might have, fewer fatalities than the instigators had hoped for, and resulted in not one dead American or European. At the time, the botched attack didn't elicit the sobering effect it should have.

After finding each other on the bridge, Karim and I sauntered off campus unchecked with a group of friends. Our house was walking distance from school, and none of our friends could get a ride home. We were exhilarated to be making our way through the Surra streets together during school hours, a crisp blue winter sky beaming over our heads, the sinister reason for our unforeseen freedom of no concern to us.

When we got home, Mom was at Mama Lulwa's for chai al-dhaha, as she was every day. She hadn't heard about the bombs, so she wasn't worried when we called to let her know we were fine.

We told her we had brought friends home with us, and she asked Aasif to prepare lunch for a crowd. It was the greatest thrill of my life so far, an intoxicating blend of danger, the unknown, and boy sweat. Half the kids who came home with us were boys, Karim's childhood pals, the other half were girls: Sana, Asha, and Hala, my three closest friends.

Our friends phoned their parents. None had been worried. They, like my own parents, never considered that a school could be a target. Who would want to attack kids, American or otherwise, in Kuwait of all places? Most of our friends' parents had experienced firsthand the brutal baton of force, abandoning homelands for the sake of their children. They had arrived in Kuwait at a time when the country needed them as much as they needed it, and those cotton-padded years allowed them to ignore the simmer of danger ahead. The last two sunlit decades and the recent bombs didn't add up.

My father was on call at the hospital, so he didn't come home for lunch that afternoon. Mom joined the eight of us at the long mahogany table that could seat fourteen. The boys ate like they hadn't seen food in months—margooga, fried samosas and batata chaps, dill rice and chicken salna. My girlfriends and I picked at our plates.

"It wasn't easy to navigate the streets back to Surra," Mom reported. "Checkpoints everywhere. There might be a curfew tonight. I'm going to phone your parents after lunch to see if they'd like you all to spend the night. If school isn't canceled tomorrow, you can take the bus with Karim and Sara. That okay with you guys?"

It was more than okay.

After lunch we followed the boys to Karim's room.

"*Avalon* is the best album ever."

"You're such a romantic, Karim. Roxy Music over the Violent Femmes? No fucking way!" If Karim had a best friend, it was Faris, short and compact with a thick head of black hair he had started to gel back that year. His parents had moved to Kuwait from Beirut in the early sixties. They had figured the period of stability in Lebanon would end, as it did, and that they should head to Kuwait, a source of wealth.

Not one to hold back, Daoud said, "You both suck. It's gotta be the Police, hands down. Copeland rules!" He eyed Lebanese Hala as he spoke. "Copeland grew up in Beirut, you know, went to a school just like ours." It was exactly the sort of detail Daoud would know. Daoud's parents had fled to Kuwait from Bayt Nuba during the 1967 war. Their village was razed, preparing stolen ground for illegal settlements. His family, Daoud never tired of repeating, had nowhere to go back to.

Of the four boys, only Nabil kept his opinion to himself. He flipped through Karim's records, pulling one out, examining the back cover carefully, putting it back, then continuing to flip.

"What do you think, Sara?" Faris asked, ignoring Daoud. "Who are you listening to this month?"

I wasn't shy around Faris when he was alone with Karim, but with all the boys together, and especially in front of my friends, I couldn't respond.

"She likes David Bowie, Siouxsie and the Banshees, and Culture Club, don't you, Sara?" Karim answered for me. "And Joy Division, Nabil, so you're not the only one."

Nabil looked up from the albums. "Not Madonna, then?" He was smirking.

I could feel my face flame up. If I said no, my friends would know I was lying. If I said yes, Nabil would think I was a joke.

"Of course we love Madonna, so fucking what?" Sana glared at Nabil, daring him to disapprove.

Nabil turned his attention back to the albums, his long fingers continuing their methodic flipping. He was the youngest of four. His father had moved to Kuwait in the early fifties from Beirut, where his family had settled after being expelled from Jerusalem in 1948. Nabil's father was the head mathematics teacher at the Shuwaikh Secondary School for Boys; he had taught my father. He was given Kuwaiti citizenship within five years of arriving in the country, had married a pretty young girl from Haifa, whose family had also escaped to Beirut, and brought her back with him to Kuwait. Nabil was Kuwaiti—his father's citizenship passed to his wife and children—but his accent when he spoke Arabic was the Palestinian of his ancestors. "Do you think this weekend's party will get canceled?" he asked without looking up.

"Who cares," Karim said. "I wasn't going anyway."

"What party?" I asked.

"Nothing you'd be allowed to go to," Karim swept in. "You know Mom won't let you go until high school."

"Do you know what goes on at those parties?" Daoud sucked in air and flicked his right hand back and forth like it was wet.

Nabil pushed away the record crate and looked straight at

me. "They're totally awesome, Sara. You should come." Then he waggled his eyebrows in his Groucho Marx way, eroding some of the cool he had been trying so hard to put on.

That wasn't going to happen. School was canceled for the rest of the week, and a curfew was instated through the weekend, so all parties were postponed. Not that Mom would have allowed me to go to a party with Nabil; Karim was right about that. The boys, apart from Karim, grumbled a little about their lost weekend, but they seemed content to spend it bantering with each other, and with us, for hours around the record player. None of us brought up the reason why we were thrown together so unexpectedly. It seemed beside the point. In our adolescent absorption we couldn't see that day for what it was: a harbinger of an annihilating future.

Noura

Bader had always been a reassuring presence to Noura in their Shamiya house. He would read the papers, listen to the radio, think about things he didn't share. He seemed to prefer solitude, but he was not uncaring, driving Noura and her siblings around town when they were younger, slipping them a few extra fils for ice cream. He was forty-one and had chosen to be alone, rejecting marriage and the responsibilities of starting a family. He worked at KOC with their father, managing ledgers, assessing financial accounts, writing reports about the future of oil.

Lulwa suspected Bader's detachment had something to do with the seven years of living under Mama Sheikha's vinegar mandate. Lulwa had done it for love. A childish belief that atoning for her exceptional happiness with Mubarak would save them, and a deep-rooted suspicion that only through her mother could that atonement be made. She had feared their return to Kuwait in 1954 would end her good fortune and that her children would be forced to pay the price. That hadn't happened. So Bader was reclusive, that was no great disaster. Lulwa's luck had persisted for over a decade more.

Bader had not complained of fever that morning, but Lulwa could tell he was feverish. Influenza, she had thought, a few days in bed. But Bader fell in and out of consciousness, not in and out of sleep. He couldn't walk to the bathroom without falling. Mubarak wanted to take Bader to the hospital right away, but Lulwa was certain that if they did, he would never leave it. Yasmine rushed to her neighbor's house, Mama Yeliz in tow. The three women took turns wiping sweat off Bader's brow and chest, alternating cold compresses with wool blankets. On the fourth night, Bader woke from restless sleep grasping his head, an unearthly howl filling the heavy night. Lulwa, slumped in a chair in the corner of her son's room, flew to her feet. She called out to Noura to get Dr. Tarek from next door.

Tarek recognized the symptoms caused by *plasmodium falciparum*, the deadliest of the malaria-causing parasites. Malaria, rare in Kuwait, was all but eradicated in the early 1900s with the advent of quinine tablets. But the summer of 1967 had been uncharacteristically humid, and the lethargic roll of air carried fat marsh mosquitoes down from the north. Tarek could detect Bader's enlarged liver and spleen with his fingers.

Tarek drove Bader to the Amiri Hospital in Sharq, not far. Mubarak went with them, his son's sick head on his lap. Noura sped after them, her mother and Yasmine clinging to each other in the back seat. Lulwa was white with terror. Yasmine tried to reassure her, making impossible promises about her son's abilities as a doctor.

Lulwa was right to be afraid. Not an hour after Bader was admitted, Tarek took Noura aside. "I'm so sorry," he said, "but your brother has cerebral malaria. He's not long for this world." Noura felt her legs buckle. Tarek grabbed her by the elbow. "Steady, Noura." It was the first time he had ever addressed her by name. His tone was low and soothing. His calm gaze centered her. She stared back at him, surprised by his familiarity. Tarek and his brother had been the handsome boys next door, a little older, away at school most of the year, and now, in this moment, he was here.

She returned to the waiting room where her parents were huddled together, staving off the inevitable. The smell of Dettol used to mop the hospital floors made her retch.

Better to die young before your children than to die old after them, the folks of Kuwait Town said. Lulwa had clung to Bader on the dhow when she believed her brother was dying. She remembered her son on the roof of her parents' old house in Jibla, chasing after sparrows with glee. She wept, aching to recover the echo of her child's squeals.

Lulwa silently blamed herself for her son's death. Mubarak reproached himself for not taking Bader to the hospital sooner. He was certain that had he insisted, his son would be alive. Swirling through his tunnel of agony was his residual fury over the seven lost years with his son, snatched away from him by Sheikha decades earlier. Brooding over his mother-in-law allowed Mubarak to endure his own guilt.

Sheikha, rattling bones in a sack of skin, sat alone during the 'azza. She mapped her daughter's every expression. Lulwa was suffering as Sheikha had suffered all her life. It did not bring Sheikha any smacking satisfaction. She was flooded with a disappointment so profound, she believed it would kill her. After the 'azza,

Sheikha sequestered herself in her house, prepared to die alone. For the first time, Lulwa made no effort to draw Sheikha back.

Through the bludgeoning heat of late August, Lulwa and Mubarak grieved for their son. It fell on Noura—the only one of the four sisters unmarried and still living at home—to do what she could to diminish the ferocity of her parents' sorrow. She took some time off from teaching to be with them. They didn't ask her to quit her television job, but Noura understood that it would be un-seemly for her to appear once a week on-screen dressed up, made up, and cheerful, for all the country to behold, while her parents suffered. In any case, Noura was finding it increasingly abhorrent to engage with the trivialities the producers thrust upon her as the region convulsed with violence. She wanted to tackle serious issues. Maybe, with persistence, she could have convinced them to give her a chance, to act against their entrenched biases, but with Bader's death, she simply quit. It was the right thing to do, but a tiny, nearly imperceptible clot of regret began to collect at the center of her being.

Tarek dropped in on the family regularly to check that Lulwa and Mubarak were not falling into what he called—rather exot-ically to Noura's ears—*melancholia*. He would sit by Lulwa's bed, ask discreet questions, and wait patiently for her to respond. He brought small gifts: a set of embroidered handkerchiefs, rosewater in a crystal bottle with a blue atomizer, white mlabas almonds. Once the heightened pitch of anguish dampened, he started stay-ing for lunch, sharing stories about his life as a medical student in Vienna, doing all the talking so that the Al-Mustafas didn't have to. Mubarak and Lulwa began to insert a few hesitant words here and there, showing interest in the doctor's descriptions of frozen lakes and ballroom waltzes. Noura understood what Tarek was trying to do.

On the last day of December, as Noura led Tarek to the front door after lunch, as usual, he paused for a second, then turned around to stare at her. Noura stared back, and when he said nothing, she shook her head inquiringly. Tarek took a deep breath. "Noura, we don't know each other well, but I've spent the last few months here with your family. I've seen enough of you—and I hope you of me—to know that we belong together. I want to marry you, Noura. Not tomorrow, not the day after, but soon. I need English lessons. I'm preparing to take exams to study in America, to complete my residency and fellowship there. Would you teach me? We could get to know each other without the pressure of an engagement. What do you think? Don't say anything yet. I've shocked you, I can tell. Consider it. We'll talk in a few days. Goodbye, Noura. And happy new year!"

He backed out the door like he was being pushed, not giving Noura a chance to respond. Not that she would have known how to. No man had ever proposed to her personally before. That wasn't how it was done. Tarek's breach of protocol intrigued her.

That evening, after seeing her parents to bed, she sat alone on the bench in the courtyard. She closed her eyes and thought of Bader. She felt her small hand enclosed in her big brother's. Over a decade ago, he had led her up the plank of the family dhow that had brought them to a place not yet home. She had been a child then, and now she was an adult, twenty-two years old, and her brother was dead. She gazed up at the black fabric of sky pricked by the light of winter stars and considered Tarek's proposal.

Tarek and Hisham, his older brother by two years, were, as their friends described, two butt cheeks in the same underwear. After the move to Kuwait, they boarded at the Shuwaikh Secondary School for Boys, its campus by the sea equipped with tennis and basketball courts, a swimming pool, gardens with benches to sit on, and a cinema. They whiled away late afternoons at a campus café overlooking the water, watching the sun go down behind a flamboyance of flamingos as they argued about nationalism, pan-Arabism, Marxism, and poetry. Their school became their sanctuary. Easygoing Hisham had learned to blot out his father's moods, but for introverted Tarek, Marwan's presence was stickier. He detected in his father a roster of traits he disliked in himself. Boarding school allowed him to push those traits down so deep, he could convince himself they were gone.

The brothers both attended the University of Vienna, Tarek to study medicine, Hisham, engineering. Tarek had mastered German and Latin in less than a year, passing the oral medical school admissions examination with a score higher than ninety percent of native speakers. He was made for medicine. A lifetime of practice wouldn't be enough. Hisham, no less intelligent than his younger brother, put his wits to different use. Without effort he earned grades high enough to win him a government scholarship, a degree in engineering from Vienna, another government scholarship to complete his doctorate in architecture at the University of California at Berkeley. Academics came easily to him, so he directed his imagination elsewhere: paying for expensive waltz lessons by skipping meals; embracing everything to do with

La Nouvelle Vague; dating Austrian beauties, blondes without exception; organizing gatherings at Café Hawelka and bierkellers for an assortment of individuals whose lives otherwise would never have crossed.

Noura had been correct to identify a hint of Omar Sharif in Tarek's piercing eyes and square chin. He had a slim build but with strong swimmer's shoulders, which he had developed in the canals of Basra, the bay of Kuwait, and the lakes of Austria. His barber in Vienna had marveled over his thick dark hair every time he went in for a haircut. He dressed elegantly, like his father, fastidious about the quality of his shoes. By all accounts, Tarek was a handsome man, but his attractiveness was often overlooked when his brother was around. Hisham strode through life with innate confidence. If Tarek's eyes shone with seriousness, Hisham's glinted with mischief. Without Hisham, Tarek would not have survived their parents' fights, their father's emotional detachment, or their mother's regrets.

Noura didn't think it would be so awful to teach the young doctor English. She thought, in fact, that it might even be ideal to marry Tarek, might be the very thing she had been waiting for.

The next afternoon, she padded after her father into his study. It had been many years since she had trailed after her baba. Mubarak knew what was coming.

"Hah, ya habibti, what can I do for you?"

"How do you know I need something, Baba?" She tried to perch on the teak bench like she used to as a little girl, but it was too narrow for the young woman she had become. She leaned against her father's desk instead.

"It's the young doctor, I presume?"

"I suppose it is."

"He wants to marry you."

"He does. But first he wants me to give him English lessons."

Mubarak roared with laughter for the first time in months. "*That* I did not expect! English lessons?"

"He's studying for an exam to continue his medical training in America. He needs English." Her father's laughter was reassuring, but Noura found herself ready to defend Tarek's unorthodox approach if necessary.

"That's not quite how it's done, habibti, you know that. But, to be honest, I don't see the harm. Let me speak to your mother. English lessons. Clever boy!"

Lulwa agreed to the arrangement, overjoyed at the possibility of her best friend's smart son and her beautiful daughter married. Lulwa instructed Philomena and Inas to place the weathered table out under the liwan, where Noura and Dana had taken Arabic lessons with Abla Samira ages ago, when time was considerate and Bader was still alive. Lulwa, playing chaperone, made a show of walking past as Noura and Tarek studied conjugated verbs, heads touching.

The two were officially engaged in August 1968 and married a month later in a ceremony nothing like the extravagant weddings of Noura's three older sisters, Bader's death being still too close. But even in the best of circumstances, Noura wouldn't have wanted that type of wedding. Her parents paid for the young couple's postponed honeymoon on a houseboat in Kashmir in January, the coldest month, the only time Tarek could take off work.

Before Kashmir, Noura took Tarek to Poona to see the home

she grew up in and to visit her aunty Hayya, the lonely keeper of that fading past. She was disheartened by what she found in Poona. The stunning old mansion and bungalows reeked of mold, and Hayya seemed adrift, swimming in clothes three sizes too big, her eyes and mind less sharp. Noura couldn't bear to stay long. After a few days, they took the train to Kashmir, then on to Dal Lake by car. Chinar trees silvered by moonlight and spiked with icicles lined the road to the lake, tinkling as they passed.

"I've seen snow, believe me, Noura," Tarek said, white breath clouding around his mouth, "but this is something apart."

The houseboat was equipped with a coal-burning stove. They spent their honeymoon in each other's arms, bundled in cashmere blankets on woven silk rugs shining like pools of amethyst and aquamarine. They held hands and watched the eternal snow come down, Dal Lake crystallizing at the shoreline. Noura fed the migratory birds, kulcha and lavasa after breakfast, sheermal after lunch. Every morning a purple moorhen returned, its flame-red bill and shimmering feathers a striking contrast against the snow. Day after day, more birds arrived. Cotton teals about to speak and green-headed mallards hustling for Noura's attention. Amid gleaming ice and the wonder of birds, Noura and Tarek made their first child.

Maria

A week after Maria met the lady with snowcapped hair from the faraway land, she returned to her mansion on Koregaon Road. Hayya memsahib was waiting for her. She offered Maria a job as ayah for a baby expected to be born soon. "You'll be working for my niece Noura, my brother's daughter. You must be ready to leave India by mid-December, three months from today."

The salary Hayya mentioned would end her troubles. Maria understood that this chance had arrived from above. "I'll be ready, memsahib."

That evening under the light of a harvest moon so large and near it seemed about to collide with the earth, Maria broke the news to Anna and the children.

"Where is this place?" Salvador asked suspiciously.

"In Arabia. Not far." Maria tried to sound reassuring.

"You'll fly there?" Josefina asked, her features a mix of confusion and curiosity.

"Yes. On an airplane."

"Will we come with you?" Christina asked.

"No, mhoje dhuve, you won't. You'll stay here with your Anna maxan. Salvador, you'll leave the factory, finish secondary school, go to university, like your pai wanted. Christie, you'll go back to school again with Josie. Then you'll both go to university, like Salvador. I'll send money every month so your maxan won't need to roll bidis." Maria smiled at her sister. Anna, terrified, looked down at her tobacco-stained fingers.

"How do you know they'll give you money?" Salvador asked.

"Why wouldn't they?"

"It happens all the time, ni? You're promised one thing and end up with something different." The past three years had depleted any optimism left in Salvador.

"You'll go back to school, baba. Everything will work out as I've planned."

That night, Maria heard her girls crying themselves to sleep. If she went to them—they were only a few fingers away— she would change her mind and never leave Poona. Then their chance at happiness would disappear. They had to learn to comfort themselves. She put their protection in God's able hands. It was all she could do.

By early December, Maria's paperwork was complete. When she felt herself wavering at the thought of being apart from her children, she redirected her attention to the months and years ahead. With their education secured, they could apply for jobs, good jobs, in Kuwait. They would be together again soon enough. She was leaving so that she could give all of them the opportunities they deserved.

Maria prayed to Lord Jesus with her eyes shut tight for the duration of the flight to Kuwait. The sky belonged to birds, not people.

A stewardess helped her fasten and tighten a belt across her lap. Her cotton sari was not thick enough. Her feet were blocks of ice. What would the weather be like in Kuwait? Would the monsoons come once a year? Hayya memsahib had told her that her brother's family all spoke Hindi. But in the streets? In the markets? At church? What place would Konkani hold in this new life of hers?

The plane landed with a thud, and soon her body returned to itself. She was able to unfasten the belt and stand on her thawing feet. She followed the passengers down a flight of rattling stairs, and when she heard a man calling, "Maria Torres? Maria Torres?" she made her way toward the voice.

The man was wearing a long gray robe and a red-and-white-checkered cloth over his head, held in place by a black rope. He looked like Pandit Nehru, which encouraged her somewhat.

She gathered herself and stood a little taller. "I am Maria Torres, sahib."

"Hello, Maria," he said cheerfully in Hindi. "Welcome to Kuwait. I'm Mubarak. You'll be working in my daughter's home. Give me your passport, and let's go."

Maria handed him her passport and followed close. The plane had arrived late at night. The cold December air whipped against her body. The maroon blouse under her sari exposed a sliver of midriff that the wind touched with icy fingers.

Mubarak guided Maria through passport control, collected her luggage, and led her to the car and driver waiting outside. He held the back door open for her, then got in front beside the driver.

Maria looked out the window of the car at the expanse of desert on either side of the straight, wide road. She had never before seen so much emptiness. No thatched roof huts, no rice fields, no coconut trees, no people. It was coal black beyond the car headlights. There was nothing to see.

"My sister, Hayya, tells me you have children of your own," Mubarak said. "How old are they?"

Maria felt a dry sponge in her throat blocking speech. Without warning tears formed small puddles in her upturned palms. The tears she had not allowed herself to shed as her daughters clung to her that morning. She could not respond.

At the house an unrolled mattress with thick blankets and a pillow awaited her in a room where someone else was already asleep. In the morning, gray light seeped through a window. The other person got up, rolled her mattress, dressed, and left. Maria stirred but did not rise. No one came for her.

At noon, she bolted awake, heart racing, eyes wide open. Her hands brushed the floor and felt cold tile, not the dirt ground she was used to. Maria rubbed her bloodshot eyes and started to remember.

She put on her sari from the night before, opened the door of the room, and stepped into an outdoor corridor that encircled a large courtyard. At the center of the courtyard was a tree with no leaves, only bony branches extending upward. Two women with a baby were sitting on a bench beneath it. The older woman stood up and walked toward her. "Hello, Maria. I'm Mama Lulwa. Did you rest? The bathroom is there, just beside the room you were in. I've left some things for you in a bag." She pointed to an Indian woman in a blue dress with pockets standing nearby. "Philomena will show you." The woman spoke fluent Hindi.

"Thank you, memsahib," Maria said.

"You'll get used to it," Philomena reassured Maria as she led her from the courtyard to the bathroom. "You'll be happy here. Noura's a good girl. I've known her since she was little."

Maria watched Philomena as carefully as she could. How to use the faucet, toilet, bath, toothbrush, and light switch. The house was partly indoors, partly outdoors, like the old wadas of Poona. It was cold in the corridors and courtyard, so Philomena gave her a sweater to wear over her sari and a pair of socks to put on with her leather slippers. "Soon you'll have dresses like this one and proper shoes, so it'll be easier for you to work, and it'll be warmer. In a few months, it'll be so hot you'll wish for this cold!" Philomena cackled.

Maria's mind felt foggy, her mouth dry, and that hard lump kept rising in her throat, making her feel like she might gag. She had tidied up her bun, taming stray hairs with frigid water from the faucet. The thick socks made it hard for her to walk in her slippers, but she thrust her feet forward, regaining some balance. Philomena led her back to the courtyard.

"This is my daughter Noura," the older woman said.

"Hello, Maria. My aunty Hayya says you have some experience with babies?"

Maria forced down the lump. "Yes, memsahib. I have three children."

"How old are they?"

"Nineteen, fourteen, and nine."

"You must be missing them."

Maria examined the lovely young woman with the baby in her arms. She saw pity in her eyes. What must she look like to her, with her cotton sari, strong arms, awkward slippers that refused to stay on? Did she look nervous or just sad?

Noura memsahib handed her the baby, lightly wrapped in a blue blanket. Maria nestled him in the crook of her arm, as she had once nestled Salvador. He gazed up at her with the grayest eyes she had ever seen, two little pools of rainwater. His arm lifted, and she gave him her index finger to grab. Maria noticed the older woman, Mama Lulwa, glancing at her daughter. The young woman looked relieved. "His name is Karim," Noura said.

"He is a perfect baby, memsahib," Maria offered.

Noura beamed. Maria was sure she believed he was the most perfect baby the universe had ever produced. Maria had felt exactly that way about each of her own.

Over the next two weeks, Mama Lulwa—that was what Maria had been instructed to call her—taught her everything she needed to know about running her daughter's house the way Mama Lulwa ran her own. Maria was an excellent cook, which pleased Mama Lulwa. She taught Maria how to make chicken mechbous and margooga. "You'll be able to cook these for them in America." Maria nodded, figuring America was another part of Kuwait.

Noura kept her distance, allowing her mother to take charge. Mama Lulwa introduced Maria to Noura's husband, Tarek sahib. He smiled at Maria and said hello to her in English. Unlike Mubarak sahib, he wore a suit and didn't speak Hindi. He came for lunch every afternoon, napped in Noura's room, then left in the evening after his son had fallen asleep. Mama Lulwa explained to Maria that she, Noura, and baby Karim would be moving back to Tarek's apartment at the start of the new year, a few days away.

"Now that you're here, Noura will have the help she needs with the baby. She won't need me under her feet."

During the day, Maria concentrated on learning everything Mama Lulwa, Charlie the cook, and Philomena taught her. She didn't speak much because she wanted to focus and because she didn't have anything to say. At night Philomena would try to engage Maria in conversation. Maria listened to Philomena's prattle, even while silently reciting her prayers, until she drifted into dreamless, exhausted sleep.

On the first of January, as planned, they moved into Tarek sahib's apartment in Salmiya. The sea shimmered a few meters beyond a sliding glass door. Maria slept on a mattress in the baby's nursery. Noura no longer worked, so she was at home most mornings with the baby. She read him books, sang to him, prepared his formula and fed him, changed his diapers, cradled him in her arms, and gazed into his eyes. She took him with her on walks along the shore and sometimes packed him up and drove him places in her car. She found it difficult to relinquish Karim into Maria's care. Maria, sensing Noura's reluctance, kept away from the baby, focusing instead on cleaning and cooking.

Maria found it almost impossible to play with the baby, to coo back at him or to laugh at the sweet things he did. She didn't dislike the baby or these people whose lives she was sharing. But to open herself to the infant felt like a betrayal of her own children. She didn't want to turn to ice whenever Noura placed the baby in her arms, but she did.

Noura and Tarek would often go out for dinner, leaving baby Karim in Maria's care. She followed every instruction to the letter.

She couldn't be faulted for her attention to the infant's physical welfare. She bathed him, fed him, swaddled him, and put him in his crib. Karim was a fast sleeper, and Maria usually didn't have to do anything other than sleep beside him on her mattress until morning.

But one night in late February, Noura went to the nursery to check on Karim after arriving home from an evening out. Maria was lying on her mattress staring up at the ceiling as Karim hollered in his crib. The light in the room blazed.

"Maria! Maria! What are you doing? The baby's crying!"

It took a few seconds for Maria to react. She had not been asleep, exactly, but she had tuned the baby out. Her mind had wandered to Lazarus. The white ceiling of the nursery had turned to blue sky. She could see her husband's fingers grazing fronds, could feel her chest clutch as he climbed the trunk of the coconut tree. His right arm held a machete, his left arm dangled behind him. She tried to warn him not to let go of the trunk, but she couldn't speak. As she sucked air into her lungs, preparing to shout as loud as she could, she heard her name being called from far away. *Maria*.

"Sorry, memsahib! I was asleep."

"You were not asleep, Maria! Your eyes were open. How long has Karim been awake? Why didn't you pick him up? His diaper needs changing. Why is the light on?"

Maria didn't know what to say. She stood by the crib, her arms at her sides.

Noura lifted Karim out of his crib and carried him with her to her room. He slept with his parents that night.

The next morning, Noura took Maria back to her parents' house. Sitting on the floor in Philomena's room, Maria could hear the young woman's voice rising and falling in her father's study as she complained to him and Mama Lulwa. She didn't blame Noura for being upset. Karim was Noura's firstborn, like Salvador was hers. Maria's delayed mourning for Lazarus was going to cost her children's futures. But it was more than Lazarus. It was, all at once, her father and Bonita, her mother and her poor sister Anna. It was the burden of a world where parents were forced to abandon their children for their survival, driven from their homes to alien lands, among strangers who knew nothing of their lives.

"Maria, please come to my study," Mubarak sahib called out to her. When she entered, Mama Lulwa and Noura were no longer there. "My daughter has informed me that she doesn't think you'll make a reliable ayah for Karim."

Maria said nothing, feeling like a trapped criminal.

"Do you agree?"

"Maybe, sahib."

"You want to return to India?"

"No, sahib, I don't."

Mubarak asked her to explain, and Maria, taking a chance on this man with the kind eyes who had met her at the airport, whose room of books smelled something like home, told her story, ending with her children's tuition fees and her desire to be reunited with them one day in Kuwait. Mubarak—true to the boy he had been, the one who had often vexed his father with actions and allegiances not always in accordance with their class, but always in accordance with his convictions—empathized. Maria, like everyone, deserved a chance, but, Mubarak thought, it was essential that she understood exactly what she was committing to. He drew her attention to a large blue globe sitting on a table beside his desk. He pointed to Kuwait. "This is where we are." He pointed to the United States of America. "This is where Noura will be moving in a few months."

"Where is Poona?" Maria asked.

Mubarak pointed to a spot, not so far from the first, distressingly distant from the second. Maria covered her mouth with her right hand.

"Listen to me, Maria. I will have most of your salary transferred to your children in Poona. And I promise, once their education is complete, I'll make sure they find jobs in this country. But you must promise to take care of my daughter's child as if he were your own. Noura is the bird of my soul. Soon she'll be far away, alone with her son in America, her husband busy at work. She'll need you. Are you willing?"

Maria looked up. The dry sponge in her throat was still there, but so was her belief that she was not alone. To work for this family was the chance she had been given by Jesus Himself, or maybe by her beloved Lazarus watching over her. Turning it down would be both unholy and unwise. "Yes, sahib," she replied at last, "I am."

"It's settled, then. I'll speak to Noura."

A few months later, Maria was on a plane again for the second time in her life, on her way to America. Buckled up on his mother's lap in the seat beside her, ten-month-old Karim flashed Maria a smile. Maria—goal fixed, faith intact—smiled back.

Sara

I'm going to the cemetery to visit Maria. It's been a week since the funeral, and I haven't been out of the house. I haven't been out of bed in four days. I feel sludgy and gross, but my phone call with Sana last night shifted something, connecting me to a forgotten sense of urgency.

I shower and change into black clothes that will attract the sun, like the abayas of my women students. I think of her, in her black niqab, and the heat that must encase her body six months out of the year, the suffocating sensation of that mask and hood. I wonder if sometimes she wishes she could move as freely as I do. I recall Sana's voice over the phone. I have not been free. I've tied myself in a million unbearable knots.

Aasif has prepared breakfast for me, leaving it out on the dining table, and I imagine he's been doing this every day I've been in bed. He was leaving sandwiches on a tray outside my door, and fruit, which I forced myself to nibble on before falling back to sleep. Aasif has been caring for me even while mourning Maria, whose company he shared for three and a half decades, the person he argued and competed with, was teased and exasperated by. Maria was with him longer than his wife and kids.

I find him in the basement folding towels, maybe the last set Maria tossed into the dryer. "Thanks for breakfast, Aasif. For everything."

He inclines his head to one side. "You're awake?"

I notice that the dizziness I've been experiencing off and on since my arrest has stopped. "I think so."

"Good."

"I'm going to the cemetery to see Maria. Want to come?"

He pauses, the middle of the towel tucked under his chin, his arms stretched out in an upside-down V, holding the two bottom corners of the towel apart. "No. I offer my du'aa for Maria five times a day. The cemetery is no use. You'll be back for lunch?"

"Yes. But I can have a sandwich."

"Chicken mechbous."

"Perfect, Aasif. Thank you." I want to hug him, but he would be mortified.

The heat at the cemetery is unbearable. My black clothes trap the sun's fire, scorching my skin. The Christian corner of the cemetery is easier to navigate than the Muslim area, and it's not hard to find where Maria is buried. The sand at her grave is packed and looks like it's been that way for years. A small stone with her name and dates indicates otherwise. *1930–2013.* I knew Maria was eighty-three, but seeing it etched in stone makes me know it differently. My mother was only fifty-six when she died; my father made it to fifty.

These calculations stop me from thinking about what I'm

here to do. To stand over the mound that was once Maria and say goodbye. Her love for me gone, like my mother's. To remember love is not the same as having it around you.

I want to find the graves of my parents and my grandmothers next, but it's difficult. The guard at the gate says I need the exact dates of their deaths, and even then it might be impossible. He asks if stones mark the graves, and I don't know. I never ordered any stones to be placed. Maybe one of my aunts or uncles did. The graves would be far-flung, and I would need to follow barely visible, convoluted paths to find them, if they're marked. If they're not marked, they might be lost for good. It makes me sad to think of our family so splayed apart, and I decide to leave without trying.

At home I swim, eat Aasif's mechbous, then crawl back into bed. My body is lead, depleted by the heat, but my mind is restless, and the past is a sprawling landscape.

If bombs shook our fortress in the winter of 1983, they didn't crack the foundation. Mama Lulwa urged me not to concern myself. Those winter bombs; the Iran-Iraq war; the Suq Al-Manakh stock market crisis; the hijacking of a Kuwait Airways plane in 1984; the assassination attack against the amir in 1985—all not worth my fear, according to my grandmother. "I don't pay attention to all this garbar, ya habibti. It passes. You mustn't be like your Baba Mubarak was or like your Mama Noura is. Politics. All the time, politics." As she spoke, she ate mango ice cream out of a crystal bowl with a silver spoon that looked like a small shovel.

On our Thursday family visits, I would trail after Mama Lulwa to her India room. We would sit on the peacock blue velvet sofa she had brought with her to Kuwait, which she refused to reupholster despite moth-eaten patches. An assortment of birdcages hung from the tall ceiling on hooks and brass chains of varying lengths installed by Baba Mubarak. Lacquered tiered cages from China; cages from India, some domed like the Mysore Palace, others painted Jodhpur blue; and lacy white specimens from Isfahan. All of them contained birds, which Mama Lulwa sometimes let out to whirl like escaped memories above her head. My favorite was Bebe Mitu, the African gray parrot she had brought back with her in the fifties. He would sit on my shoulder repeating, "Mama Luuuluuuuu . . . Mama Luuuluuuuuuuuuuu!" I was the only person, apart from Mama Lulwa, Bebe Mitu allowed to pet his beak without risk of a severed fingertip.

Once, when I was twelve, Mama Lulwa asked me, "Do you remember Baba Mubarak's voice? How old were you when he died?"

"Seven." I remembered Baba Mubarak's death vividly because it followed so soon after Baba Marwan's. The deaths of my two grandfathers, one after the other, had launched my anxiety over Maria, my transposition of her death onto those of the white-haired buddis in the Friday Hindi films. "Baba Mubarak sounded just like Bebe Mitu does when he calls your name. I remember his voice." I paused for a second. "Mama Lulwa, why did Mama Sheikha kidnap you and Uncle Bader for seven years?" Rumors had always circulated among us cousins about wicked Mama Sheikha, but none of us knew the truth. I had asked Mom but, as usual, my mother refused to get into it.

My grandmother took a deep breath. Her chest filled out like a lateen sail. "Aakh, ya Sara, what a question." She remained silent for a long time. Then she began to speak, and it was like I wasn't even there.

"To all those who know me, the great mystery of my life is why I stayed. One month, six months, up to a full year, they might have been able to rationalize, but not seven years. Half of Bader's childhood, practically. I knew where Mama Sheikha hid the skeleton key. I could have gone any time. But I didn't. Not until she left the door open for me."

She told me about how she was raised more by her older siblings than by her mother. "Without my sisters and my brother, I would have died, as so many babies in old Kuwait died. Nobody would have blamed my parents, but it would have been their fault. How I found the audacity to marry Mubarak, I'll never know. But that's what saved me. I wish my mother had been more like me." She stopped, and I hoped she wasn't going to end there. "Which is why I'm telling you, ya Sara, ya habibti, don't mind these things that are happening around us. Everything passes, and life goes on."

The September I started ninth grade, I returned from California with an asymmetrical bob, a thin braided tail, and a set of hand-tailored, pleated navy skirts—my new high school uniform. I ran into Nabil at the water fountain on the first day of school. "Look at you!" he said. "What happened to you? Karim stretch you out on a rack this summer?"

"Something like that." I didn't think the few extra inches made much of a difference. He still towered over me, tall and lanky, his unkempt hair obscuring his impish eyes.

"And your hair. I like it. You look like someone on MTV."

"Yeah?"

"The girl in 'Til Tuesday."

"Aimee Mann. I love her."

"Good for you." That customary sarcasm. "So, you allowed to go to parties this year? That brother of yours won't come anymore. Always with his sketchpads. If you want, you can tag along with me."

"Thanks." My palms were sweating. I was twelve again, reduced to monosyllabic responses. I tried to pull it together. "That would be great." I bent down to drink from the fountain. Nabil reached over my shoulder and flicked water into my eyes. "Hey!"

He smiled, lopsided, revealing the slight gap between his front teeth, and I knew, with the certainty of my almost fourteen years, that this was the start of the best year ever.

By the eighties, the Salmiya Sea Club had replaced the Gazelle Club in the hearts of teenagers enrolled in elite private schools. The Gazelle Club never lost its civilized cachet, but it lacked the frenetic appeal of the Sea Club—its pulsating music on the beach; its windsurfing; its tolerance of barely disguised bottles of gin and young people in various states of undress; its central location in Salmiya, where the cool kids, including Nabil, lived.

On a sunny October day at the Sea Club, in the water far from shore where no one could see, Nabil and I first kissed. It happened maybe a month after the water fountain splash. He looped one leg around my torso like an octopus and pulled me to him. His skin against mine felt hot in the autumn sea. With his hair slicked back out of his storybook eyes, Nabil looked more earnest than I had ever seen him. I wrapped my arms around his neck, my legs tight around his waist.

"Beautiful Sara." We kissed once, lips just touching. I looked over my shoulder, back to shore. "Nobody can see us from here, don't worry."

"I'm not worried," I said, though I was a bit, about Karim. Nabil cupped my face in his hands and kissed me again, longer this time, his salty tongue in my mouth.

We unlatched, and he pulled me underwater with him. We both kept our eyes open. He raised and lowered his eyebrows at me, the way he had been doing since we were kids, and I laughed, as I always did, gulping down water. We shot up to the surface together, coughing and slapping each other on the back like the old friends we were.

Nabil took me to my first party. At a stranger's mansion overlooking a moonlit shore in Messila, I experienced myself untethered from my brother for the first time. Nabil pulled me by the hand out of the house and toward the sea. He took off his shoes and plopped down on the damp shore. "Sit."

I slid down next to him, slipped off my shoes, and aligned my left foot against his right one. Every few seconds, foam silvered our toes. I pulled my knees in tight against my chest. It was chilly. Nabil put his arm around me.

"Is it what you imagined?" He squeezed my shoulder.

"Mes-si-la. It should be the name of an island in the Cyclades."

"We should go to an island in the Cyclades together."

"I'm sure my parents would agree to that immediately."

He chuckled, then added longingly, "I wish I had your parents."

I turned to squint at him. "Really?" After all the years of being friends with Karim and me, it was the first time he had ever said anything about our parents.

"They're so hands-off. They treat you and Karim like adults. My parents are such a mess, and it's coming at us twenty-four seven. Your parents—" He stopped for a second. "They give you space to breathe." He paused again. "Am I wrong?"

"You're half-right." As for that other, unarticulated half, it kept Karim and me alone in ways that hurt.

"What do you want, Sara?" He sounded suddenly impatient. I shrugged, and he leaned in and kissed me like he wanted to obliterate something. "There's more going on in this country than you know. It's going to be us who pay the price." I could hear Nabil's father in his words, and I understood that by *us* he meant Palestinians. "Still"—his tone lightened—"the world is a big place."

I stood abruptly and lifted my dress over my head.

"What're you doing, Sara? Someone might see!"

"The world is a big place, Nabil. A big, wild place." I ran into the icy, inky water, free as I would ever be.

Nabil and I were inseparable for the two years that I was in ninth and tenth grades and he, like Karim, was in eleventh and twelfth. We wrote long letters to each other, pages crammed with intensity. We shared books with marked passages, decoded as secret messages. We exchanged mix tapes, songs carefully selected and deliberately arranged. An energy charged between us, glorious and insatiable, the kind that thrives in the young. We would find each other at lunch and sneak behind the gymnasium to make out like the world was ending. Our weekends were full of parties, the skating rink, the Sea Club, each other's houses, Faris, Daoud, Sana, Asha, Hala, and sometimes a reluctant Karim.

If I was Karim's ready excuse in California, enabling his access to Matt, Karim was mine in Kuwait, making it possible for me to be with Nabil without my parents' knowledge. At least, I didn't think my parents knew; they certainly seemed to want to be kept out of it.

But Maria knew all about Nabil and me. Her inclination was to condemn what she knew my maa and bap would disapprove of, but she would never have tattled to them. "I've known that boy since he was a shrimp, and I'll knock his head off if he does anything bad," she told me. And she told Nabil too, every chance she got. Nabil loved Maria. He would hug her and kiss her hands and get her to laugh by wagging his finger at himself as she scolded him.

Nabil's parents fought like rabid rodents every day. "They scream at each other, and she claws him with her nails," he told me. "He cheats on her like a fucking hound." His parents had never felt Kuwaiti. ("Forever exiles is what we are," Nabil quoted his father.) His father supported countless members of his extended family in Lebanon and Palestine, which his mother resented. His mother, in an attempt to displace her resentment, smothered her sons. Nabil had let slip that his mother believed I must come from a low family because my parents were so permissive.

"But I'm not allowed to do half the things I want!" I protested, offended.

"Yeah, but you're allowed to go to parties, to be on the phone with me at all hours."

"But they think I'm with Karim."

"My mother doesn't know that."

"Why don't you tell her?" *Sharmouta* is the word I'm sure she used to describe me. It bothered me that Nabil's mother saw me that way; it bothered me more that Nabil didn't defend me.

"Who cares, Sara? I don't give a shit what my mother thinks about you or anything."

I didn't respond, but it stuck with me, Nabil's mother's judgment. It must have stuck with Nabil, too. Her hostility probably intensified my appeal when we were together, his antipathy years later, when we were far apart.

Nabil's father was hard on the brothers, not averse to swiping them across the back of the head if they didn't get straight A's. The brothers didn't get along. The undercurrent of violence in their home affected their relationships, and Nabil was often at the receiving end of his older brothers' fists. The calm of our Surra home had been a refuge for Nabil growing up, and he wanted his own version of our life.

"I'm going to make so much money, I'm going to be secure forever. There's a way out of this. It's going to be different for me, for your brother, too." Then, as if it dawned on him that he had missed some crucial point, he added, "And it's going to be different for you, Sara. Just wait."

Noura

"**G**ive me a shank, ten pounds of brisket, eight pounds of short ribs, and ten pounds of ground chuck. That one, please, Tony." Noura pointed at one of two dozen beef carcasses hanging in the refrigerated warehouse in East St. Louis.

"You got it, ma'am."

Vaccaro & Sons dealt mostly with beef, but for Noura they sourced interesting cuts of lamb—including trotters for Tarek's favorite pacheh—and farm chickens. They wrapped the meat in butcher's paper, never plastic, ready for her to collect on the first of the month.

Noura had traced a circuitous route to Vaccaro & Sons a month and a half after she, Tarek, Karim, and Maria had arrived in St. Louis in August 1970. The meat at Schnucks tasted of the plastic it was packaged in. Noura adored Schnucks, its twenty options for every item, its colorful aisles of unimaginable foods. She couldn't, however, stomach its meat.

When Noura told Tarek she had driven down alone to East St. Louis to find Vaccaro & Sons, he was horrified. "Noura, you can't just go off to these places we know nothing about. We hear about shootings on the news every night. What if something had happened?"

"But nothing did, Tarek. Except now we have this fantastic meat! You should've seen Maria when I brought it home, and she doesn't even eat meat."

Tarek sighed. "Look, Noura, it's great you're getting to know this place, but next time tell me first."

"Nothing's going to happen to me. Focus on your work, and I'll take care of the rest." Noura kissed him on the mouth.

Tarek's days and nights were consumed by his residency. When he wasn't on call, he was asleep; when he wasn't asleep, he was studying. Making things work for them in America was left to Noura. After a week's stay at the Holiday Inn on Lindell Boulevard, they moved into a redbrick colonial-style townhouse with a wide balcony in Shrewsbury. Tarek received a scholarship stipend from the Kuwait Ministry of Higher Education, a salary from the Ministry of Health, and modest pay for his residency at St. Mary's Hospital. This meant they could afford a three-bedroom townhouse with wall-to-wall carpeting. They bought a used, dusk blue, 1969 Chevy Nova sedan, and Noura passed the driving test on her first attempt. Tarek didn't bother to take the test, relying on Noura to drop him off and pick him up from the hospital.

Commandeering the car, Noura explored the city. She discovered Forest Park, with its zoo, planetarium, botanical garden, and museums. She found Eckert's Farm for apple picking in September and pumpkin patches in October. She read *Good Housekeeping* and staged every holiday as prescribed. She organized summer picnics in parks and boat rides on the Mississippi, in honor of Baba Mubarak's love of Twain. She hosted elaborate dinner parties for

Tarek's colleagues, who believed she was an Arabian princess. As Noura settled into the expanse of her new life, St. Louis began to feel like home.

In late October 1971, Noura boarded a plane to Kuwait to deliver her second baby in the same country her first baby had been born, wanting them to share a connection to a place from which she was feeling increasingly removed. On the tenth of November, Sara was born. Noura returned to St. Louis with the baby a few weeks later.

Noura hadn't wanted to leave Karim for long, but he was more independent than she would have imagined a child his age to be. He didn't cry when Noura left him at daycare, and when she put him in his playpen with books and toys, he kept himself entertained. She sang to Karim, nursery rhymes he learned by heart and then sang to himself in his room, putting himself to sleep. When Sara arrived, a pink screeching thing, Karim was curious but displayed none of the jealousy Dr. Spock had prepared Noura for. He called her *little sister*.

Sara was almost as much Maria's as she was Noura's. "With Saru beti, I get to have what I missed with my own," Maria confided wistfully to Noura, the baby's cheek pressed against hers. It wasn't long before Sara was sleeping in the nursery with Maria, not her mother.

By June, seven months after Sara's birth, Noura began to feel listless. She decided to go for a drive, something she hadn't done since Sara's birth. Passing through a tree-shaded neighborhood, she noticed a sign for Webster College.

"Your father will be ecstatic," Tarek said that evening, when

Noura shared with him her plan to enroll. The next morning, she went to see the registrar and was told that she could sit in on a class over the summer while she waited for her transcripts to arrive from Kuwait. In Intro to Political Science, Sister Mary Margaret discussed slavery and racism and the war in Vietnam. She mentioned Gandhi and pacifism and alternatives to violence she believed were viable in contemporary politics. "As a nation, we can take other directions," Sister Mary Margaret explained, "political practices different from those that have bloodied our history." Some of the seventeen- and eighteen-year-olds listened attentively and took copious notes. Others gazed out the window, distracted by the promise of the summer night ahead. Noura, who had recently turned twenty-seven, was riveted.

She was initially intimidated by the brash confidence of the young American students. They interrupted Sister Mary Margaret, which she didn't seem to mind. They asserted opinions without evidence. But the discussions were so interesting that Noura soon plunged in, posing questions, presenting arguments, making links between the experiences of the native inhabitants she was learning about and the people of Palestine, whose 1967 expulsion she remembered so vividly.

Noura was accepted into the Class of 1976. She registered for a range of classes in political science, including another one with Sister Mary Margaret on the history of social justice. She was done at noon, picked up Karim from daycare, ran errands, and was home in time for lunch. During the day, Maria cleaned the house, prepared meals, and took care of Sara, until she joined her brother at daycare. Noura spent most afternoons with Karim and Sara, taking them to the zoo or playgrounds or dancing with them in the living room to Three Dog Night. She spent evenings immersed in study. She couldn't have managed any of it without Maria, who made herself available to her children in a way she couldn't, or didn't want to.

One night in October 1972, there was a sharp knock at the door. Tarek and Noura had just finished dinner. The children were asleep, and Maria was in the kitchen doing dishes. Noura was reading for class; Tarek was watching the news. He got up to answer the door.

Two hulking police officers were on the other side. "Are you Dr. Tarek Al-Ameed?" one of them asked.

"I am."

"You'll have to come with us."

"What for?" Tarek asked. Noura rushed to his side.

"We'd like to ask you a few questions. Ma'am, there's no cause for alarm."

"What's this all about?" Noura asked.

"Munich," the other officer muttered, speaking out of turn.

In early September, like everyone, Noura and Tarek had watched in horror as the ugly arrow of European history pierced through unpaid debts. In Germany—the country where their troubles had originated three decades earlier—Palestinian terrorists captured and killed Israeli Olympic athletes. Noura and Tarek were disgusted, but they understood the roots of the men's ill-considered motives and their vicious tactics. Kuwait had been at the receiving end of Palestinians displaced by the Israeli Haganah and Irgun, no strangers to terror. The masked men had learned their lessons well, and the unsuspecting paid the price.

Noura pondered how the event would reshape U.S. relations with the Arab world. "This," she had remarked to Tarek, "is the start of something monstrous."

Tarek returned home by taxi after midnight. He had been interrogated by a detective about any connections he might have to Palestinians, whether he supported the PLO, whether he would carry arms against Israel, whether he was a member of the Black September Organization.

"And then they asked me the stupidest question I have ever heard in my life. Would I help an injured Jew. They asked me that, can you imagine? I explained the Hippocratic oath to them. Then I told them about our Jewish neighbors in Basra."

"What did they say?"

"Not much. They had no idea where Basra was. They left me alone in the room. Someone came in with water, asked if I needed to use the toilet. Then it was over." Tarek was serene as he spoke, unfazed. Noura was certain he must have been exactly that way during the interrogation. He was levelheaded and matter-of-fact. It was one of the things she loved about him. If one of the kids bumped their heads, spiked a fever, choked on a carrot, Tarek would remain unflappably efficient. It was a quality that instilled complete confidence in his patients; it had steadied Noura when her brother died.

Tarek displayed total indifference to the episode. He put Noura's apprehension out of mind and got on with his routine.

Noura adjusted to life in St. Louis with an ease that convinced her America was where she belonged. She felt autonomous and capable. The incident with Tarek and the police confirmed to her that she wanted to major in political science, to specialize in the convoluted, volatile politics of her region. She excelled in her classes and wanted to continue with graduate studies. The idiocy of Middle East experts in the U.S. astounded her, and she was convinced that the advice they gave their government was going to lead the Middle East down a path of destruction from which there could be no reprieve. Noura believed she could play a role in altering that course. Not by returning to Kuwait, but by putting her insights to work from the outside. She was perfectly positioned to do it, comfortable in the irreconcilable gaps that made others squirm.

The children attended an elite preschool in Kirkwood surrounded by a copse of red maples and honey locusts. They rode horses, went swimming, sang songs about the grand old flag. Karim and Sara were closer to each other than to anyone else, even Maria. They spent hours in the park with Maria playing pirates. They lived in books, watched *Sesame Street* and *Mister Rogers' Neighborhood* while holding hands on the couch. They spoke to each other in English and Hindi. Noura and Tarek spoke to each other in Arabic, to the kids in English. Noura figured her children would pick up whatever Arabic they needed by osmosis, and since her plan was to remain in America, she believed they wouldn't need it. She wanted to stay for them as much as for herself, not wanting to uproot them the way she had been uprooted from Poona. This was the only home they knew.

Noura had pulled a sheet over Kuwait, and, she was ashamed to admit, over her family in Kuwait. She felt beholden to no one but herself, her children, her husband, and Maria. Maria had gone to India to visit her own children during the third and fifth years of their stay, but apart from Noura's brief trip back to deliver Sara, she and Tarek hadn't returned to Kuwait at all. It was too far to go with young children, Noura decided, too hot in summer. Her father sent a torrent of letters, bursting with news about Lulwa and their grandchildren; about his sister Hayya's untimely death in 1973 (from heartache, he believed); and about a metamorphic Kuwait. Noura wrote back sporadically, telling herself she was too busy to keep up, seared with guilt knowing she didn't want to.

In response to his daughter's dearth of letters, Baba Mubarak decided to visit in January 1975, Noura's junior year at Webster. He brought with him folders of newspaper clippings he had collected since he was a university student himself, eager to pass them down to his daughter. It was still his habit to spend hours each week combing through papers from all over the Arab region and beyond, cutting out articles, ordering them chronologically in folders labeled by topic. Mubarak was sixty-seven. He was retired and could finally focus on the things he enjoyed.

Mubarak walked unsteadily off the jet bridge of the TWA flight from Kuwait via London looking worn and bewildered. He was weighed down by the bag of folders he had insisted on carrying by hand. Noura was shocked to see her father had become an old man. That bag of folders made her sob into his shoulder, right there in the terminal.

Mubarak, disconcerted by his daughter's tears, stroked her hair with the hand that wasn't holding his precious bag. "Calm down, ya binayti. All this because you're happy to see me? If I had known, I'd have come years ago."

Noura brushed away her tears, not wanting to upset her

father. She took the bag from his hand and smiled. "Come, Baba. You've got two very excited grandkids who can't wait to see you."

During his monthlong stay, Mubarak came to understand Noura's tears and her reluctance to visit or write. He understood that she was claiming a freedom she couldn't have in Kuwait. Her time there would dissolve into duties to extended family and society—acknowledging births, marriages, deaths—and not into the things that mattered to her. Mubarak recognized that as a woman, Noura wouldn't be able to put her degree, maybe degrees, to use the way she could in America. It had come naturally to Lulu to fulfill domestic duties, she seemed to thrive on it, but his monkey girl was different. She was like him. He had been forced into his own family's business obligations against his desire to study. The last thing he wanted was for his daughter to feel obligated to do anything she didn't want to.

"Habibti, Noura," he began as she drove him back to Lambert Airport, waiting until the last possible minute to recite the speech he had been preparing almost since his arrival. "Don't return to Kuwait. Something wicked that way comes, I'm convinced. India was my home, and I left. Looking back, it wasn't worth it. Stay here, both of you, and shine for us."

Noura sobbed in the car all the way back from the airport. She knew her baba was right.

Noura's senior thesis was titled "The Politics of Partition in Palestine, India, and the United States." At her oral defense, she was asked by a member of the panel of three examiners: "In your paper you make a hyperbolic link between the colonial politics of Israel, Britain, and the United States. Could you please articulate your grounds for this rather far-fetched comparison?" In response, Noura weaved her way through a complex of caveats and connections. When she stopped, an hour later, the panelist who had asked the question turned to the others and said, "Well, that about covers it." She graduated summa cum laude.

Noura insisted that Tarek apply for as many top positions around the country as he could. He resisted at first but gave in to appease her. He was offered jobs at New York–Presbyterian Hospital, Cleveland Clinic, UC San Francisco Medical Center, and St. Mary's in St. Louis. He had no intention of accepting any of them. Whenever Noura brought up the possibility of staying in America permanently, of wanting to earn a doctorate, Tarek would dismiss it.

"I have a right to decide, too!" Noura was becoming more and more adamant as their departure date neared.

Exasperated, Tarek shot back, "Noura, we don't belong here! Remember that night?" He had never before brought up the interrogation, but Noura knew what he was referring to.

"I remember that night, but so what? That night is exactly why I need to stay. You're doing so well here. And the opportunities for the kids—"

"There are opportunities in Kuwait. Things are developing fast. I want to be a part of it. This is a once-in-a-lifetime chance for physicians—for anyone—to build something for a country from the ground up. It's so exciting, Noura! Think of what we'll be able to do."

Noura wasn't convinced, her father's warning about Kuwait fresh in her mind. She tried to explain to Tarek that her life would be swallowed up by social obligations, which she detested, and that she wouldn't be able to engage in politics the way she wanted to. He listened but assured her that times were changing. "You'll do whatever you want to, Noura, just like here." She didn't believe him. With one month left before their planned flight, she was running out of time.

Noura remembered the willful indifference the producers of *What's What?* had to any of her suggestions, their emphasis on her looks over her intelligence. She remembered quitting her job to care for her grieving parents, doing so with love, but with an awareness that this was what was expected of her. Noura's aspirations did not involve Kuwait's national development. She felt, for the first time, resentful that her husband would be the one to decide, like the television producers had decided, the shape her life should take.

Tarek didn't cave to Noura's pleading. He was not unfeeling, but he was convinced that his version of the future was correct. Noura couldn't figure out how to accommodate both her unwavering love for her husband and her ambitions for herself. She couldn't give up Tarek and a stable life for Karim and Sara. Divorce was unthinkable; despite Tarek's intransigence, Noura didn't want to be without him.

Then, in late June, about a week before they were due to leave, the phone rang in the middle of the night. Noura held her breath as Tarek answered. Tarek positioned the earpiece so that they both could hear.

"Taruki? Ya mel'oon, wainek?" Hisham's buoyant voice crackled across the long-distance line. "I bought two plots of land next to each other in Surra. One for me. One for you. Tell Noura I'm going to design the house of her dreams. We're going to be neigh-bors, brother! Yallah, hurry back!"

Hisham's unsought generosity blurred Noura's vision. Karim and Sara would have cousins their age right next door. Tarek, so isolated in St. Louis, would have his brother again. They had no ties here, no family. If something were to happen to her and Tarek, what would become of her kids? Noura felt herself being drawn back into the fold of the country she had been on the verge of giving up. Against her better judgment, she decided to give it a try.

M a r i a

Maria stared out the window in the direction of the green dome of a cathedral she had spotted on their way to the Holiday Inn. They had been in this new country for three days. Her eyes refused to shut when it was dark outside. She remembered Mubarak sahib's finger sliding from one side of the globe to the other, where she was now, as far away from her children as she had ever been. She ached for them differently than she had in Kuwait, knowing the distance between them. She would slip out of bed and peek through a crack in the curtain, careful not to let in too much electric light and wake Karim, asleep in a crib beside her. The empty streets reflected the emptiness she felt in this place so far from home.

By the time they checked out a week later, Maria's sleep had returned to normal, but her longing for her children remained an anvil in her chest. Noura arranged for Maria to speak to them. Eight months had passed since her departure from Poona. She could hear her voice ricocheting on the line, coming between herself and them. "Tumi kosi asat, baba? I miss you so much, my darlings!"

"Mai, where are you?" Salvador's voice sounded thicker.

"I'm in America, puta. How are the girls? And your Anna maxan?"

"They're fine, Mai. All here."

"Mai, we miss you!" Christina's voice was edged with womanhood.

"Mai, Mai!" little Josie sobbed.

"Take care of each other!" Maria fought back her own sobs. "I love you all!"

A lag, then silence. The line had cut. Had they heard her last words? Maria wept, and Noura, who had been waiting in the hall, came in and put her arm around her shoulder.

The next morning, Noura took Maria to the cathedral with the green dome. Maria crossed herself and made her way toward the altar, glancing back nervously at Noura. She went down on one knee, murmured a short prayer before rising to sit on a pew in the front row, where she crossed herself again and prayed to Jesus to protect her children and sister. She prayed for the strength to live in this country, to make herself available to the Al-Ameed family. As prayer after prayer ticked through her head, she felt Bonita's resilience seep into her like smoke. She lit a candle for Lazarus, then made her way back to Noura. Visits to the Cathedral Basilica of St. Louis became a monthly ritual, one of the few things she liked about the city.

Maria cried herself to sleep every time she spoke to her children, about once every three months, but the longer she was away, the more her sadness numbed. Noura helped her navigate the strangeness around her. A machine that washed clothes, one that washed dishes, another that sucked up dirt, one that browned bread. Carpets that could not be rolled up. Meat wrapped in plastic. Noura encouraged Maria to take Karim out in his stroller. She explained about sidewalks and crosswalks, but Maria was terrified that one of the locals would speak to her.

English was, at least, more familiar to her ears than Arabic, which Maria couldn't make out at all. English was the language of her children's education and the Lord's Prayer. When she was alone in the house, Maria watched game shows and afternoon soaps, *Days of Our Lives* and *All My Children,* turning up the volume so she could hear from the kitchen as she prepared lunch. English revealed itself to her through commercial jingles.

That first year in the new country, Tarek sahib was more a spirit than a physical presence. When he was not at work, he was in his bedroom reading thick books. He was not unfriendly, often complimenting Maria on her cooking, but Hindi was a fence that kept her, Noura, and Karim on one side, Tarek on the other.

Sara changed everything. The love Maria felt for her broke something open inside her. She felt that she was betraying her own children. She loved them more than life, but her love was curbed by work and death and fear. With Karim at daycare, Noura at college, and Tarek at work, Maria and Sara were alone together with nothing but time between them. Maria began to turn the sad stories of her life into fairy tales for Sara. The story of Bonita the cow and the sprightly little girl from Goa. The story of the handsome magician who handed out coconuts to poor villagers. The only story she never told Sara was the one about the children left behind.

In 1972, three years after leaving Poona, Maria planned to return home for Christmas. She imagined her daughters taller, their skin gleaming, hair on Salvador's twenty-two-year-old chin. A thorn of foreboding poked her awake at night. What if they had forgotten her? What if they loved Anna more?

A week before her flight, Noura drove Maria to Northwest Plaza to buy gifts. Maria bought yellow raincoats and rubber boots for Christina and Josefina to wear during monsoon season; unsuitable woolen dresses because it was winter in St. Louis and there was no other choice; a tweed jacket, a button-down shirt, and a pair of leather shoes for Salvador. For Anna, Maria chose a gray-and-white shawl. Noura bought butterfly pendants for the girls, a Timex watch for Salvador, a beige cardigan with wooden buttons for Anna, and a blue one for Maria.

There was just one thing missing. "Memsahib, could we stop at a toy shop? On television I saw some pretty dolls." She had seen a commercial for dolls with eyes that miraculously changed color.

"Girls love dolls. Let's go."

Noura took her to Famous-Barr, its white roof the shape of a wide-brimmed hat. The dolls were on prominent display in the toy department. Their saucer eyes reminded Maria of Gita in the bidi bungalow. A flux of acid singed her throat. What would Christina and Josefina think of these doe-eyed dolls, their flowing hair and fancy clothes? They belonged to a world where young girls—girls like Sara—could do as they pleased. They could have purple eyes. They could change clothes five times a day.

"Is this the one you'd like, Maria?" Noura asked, holding up a brunette doll.

Maria thought for a second. The brunette matched the color of her daughters' hair, but the blonde was the one she believed her girls would want. An American doll. "No, memsahib, this one," she said, pointing to the blonde.

Noura took two of the blond dolls off the shelf, along with a few small boxes containing tiny clothes, and two cases with handles to store each doll and her things. It was more than Maria could afford. She had been planning to buy one doll for her girls to share. As promised, Mubarak sahib transferred most of her salary to India every month, but she had been carefully saving the remainder to buy gifts to impress her children with, so they could hold in their hands the reason for her absence. Maria knew she only had enough money left for one doll, not two, but she didn't want memsahib to think she skimped on her girls. She didn't object as Noura added the second doll, even as her hands shook.

At the cashier counter, Noura swiftly took out her wallet to pay for the fire engine she had picked out for Karim, as well as for Maria's two dolls and their accessories.

"Memsahib, no!"

"It's from Tarek and me, Maria. A gift for your girls."

Noura's generosity unsettled Maria. Three years gone. Her girls were at the top of their classes, and Maria knew they were both eager to attend university. There was no longer any problem with tuition payments. Anna had not rolled a bidi in years. But that winter, the blond dolls she couldn't afford made Maria feel that as much as she was doing, it wasn't enough.

The smell of Bombay slammed against her as she disembarked the plane. Fragments of the life she had left behind began to fall into place. On the train ride to Poona, disquiet seized her again. What if her children didn't recognize her? What if they didn't reciprocate her desperate, guilty love? At one of the stops, Maria climbed off the train and threw up.

They were at the station waiting for her, smiles brightening their faces, worn shoes shined to mirrors. The girls flung themselves into her open arms, the white bows in their braided hair coming untied. "Mai, Mai, Mai, Mai, Mai!" their church bell voices chimed. They covered Maria's wet face with kisses.

Maria glanced up at Salvador. He had retrieved her heavy suitcases from the train, one in each hand. He was grinning widely. She reached out and pulled him in tight, inhaling the metallic adult smell of his sweat.

Anna looked ten years older than her fifty. She flung one arm around Maria, resting her other hand on her cane, and kissed her sister on the cheek. "Dhakte bhoini, you look well, praise the Lord."

"You do too, vhoddle bhoini. You all do, praise the Lord above."

They rented three bicycle rickshaws from the station: Maria in one, her arms tight around her girls; Anna behind them in another; Salvador ahead of them with the two suitcases, his back straight as a pole. Everything looked familiar but nebulous. The weather was balmy after a wintry St. Louis. What would Anna do with the sweater Noura had bought her?

Never in her life had Maria taken more pride in anything than she did in presenting her family with the gifts she had brought back. Josefina cried out with joy at the flaxen-haired American dolls, and Maria knew she had picked the right one. When Christina lifted the lid off the white square box that contained her butterfly necklace, she gasped. "It's lovely, Mai! Thank you."

"The dolls and necklaces are gifts from Noura memsahib.

Salvador, do you like your watch? That's from sahib and memsa-hib as well."

"Thank you, Mai, for everything." Salvador smiled at his mother, less effusive than his sisters. Maria had detected at once that Salvador was holding something back. She did not pester him with questions; there would be time enough. For the moment, she wanted to relish her children being within arm's reach, her love for them unencumbered by erratic telephone lines and the span of continents.

Days zipped past with the speed of a spring fly. Maria couldn't get enough of her daughters, and while Christina indulged her, at seventeen she was too old to be sitting on her mother's lap, too old to be playing with dolls. Maria saw Christina's doll abandoned in a corner of the hut, plastic intact. She had misjudged the years. Christie at fourteen, the age she had been when Maria left, would have loved the doll, just as twelve-year-old Josie did now. But Christie at seventeen, one year younger than Maria had been when she married Lazarus, had outgrown dolls and yellow raincoats. Time in Poona had not stopped while Maria was away.

Salvador was avoiding being alone with her. He was evasive when she asked him questions about his job. She assumed he was still working at the auto factory, but she couldn't get anything out of him. Anna also seemed to want to sidestep the question. But one evening, with Anna and the girls outside preparing a spe-cial dinner of xeet kodi and rice, Maria and Salvador were finally alone together in the hut. She held his hand in hers. "Salvador, baba, what's going on at work?"

"Nothing, Mai. I work. I come home. I go to work again. I get paid. Not much, but enough." He tried to extricate his hand from her clasp.

Maria held on. "Where are you working?"

"Auto factory, same as always."

"You're hiding something." Salvador shook his head. "Are you unhappy at work?"

"Better than no work."

"You're twenty-two, Salvador. Do you want to get married? Is that why you're acting funny?"

"I'm not acting funny, Mai. I don't make enough to support a family." He stared past Maria, refusing to meet her eyes.

"Do you want to go to Kuwait? I thought we should wait for Christina to finish college so that the two of you could go together. But if you want to go, I can ask memsahib's father."

"I don't want to go to Kuwait without you there. I'll wait for my sisters. I'll survive, Mai."

Back in St. Louis, Maria managed to set aside her trepidation for days at a time, sometimes weeks, by focusing on Karim and Sara. Noura was, by then, preoccupied with university, and the children were almost entirely in Maria's hands. They came to her for solace after nightmares, for the comfort of her arms around their little bodies. She lavished them with love, not allowing herself to succumb to the guilt of knowing that this love rightfully belonged to Salvador, Christie, and Josie. The tenderness she felt for Karim and Sara when she bathed them, took them to the park, fed them, told them stories, put them to sleep, she did not feel for her own children. What she felt for her own children was a torturous responsibility, an unrelenting need to lay out a protective plan for their futures. To simply relax and enjoy their existence in the world was impossible.

Maria returned to Poona again in December 1974, two years after her first visit. This time the girls, in high spirits initially, grew increasingly sullen as the days passed. Her gifts kept them politely obliged for a few days, but they soon fell silent, providing stilted responses to their mother's avalanche of questions. Christina had one more year left at university, where she studied accounting. She lived in the hut with Anna and Salvador and took the bus to university daily. Josefina was in her first year at secondary school and continued to board, coming home on weekends. Salvador was still at the auto factory, but he spent most of his evenings out of the hut, returning past midnight, reeking of alcohol.

Maria confronted Salvador about his drinking, but he denied it. Anna confirmed that Salvador no longer contributed any part of his pay to the household, that he came and went at odd hours. He was disengaged from his sisters, not watching over them as he used to.

Maria wandered around her husband's village at a loss. They were slipping from her. Anna was a sad, tired woman. Salvador was not slightly frustrated, as Maria had thought two years earlier; he was eaten up by discontent. The girls were irritable, impatient with her. She thought she detected embarrassment in the near-imperceptible roll of Christina's eyes.

Nothing was resolved before Maria's departure. Her daughters gave her fleeting hugs, Josefina clinging a few seconds longer than her older sister. Salvador carried his mother's bags onto the train, helped her climb on, then kissed her somberly on the forehead.

If he had looked back, he would have caught Maria waving to a vacant platform.

In St. Louis, Maria was as glum and silent as her daughters had been in Poona. When Noura inquired how her visit had gone, Maria couldn't bring herself to share her colossal sense of failure. She had left behind everything to secure a future for her children, but they didn't seem to appreciate her sacrifices at all. She could feel their clammy resentment beading on her skin from over eight thousand miles away.

Noura had started to mention the idea of staying in America, how marvelous it would be for the children, for Tarek's work. "Just think, Maria, you could bring your kids here, too. They could find work, become American!" Every time Noura brought it up, Maria felt a jet of panic shoot through her. How could she bring her children to this land of hush and ice? She could hardly bring herself to negotiate the desolate streets outside their townhouse, let alone the distance between India and here. Kuwait, she could manage. In the eight months she was there, she had found a place for herself at church, had made friends who spoke her language, located acquaintances she had known in Poona, friends she had grown up with in Goa. She had seen Indian laborers and domestic servants in Kuwait, but she had also seen Indian bankers and businessmen. It was this future she was preparing for Christina and Josefina, and, she hoped, for Salvador, too. Her children would meet eligible partners in Kuwait, and they would all live together in the purifying heat.

Late one night, about a year after her second trip to Poona, Tarek woke Maria in Sara's room, where she slept. "Maria, Maria. It's your sister calling from Poona."

Maria flew to the phone in the kitchen. One of her children must have died.

Anna's voice on the other end of the line was strained. "Maria bhoini, we're all safe. But Salvador—"

"He's dead."

"No, no! He was fired. Spends his days and nights drinking with the money you send. When he worked at the factory, he used his own money. Now he's pinching your transfers. We won't be able to pay the girls' tuition and food."

Maria felt her head being pulled from above, her neck stretched thin, so that when she spoke, it was as if from miles away. "Is he there? Let me speak to him."

"I'm at the post office. I don't know where he is. I'm sorry, Maria. I can't control him."

Maria's neck sprang back into place, and a habituated resolve took over. "I'll speak to memsahib. Please try to keep him safe. How are the girls?"

"Girls are fine. Don't worry about them."

Tarek came into the kitchen to ask Maria if everything was all right, but she did not have the Arabic or English words to explain that things were far from all right. Instead she said yes and thank you. In the morning she would ask Noura for help.

It took six months but, as promised, Mubarak sahib found a clerical job for Salvador at the Kuwait Oil Company. He would teach Salvador how to type and perform basic office tasks before he started work there. He also found an accounting job for Christina. When the Al-Ameeds returned to Kuwait in July, Maria would continue on to Poona. She would stay there for a month, then the three of them would fly to Kuwait at the beginning of August. Maria clung to this plan and to her faith, against misery, against Noura's exhortations about immigrating to America.

Then, a week before their return, a second phone call ripped through the night. Maria instantly saw her son in a ditch with a broken neck. She raced to Noura and Tarek's bedroom, hovering outside their door, but nobody came to get her. She heard an unknown male voice speaking Arabic, then the click of the receiver placed back on the cradle. Noura and Tarek were chuckling. *My son is not dead.* Her breathing returned to normal, her pulse steadied. A few more days and her magic carpet would soar.

S a r a

Mr. Al-Baatin's request to lift the travel ban has been denied. I shrug my shoulders in response to the news, but he's furious. "You haven't murdered anyone, embezzled millions like so many we know tucked away in their London penthouses! The prosecutor was bought, it's as clear as day."

"Does that happen?" I have naively believed the judiciary to be fair. I remember my parents often saying, *At least our courts are clean.*

"It happens." The lobes of his ears turn crimson. If I touch them, they will be hot little embers. How would Mr. Al-Baatin react if I were to cup his ears with my freezing hands? Compulsive thoughts have been surfacing with increasing intensity. Thoughts about not retracting the blasphemy, making the prosecution argue their case to the end, forcing the state to reveal its barbarity or to rescue its humanity.

"So, what's next?" Lola, who has been at Mr. Al-Baatin's feet since his arrival, jumps gracefully onto his lap. He scratches under her chin, and she purrs as loud as an engine.

"The petition to dismiss before trial hasn't been ruled on.

They tell me it's in process, but who knows." Mr. Al-Baatin expels air out of the side of his mouth like it's the blowhole of a whale. "A trial date hasn't been set and you haven't been called in for questioning, so my sense is this is going to drag."

I open my mouth to tell him what Sana had said about parliamentary interest in my case, then stop myself. Mr. Al-Baatin is here. Sana is in London. Maybe she's wrong. Surely my lawyer would know if my trial date were near.

"Is there anything about Wassmiya you can tell me that might help?" he asks.

"Like what?"

"Oh, I don't know. A secret boyfriend? A secret girlfriend? Putting on makeup and changing out of her abaya in the bathroom after her father drops her on campus?"

"How do you know about that stuff?"

Mr. Al-Baatin grins. "I do have a daughter who teaches at Kuwait University too, you know."

"Right. I forgot." Mr. Al-Baatin has become Mr. Al-Baatin my lawyer, not Mr. Al-Baatin Hanan's father. I think about Wassmiya, controlled from the day she was born, no swimming at the Gazelle Club, no riding bikes with boys. *No space to breathe.* Nabil's approving words about my parents that night at the beach a million years ago surface without warning. Wassmiya's parents would not have given her the space to become anything other than a replica of themselves. "She's a true believer. Walks the straight and narrow. She's not a hypocrite, just deluded." I'm sure she'd say the same about me.

Mr. Al-Baatin blows air out the side of his mouth again, and I'm concerned this will settle into a habit he'll use in court. It's not attractive and won't win him, or me, sympathy. "'True believer.' I don't know what that means."

I shrug for the second time that evening. Aasif is a true believer. Maria was, too. Neither used their beliefs to harm a fly. We never imagine ourselves caught in the bloody jaws of true belief, yet here I am.

Mr. Al-Baatin gets up to leave. Lola heads out of the sala, her displeasure visible in the sharp arch of her back.

"Call if you need me, Sara. Until next Wednesday."

Four weeks since my arrest. One full month. I've spoken to Karl but still haven't told him. He suspects something, but I blame my distance on Maria's death and change the subject. If I tell him, still more will shift, and I'm not ready. Complicated knots of grief bind us together, knots we don't attempt to untie. Karl remains in Norway, visiting a few times a year; I stay in Kuwait. Maria and Karl got along. They took to each other over the years, sharing a mutual fondness that reminded me of her fondness for Nabil. Nabil—one of the knots that binds.

It was on a bare kashi floor in a pitch-dark room at one of our parties that I lost my virginity to Nabil my sophomore year, a month before his graduation. There was no pain, no blood, and no condom. We were at the edge of delirium. There was no lock on the door. I had to be home by midnight.

The floor was dusty, dried insects collected in forgotten little mounds waiting to be disposed of. The furniture was draped in muslin. Nabil, usually slow and exact, urgently pushed up my skirt, fumbling his way in. I knew what was happening, and I didn't want it to stop. I had been waiting for it. "Beautiful Sara," he panted in my ear, though he couldn't see my face. He pulled out when he came, so fast I wasn't sure it had happened.

That night, when I got home, I grabbed my blanket and pillow and snuck into Karim's room, as I had hundreds of times before. Instead of kicking me out, which he had been doing more frequently, Karim scooched over. I nestled against him, my back to the wall, my chin on his arm. His breathing was steady, but I knew he was awake, like I had known it as a child, fretting that if he fell asleep before I did, I would be the last one with eyes open in a silent house.

"What's up, little sister?" He knew me well enough to know something was up.

"I was with Nabil tonight."

"What else is new?" Karim had never said a harsh word about Nabil and me together these last two years. He acted bored around us, indifferent, but I knew there was something there. I hadn't probed because I suspected that if I did, it would come between us—Nabil and me; or Nabil and Karim; or, most dreaded of all, my brother and me. I had chosen to be selfish, convincing myself I was being kind. But that night was different. Guilt cut through my veins like little razors. I couldn't say anything, but Karim did. "You had sex." He wasn't asking. I could feel his breath on my hand the way, a few hours earlier, I had felt Nabil's on my neck. "Fuck you, Sara," he groaned, his voice catching in a sob.

"I'm sorry, Karim," I said, knowing in my bones what I was apologizing for.

He got out of bed, flopped down on the carpet, and fell asleep instantly. The next morning, things between us seemed normal, but Karim never spoke to Nabil again.

———

We had a month of days to fill with each other. We tucked our-selves in his room, managing to sneak past his nosy mother. My parents believed I was with Sana or Karim, not because I said so, but because that was how it had always been. We learned each other in parts, stared into each other's eyes. He put *Avalon* on re-peat and drew his curtains against the afternoon sun. Our skin glowed indigo.

All it took was that first time without a condom. I said noth-ing to Nabil when my period was late those last two weeks we were together. Nabil was going to study economics at Harvard, far away from Karim, who was going to study architecture at UC Berkeley, like our uncle Hisham. I didn't think about being left behind. I didn't think about my late period or what I could feel tingling inside me. Nabil wouldn't have known how to deal with my pregnancy. He had been plotting his exit from Kuwait and his family his entire life. Even his attachment to me wouldn't have been enough to change anything. I knew him well enough to know that.

Together we went to all the graduation events, and I allowed myself to believe that I was graduating along with them. Nabil was leaving in a few days, and Karim, Mom, and I were heading to California again for the summer. As we swayed in the dark to "I'll Fly for You" at the after-graduation party, neither of us made promises we wouldn't keep or offered reassurances we could cling to in a lonely moment. Maybe Nabil was being mature, his two years on me giving him insight about long-distance relationships. I was not being mature. I was being a scared kid, suddenly unsure about all the non-kid stuff we had been doing together in his bedroom that last month.

Nabil whispered only one thing to me before the slow song ended. "Another time, Sara. Another place." It took everything in me not to weep.

Karim spent that summer in California sprawled on the couch reading or drawing, and I spent it alone by the pool. Our mother, like my brother, spent most of it reading. I remember Edward Said's *Covering Islam* and Gramsci's *Prison Notebooks* splayed on chairs out on the balcony. She didn't like to swim, and she despised television. She had a few Iraqi and Palestinian friends she would meet for dinner once in a while. Maria went to India, as she had done every summer since our return to Kuwait from St. Louis. Dad would arrive in August.

Matt still lived in his parents' basement. He was twenty, hadn't gone to college, smoked more pot than he did before, and hadn't grown an inch. My brother towered over him. Karim saw Matt a few times the first few weeks of our return but then kept mostly to himself. I still hung out with Matt because by then, with or without Karim, we had become friends. It was Matt I turned to when my second missed period confirmed what I already knew.

Karim was planning to head to Berkeley the last week of July; he said he wanted to get acclimated early. Mom said she would drive him. I started to work on her about staying behind in the condo. At first, she wouldn't hear of it. "I'm not leaving a fifteen-year-old alone for a week, Sara. Forget it."

"I'll be sixteen in a few months. I won't go out, just to the pool. I'll be home the whole time. I don't want to be in a car for hours and then have nothing to do as Karim gets settled."

"Don't you want to say goodbye to your brother? See what it's going to be like for him there?"

"I can say goodbye to him here." I was terrified that Mom could sense my pregnancy or that Karim might notice I was somehow different. But they were absorbed in their own thoughts, leaving me with mine. I swam endless laps in the community pool, sat in the steaming Jacuzzi until I almost fainted, jumped up and down on hard concrete, hoping to dislodge the grain of rice clinging to my womb. I checked my underwear compulsively for drops of blood. I inspected my flat stomach in the mirror, imagining a bump that wasn't there.

For weeks it was *No means no,* but then, abruptly, Mom changed her mind. "Stay, then, Sara," she said one morning over breakfast, without any pestering from me. I tried to hide my relief as I casually buttered my toast.

Matt arranged everything, drove me to the clinic and back, even spent one night at the condo with me. I remember asking him repeatedly, "Is it gone? Is it gone?" like the pregnancy was an unwanted wart.

"Yeah, sweetie, it's gone." He filled and refilled a hot-water bottle for my cramps. He made me sandwiches out of the bread and cheese Mom had stockpiled before she left. He slept on the floor beside my bed, holding my hand.

I felt mostly relieved, not permitting myself to feel the regret that lined that relief. I didn't feel guilty for not telling Nabil. As far as I was concerned, I had saved his neck.

I thought I wouldn't survive Kuwait without Karim and Nabil, but I did. Sana, Asha, Hala, and I were inseparable our junior and senior years. Sana was obsessed with the intifada. Her family, like Daoud's, was one of the '67ers. Their roots in the village of Imwas could be traced back hundreds of years, their dead buried in ancient Roman cemeteries. In 1967, the villagers were ordered to march or die. They marched, leaving behind steaming cups of coffee and half-eaten meals. Soon after, they were told they could return, but when some did, they saw their homes razed, their village surrounded by tanks. "There's a park there now," Sana informed us. "A fucking Canadian-sponsored park for occupiers to picnic on my family's land."

Sana, with her anger and verve, and Asha and Hala, with their easy affection, wrapped me in the friendship of girls. Their parents were strict, and without Karim to chaperone me, my parents had become stricter, too. I objected to this on principle, but in fact, without Nabil, those parties weren't fun anymore. The four of us had rotating slumber parties every weekend. Wednesdays after school we ambled down Salem Al-Mubarak Street in Salmiya under a canopy of sidr trees. We bought bootleg cassettes and mix tapes from Swan Lake, Chinese slippers with black straps and terra-cotta-colored soles from the Union Trading Company. We met up with friends for dinner at Pizza Hut. At twilight, residents of the apartments above the rows of shops and restaurants would unwind on their wide verandas, taking in shoppers and kids roller-skating or shooting footballs.

A medley of languages would drift over us, a seamless blend we took for granted.

But even then, lines were being drawn. Police had started rounding up boys for loitering or wearing shorts or other unspecified transgressions. Parents would be called to collect their sons from police stations, only to find their heads shaved. We heard rumors about perverts at the police stations, and I was afraid for our friends. I was so relieved Karim was gone.

Because of the strident opposition of respected parliament members and their supporters to the increasingly anti-democratic practices of leadership, Kuwait's National Assembly was suspended by the amir and, against the constitution, new elections weren't called within two months. Prominent activists in support of the opposition petitioned against the decision, threatening to take their objections to court. Private diwaniyyas were attacked by police armed with tear gas and dogs, violated for the first time in the country's history. My parents, like everyone, were shocked. Videotapes of the violence circulated around the country, and copies traveled up to Saddam Hussein, giving him ideas. Those fighting for the constitution in Kuwait were inspired by those fighting for their lives in Palestine. Kuwaitis, including my mother, started showing up at pro-intifada demonstrations in Hawalli, side by side with the Palestinians who had helped build their country.

My friends and I were part conscious, part oblivious. We were busy prepping for SATs, APs, filling out applications, writing personal statements, waiting for results. I had seen Nabil a few times over winter breaks. He hardly said two words to me, made sure we were never alone together, but sometimes I caught him staring at me like he used to. It was infuriating and devastating. Still, I applied to schools exclusively on the East Coast—near Harvard but not Harvard, close but not too close. My choices, I convinced myself, had nothing to do with him. There were great schools on the East Coast, and I wanted a fresh start.

My mother also made me apply to Berkeley.

Noura

"**W**atch it!"

Noura caught the ball before it hit her face. She sat up on the lounger, pushed her sunglasses onto her head, and squinted against the noon sun to confirm the culprit.

"Sorry, Mom!" Karim yelled up from the beach. "Can you throw it back?"

"Say, *please*."

"Puh-*lease*?"

She tossed the ball to her seven-year-old with one arm. He caught it and ran to the waiting kids. Noura looked for Sara, finding her in the pool with Tarek. Not the kiddie pool, the gigantic, Olympic-size, saltwater pool the Gazelle Club was famous for. At five, Sara was comfortable in the deep end without arm puffs.

Although the Gazelle Club first opened its doors in the early sixties, Noura's parents hadn't been members, so Noura had never seen it before her return from St. Louis. It reminded her of Beirut, of the Saint George. Clear sea, beaches and pools, a bowling alley, a nightclub where bands played live every weekend, where couples danced and drank martinis. Handsome, successful men from all over, their lovely wives stretched out like blades of grass. Young families enjoying their weekends at a beachside club in this sudden country. It only felt sudden to Noura and Tarek because they had missed the buildup to the boom. Four months in Kuwait was enough for them to realize everything had changed.

A few weeks after Noura and Tarek arrived from St. Louis, in July 1976, they had huddled with Hisham over blueprints for their new home. Hisham had designed a contemporary house guided by the lines of Kuwait's traditional courtyard structures. The courtyard would be covered instead of open. In place of a central garden, there would be a deep swimming pool. Rooms would circle the courtyard, as in the past, but everything would be far more spacious, accommodating their young, post-oil family.

Hisham's plans were impressive, and the house itself, completed a year later, did not disappoint. Noura's new home, along with the Gazelle Club, allowed her to release some of her misgivings. Hisham; his Austrian wife, Clara; and their two children, also a boy and girl, lived next door. Karim and Sara had convenient companions in their cousins, and Tarek and Hisham were two butt cheeks together again, as if no time or distance had ever separated them.

Noura had decided to enroll Karim and Sara in the American School of Kuwait at a time when very few children of both Kuwaiti parents attended, especially not girls. But Noura wanted her daughter to enjoy every opportunity her brother did. If Noura couldn't complete her own American education, her children would be given that chance. Tarek went along with his wife, believing that when it came to the children, he should leave it to her.

Tarek worked hard, as he had been eager to do, developing Kuwait's medical system and its university's medical school. He came home buzzing with plans. When he noticed young Egyptian workers dying unnecessarily of heatstroke, he established a heatstroke unit at the Amiri Hospital, then met with the minister of labor to change shift durations for workers during the summer months. Tarek was discreetly persuasive, so that under his direction, departments were established, expensive equipment purchased, protocols, even laws, adjusted, without those in power feeling forced. People would do what Tarek wanted, believing his ideas were their own. Tarek didn't mind eschewing credit, as long as the work got done.

He and Noura attended and hosted dinners for six, as well as glamorous parties thronging with people who seemed untouched by loss. She challenged herself to arrange parties that heightened the senses, so that an evening would imprint itself indelibly in the memories of her guests. She regularly hired a sitar player her family had known in Poona, who had moved to Kuwait, enchanting their visitors. Noura put aside still more of her doubts and disappointments, allowing herself to get caught, for a time, in the exhilarating, breezy rush of life in new Kuwait.

Once the novelty of settling in began to fade, however, Noura started to feel listless, like she had after Sara's birth. Her qualms about returning to Kuwait resurfaced. With the children at school, Tarek at work, house chores covered by Maria and Aasif, the recently hired cook from Uttar Pradesh, Noura was left with nothing to do but visit her parents, drop in on friends for chai al-dhaha, or fulfill the social obligations she had so dreaded in St. Louis. Real politics, the kind she wanted to engage in, remained forbidden to women, who were not permitted to vote, run for parliament, or visit diwaniyyas, where most of the country's plans were hatched. She wanted more than to fight for women's enfranchisement, important as that was. She wanted to think about the wider, long-term ramifications of current political decisions. She wanted to make connections between what was going on in Palestine, for example, and what might happen in Lebanon or, for that matter, in Kuwait, and what the United States might have to do with all of it. But there was no place for her to do this. Kuwaiti women could go far in the fields of education, business, and social and cultural work. Kuwaiti women, Noura included, had been driving and dressing as they pleased for decades. They were educated and active. Noura could travel freely and own as much property as she could afford. But when it came to politics, there was a line that couldn't be crossed. This hard limit was starting to feel like a noose around Noura's neck.

Mama Yasmine, still her mother's best friend, was often at her parents' home, and Noura wished she had a friend like her or a sibling as close as Hisham was to Tarek or Sara to Karim. Her sister Dana, who had divorced her first husband and married a diplomat, was living abroad. Her other siblings were all involved in their busy, conventional lives, and while she loved them and saw them regularly in her parents' home at Thursday lunch, she knew they wouldn't understand her. She wished she had someone with whom to share the fact that she felt the tentacles of her life choking the ambition that had fired her youth. How the incessant demands of children, husband, parents—which never came across as demands—clung to her like stubborn burrs until, one by one, she dutifully performed whatever was asked of her. How she could feel the years disappearing without anything to show for it, apart from her children, whom she adored, but whose existence in the world wasn't enough to make her feel complete. A friend to whom she could reveal that when she had these guilty thoughts about her children, she would dream of their bodies floating facedown in their fancy indoor pool. How those dreams would jolt her awake in the middle of the night, her head throbbing on a sweat-soaked pillow, and how she would tiptoe into Karim's room, then Sara's, to watch their blankets rise and fall.

The only person she mentioned some of these things to was Maria, who listened without judgment, who seemed to understand exactly what she meant.

The idea for Noura to open a small, foreign-language bookstore was Hisham's. He had noticed she was more on edge, and in that way he had of wanting to fix things for his brother—understanding that Tarek's well-being was inextricably bound to his wife's—one afternoon at the Gazelle Club, he announced: "Noura, habuba, you should start your own business."

Tarek and Clara exchanged puzzled glances as Noura asked, "What do you mean? What business?"

"Oh, I don't know, anything you like. A beauty salon. A clothing boutique. A bookstore. A coffee shop. A joke shop!" Hisham winked at his brother. "You're an exceptionally intelligent woman, Noura. I'm sure you'll figure something out."

"What do I know about starting a business?"

Hisham gave a knowing grin. "You come from a family of merchants."

"Baba Mubarak isn't like that. He's a dreamer."

"But your mother is." Hisham was resolute. "I'll invest the starting capital. Do something you love."

So, with a nod to Dickens and her father, Noura opened Curiosity Bookshop in September 1978. She wasn't going to make a fortune selling books, but the shop would cover its expenses, at the very least, by selling English and French titles, international magazines and newspapers. Noura avoided using wasta, though her well-connected brothers insisted they would be happy to help. As a point of pride, she forged relationships with bureaucrats who, like the men at Vaccaro & Sons, were disarmed by her beauty and tenacity. They let pass more than they normally would have. Translations of Naguib Mahfouz and Qasim Amin were prominently displayed for all to see.

On the night of the opening of her bookshop, after friends and family had left, Noura and Baba Mubarak were alone together. Tarek had taken Karim and Sara home for bed and would return to collect his wife and father-in-law. Mubarak sat on one of the wooden benches parallel to the shelves. "This reminds me of my study."

"It's a bit like it, isn't it, Baba? I've always loved that study of yours."

"I'm proud of you, ya binayti. Proud to have a daughter surrounded by books. They were always my first love, you know. Well, second, after Lulu." He smiled as he said Lulu's name. "I've been happy, binayti, despite everything." He paused, sighing heavily. "It's all rushing by. I'm afraid for you."

Noura looked up from tidying her desk, startled by her father's downward shift in tone. "What of, Baba?"

"It's clear from the clippings," Mubarak said faintly. "Why did you come back here? Why didn't you stay on the banks of the Mississippi like I told you to?" He was staring down at his feet.

"Baba, what are you saying?" Noura hurried to his side. "Are you all right? What are you so worried about?" But she understood instinctively—she feared it, too.

Mubarak gazed at his beautiful daughter sitting beside him, concern in her warm eyes. In her: his India, his Lulu, his fearless youth and abandoned dreams. He bumped up against her shoulder and smiled, took her hand in both of his. "Don't pay any attention to me, my monkey girl. I'm old, that's all. I worry about everything. This bookshop is glorious. Like the bookstores on Charing Cross Road. I wish we had spent more time in London. Do you remember all of that?"

"How could I forget, Baba?"

Tarek walked through the door, ringing the old-fashioned bell Noura had insisted on. Noura jumped and swiftly wiped her wet eyes. "Are the kids in bed?"

"Is everything okay?" Tarek asked.

"Everything is just fine, ya Duktor," Mubarak replied, getting up cautiously. "Just fine."

Mubarak died of a heart attack in his sleep a few months later. After his 'azza, Noura sat cross-legged on the floor of his dusty study, walls of his books towering over her. She inhaled the smell she knew as well as she knew the scent of her children's skin. The smell of tobacco and pencil shavings and gripe water.

Her father's files—the ones he had brought to St. Louis, which she had returned to him after her graduation—were all neatly labeled and categorized according to Mubarak's own inherent logic, packed into a carton box tucked under his desk. The collection had thickened over the years. Noura lugged the box out into the center of the room and lifted up the four flaps to reveal the files. In front was a divider labeled *IRAN* and behind it: *Pahlavi Dynasty; Mohammad Reza Shah Pahlavi; United States; Ayatollah Ruhollah Khomeini; Tobacco; Marxist Groups; Goethe Institute; Ali Shariati; Oil Corruption (see, also, KUWAIT: Oil); Savak; Cinema Rex; 1953 Coup; October 1977; 1978—Ongoing*. Behind *IRAN* and its attendant files was *IRAQ*, then *PALESTINE*. Behind *PALESTINE, LEBANON*. Behind *LEBANON* was *KUWAIT*. Each country had its own series of topical files. Inside each file, a glut of clippings in Arabic, English, Urdu, French, German, Farsi.

Noura flipped through them. One catastrophe after another, her father had been tabulating. The puzzle she had been piecing together for years was instantly complete. The end was violent, sweeping everything in its wake, leaving behind nothing but the bitter stench of sulfur and charred flesh. She broke out in a cold sweat. *My children.* But the present reasserted itself, releasing her from the hold of her father's forecast and her own informed grasp of that trajectory. *It hasn't happened yet. It doesn't have to happen.* Noura repressed her fears and tried to reconcile herself to the fact that she was her father's monkey girl no more.

A few months before Baba Mubarak died, Baba Marwan, Tarek's father, had died of a stroke in the middle of family lunch. He died in the arms of his son, the cardiologist, who was unable to save him.

A few months after Baba Mubarak died, Mama Sheikha died in her sleep. After Bader's death, Lulwa had refused to see her mother for a few years, but eventually she was drawn back, the only member of her family to visit the unlikable husk of a woman. After Baba Mubarak's death, Mama Sheikha had moved in with her daughter, slept in her bed. Noura had forgotten that Mama Sheikha, by then ninety, was still alive. She and her siblings were uncomfortable with Mama Sheikha's presence in their parents' home, but they didn't have a say in it. Before they had a chance to get worked up, Sheikha was dead.

Baba Mubarak, Baba Marwan, Mama Sheikha. Noura shoved the pile of deaths to one side. But once in a while as she shelved books in her shop or hung her clothes up after a long day, the bodies toppled down. It was a struggle to stash away the catastrophes her father's files tabulated. The pattern, once understood, could not be ignored, and Noura felt like she was biding time.

The Islamic revolution crashed down on Iran, shaking the entire region. Noura was grateful her father was not alive to witness it. Snapping at its heels, the war between Iran and Iraq. As the problems arrived, petroleum prices soared, enabling the residents of Kuwait to press on despite the dirty war next door. American hostages in Iran did not spur a mass exodus of expats out of Kuwait. How could anything happen in a country where the Gazelle Club existed? And the Equestrian Club and the Yacht Club and the Salmiya commercial strip and the American School and the French School and the cathedral and Christmas decorations every year and high salaries and impossibly rising stocks?

Noura tried to succumb, like the Americans, to a gilded life in their desert town. She had two kids to raise, a house to oversee, a business to manage. She loved Tarek, trusted in his steady ways, holding his hand tight in bed at night. The ooze of oil spread blindness, affording the luxury of delusion. The reassuring details of Noura's everyday life, of Tarek's soothing hand, dulled her naturally keen political acumen.

Still, every so often Noura felt like a fox with its leg in a steel trap. She lamented St. Louis, the freedom that had filled her chest when she breathed in frosty air. In such moments, regret would overwhelm her. Her trust in Tarek would falter, and rage at his authority——an authority he would neither acknowledge nor recognize——would thud in her ears. She would silently blame him for their return, for his loyalty to his brother over her, for his inability to read the glaring signals flashing around them. And then she would blame herself for not doing a damn thing about it.

Noura had taught Karim and Sara to be independent, so she couldn't complain when that was what they became, even when it meant that they relied on her and their father less than other kids their age. They both did well at school——apart from Arabic and religion classes——had a small but tight circle of friends, and kept themselves entertained for hours. Karim was inclined to brood, but Sara knew how to comfort him. They would disappear, taking Noura to the edge of panic, and then they would reappear, and Karim would be fine. Noura forced hugs on her son, which he put up with until he was ten, at which point he accepted physical affection only from Maria. It stung Noura a little, but Maria had given her son baths until he was eight, had tucked him under her arm like a baby chick his whole life. Maria had been at the center of her children's lives as Noura studied, socialized, started a business. It was a price she had been willing to pay.

When Karim started high school, there was that locker room

fight. Even before she got the call from the principal, Noura had suspected something was up; after their annual summer trip to California, Karim had transformed into another person. "It's puberty," Tarek assured her. Noura was positive it wasn't that. Sara, at twelve, was going through the kind of puberty Noura recognized. She was developing small breasts. She bounced with euphoria and crashed into gloom within the same half hour. She was obsessed with her friends, who could do no wrong, and had started thinking boys were cute. But Karim was going through something else. Noura tried to coax it out of him, to no avail. She asked Maria if she knew anything; Maria said she didn't. She asked Sara, who she was certain knew the whole story, but her daughter, her loyalty to her brother unimpeachable, remained chup chaap.

Through it all, Tarek made light of what Karim was going through. "I'd be worried if he didn't know how to throw a punch," he said. In those moments, Noura's anger toward Tarek would spike. What she had accepted, even admired, about Tarek in the past—his calm demeanor, his surgeon's distance—would grate on her. They would fight about it, her hard, angry words likely overheard by the children. But after their arguments, rather than coming to Karim's rescue, she would shield herself with her husband's reserve, using it to produce an equilibrium within herself she knew was both false and wrong.

Karim never got into another fight, but he walked around like he was carrying the secret of the universe inside him. Life maintained a delicate balance for a few more years, allowing Noura to pretend that everything—her son, her life, her country—was fine. During their summers in California, Noura would have her son back, more or less. In Kuwait, he switched. Then one summer, when he was fifteen, she saw Karim kiss a young man in a VW, and the mystery was solved. She couldn't bring herself to ask him about it or to share what she knew with Tarek. Her uncle Ahmed was gay. He had never married or had kids, and nobody asked why; it was understood. Noura didn't want that for her son—a life shrouded in secrecy and silence. But she had learned from her mother that some things—the hard, real things—should remain locked in a heavy box hidden inside a mud hole. Noura couldn't be for Karim the mother he needed. She didn't know how.

She forced Sara to follow Karim to UC Berkeley.

"I'm going to Brown," Sara countered, exhausting Noura with arguments about why the East Coast, not California, was where she wanted to be.

"I want you to be with Karim. It's safer. You'll live together. He can keep an eye on you."

"I don't need anyone to keep an eye on me! Certainly not Karim. Karim hasn't had his eye on me in years. I want to go to Brown."

"Look, Sara, things aren't the same here for girls as they are for boys. I've done you a great disservice if all the freedom I've given you has made you believe they are." This was not what Noura had ever believed, not what she had taught her children, but she said it anyway because she couldn't tell Sara the real reason she wanted her in California.

"I'm not going to be here. I'm going to be in the States."

"But you're still Kuwaiti. It's not acceptable for seventeen-year-old Kuwaiti girls to live on their own in the States."

"Since when, Mom?" Sara looked utterly confounded. "Karim went off alone. It's not fair I can't just because I'm a girl!"

"Life isn't fair." It was the ugly flip side of *Life goes on,* and it was the last word on the matter. Like it or not, Sara would go to Berkeley.

Noura couldn't stop herself from exerting undue pressure on her daughter to atone for her failure with her son, mothering her son through her daughter. She wanted Sara with Karim because of what she understood about the future. To give them back to each other—against secrecy and silence, tabulated catastrophes and death. She believed, for them at least, it wasn't too late.

Maria

Maria arrived in Poona from St. Louis in July 1976 to a son pickled by alcohol. Anna had said that her nephew frequented the slums around the railroad, so that was where Maria started searching as soon as she debarked the train. Within hours she had located Salvador, passed out on the dirt floor of a collapsing hut that sold drinks chemically closer to lighter fluid than to whiskey. She dragged him back to the hut, supporting his full weight, first on one shoulder, then the other. His skin was sallow, his once-radiant eyes bloodshot.

Maria spent the next month sobering up Salvador, while Salvador tried to flee into the blue-black night every chance he got. When he was successful, Maria was forced to call into the darkness, waking not only her daughters and Anna, but also her in-laws, the disgrace exposed. Sometimes her shouts drew out a cousin or nephew, who would help catch Salvador before he ran away.

Getting Salvador on the plane to Kuwait in early August was Maria's only objective. She became obsidian hard, bullying her son back to health. When Salvador's attention strayed to the entrance of the hut, Maria slapped him on both cheeks, grabbed his face in her hands. "You will not leave this hut, do you hear me? You will not step out until the need is gone."

"Mai, don't you understand? It never will be."

"You are coming with me to Kuwait. You will get married. You will become a father. Is this the way you would want your own son to behave?"

The violence in her sister's tone cut Anna. "Please, Maria, dhakte bhoini. Let the boy rest. He won't do it anymore, will you, bachea? Think of Kuwait! You, Christie, your mother, together at last. And soon Josie, too." Anna lifted Salvador's exhausted head onto her lap, offering the affection Maria withheld. "Don't worry, baba, everything will be fine, like galloping through fields on an imaginary horse."

For the first time since her arrival, Maria saw her son smile.

By the start of her fourth week in Poona, Maria began to believe it might be possible for Salvador to recover in time for their departure. He started to wake up earlier than his mother, to roll up his mat and heat milk for their tea, to sit beside his aunt as she flipped their breakfast bhakris. The movements of his body eased into a recollected rhythm.

Josefina was home from school that final weekend. She rose at dawn and stepped outside the hut to sulk. She resented her brother for stealing her mother away from her during her precious month in India. Salvador followed his sister out, and her features darkened like a solar eclipse. "We're not leaving you behind," he offered gently. "You'll join us in a few years."

"Five years," Josie hissed. She stood up and stamped her feet, kicking dirt at her brother.

Salvador remembered time's sludge at sixteen. What would it do to his sister to spend it without siblings, without her mother? He spit out the guilty bile that filled his mouth.

In the fire of August, Salvador started work as an office boy at KOC, Christina as an accountant at the Kuwait Trading Company. Maria had arranged for Salvador and Christina to lodge in a room let by a Goan couple. Both returned to their shared room exhausted, scarfed down a meal, then went straight to bed. On Fridays they met their mother at church in Kuwait City. Maria didn't have to be back at the Al-Ameeds' until late, so she spent hours after church preparing meals for Salvador and Christie in the small kitchen of the Goan couple's apartment. She stuffed their freezer with portions of food for the week ahead.

Within two years, Christina managed to attract a suitable husband. Anthony was fourteen years older than her. He had been in Kuwait for seventeen years, had a steady job as a bookkeeper with one of the Kuwaiti merchant families. He was even-tempered and dependable, spent his evenings meticulously going over his company's ledgers. He was not lively the way Christie remembered her father being, but he was as good. The fact that Anthony was Goan was enough for Maria. Her plan was on track.

Between them, Anthony, Christina, and Salvador soon were making enough to rent a modest two-bedroom apartment in Salmiya, with a larger kitchen than the one they had shared as lodgers and a freshly tiled bathroom. Maria didn't contribute to the rent, but she spent money on their food, and she continued to send money for Josie's tuition and for her and Anna's expenses.

Maria remained with the Al-Ameeds. She had her own

children—Salvador, Christie, Josie—and she had her other children—Karim and Sara. It didn't bother Salvador to hear his mother talk about her other children. It bothered Christina, but she didn't say anything to her mother during their weekly visits. Christina had her own life, her job, her husband, and soon, she hoped, her children. She began to let her mother go.

Maria returned to India in July 1978 with the objective of finding Salvador a wife. Josie was not waiting at the railway station to meet her when she arrived. Anna explained that she had an exam, but Maria knew that was an excuse.

Josie stomped into the hut in the early evening, childish braids gone, hair cut fashionably short. She planted a perfunctory kiss on her mother's cheek, and Maria was forced to confront the cost of being away for almost a decade of her child's life. Josie was eighteen years old, a tall young woman, a smoldering force in their shadowy hut. As Anna prepared a simple dinner of bhakris and bhaji, she rattled as many pots and pans as she could, a musical distraction allowing mother and daughter to postpone speech. At last Maria asked Josie about her exam that day.

"Fine," Josie said curtly. Always first in her class, she was studying accounting like her sister.

"What subject?"

"Mathematics."

"You've always been good with numbers."

Josie picked at a scab on her knuckle.

"You'll get an excellent job in Kuwait. Maybe at Christie's company. Or maybe with Salvador at KOC." Josie hadn't asked about Christie or her new husband. She hadn't asked about Salvador. "While I'm here, I'm going to be looking for a wife for Salvador. What do you think?"

Josie bit her cheeks. Her resentment of her brother was palpable, even after two years. She got up to help her aunt.

"Anna bhoini, what do you think?" Maria turned to her sister. "Anyone in mind?"

Anna stopped what she was doing, leaned forward on her cane. "We'll ask around. So many will come out of the jungle for a chance to skip up to Kuwait. We have to be careful."

"I'll go prepare the bhakris," Josie muttered. Maria smiled widely and started to thank her, but Josie was already gone.

Maria thought of those blond dolls with the changing eyes. On this return from Kuwait, she had brought back all sorts of things for Josie: clothes, shoes, chocolates, perfumes, pretty barrettes, which she might still be able to clip on behind her ear. Josie had thanked her mother briskly, hardly glancing at the heap of things Maria had collected so painstakingly in the weeks before travel.

Maria chose to believe Josie's mood would pass. Josie's feelings had no place in Maria's plan. Josie would finish school, come to Kuwait, get a job, find a husband. Her path was clear. For the moment, Maria's focus was Salvador.

Salvador felt like an interloper sandwiched between his sister and her new husband. He started staying late at the office, washing each teacup twice, wiping clean the daily accumulation of dust on every surface. Alone with the lights off, Salvador prayed like he knew what was coming.

What came, about two weeks into Maria's absence, was a wiry

man who worked in the department next to Salvador's. Alfonso cackled obnoxiously in the presence of the cleaners, office boys, and security guards, most of them Indian or Egyptian. He threw back his head, with its flat, greasy forehead, as he laughed. Salvador didn't ask what he was laughing at or how he could afford to pay for the gold rings weighing down his pinkies. He recognized Alfonso's type, the ones who delivered what was needed with a wink and a pat on the back, at first. Soon enough, the Alfonsos would stop winking and start pummeling, demanding their money.

Alfonso sidled up to Salvador in the empty office. He snickered as Salvador prayed to Jesus. "Pray all you want, boy. I have it for you by the bucketful." Alfonso inserted an unlabeled glass bottle with amber liquid into Salvador's clasped hands. As he took his first sip, Salvador didn't think of his mother or the wife she was seeking for him. He didn't think of Christie or her new husband. He didn't think of his poor aunt or his angry little sister. He was amazed at how automatic it was to harden what, over the last two years in Kuwait, had gone soft. As he focused on the heat in his guts, his mouth went to the bottle a second time. He had missed this fire.

He was caught two weeks later by one of the Kuwaiti managers at KOC, someone who knew Mubarak. The man took away the bottle and ordered Salvador home. That night, Salvador lay in bed shaking. Mubarak sahib had taught him how to type. He had found him his job. His daughter was his mother's employer. Everything was on the line.

The next morning, he went to work as usual. The Kuwaiti

manager summoned him to his office and told him to go see Mubarak after work.

That evening, old Baba Mubarak was waiting for Salvador in his study. "Beta, what are you doing?" Salvador hung his head. "Think of your poor mother. How hard she's working for you all."

"Sorry, sahib," Salvador mumbled.

"This must stop. The manager who caught you promised to give you a chance, but only because of me. Next time—and there can be no next time—he'll call the police and you'll be deported. Your mother will not survive it. Do you understand?"

"Yes." Salvador swallowed. "Please, sahib, don't tell Mai. I promise not to do it again. She mustn't know about this. Please."

"I won't tell her. Just don't do it again."

When Maria showed Salvador the photograph of the girl she had chosen to be his wife, Salvador took a glimpse and nodded. Marriage was going to be the bond that saved him. After the disaster averted by Baba Mubarak, Salvador would do whatever his mother wanted. The girl had long ebony hair, a sharp parting down the center. "She's twenty," Maria shared. "She looks younger than she is. What do you think?"

"She's pretty. What's her name?"

"Lucilla. We know her family. A good girl. No schooling but hardworking. I'll ask memsahib if she knows a family looking for a maid."

The wedding in Poona in early December was small and bright. Even Josefina was all smiles. Salvador was jolly with everyone, Lucilla grinning shyly on his arm. Once they were back in Kuwait, Noura found a home for Lucilla to work as a maid. She and Salvador spent their Fridays together. Maria was gladder than she had ever been.

Josefina arrived in Kuwait in July 1981, after completing her degree in accounting. She was hired by the National Bank of Kuwait, the top bank in the country. Her hair was long again. Anger no longer misted off her. She joked with Lucilla, played happily with her nephew and niece. By then, Salvador had a baby boy named Lazarus; Christie, a daughter named Natalia. Everyone at work predicted Josie would be promoted fast. It wouldn't be long before a husband came around. Sure enough, she was soon married to a Goan banker named John, who also worked at NBK, and they moved into their own apartment in the same building as Christie and Salvador.

Sixteen years after the death of her husband, Maria finally gave herself permission to exhale. She continued to send money to Anna and, at last, started to tuck away something extra for the house she planned to build in Poona for herself and her sister.

A week after Karim's peculiar fight at school, Maria found out that Salvador had started drinking again. Lucilla, Christie, and Josie had been keeping it from her. The whiff of whiskey on his breath had seemed insignificant to them at first, with no negative effect on work or home. Anthony had taken him aside and Salvador had made promises, but nothing changed. Then one Friday, while Maria was visiting, Salvador snuck into the bathroom and came out unsteady on his feet. Maria took one look at him and knew. She put her nose to his mouth. "When? When did this start?" She looked at the three women's blank faces, at Anthony, at John. The children playing on the carpet fell silent.

"You will stop this, Salvador. Do you understand? You will not ruin us."

"I promise, Mai. I'll stop."

Salvador couldn't stop. He drank himself out of a job. An ambulance was called to work. He was admitted to Amiri Hospital—Tarek's hospital—for alcohol poisoning. Tarek kept Salvador admitted for as long as he could, ten days. After that he was deported, his passport stamped *Permanent No Entry*. Noura tried to use wasta, to no avail. Lucilla and little Lazarus went with him. Maria blamed her daughter-in-law for not being enough to keep Salvador away from drink. She blamed Christie and Josie for not telling her. But inside she knew that no one could save Salvador but Salvador.

Over the next few years, the news from Anna was sometimes good, sometimes not. Salvador went for periods without drinking and then he fell back in, nearly to death. He sobered up, made promises to Lucilla that lasted a month, maybe two, and then it would start over.

Maria sent money to Lucilla and to Anna, never to Salvador. She paid for her grandson's school and all their needs. Salvador worked when he could but didn't bring in much. Maria preferred it when he wasn't working because then he didn't have money to spend on alcohol.

When Kuwait was invaded by Iraq on the second of August 1990, nobody was prepared. It was a Thursday, the first day of the weekend, so Maria's daughters and their husbands were not at work.

There would be no work during the invasion with Kuwaiti banks and businesses closed. A week later, Noura, risking danger at checkpoints, drove Maria to her family. "If you get the chance, Maria, leave. War is not for children." They held each other tight for a few seconds in the car, without tears. Maria would not see Noura again for nine months.

In September, Maria, Christina, Josefina, and their husbands and children made their way back to India via Jordan with nothing but the clothes on their backs. Every last one of their fils was frozen at NBK. They all wanted to believe that their savings would be recovered, that the lives they had built with such care and sacrifice over the long years could not be so easily wiped out. But it was only Maria, contrary to her history, to her entire disposition, who actually believed it to be true. "Faith," she insisted, "will see us through."

By then Salvador had not had a drink in three years. He couldn't provide a clear reason behind his abstinence, but by his mid-thirties, the urgency to drink had started to dissipate. The change had come gradually, one less drink at a time, until he hadn't had one in weeks, then months, then years. Salvador had a modest store of rupees, and it filled his whole being with the lightness of clouds to be able to share it with his family. When they arrived, a tribe of broken refugees, dust in their hair, skin beaten by the sun, it was his turn, at last, to save them.

III

Sara

III

1989 – 1992

Mom made me go to Berkeley. "The alternative for most Kuwaiti girls is Kuwait University, Sara. Don't forget that." I cried. I shouted. I moped. She wouldn't budge. My father kept out of it. Her insistence felt violent, his reserve, customary.

Karim, by then a junior, had his own apartment in Northside. I was going to be living with him, not in the dorms I would have preferred. Karim, to his credit, never behaved like he didn't want me there. He gave up the only bedroom in the apartment for me, sleeping on the futon in the living room. We slipped back into something we recognized, and it felt like a recovery.

My first year at Berkeley passed without much to distinguish it. I found my bearings, made a few friends, declared my major in philosophy. Living in the States was what I had been yearning for since childhood, but the reality didn't match the fantasy. My brother seemed at home, more relaxed in his skin than I had ever seen him. I tried to mimic his ease, but mine felt phony. No one would have guessed me to be anything other than American, precisely what I had always wanted, and yet, there I was, in the place I had longed to be, inexplicably, decidedly, out of place.

By then I had stuffed Nabil and our unfinished business out
of sight and mind, but one night, toward the end of the academic
year, I had a dream about him—a dream like a premonition or a
call for restitution.

Karim was preparing coffee as I ambled into our tiny kitchen.
"Any word from Nabil?" I asked, sounding artificially casual.

Karim's shoulders tensed up defensively. "No. Why?"

"I don't know." I studied my brother. Three years had passed
without Nabil, yet the mere mention of his name made Karim's
body rigid. He continued to stand over his pot, waiting for the
coffee to percolate. "Did you love him, Karim?"

Karim spun around, his eyes full of a childish anguish I had
believed was long gone. "Why didn't you ever ask me that before,
Sara? What's the point now, when it doesn't matter?"

"Why would it have mattered then?" I asked disingenuously.

My brother shook his head, poured his coffee, and retreated
to the bathroom. I'm not sure if he caught my pathetic little sorry.

Iraq invaded Kuwait a couple of months later. By the end of August, the phone lines went dead. Our mother's final words to us
before the lines cut were: "Your father goes to the Amiri Hospital every day. But he'll be fine. Your uncle Hisham shadows him
like a hawk, his own personal bodyguard." She laughed, and her
laughter reassured us. "We have enough food. Water still flows
from the taps. We've heard rumors it might stop. Let's see. I've told
Maria to go to India with her grandchildren, and Aasif left with
his nephew a week ago. You two stay put and study hard. Take
care of each other. This will be over before you know it."

The invasion coincided with my sophomore year at Berkeley.

So many voices, true to Berkeley tradition, clamored against the war to save Kuwait. *It's about oil. Why should we risk our men and women to save a bunch of camel-riding sheikhs?* Oil, I understood, was the lubricating force, but it was my mother and father they were willing to let die.

After a particularly heated class discussion, my Continental Philosophy professor took me aside. "They don't mean harm. Most of them hadn't even heard of Kuwait before this August."

I couldn't respond, my eyes filling with unexpected tears. I had mentioned in class that my parents were still inside. Even that hadn't been enough to stop the arguments.

"Any word from your parents?"

"Not since the end of August."

"I'm really sorry to hear that."

He did sound sorry. I glanced up at his well-intentioned face. Professor Byrne would have been draft age during Vietnam. Who knew what this buildup of a military shield in someone else's desert stirred in him.

"It must be tough dealing with all this and school."

"School is my savior."

He laughed at that and told me to come see him if I ever needed anything. I thanked him but didn't take him up on the offer. I worked diligently that year as I waited for the liberation of a country I had never before thought of as mine.

Karim and I were in the kitchen of our apartment in early March 1991 when the phone rang. I picked up and heard our mother's voice. For six months our parents had been Schrödinger's cat, simultaneously alive and dead inside a country we couldn't look into. I put her on speaker. We hovered over the machine like it was a warm fire. I could feel the raised hairs on my brother's arm prickling my own.

"Your father's dead. So is Uncle Hisham. My brothers buried them. It was quick. There are so many 'azzas these days, we've decided to forgive each other for not turning up." She paused. "It's been raining, and the rain that falls is black." Our mother's voice was faint, chopped up by static on the line. I checked Karim's face to confirm he had heard what I had. His eyes were saucers.

Our mother provided no words of explanation or commiseration. There wasn't time, satellite phone minutes as precious as gushing, uncapped oil. "You've seen the wells? It's all true. Black as night during the day. Mama Yasmine is suffering, like Mama Lulwa after Bader." Another pause. "The streets are chaos, really dangerous. I'll call again, soon as I can." The phone clicked dead before we could utter a word.

As American bombs decimated Iraq, my father and his brother laid out plans for the new Kuwait. "We'll get it right this time," Hisham pledged to Tarek, "all the things we got wrong the last." Their first project would be to rebuild the medical infrastructure: Hisham the architect from the outside in, Tarek the physician from the inside out.

As they made their way from the Amiri Hospital to Mama Yasmine's house on foot, they spoke louder than they had in months, carried away by the release of not having to hide under black abayas in the footwells of cars in order to sneak past Iraqi checkpoints. They walked under the black smog of burning oil wells, which they could smell but couldn't see because it was night. They spoke loudly with their strong enemy accents. Their Basrawi drawl captured the attention of two young men with the plugged-up eyes of true patriots. The brothers chuckled at first when the scruffy boys ordered them to put up their hands and surrender like television bandits. Then they noticed the guns. "We're Kuwaitis, ya awlad, ya-l-taybeen, just like you. Haven't you heard of the Al-Ameed family? Go ask your fathers, your grand-fathers."

Nothing the brothers said could penetrate the boys' snare of ignorance, their moral certitude. The two boys spit curses at the two middle-aged men, old enough to be their fathers. They kicked them in the backs of their knees, and the brothers folded to the ground like cards, as so many would fold in the months to come at the hands of vigilantes with no hold on the history of their own country. Hisham reached for Tarek's hand, and this made the boys jeer, "Fags as well as traitors! We've hit the jackpot."

Hisham whispered to Tarek, "Can you believe this is what it comes down to, ya Taruki? Surviving the invasion only to bite it in a dusty lot?"

Tarek laughed, as he had countless times at the words of his wonderful, wonderful brother. Two shots cracked simultane-ously. The brothers fell forward, still holding hands. Their bodies, left to rot, were recovered two days later by apologetic members of the neighborhood resistance. A misrecognition, an irreversible mistake.

After Mom's phone call, Karim and I held each other and sobbed. He had been removed, our father, more captivated by medicine than family, closer to his brother than to anyone else. But he had taught us to swim, had gone to the trouble of buying us forbidden comic books on the way home from work, leaving them for us under our pillows where our mother wouldn't find them. He was our father, who had loved his indoor plants and our mother, and now he was gone, and we, his children, had been so far away.

Our mother, in her subsequent phone calls, ordered us to wait. "I don't want you breathing in this toxic air," she said, but that wasn't the reason we didn't hurry back. When we asked her to come visit instead, for Karim's upcoming graduation, she said she couldn't leave the house for fear of looters, and she couldn't leave Mama Lulwa alone with Mama Yasmine. "It's too much for her to handle on her own." We knew that wasn't true; Mama Lulwa could handle anything.

I convinced myself it was okay to postpone a trip to Kuwait because Maria was back. She had returned in May with her two daughters and their husbands, all of them prepared to begin again. She moved back into the Surra house, and she and my mother set to work bringing it to order. The first thing they did was to trim the overgrown mejnooneh. A wall of unruly fuchsia flowers and thorny shrub had exploded across the front walls of the garden, indifferent to the black air and oily rain. Mom and Maria attacked the oven with steel wool, soaped down every inch of the refrigerator; cleared the kitchen shelves and drawers of glasses, china, cutlery, pots, and pans; and wiped down the emptied cupboards with Dettol-soaked sponges. They washed and dried everything, then returned each object to its place. They hand-washed sheets and towels because the drive belt of the washing machine had cracked, and there were no spare parts. They dipped yellowed lace into bowls of diluted bleach. They hung everything to dry indoors, stringing up a labyrinth of laundry across the house, protecting their clean washing from the devastated environment in a way they couldn't protect themselves. They dusted every surface, dusted again the following day, then the next, every day for a year. The oily grime stuck their feather dusters together exactly the way barrels of spilled crude clumped together the feathers of seagulls and cormorants. Migratory birds that had instinctually returned to the Gulf for hundreds of years found themselves, without warning, flightless, at the mercy of the toothbrushes and cleaning agents of despondent animal rights activists on the ground. Day after day, my mother and Maria cleaned in an effort to scrub away despair, to persist despite the intolerable.

Mom finally agreed to visit us for a few weeks in August. We decided to meet in our Orange County condo. Our mother, her beauty ravaged but sublime, said little about our father, so, following her lead, neither did we. Instead, she spoke about the political situation in Kuwait. "It's a Kuwait I no longer recognize. We want to pit democracy against itself. We fought for freedom only to give it up. And what we've done to the Palestinians. It's—" She shuddered, unable to complete her thought.

"Why don't you just leave, Mom?" Karim interrupted, obviously annoyed. "They'll never change."

Mom seemed gutted by Karim's question, or maybe by his use of the word *they*. "You know," she began haltingly, "in December, just before liberation, I suggested to your father that we leave. By then we knew the Americans were coming. 'Let's go to California,' I said. 'You could start a practice. We'd be near the kids. This nightmare will take forever to mop up, if it's even possible. There's no future here.' And do you know what he said to me?" We shook our heads. "He said exactly what he did that first time in St. Louis. 'I can't do it, Noura. I have to help rebuild the country.'" She exhaled hard. "And just like before, I didn't push for the decision I knew was right."

"You could come now, Mom," I ventured.

My mother looked up at the ceiling. "Mama Lulwa. Mama Yasmine. Maria. And my bookshop. It's too late."

It wasn't, but it felt that way to her. So we let our mother go back to the country she always knew wasn't right for her, to mourn the husband who had tied her to the place that ate him up.

On the one-year anniversary of Dad's death, my phone rang. By then I was living alone in the apartment. Karim, newly enrolled in the Ph.D. program in architecture at Berkeley, had recently moved out.

"Sara?" My fingers around the phone turned to glass. The last time I had seen him was just over two years earlier, in 1989, during my final winter break in Kuwait before the invasion. We had scarcely exchanged two words, eyeing each other from across rooms belonging to various friends.

"Sara? You there?"

"Yes," I whispered.

"Sara. I'm sorry I didn't call you about your dad right after Faris told me. I kept postponing, then months passed, and then it felt wrong. Now it's been a year. How are you? How's Karim? Your mom? Is Maria okay?"

"I don't know" was the only response I could summon. He didn't sound like himself anymore, his accent so much more American, his pace fidgety, no longer languid.

I wanted to tell him everything. That we couldn't speak about our father and that my mother was trapped in Kuwait. That my brother was free and on his way to happy. That I was applying to Brown, and only Brown, for graduate school. Instead, out of nowhere, I said, "I've been missing something about you lately. And about myself."

I heard a sharp intake of breath, and then, after minutes that felt like hours, he said, "I'm so sorry, Sara. I really am." After another interminable silence, he added, "Nothing stays the same."

I hung up without saying goodbye.

July 2013

Once upon a time, I dreamed of being unbound. I wanted to be free but couldn't manage it. My brother could. My mother could not. My father could. My grandmothers could not.

I spend my days sleeping, reading, swimming, watering my father's indoor plants. I anticipate Mr. Al-Baatin's weekly visits. I eat food Aasif prepares. I await Sana's imminent arrival and, in the next few weeks, Karim's. I still haven't told Karl because telling Karl will force a decision that can only be terminal. I imagine coming unstuck and wonder whether that will necessitate coming undone.

"Your trial date has been announced. Sooner than we thought." Mr. Al-Baatin is out of breath and sweating as he lowers himself onto his creaking love seat. For once he doesn't automatically reach down to pet Lola.

The corner of my left eye starts to twitch uncontrollably. I shake my head inquiringly because I know that if I open my mouth to speak, no words will come.

"The fourth of August."

I gasp. Sana was right.

"I know. Just over three weeks away. Believe me, Sara, I haven't been doing nothing these last five weeks. We've covered every angle—the fundamental unconstitutionality of the new law, precedent cases, the specifics of the accusation against you. I'm confident we could win this in court. But, as I've always maintained, we don't want to put you through that. We want this over as soon as possible. No long, drawn-out trial."

"So?" I croak.

"So you retract your statement. One of the provisions of the amendment stipulates that if the offending statement is retracted, the judge can dismiss the case out of hand."

"That can't happen before trial?"

"They still haven't ruled on that request, but because the public prosecution accepted the case, it's unlikely. But the judge can still dismiss the case in court, before the trial really begins. Why they haven't called you in for questioning, I don't know, but I read it as a sign they're planning to dismiss the minute you retract."

My head is spinning. I lower it onto my knees and remember the move from a couple of weeks ago at the hospital. It's good Maria's not here. "My friend Sana arrives in a few days. She's a human rights lawyer based in London. Could she meet with you?"

He winces but says, "Of course."

I feel bad. He has been nothing but kind to me. "Please, Mr. Al-Baatin, I have no doubt in your abilities. She's my oldest friend."

Mr. Al-Baatin gives me an exhausted smile and nods. "You've been through a lot, Sara. I look forward to meeting your friend. Any input she provides will be in your best interest. We all want the same thing here. For this to be over so that you can go back to your old life."

Half of that statement, anyway, is true.

I water my father's plants and cry. These plants were alive when he was. I didn't witness my mother grieve for my father, and she never encouraged me to share my complicated sorrow. I'm not sure Karim or I mourned him the way he deserved. The shock of it obliterated our capacity to process his loss.

It took me years to gather together the story of my father's death after my return to Kuwait, in snippets collected from Maria and Mama Yasmine. To gather together does not mean to make sense of. The event will remain forever senseless. But even the senseless deserves to be marked, and because I may be running out of time, the time to mourn my father—cultivator of indoor gardens, surgeon of broken hearts—is now.

Maria told me about those days of brushes and bleach after the invasion and of the quiet exchanges between her and my mother. It was Maria, not my brother or me, who healed my mother after my father's execution. Maria told me about her own escape through the desert to Baghdad. Bussed from Baghdad to Amman, then airlifted to India. A procession of pickup trucks and cars strapped with luggage, bent human beings on foot, heavy bundles on their heads. "Men falling flat from thirst, Saru beti. Families with nothing but the clothes on their backs. Thank the Lord we had our own cars and water and food, but all our money was stuck at the bank! I knew we would be back. Apka maa, Noura memsahib, was still inside. And your baap, bechara." She would shake her head at the mention of my father.

Mama Yasmine gave me another snapshot of my mother's despair. After dropping off my father and Uncle Hisham at the Amiri Hospital every morning, my mother and Mama Yasmine would wait at Mama Lulwa's house in Shamiya for their return. My father refused to allow my mother to pick them up, not wanting her to risk driving at night through soldier-thick streets.

My mother would wait in Baba Mubarak's study, sit at his desk with an open book in front of her. "It looked like she was reading," Mama Yasmine told me, "but I never saw her turn a single page."

My mother waited in her father's old study until she heard the doorbell ring, at dusk on good days, past eight or nine in the evening on bad ones. She refused to eat. She was, Mama Yasmine thought in retrospect, grieving for my father before his demise. And when the news arrived, my mother didn't collapse. She didn't wail the way so many wives in old Kuwait Town had wailed for their perished sailor husbands and brothers, the way Mama Sheikha's mother must have done for her son.

"When the news came, your mother, who had starved herself through the invasion, sat down at the mat in the sala—her legs arranged in that unholy M shape you and Lulwa could also manage—and served herself a mound of rice. If I didn't know better, Sara, I'd say your mother was relieved."

Relief, like stony rigidity, is a version of shock. Or maybe my mother's relief was relief. Relief at no longer having to pay the price for my father's obstinate connection to a country that had stolen her ambitions and then flushed her sacrifices down the toilet. Relief at not having to go through it all again, this time without the delusion that something good would come of it. But my mother did nothing to channel that relief into action. She, like me, stayed put.

Sana marches into the house as she has hundreds of times since she was six years old, and it's like the air begins to swirl again, like everything that has been on pause since Maria's death is reanimated. It takes all the strength of my muscles not to give in to the pull of gravity.

She has a small overnight bag in hand, and I feel the relief of centuries wash over me. I haven't seen her in a few years, but she doesn't look older. Sana, eternally fifteen. At seventy she'll still look fifteen to me. I see Karim that way, too.

"You're a toothpick." She hugs me, and all at once I am aware of my bones. "We'll plump you up in the next few weeks."

"Like a goose," I manage.

"Exactly like a goose." She doesn't let go. "It's going to be okay, Sara. Everything's going to be okay."

Sana has only one aunt and uncle left in Kuwait. She's staying with them. Everyone else has scattered to the far reaches of the globe. Family in Beirut, London, Santiago, and, of all places, Lubbock, Texas. "We are the diaspora," she says.

We don't make small talk. We never have. We go straight to my room and sit together on the two-seater sofa where we used to spend hours discussing everything under the sun. We begin again like no time has passed.

"I'll go see Mr. Al-Baatin in his office tomorrow morning," she announces.

"He says I should retract."

"Of course you should. We'll write the retraction together, and we'll practice until it rolls off your tongue."

"You don't think I should fight this?"

"Absolutely not."

"For the good of the nation?"

"Not for the good of the universe. Don't be nuts, Sara. There's nothing but to retract."

"And that will work, you think?"

Sana hesitates. "I'm going to be honest with you, Sara. I don't know. I don't know what's happened to Kuwait. I don't know whether this is the beginning of something or the end." I feel the blood drain from my face. "Sorry, habibti. But let's be logical here. Of the thirty or so executions since 2000, not one has been over ideology. Murder, rape, drug trafficking, nothing less than that."

"But this is a new law."

"It is. But even going back to the sixties, it's only ever been for murder. Regardless of this shitty new law, I doubt that will change."

"You're sure?" I watch my friend's expression closely. She isn't.

"What will you do after?" she asks to distract me.

After the trial is a wide-empty slate. I can't see myself returning to Kuwait University or any university. I can't see myself in Kuwait or the States. I shake my head.

Sana bites down on her lower lip, a habit she's had forever. "Why did you come back, Sara? I couldn't ask you at the time. Nabil, then your mom so quickly after him, it was inhuman. But your decision to leave California, what for? By then everyone was gone."

"Maria was here," I respond. "One of my grandmothers was alive. Mom's bookshop." I recite the routine litany, no longer convinced.

She purses her lips sideways in disbelief. "For them you came back? For a bookshop?"

"I'm not sure what I was thinking at the time. I wasn't thinking. It was compulsive."

Sana nods in an effort to appear sympathetic. "And staying over a decade?"

She can't help her lawyerly ways. I smile. I try to think of a way to explain to my oldest friend what I haven't been able to explain to my brother or to myself. "It's like torpor," I begin. "I've been in torpor for eleven years. Do you know that word? It's a sort of bird hibernation. When they're under threat of cold weather or starvation, some birds fall into torpor. Their heart rates decrease, their body temperatures drop, and they enter a sleeplike state. This allows them to survive harsh conditions. But," I suddenly remember, "it leaves them vulnerable to attack."

Sana shakes her head. "What's the alternative? For birds?"

I think of Karl. "Migration."

1993-1999

Providence was a compact city covered with historic plaques, including my redbrick apartment building on Benefit Street. I didn't own a car, so I walked everywhere. From my apartment to the philosophy department in Gerard House, to Eastside Marketplace for groceries. Sometimes I walked across the College Street bridge into downtown, wandering through eerily deserted cobblestone streets. At night, warm light poured out of casement windows I peeped into, catching glimpses of tangled lives that had nothing to do with mine. I mapped the unfamiliar with the soles of my feet.

My mother was doing exactly the same thing in Kuwait, trying to make her unfamiliar, postwar city familiar again on foot. Walking bound the two of us together. Separately we walked the same solitary path, committing to an isolation that felt necessary.

Over a year and a half after that awful phone call with Nabil, I opened my front door to him.

"You're here," I said in disbelief.

"I'm here, beautiful Sara."

"What're you doing here?" Ever since I had arrived in Providence, knowing he was nearby, the past had reignited in me. Nabil at eight riding his bike down the recently paved streets of Surra, raising his eyebrows and beaming as I trailed behind. Nabil at the Gazelle Club under the jetty. Nabil as a teenager, spectacular as summer. It felt like I had conjured him into being.

"Visiting friends for Thanksgiving. Can I come in?"

To see him in the flesh after four years was strange. He seemed different, broader, filled in, yet so much the same, eyes sparkling like no time had passed. More astonishing was the rush the sight of him stirred in me. No amount of imagining Nabil had the effect of his physical presence standing before me, the awakening of a misplaced vitality.

I opened the door wider for him to step through. He bent down and kissed me on the mouth for a long time, cuffing his hands around my wrists like a guard. Willing prisoner, I kissed him back.

Facing each other on my bed, propped up on our elbows, we slipped back into neglected habits like we were slipping into childhood dreams. It was more effortless than it should have been to talk to each other, so easy to accept the warmth of his breath against my skin. We discussed our lives in broad strokes before inching toward the essentials. His parents were back in Kuwait, as was their right as Kuwaiti citizens, but with so many of their Palestinian friends prevented from returning, it was lonely for them. He had been in Massachusetts during the invasion, his parents and siblings in Beirut, stuck there after their summer holidays. Daoud was at the World Bank in D.C., his parents permanently expelled to Jordan. Faris was a banker at Lloyd's in Geneva; his family had migrated to Canada.

"How's Karim?" He squirmed, suddenly awkward.

I had been waiting for the question. "Working on his Ph.D. at Berkeley. He's seeing someone. Jonathan. Serious, I think."

Nabil grinned his toothy grin, visibly relieved. "I'm really glad."

"He loved you, you know."

Nabil looked away. "I know." He paused. "Did he ever tell you about us?"

I remembered my brother's face from a few years earlier, when I had finally stated openly what I had always secretly known. "No."

"It was after that fight with Sami. Karim told me he was gay."

"What did you say?"

"Not much. I didn't care. I never again left him alone in the locker room, made it clear to those shitheads that if they ever touched him, I'd kill them. But when you and I started going out, Karim stopped talking to me, started acting distant. When I asked him what was going on, it was a mess. I didn't want to hurt him, you know? But I wanted you, Sara. That's what I told him."

"You said, 'I want Sara'?" My stomach turned with guilt at the thought of my vulnerable brother hearing those words at that time.

"Yes." Nabil pulled me to him, wrapping his legs and arms around me so I couldn't move. "I still do." And I still couldn't resist him. We kissed, and it made me realize how small I had been living. Then he said, "I just got offered a job in Manhattan, only a few hours from Providence."

His words jerked me out of the sinkhole his arrival had sucked me down. What was this deus ex machina after six years of almost total disregard?

"Look, Nabil." I sat up, my back straight against the headboard. "Where the fuck have you been?"

He looked away, blinking fast like he'd been caught in a lie, before sitting up against the headboard beside me. He was silent for some time, then tentatively started to explain. "It was too much, Sara. Feeling like an outsider in Kuwait. And my parents, always with their pressure on us to excel, to not make any mistakes because we were setting some kind of example as Palestinians. Then the invasion, and everything becoming a thousand times worse for them, and so for me, too. All I wanted was to escape, to find something for myself." Freeing himself from all of that, finding his footing elsewhere, he said, necessitated a guillotined severing of the past. "It was the only way I knew how to do it. I couldn't be two people at once, Sara. Not even for you."

His words could have been my brother's, and that made them even harder to hear. "And now you can?"

"Now I don't need to. I'm here. And you're here. You could have gone anywhere, could have stayed in California. But you came here, close to where you knew I was. Am I wrong?" He wasn't wrong, and his words made my insides roil, but I couldn't give in to it yet.

"Nabil—that summer after you graduated, I had an abortion." I sketched out what had happened without emotion, with the fewest possible words. As I spoke, I looked dead ahead, but I could sense Nabil stiffen.

"Why didn't you tell me?" he asked.

"You were already gone."

"You could have called me."

"I didn't have your number in the States. You didn't give it to me."

"You could have gotten it from my mother."

"Your mother would never have given me your number, Nabil." He knew I was right about that, which gave me some satisfaction. "The point is, you were gone. Would you have come back if I had told you?"

He exhaled heavily and ran his hands through his hair. "Why are you telling me this now?" He left my question unanswered, and I couldn't tell if he was angry or just confused.

I thought for a second. "If we're going to start again, you need to know. I don't want to carry it alone anymore." What I had done had saved us both. I needed him to acknowledge that. He didn't, but I decided to give him time.

We spent the next two days naked in bed. We left only to shower, to make tea and sandwiches, which we brought back into bed with us. We talked about friends we knew, what had happened to them during and after the invasion, about the people we had been with since each other, which didn't arouse jealousy because it felt so remote, like it had happened to someone else. Mostly what we did in that bed was fuck, over and over again, like we were starving. He kissed me with his arm hooked around my back, pulling me in tight, planting his lips on mine so long, the only breath I could inhale was his. We stared at each other for hours, like we had when we were teenagers, noticing small changes. His eyes had fine lines at their corners because he squinted when he concentrated and when he smiled. He had a scar near his temple where his cat had scratched him when she was a kitten. My hair was longer, and he curled a stray strand around his fingers, gently moving it out of my eyes. He slid his hands down my legs, tracing the muscle that had developed from my incessant walking. We did everything to each other to the point of exhaustion, and then all we said was *Don't stop*. It felt overfull, and—though I couldn't have admitted it—it felt like the last time.

Neither of us brought up the abortion again. Nabil didn't say what I needed him to say, and I couldn't bring myself to prompt him. I went with him to the train station, and we kissed on the platform like in the movies. The last thing he said to me was sorry.

I didn't immediately understand what his sorry—yet another one—meant. At first I figured he was sorry about the abortion. Then I thought maybe he was sorry he hadn't been able to discuss it that weekend. Every time the phone rang, I anticipated his voice, but it never was. I refused to call him. Weeks passed, and my confusion sparked to anger. Who did he think he was? Materializing at my door after six years like nothing had happened. Assuming I would take him back, no questions asked. And then, after learning what I had gone through, turning himself into the injured party, the one who hadn't been told. This was Arab male sexism at its finest. For all his talk about separating himself, finding his own way, Nabil had turned into his judgmental mother. If this was how he was going to react to a decision that had saved his ass as much as it had saved mine, that was tough shit. This time, I thought, I was done with him for good.

I met Ethan in the fall of my second year at Brown. He was a graduate student in the Department of Modern Culture and Media.

We were in a seminar together on theories of modernity and post-modernity. After one of our classes, he told me that he had liked my presentation on Lyotard and the future anterior.

"Nobody asked any questions," I said.

"We were stunned silent."

I checked to see if he was kidding. "That might not be a good thing."

"It was pretty impressive, Sara. It's Sara, right?"

"Yeah. And you're Ethan." Ethan looked like a young Elvis Costello, with his obligatory heavy-framed glasses and striped scarf. "Thanks. About my presentation."

"It's true. Want to go down to Wickenden for sushi?"

"Sure."

It was as simple as that, without the baggage of a shared past, shared brother, or shared fetus between us. Ethan was sunny and sweet. Soon we were cooking meals together, doing each other's laundry, watching films we rented from Acme Video, reading in bed late into the night. Together we went to the very first Water-Fire, an installation of bonfires on the downtown rivers.

He asked me questions about Kuwait and the invasion, which I answered formally, like I was giving an interview. He asked about my father, and, surprising myself, I was able to articulate my mixed feelings. Dad had been a distant man. Karim and I had never doubted his love for us, but it was not a love that cuddled or consoled. In answering Ethan's questions, I discovered that I was mad at my father for letting my brother down and, I suspected, my mother, too. But I discovered, also, that I missed him. His calm, stable presence, his reliable, problem-solving self. Ethan's questions took me to the edge of my father's violent end, but I didn't want to talk about that. When I tried to, my lungs filled with phantom water I couldn't expel.

Ethan and I had been together only six months when Mom called in the middle of a cold night in March to tell me that Mama Lulwa had died in her sleep. "The best kind of death, Sara. We should all be so lucky." Mama Lulwa had followed the path set by her siblings. Her brother, Ahmed, had died at the age of eighty-nine in 1992. Her sister Sumaiyya died a year later at the age of eighty-eight. Hussa went next, in 1994, aged eighty-seven. Mama Lulwa was certain— as she had shared with Mama Yasmine over tea—that her life would end, as it did, in 1995, a few months short of eighty-six.

I thrust my frozen feet into the flannel-covered duvet. The heat must have switched off. I closed my eyes and saw Mama Lulwa's birds. "Will you take Bebe Mitu?"

My mother hesitated for a second. "Okay."

"I'm sorry, Mom."

"Life goes on, Sara. It does until it doesn't." She chuckled, and it was peculiar to hear her so close in the brittle New England night.

"I should come," I said. I tried to remember my spring break dates.

"Don't you dare. Your job is to study. Come in summer, if you must."

"Why don't you come here after the 'azza? The weather's turning already." I lied; it was snowing, not a hint of leaf buds on trees. "It'll be spring in April. Come then. You need a change. We can go to New York or Boston for the weekend."

"I don't want to leave Mama Yasmine. She's taking it harder

than any of us. Maybe I'll come back with you in the summer for a few weeks. We'll see."

She wouldn't come. She never traveled anymore. Much as she complained about everything in Kuwait, my mother stayed. She stayed the way Mama Lulwa had stayed, willing captive of Mama Sheikha.

Unhinged time, I decided, was what I wanted to write about in my dissertation. "Traveling Through Time in the Middle East: Memory, Becomings, Futurity" journeyed through philosophical conceptualizations of time, bringing them to bear on how we might reconsider the region's colonial past, its neocolonial or globalized present, and its unknown, potentially better future. I used Spinoza—prince of philosophers—and Nietzsche. I navigated through Bergson and Deleuze to examine the Middle East through the lens of time. Not l'étendu—chronological, normative, forward-thrusting clock time—but la durée—time in motion, in flux, refusing to persist along any given line, gliding out of the past into the present and future.

I explored these paradoxical shimmers in the contexts of Palestine before 1948, Iraq before 1979, and Kuwait before 1990. I traced the unseen path of marginal, incidental, but nonetheless promising moments in order to consider if, where, and when they had emerged and might emerge again. I made connections between events and people that appeared unrelated or far-removed. I was on the prowl for discarded secrets in the detritus of history. Overprint colonial stamps circulating in Jerusalem, Jaffa, and Haifa years before the British Mandate. Remnants of the arched reed homes that once flourished in the marshlands of the Tigris and

Euphrates. The music of Saleh and Daoud Al-Kuwaiti, Kuwaiti Jews of Iraqi origin, superstars of their time in the Arab world. Their first oud and violin were gifts brought back from India by their uncle, a merchant, who, it's not impossible to believe, may have dealt with my great-grandfather.

My dissertation collected such fragments and illuminated them from the perspective of durational time, Proust's time. The narrative developed through the process of becoming, disappearing, then appearing again, only to vanish once more. From form into formlessness, from the actual into the effervescent virtual.

Time is, as Hamlet declared, "out of joint." It cannot be contained and that, I argued, made it politically and ethically relevant to analyses of contemporary geographies under threat, such as the Middle East. If time is not linear, then the potential for some untimely seed from the past, something singular and mercurial, is eternally present. Anything can happen at any moment and never in the same way as before. Nothing is definitively predetermined, and this opens up a potential future different from the one anticipated by those in power. Mine was an optimistic, affirmative study, one that advanced the full glory of what life in the region could yet become.

I was offered a tenure-track position at UC Berkeley set to begin in the fall of 1999. The job market in philosophy was brutal, so I understood exactly how lucky I was. I was ecstatic. Karim and I spoke on the phone more regularly, saw each other whenever we could. He was still with Jonathan, whom I adored. My return made sense.

Ethan was less lucky. In the process of writing his dissertation, he had become more balled up and unsure. He read and read, took notes and made outlines, but he couldn't seem to move beyond that. He went to conferences and came back convinced that everyone in his field was smarter than him, that they would snatch up every scarce job before he finished a single chapter. I tried to convince him that a dissertation was the start of a career, not the end of it, to no avail.

I had kept Ethan a secret from my mother all through graduate school. He accepted my decision because he believed it had something to do with Islam. He never asked if he could come with me to Kuwait. He dutifully respected cultural differences that weren't there.

By the time I got the offer, we were more friends than lovers. Our platonic companionship seemed enough for him, and in the throes of dissertation writing and job applications, it had been enough for me. My upcoming move to California felt like a natural conclusion to what was already over. Since I had been hired, I hadn't said a word to Ethan about the possibility of his joining me. I thought my intentions were clear, but one afternoon, Ethan disclosed that he was moving to Berkeley, too. He could write from anywhere, he said, would look for an adjunct position at Berkeley City College or some other community college.

I didn't dissuade Ethan from coming with me. I put my inaction down to academic exhaustion. I lacked the energy for confrontation, I told myself. So that summer I said yes to everything. To Ethan picking where we would live, to his saving mementos I would have tossed. To our driving cross-country, U-Haul in tow, when I would have paid for airfare and shipped our books and papers. I said yes, yes, yes, fixing time in a way I should have known by then was impossible.

July 2013

I've been practicing the retraction with Sana every day. The classical Arabic is tricky for me, so we repeat, and repeat again. I remember the story of my young mother and her sister repeating their names with their tutor to erase their British-Hindi accents. My Arabic is accented too, though more American than British-Hindi.

"We need it to be as smooth as possible, so in the heat of the moment, you don't have to think about the words. As automatic, Sara, as the breath that gives you life."

"You're a poet," I say dryly.

Sana winks at me. We're in the sala waiting for Mr. Al-Baatin. Sana has been visiting his office most mornings, going over details I suddenly want nothing to do with. I hand over my fate to them on a silver platter. My mind has become a wandering vine, without the type of focus required to save myself.

Mr. Al-Baatin doesn't ring the bell anymore. He walks into the house and assumes his usual place in the sala, his hand extending down toward Lola. "Well. Eighteen days to go. How are you holding up?"

I shrug.

"She's fine, aren't you, Sara? Recite the retraction for Mr. Al-Baatin." Sana sounds like one of our elementary school Arabic teachers, asking me to recite a poem I hadn't bothered to memorize. But this time I have bothered, and I do as she asks. I deliver words to the effect that I understand the accusation against me and I officially retract the blasphemous statements I made. I've repeated the lines so often they've become meaningless, words blending into the nonsense they are.

"Good. And that will be the end of it."

A pin of doubt pricks me. The judge could see fit not to accept my retraction, forcing the trial to continue; he could find me guilty. My case would then go to the Court of Appeals and, if rejected there, on to the Court of Cassation. If the Court of Cassation rejects my contestation, then my guilty verdict stands. After that, a higher approval must be obtained before execution. By which authority, I'm not sure. I don't want any clarification on this point. I hold on to the retraction like it's a raft in the Indian Ocean.

"Any word on early dismissal, Mr. Al-Baatin?" Sana asks. I'm certain that request won't be granted. They want this to go to trial, a chance for theater.

"I suspect it'll be denied days before trial," he says, and Sana nods.

I look away, my attention distracted by a ringing neither Sana nor Mr. Al-Baatin seem to hear. The house phone. Very few people call on the house phone these days. Aasif must be out in the garden. It rings and rings, then stops.

"Is there anything worrying you, Sara, other than the obvious?" Mr. Al-Baatin leans forward and moves his hands toward mine, almost as though he's going to hold them. Unthinkingly, I reach forward and grab them. I see his alarmed eyes and offer him what I hope is a look of gratitude.

He gently squeezes my hands then retrieves his from my grip. "Well, in that case, I'll get going. You'll visit my office again this week, Sana?"

"If that's okay with you?"

"Always." He gives Lola one last scratch and heaves himself up. Sana gets up to go, too.

I walk them to the door, then out to the black iron gate. My entire life this gate has always been left open, but since the accusation, I've started locking it. I see Aasif watering the mejnooneh and remember the unanswered phone call. I reach into my pocket for my cell phone. Six missed calls from Karim. It must have been him who tried to call the house.

I walk back inside and phone my brother.

"Is everything okay?" he asks. "I've been calling. Even the house. You okay?"

"Sorry. My phone was on silent. I was with Mr. Al-Baatin and Sana when you called."

"I was worried." He does sound worried, which I find surprisingly gratifying. "Any updates?"

"Not really. Everything's hunky-dory." I try to lighten the mood.

"I've got some bad news, Sara. I can't get there until early next week. This project. I've tried everything, but it's not possible."

"Early next week is fine." I can't mask my disappointment.

"Is Karl there?" he asks. When I don't respond, he says, "You haven't told him yet, have you?"

"No."

"Sara." My name is a sigh. "Why not?"

"I'll tell him when you're here. I want you to be here for it."

"You do it the way you need to, little sister," he says with a tenderness that breaks me. "I'll be there. Later than I had hoped, but soon. You'll be all right until then?" I nod, believing he can see. "Call me for anything, promise?" I nod again as he hangs up.

What Karl and I share is the dark intimacy of violence. When he pins my arms over my head, his body heavy on mine, all the air rushes out of my lungs. I pull him in deep. I am hungry for his weight, desperate for the stillness he offers as a gift. Only in those blackening moments do the lost ones flicker into the periphery of my vision like stars.

In me he finds a pocket of sorrow deep enough to contain his own. His father blew his brains out in the family room when Karl was sixteen. The why of it remains inexplicable to him and to his mother, the two left behind to wash blood and brains and bone off walls. There was no history of depression or suicide, no extraordinary blowups between husband and wife. "It felt like a murder," Karl told me once. "Like someone took over his hands and murdered him with his own rifle." But it wasn't murder. My father's death was murder, and when Karl asks me to tell him what happened, I do, in excruciating detail, without hesitation. Not only do I tell him about my father's murder, I also tell him about my mother's and Nabil's, and telling him opens up a world.

Karl collects my pain in his hands, which becomes the restorative element he needs in order to make an imperfect peace with his father's suicide. For years we have been together while mostly apart. And yet neither of us lets go.

I pick up the phone to dial his number, only to put it down again.

2000 – 2001

It was a relief to be back at Berkeley. Professor Byrne was still there. Karim was earning a reputation for himself at a top firm in San Francisco, working on large-scale projects. He and Jonathan had Ethan and me over most Friday nights. Karim would pop open a bottle of champagne, and Jonathan would bring out olives and almonds in small ceramic bowls. Karim would slip back inside to stir whatever was on the stove, while Jonathan quizzed Ethan about obscure films only the two of them had seen. Karim would rest his hand on Jonathan's wrist, and Jonathan wouldn't notice because it was the most natural thing. Jonathan would kiss my brother if he said something clever, and my brother would grin as though the world belonged to him. They exchanged glances and private smiles, filling with intimacy interstices Ethan and I wouldn't have known what to do with. I couldn't end it with Ethan. I had allowed him to come with me all the way to California. He was a grown man making his own decisions, but I felt responsible.

My life appeared solid. My manuscript was complete, book proposal ready to submit. My essays were being accepted by peer-reviewed journals. I attended key conferences, along with more specialized symposia. My student evaluations were encouraging, and I was a valued member of various departmental committees. I was, in short, on track for a speedy promotion. Still, I couldn't shake the feeling that something was about to drop.

When the Twin Towers fell, I thought that was it. I heard about it on NPR, a few hours after it happened, and was dumbstruck by the magnitude of grievance a person could harbor to attack his own country in such an apocalyptic way. I was certain it was an inside job. "There's no way this could have been organized by Arabs. It's too sophisticated, required too much advance planning. Don't look at me like that, Ethan. I can say it; I'm Arab. And thank God! Can you imagine what would happen if this were an Arab plot? It would mean the end of the world."

How wrong and how right I turned out to be. Arabs brought down those towers. Arabs from the very country my mother had been blaming for its stranglehold on Kuwait since its liberation; for the rise in conservatism; the change in our demographic; our uncharacteristic insularity. There was going to be a long-delayed reckoning for our neighbor to the south, its arrogant pressure on the region, its defiant vying for supremacy. But that didn't happen. Instead, U.S. attention was directed toward the unfinished business in Iraq, initiated by the forgotten war that had liberated Kuwait. Saddam Hussein, who had nothing to do with 9/11, was a convenient target.

During the invasion, I had blocked out what must have been going on inside Kuwait—brutality, torture, fear, and, after liberation, the scapegoating of innocents. My father had been a victim of it, and yet even that I had managed to seal up tightly and tuck away so that I could proceed with the course I was on, the course that had taken me from Berkeley back to Berkeley, away from Kuwait, far away from my mother. I listened, on the radio Ethan insisted we leave on every second of the day, to stories about victims and culprits, about who had done what, and what would be done for revenge. That word wasn't used, but it was intended. As hours passed, I fell deeper and deeper into what the invasion must have felt like for my mother, counting the minutes in my grandfather's study, waiting for my father. Descriptions of 9/11 blurred in my mind with images I remembered from CNN of the aerial attacks on Iraq, those uncanny green, night-vision videos of exploding buildings that contained who knew what or who. I remembered images of hundreds of burned bodies, not all of them military, along Highway 80, the Highway of Death, where Iraqis and others retreating to Basra, my father's former home, were pulverized by allied forces. A cease-fire was called the following day, of no use to them. I hadn't allowed myself to think of them, incinerated from above, but the recently incinerated in New York were bringing it all back, and the somersaulting of time left me uncertain and afraid.

"We have to buy a TV," Ethan announced on the fifteenth of September.

I glanced up from Spinoza's *Tractatus Theologico-Politicus*, which I was reading for solace. "What for?"

"There's going to be war. I need to be able to follow the news as it happens."

I bristled at his certainty, feeling the resistance my peers in Professor Byrne's class must have felt. "You can follow it on the radio."

"I need images. This is going to be a war of images." It was a very Modern Culture and Media thing to say.

"So was the Gulf War. Nothing but images covering up dead bodies. Trust me, these are not images you want in your head. You'll end up like me." The words had formed without my control. *Like me, numb. Like me, detached. Like me, slow to change course.* I didn't say these things out loud, but I thought them for the first time. "Is that what you want?"

Ethan didn't ask what I meant. He grabbed his gray hoodie and left the house. He went to Best Buy and bought a huge television set our living room couldn't possibly accommodate. It was a patriotic act. He would have to figure out on his own that no amount of CNN would provide elucidation or consolation. There could be no return to the tenth of September 2001, just as there could be no return to the first of August 1990. But Ethan needed to reel with his country, so I put on headphones and left him to watch his TV.

Toward the end of November, I got a call from Sana, with whom I had reconnected via email a few years earlier. She was crying so hard I couldn't make out what she was saying. I heard "One of the planes." Then I heard "Nabil."

Instantly, I knew.

"What about Nabil?" I asked anyway.

"You don't know? Karim didn't tell you?" She was stalling, but it didn't matter. I knew. I knew.

"Tell me what?" I needed her to say it.

"Nabil worked above the ninety-second floor in the North Tower. Sara, he's dead." I hung up on her. There was nothing left to hear.

I hadn't gone looking for names after 9/11. I figured names would find me if they were meant to, like a trail of crumbs. I had thought about Nabil, but when no one had mentioned him those first few days, I thought he must be safe. He'd been dead for two months. I picked up the phone and dialed my brother's number.

"Karim." I couldn't say another word.

"You heard." His words stabbed me.

"You knew?"

"Faris told me."

"Why didn't you tell me, Karim?" I fell to my knees. "Why didn't anyone tell me?" I wailed so loudly Ethan rushed to the room, his eyes and mouth in circles of shock. The sound emerging from my throat was the sound a frightened forest animal makes in the darkest night. It was a sound impossible to imagine a human body capable of.

"I didn't tell you, little sister, because I couldn't be the one to hurt you like this. I'm so sorry. I really am."

For the second time that night, I hung up without saying goodbye. Ethan kneeled beside me on the floor. As my head spun to black, I could hear him murmuring words he must have thought were soothing. He didn't touch me. I wished that Ethan's arms around me could provide comfort, but I recognized with the cruel insight only death affords that Nabil's arms were the ones I wanted, and those arms I could never have.

We spent every Thanksgiving with Ethan's family in D.C., but that year I told him to go alone. I was churning with an out-of-control resentment. Ethan's country had been attacked, his home district directly hit. But I was the one who had suffered the bloody loss of an actual human being I loved. What were the chances? My fury kept me company until Ethan left, interrupted only by the horror of trying to imagine what a brain can piece together in the seconds before hitting the ground.

Karim came to stay while Ethan was in D.C. He crawled into bed with me and held me in his arms for days. I couldn't speak, but that didn't matter; my brother was my brother again. I slept because he rocked me to sleep, and when I woke up, still in his arms, I would remember what had happened to Nabil and moan.

I couldn't rein in the enormity of my loss, all out of proportion with the reality of what had transpired between us. It wouldn't make sense to anyone, not even to me, if logic ruled my sense of Nabil. A teenager I had once loved and who had once loved me. A man who had ignored me for years and years. Who had made one phone call late at night to condole and apologize. Who had visited once and made love to me for days. Who had fucked off after learning about an abortion I had suffered alone. This man, making money in a tall building to purchase a freedom he could never fully own as an exiled Palestinian, surely was not worth the sorrow that would have shattered me if my brother wasn't holding me together.

I spent the next month, ahead of my annual winter trip to Kuwait, scouring images. Nabil worked at a desk high in the sky. He was killed when the buildings fell. These were the facts. But I believed he would have made the decision to jump. I examined every image I could to confirm my hunch, desperate to recognize something of Nabil in an arched back or bent knee.

There weren't many in newspapers. I had to actively search online. I made special requests to photographers, who reluctantly sent their photos by email, figuring they were providing closure to some tormented soul. I examined the photos, vomited into the wastebasket beside my desk, wiped my mouth on a tea towel, then continued my investigation. I held a large magnifying glass in hand, a sad caricature of a crack detective. I sat hunched over my computer for hours, from the minute I returned home from my classes until dawn. I dozed at my desk, woke to my alarm clock, got ready for another day of teaching, then returned home to more investigating. I was trying to solve a crime so that I didn't have to consider what that crime was sure to unleash in the region where my mother, Maria, and Mama Yasmine resided.

Ethan watched, helpless, as I spent night after night at my task. I had described Nabil to him as an old school friend, but Ethan knew from my howl that night that Nabil was more than that. I had made no move to reconnect with Nabil in eight years, nor had he with me. And yet knowing he no longer existed in the world was intolerable.

Karim had mentioned to Mom that he was coming to Kuwait for Christmas. "Can you believe it, Sara? He said it like it was not the most unbelievable thing. 'I'm coming to visit, Mom, if that's okay?' How could it not be?" Mom had sold the condo in Orange County years before and no longer visited the States. Her contact with my brother was a phone call twice a month.

"Don't get your hopes up. It could be a 9/11 moment. That sort of thing has been happening, you know." I found it hard to believe Karim would follow through with the visit, and I didn't want Mom and Maria to be disappointed when I got off the plane alone. "I'll be there in a week. You can count on that."

"I'll pick you both up at the airport."

"You don't need to do that, Mom," I said, but I wanted her to. I missed my mother with an ache the size of a galaxy. I wanted to tell her about Nabil and about Ethan and about the mess I had made of it. I wanted us to fling open everything we had so tightly sealed in compartments for too long.

"I'll be there."

When the phone rang in the middle of the night two days later, I braced myself. It was Karim.

"Sara?" His voice was hoarse. "Sara, it's Mom. She was hit by a car. She's dead, little sister. We need to go back. I've booked tickets. We leave tomorrow night."

Those words had no business coming out of his mouth. I ignored them. "I already have my Christmas ticket."

"Sara, did you hear what I said? Mom's dead. I've got tickets. Forget your ticket. I'll pick you up tomorrow night at six. Do you understand what I'm saying?"

"Yes."

"Is Ethan there with you?"

"Yes."

"Okay. See you tomorrow."

I remember taking a searing shower and shaving my legs. I remember getting down on my hands and knees and scouring the gray ring around the tub. I remember taking down jars full of coins from the shelf over the fridge and sorting them into roll wrappers I had picked up at the bank months before. Ethan found me cross-legged on the kitchen floor the next morning, sorting coins. I told him about my mother. He held me, but I didn't cry. I told him I would be returning to Kuwait that night.

"I'll go with you."

"I'm going with Karim."

"I'll come as well. You need me."

"I need to do this alone," I said.

We had been together seven years. He didn't say anything, but he was thinking: *She needs to do everything alone, and since she needs to do everything alone, what's the point of me?* I could read his earnest green eyes, and in my closed heart I responded: *None.*

On the flights back, I drowned in sleep, my head glued to Karim's shoulder. My body was rubber, my exhaustion boundless. His smell was as familiar to me as the smell of dust in central air conditioners switched on in early spring. His smell was what made it possible for me to sleep on those planes as though my mother hadn't been hit by a car, like she'd be at the airport to greet us. To sleep as if we were returning home, and home was an unravaged place.

Only when the airplane began its descent into Kuwait did I start to wake up. I couldn't stop shivering. The sound of my chattering teeth alarmed the flight attendant. Karim assured her I was fine, that another blanket would do the trick. I gazed out the oval window for the first time since boarding in San Francisco, hand against jaw to still my teeth. I saw fields of twinkling amber lights. I shut my eyes, and points of cobalt flickered in my head.

Berkeley and Ethan, Mom's body and Kuwait. I pulled the paper bag from the seat pocket in front of me and vomited acid. Karim handed me his handkerchief and looked away.

Karim and I arrived late at night. Maria was waiting for us, leaning against one of the arched pillars surrounding the indoor pool, her face streaked with sorrow. I kissed her, and she shed the tears I could not. We trudged to our rooms and slept.

Early the next morning, an hour before sunrise, I was driven by someone—I can't remember who, but it wasn't Karim—to the washroom at the Sulaibikhat cemetery. It had been arranged for my mother's body to be transported there by ambulance from the hospital morgue. Waiting for me were two Pakistani ritual washers employed by the municipality to wash the bodies of dead women and girls.

"'Atham Allah ajritch," they said, expressing their condolences.

"Ajirna-w-ajritch," I answered mechanically.

"If you prefer, you can wait here in the entryway until we're done. But if you'd like to join us in the washroom, you may."

I nodded, and one of the women, around my mother's age, held me by the arm, concerned I might fall. She whispered near my ear, "We're with you."

The room was fully tiled. Even the ceilings. Tiles diamond-shaped and blue like an open sky. My mother had been placed upon a long, tiled slab. I went to her. The same woman was at my side again, her arm hooked with mine. I remember bending down and kissing my mother on the forehead. I did not fall to the ground. I did not cry or make a sound.

"I'll watch first," I said. "Let me know what to do."

They set to work.

The washing of bodies is work our government pays people to do. I held up my mother's arm or my mother's leg so that the two women, Faiza and Firdous, could perform the rites. I placed camphor-soaked cotton into my mother's mouth. I lifted her body to one side, then the other, so that the white shroud could be slipped under her and over her and under her again. A mother becomes a body to lift and shroud.

I knew on that first night I walked through the French doors of our motherless house that I was going to stay. The house had not shrunk the way childhood homes are supposed to with time. Over the next two weeks, Karim took care of the paperwork that attaches to death like a barnacle. Signatures and transfers and the agony of dealing with the family of the boy without a driver's license who had killed our mother on one of her evening walks.

When I told Karim that I planned to remain in Kuwait, he put the house in my name. But after Mom's 'azza, he tried to convince me to leave with him. We sat barefoot in the wet grass of our dead mother's garden. I pressed the soles of my feet against his. It was a cold morning, but we had walked out with no shoes on, the way we had as kids.

"Don't you get it, Sara? We're free. We'll sell the house, Mom's bookshop. Return to your life in Berkeley, to Ethan, your job. You're happy there, aren't you? She's gone. If you didn't come back for her when Dad died, why would you now?"

I had no answer for him. Neither of us spoke for some time.

"Mom knew about Matt and me, you know." He rubbed his

feet against mine distractedly as he spoke. "I saw her following us once, the third summer I was with him. She dropped me off at Mission Viejo Library, Matt picked me up, and I'm pretty sure I saw her car in the rearview mirror."

I hesitated. "So what if she knew?"

"She never said anything."

I remember Mom interrogating Karim after his fight with Sami. He hadn't opened up to her, and she wouldn't have known what to do with it if he had. "What did you want from her?"

"I don't know." Karim shrugged. "I needed Matt. He showed me what was possible. But once I realized Mom knew and didn't say anything, I understood that what I wanted could never happen in Kuwait. I felt cut off—from her, Dad, the whole fucking country."

"Maybe if you had said something to her."

"Maybe." He shrugged again. We both knew it would have changed nothing.

"There were those arguments with Dad, remember? Those were about you. Even after you left."

Karim flinched. "How could that have made it better, Sara?"

I had read Mom's outbursts with Dad during that period as evidence of her devotion to Karim. To Karim, their arguments, which we listened to cowering together like broken-winged birds outside their bedroom door, must have felt like emotional destruction, not maternal loyalty.

"What does it matter?" He stretched out his long legs, severing our connection. "They're gone. What matters, Sara, little sister of mine, is that we're free. No family, no country, no nothing. You can do whatever you want." He sat on his knees facing me and said solemnly, "I want you to leave."

But against everything I thought I knew about myself, against my brother's wishes, against my better judgment, that was not what I wanted. I studied my brother's searching eyes and did not say a thing.

July 2013

I have been as unlucky as anyone, luckier than most. It has been as unfair or as fair for me as it has been for all. This morning I remember one of the few things my mother said about my father's murder: "They were executed, Sara. Let's not disinfect reality. Their deaths are like deaths in Palestine or Chile, all the damaged elsewheres. The millions of lynched, massacred, gassed, and bombed." Commonality, not exceptionality, consoled my mother. It was personal, but also it really wasn't. By depersonalizing the personal, the present begins to make sense.

Mr. Al-Baatin's weekly visit is unremarkable. As the date of my trial grows nearer, the acute urgency of the early days seems to diminish for both him and me. It's like we're swimming in a fish tank surrounded by glass walls we believe we can glide through, stunned when we bump up against them, unable to pass into the sea beyond. That I should be feeling this way is at least moderately understandable. That my lawyer has landed in a similar funk is troubling. I put it down to the calm before the storm. He's gearing up, I tell myself, preparing for the fight of his career, maybe his last.

Sana visits his office every morning, and afterward, most days, she comes to update me. There's not much to report. The parameters of the case are known. Brief notices appear sporadically in the newspapers, but the supportive editorials are gone, which likely has to do with the fact that the majority believes that what's happening to me is right. Populations end up with the governments they deserve. My California colleagues would burn me at the stake for saying so, but California is a different planet—my brother's planet, no longer mine.

My retraction has become so much a part of me, it echoes in my sleep. I recite it through my waking hours, during my long swims. I think of my mother, who knew that her impulse to leave Kuwait after the invasion was right, and stayed anyway, choosing the path she thought she should rather than the one she wanted. She was without a husband, children, grandchildren, with few social obligations, few friends, in a country nearly unrecognizable to her. She walked alone, and she died in an ambulance surrounded by strangers.

My decision to return to Kuwait after Mom died was an extension of her decision to stay. It's what I believed was right at the time. For Maria, I told myself, whose son, Salvador, had died of a heart attack in 1995, her sister Anna a year before that. For Maria, who had nowhere other than Kuwait, and who needed my kefala in order to maintain her residency permit. For Mama Yasmine, who wept on my shoulder for my mother the way she must have wept for her sons ten years before. Maria, Mama Yasmine, our Surra house, Curiosity Bookshop—I'm beginning to see that these were not the only reasons I stayed. It wasn't out of duty. *You're still Kuwaiti*, my mother had said, a lifetime ago, when she forced me to go to Berkeley instead of Brown, when there still might have been a chance for something with Nabil. The difference between my mother and me is that Mom always knew what she wanted, even if she didn't act on it. I haven't known my desire for a long time.

I came back to Kuwait to collect shards, as many as I could, to piece them into a shape that might add up to something worthwhile.

I head to the airport to pick up Karim, who hasn't been back here in over a decade. The first thing he says is "You look so much like Mom."

"I do?"

"Yeah, you do." He kisses me on both cheeks and pulls me in. I hug him tight and don't let go. Let them arrest me for it. I can smell the stench of flight on him, but under that I smell my brother, and for the first time since this mess started, I feel safe.

Reluctantly we pull apart. As we head out to the car park, he points around us. "What's all this?"

"What do you mean?"

"Who are all these people?" I realize he means the women in black, the men in red and white.

"Haven't you heard? This is the new Kuwait."

If I'm disconnected from the reality of this country, my brother is in outer space. We arrive home from the airport, he takes a quick shower, and we walk around the garden in the barely tolerable evening heat. He listens to the story of my case with the self-righteous ears of an American, and I find myself defending the other side.

"She's a bitch."

"But a victim, too."

"Fuck that, Sara. I'm sick of hearing about these women as victims. It's condescending and way off target."

"Give me a little credit, Karim. I know these girls. Their lives are nothing like ours were."

"So what? There are all kinds of families. There always have been. It doesn't have to turn into this."

"It's"—I remember the chair of my department all those years ago and smile—"complicated?"

"That's a cop-out."

"I don't know, Karim. Life is more nuanced beyond the coastal U.S." I don't understand why I feel so defensive all of a sudden.

"But your lawyer thinks everything will go according to plan, right?"

I try to think of the best way to explain to my brother, away for so long, how nothing can be relied on here anymore, how unstable the foundation has become. And then it hits me: Karim has known this since he was a kid; I'm the one playing catch-up. "Mr. Al-Baatin said something a couple of days ago about courts being more unpredictable, that it's difficult to gauge things like before. I think he was just comparing things in general to the past, not assessing my particular chances. But the encounter left me . . . a bit less assured. Maybe *assured* isn't the right word. Things feel a little dangerous."

"Sara, you've been telling me everything's under control, that your lawyer is confident that a retraction will be accepted and that will be the end of it." The terror on my brother's face awakens a terror in me that has been lying dormant. I've been coasting along, when, in fact, I should have been plotting a dramatic get-away or garnering a more international defense, anything other than passively twiddling my thumbs.

"Maybe I've misjudged." Tears blur my vision. How can Maria be dead? How is Karim in Kuwait? How is it that I might hang? I feel like the wind has been knocked out of me.

"I'm going to phone Sana. She would have called me if she had doubts. This must be under control. She wouldn't let you down." I'm sweating buckets and shivering. Karim wipes down my forehead with his handkerchief, which I can't believe he still carries. "Let's get you to bed."

If my mother had crossed the road one minute earlier or later. If Nabil had woken up with a cold and skipped work that Tuesday morning. If my father's accent had been Kuwaiti, not Basrawi. A violence in our lives so persistent, it's the stuff of fairy tales, the ones where children end up in ovens or inside the stomachs of wolves. These shards I've been collecting, fitting together one by one, are rapidly coming apart. And they're sharp enough to slit wrists.

2002–2005

It was easy to vacuum up my life at Berkeley. My colleagues were sorry to see me go, but not sorry enough to say the words that would have convinced me to stay. When I returned in April to resign my position, the chairperson of our department sat me down on a teal leather couch in her office. Teal struck me as an odd color for leather. I noticed that the paint was peeling in the upper right corner of her otherwise unblemished office walls. I remember debating whether I should point it out to her. I also remember one of the things she said during our hour-long meeting: "They say not to make any life-altering decisions in the first year of grief."

"Who says that?"

"Psychologists."

"And what do philosophers say?"

"The same, I would think." She smiled and rubbed her eyes. She seemed thoroughly perplexed. "Stay in Kuwait for the year, Sara. One year to grieve your mother. If you feel the same at the end of it, I'll happily accept your resignation." I refused her generosity, tendered my letter of resignation. Soon after, I secured a job at Kuwait University, where philosophy professors were at a premium.

Ethan knew it was over when I boarded the plane with Karim, not him. By the time I returned to settle things in Berkeley, he had already packed his bags and gone.

I sold my car, the few things I owned. It was easy to throw out or donate most of what I had accumulated over the last twelve years in the States. I boxed up and shipped my books and papers, the only belongings that mattered.

I didn't consider which books were at the top of the packed cardboard boxes, so when the customs officer in Kuwait sliced one open for the obligatory inspection, he got an eyeful of naked bodies. It was my Orientalism box. I made a joke about nineteenth-century European desire and young Arab boys. The man looked at me like I was insane and glared at the books with the eyes of a rabid goat. I noticed his scraggly beard and his prayer mat unrolled in the corner of the room, as though prayer time was continuous, not five times a day.

"Who are you?" he asked.

I pointed at my Civil ID card in his hand. "What do you mean?"

"Who are you to bring in this filth?"

"I'm a professor at Kuwait University."

"You teach these books at Kuwait University?"

"I will."

"Shame on you. Shame on Kuwait University." He looked like he might spit. "This won't last. You wait." He taped up the box and signaled to the heavy-eyed Bangladeshi porter to come collect the boxes. "Yallah, rouhay!" He ordered me to go through gritted teeth.

At the time I didn't understand the stakes of his gelatinous disgust. I didn't realize how lucky I was that he didn't take that disgust as far as he could. I was glad to have my books intact and didn't give him or his beard much thought. In retrospect, this man was my welcome party to the new Kuwait.

I tried to figure out how Kuwait could have gone from bikinis at the Gazelle Club to niqabs in mosques in the span of a single decade. I put my best academic skills to work, probing colleagues in various departments, taking notes, reading newspaper articles, interviewing the few remaining parents of Palestinian friends, as well as members of the Kuwaiti resistance to the Iraqi invasion.

Occasionally, at the neighborhood co-op supermarket, I would run into my parents' old friends. They would kiss me on both cheeks, tell me how much my parents were missed. I would wait for them to finish, then bombard them with questions about what they remembered about the invasion, how it had changed them. Inevitably they would take a step back, their wooden responses almost identical. *That's behind us. You don't want to know about all that.* No one gave me the answers I needed.

One morning in early January, during my first mid-year break from teaching at Kuwait University, I woke up with the notion that if there was anywhere I could find the elusive thing I was seeking, it would be at the Gazelle Club. Encouraged by the cobalt blue skies and cool temperatures of a desert winter, I drove the familiar route toward Abu Hulaifa—no longer called Abu Hulaifa, renamed something that sounded like the word *crazy* in Arabic, which seemed apt.

The Gazelle Club had been destroyed by Iraqi troops during

the invasion, and the owners hadn't wanted to rebuild, for reasons having to do with the sanctification of the country. The old hand-painted sign still hung over the entrance, sun-faded red script in Arabic, blue in English. The entrance itself was bricked up, so I scrambled over the adjacent wall; there was no security guard to stop me.

The vast swimming pool—my memory had not exaggerated its size—was partly stripped of its blue tiles. The modern Art Deco building, which had housed the reception area, the restaurants, bowling alley, cinema, and nightclub, remained standing, but the windows were shattered, the ceiling panels removed and scattered over the floors like a clumsy magician's deck of cards. Indoor furniture was missing, walls graffitied. Palm trees lining the swimming pool carried the dry weight of a decade of unpruned fronds. The concrete jetty that ran along the beach, parallel to the length of the club, was the least altered of the club's structures; even when I was a kid it had seemed a kind of ruin, with its sharp broken stones and jutting steel girders.

The beach was empty that morning. A colleague had warned me that all the beaches had been sown with mines during the invasion, and that after liberation, small, carefully placed red flags had signaled danger to the unsuspecting. There were no red flags on this beach, so I walked on the sand and crawled under the jetty. I sat in the place where Karim and I, and often Nabil, used to sit for hours, listening to the vicissitudes of time in the echo of eroding waves.

That morning those waves carried the sound of my mother's voice commanding Karim and me to return to the pool area to dry off before we headed home. Nabil's hollering until he found us, and then the sound of his breathing harmonizing with ours. Karim's patient explanations about undulations and constellations and winds, wisdom passed down from our seafaring ancestors as a murmur in the blood. Sitting under that jetty, enclosed in the lull of waves, I remembered how much we had loved it here. At the time we wouldn't have identified what we loved as Kuwait. It was the Gazelle Club, our Surra home, our school, our mother's bookshop. It was Maria, our parents, our grandparents, our friends. But it was Kuwait that had made it align as it had for us and for so many. We had taken it for granted, my mother, my brother, and me. My father alone had sustained until the end a golden vision of the whole.

It was that gold I was hoping to reclaim at the Gazelle Club, and I did find filaments of it. But I also found chunks of scrap. In Kuwait I had been half American, half something else, maybe Kuwaiti. My language had been half English, half Hindi, maybe some Arabic. Half American School values, half Arab. I was half St. Louis, half Surra. Half my mother's daughter, half Maria's. Half my own person, half my brother's little sister. This was not a new realization, but my time in the States had blunted how bifurcated I had always felt here.

Kuwait was bifurcated, too. Half seafaring, half desert. Half pre-oil, half oil. Half traditional, half modern. Half cosmopolitan, half Islamist. Half democratic, half monarchist. Half consumerist, half religious. Half Kuwaiti, half non-Kuwaiti. Halves that multiplied ad infinitum. And as they multiplied—with their divisions and splits—the country disintegrated under our feet. There was no going back, but going forward was fraught with peril. This story was old, not mine or Kuwait's alone. Even the greatest of empires fall, and little Kuwait was no empire and, for a long time, far from great. After some futile flopping and fluttering, all struggle would cease. I inhaled the salty air into my lungs, then crawled out from under that obsolete jetty.

The American invasion of Iraq began a couple of months later, in March. Sirens went off a few times a day, warning of possible Scud attacks. A few Iraqi missiles landed in Kuwait, none with the chemical warheads that had allegedly necessitated the attack in the first place. I turned Maria's bedroom into a safe room, using duct tape to seal the windows. At each scream of the siren, Aasif would rush down from his annex to join us, and I would quickly seal any openings around the doorframe where deadly gas might seep through.

At night, Maria slept upstairs in my bedroom. During the day, we watched TV in the basement, near the safe room. We were glued to CNN, duly shocked and awed. Maria tapped her forehead, repeating a thousand aré bap rés. What else was there to say? I remembered the images on CNN from the first time, the forgotten war that marked the start of the ensuing avalanche, including this. Surgical strikes are never clean. Dust kicked up by foreign tanks in the desert dyed our cold, clear skies russet. Circles of fire asphyxiated Iraq, cradle of civilization, as civilization cheered from the sidelines. Any fool could see the outcome of this clusterfuck in advance, but the planes kept on coming.

I was curious what Ethan thought of all this. I couldn't imagine him supporting the war, but it was possible. People, even good ones, get swept up by beating drums. Karim called every day, pleading with me to leave, "At least until things die down." But we could already tell things weren't going to die down as quickly as the Americans hoped. This was just the beginning, and I felt tied to the outcome, unwilling to extricate myself from the fray. I had distanced myself during the invasion, physically and emotionally. I had been outside when my father and uncle were murdered, while my mother grieved. This time I was going to stick around.

About a week into the madness, I switched off the television and got into my car. When I was a girl, my father had told me about flamingos at the mudflats of Shuwaikh. He remembered them from when he attended secondary school there, but neither he nor Mom ever took us to see them. Now I wasn't sure if I had dreamed them up.

Kuwait was not under curfew, but the government had set up strategic checkpoints to discourage unnecessary driving. The Fifth Ring Road to Shuwaikh was almost empty. The Shuwaikh free-trade zone had been declared off-limits since the invasion of Iraq began. I managed to bypass the few guards wandering around the zone by parking on Kuwait University's Shuwaikh campus—once my father's old boarding school—and walking to the mud-flats on foot. The skies were rain gray, the mudflats the same color, and it would have been hard to distinguish sky from land if not for the unearthly pink of the flamingos.

I sat on my haunches at the edge of a paved road that ended abruptly, as if the builders hadn't realized until too late there was nowhere for it to go but into mud. There were hundreds of fla-mingos, seemingly unaffected by the fire raging up north. The place was silent apart from bird screeches and honks. It made me happy to watch them fly, legs trailing behind like paper streamers. That my father's story was true felt like grace. I was more similar to him than I would have thought back when his reserve was the quality I resented most, believing it had kept my brother apart. What would he have said about the devastation of the land of his birth? My eyelids drooped for a second to consider, lines of pink still zooming in my head, when someone behind me exclaimed, "Greater flamingos!"

I spun around. A man as tall as an iceberg with sandy blond hair stood behind me. What was he doing in the empty trade zone in Shuwaikh? "You shouldn't sneak up on a person," I rasped, hand on pounding chest.

"Forgive me." He bowed his head, his hair brushing his cheeks. "I didn't expect to see anyone here. I'm Karl." He had an absorbed look on his face. "You know, there's not that much difference between greater flamingos and lesser flamingos. More dark purple on the beaks of the lesser flamingos. And smaller."

"Are there *less* lesser flamingos than greater flamingos?"

He smiled at my ungrammatical, unfunny joke. "Yes and no. Lesser flamingos outnumber greater flamingos generally, but they're vagrants to Kuwait. For example, these are all greater flamingos. There aren't any of the lesser variety here today. But look over there." He pointed at a bird with a long, thin black beak, dull-brown feathers that made it almost invisible pecking at the mud. I hadn't noticed these birds at all until that moment. The bird let out a cheerful trill. "That's the broad-billed sandpiper. *Limicola falcinellus*. That's my bird."

Karl, it turned out, was an ornithologist from Norway with

a theory about the seasonal passage of broad-billed sandpipers through Kuwait and the Gulf region during winter. They were shore birds, satisfied with the abundance of crustaceans their long bills were so well-adapted to consume. He had been tracing their path from Sri Lanka up the west coast of India and Pakistan, farther up the Persian Gulf, then back to the top of the world.

"They leave the Arctic Circle—parts of Finland, Sweden, Russia, even Norway, my home—around July, after breeding in May and June, and head south, as far down as Tasmania, if you can believe it. I'm particularly interested in the broad-billed sandpipers in the Gulf region, Pakistan, and India. When and where exactly do they arrive, and when do they depart? Do they all continue south, or do some overwinter in place? Kuwait contains a number of Important Bird Areas, you know, exceedingly diverse. It's the southernmost boundary of the Western Palearctic. Norway forms the northernmost boundary. Kuwait is also at the heart of the Eastern Flyway."

I thought that if I didn't interrupt him, he'd never stop. "Are they going extinct? The broad-billed sandpipers?"

"No. They're a species of Least Concern—the best category for birds to be in. But their numbers are diminishing. It's not unthinkable that they might be Near Threatened in the next twenty years. That's distressing."

Iraqis were diminishing by the thousands as we spoke, and he was distressed about a bird? Maybe he sensed my annoyance because his tone softened as he went on.

"When I was a boy, my father and I used to go birding every

day in the summer months. I was attracted to the fancy birds, the king eider, for example, but my father drew my attention to the plain-looking broad-billed sandpiper. He'd say, 'This bird has traveled to Africa, the Middle East, and India. All the way to China and Australia. *This* is a bird.' My father never left Norway." I noticed his bright blue eyes darken to black. "I follow the bird and see the world."

Karl's bird-tracking trip had been cut short by the start of the war. He had been planning to go to Basra to see for himself if broad-billed sandpipers made it up there at all. His visits to reserves and seashores in Kuwait had been impeded by checkpoints. The two-star hotel he was staying at was, I knew, miserable. Without thinking, I invited him to stay with me for his last three days. He lifted an eyebrow, as did Maria when she saw a towering man with blond hair enter the French doors of our house. She asked me in Hindi if I had decided to bring home one of the birds as a pet. I laughed and introduced her to Karl.

I taught, I wrote, I maintained Curiosity Bookshop. I went to dinner parties hosted by my small group of friends, colleagues from university. I lived with Maria in my childhood home, taking in her stories about her life and my mother's. I visited Mama Yasmine, listening to her stories too, every version revealing a previously hidden angle of the people I thought I knew. All the things I hadn't asked my mother, all the things she had never told me, so much of it stored in Maria and Mama Yasmine. There was an ocean of words, a repository, waiting for me in Kuwait.

A few years after my return, I ran into Nabil's mother at the produce section of Sultan Center in Salmiya. I saw her before she saw me because I saw his eyes, thought with wonder and exquisite joy that there must have been a terrible mistake, that he wasn't dead after all. It took seconds for the disjunction between his eyes and the hijab on her head to reconnect, but those seconds felt like years. Time enough for me to compose myself.

She lost her grip on the plastic bag she had been filling, and potatoes rolled in all directions. Ignoring them, she walked up to me, took my face in both her hands and held tight, looking into my eyes with her son's eyes. She held me that way for minutes, and I let her, though I could feel people around us staring. Soon her hands fell limply to her sides, and she gazed down at her feet. "He loved you," she said, still staring down. "We crushed him, and none of it matters. None of it." She looked up at me, and this time I didn't see Nabil, I saw a mother who had lost her son. I too had lost her son, and I wondered if she could see my pain as clearly as I saw hers. "He loved you until the end."

I reached down and squeezed her hand. It was, I understood, for her that Nabil had left me. She had ended up in a country not her own because a man had chosen to deposit her here. I understood her rage, like Mama Sheikha's and Mama Yasmine's; her sense of impotence, like Mama Yeliz's and my own mother's; her blinding fear for her children, like Mama Lulwa's and Maria's. Their lives an outcome of being corralled by the men they married—and the families those men carried on their backs and in their hearts—because that was their only way forward.

But there was more to it, something to do with the damning quicksand engulfing our part of the world. It had caught hold of

Nabil from over six thousand miles away. His mother's words that day provided relief, enabling me, finally, to let him go.

My life was comfortable and discreet, and the years passed. Karl returned to Kuwait for his birds, and for me. He came into the country with a swoosh of exuberance that reminded me of the past. Kuwait remained for him a place of enchantment, where miracles happened through the birds he tracked. Iraq was off-limits because his mother insisted that no bird was worth her son's life. He came up as far as Kuwait, stayed with me, then flew home.

At first I thought of him as a diversion. When he returned, I was swept up, drawn into the present. He took me on what he called *adventures,* birding in protected areas of Kuwait I didn't know existed, full of trees and fanciful ponds. He pointed at birds I couldn't name, took notes I didn't read. He pulled out his thermos of coffee, and we sat for hours in agreeable silence.

Karl described the beauty of his homeland in words that made me wonder how he could see in Kuwait the eccentric beauty he did. He didn't probe me about my life, but his open curiosity made me want to share with him what I hadn't shared with anyone else. I narrated my story in chapters, like Mama Yasmine, and doing so allowed me to call things by their name.

Karl and I learned each other geologically and geographically. He too came from a land of oil. His land, unlike mine, managed to bypass the curse of it, making good on its promise, keeping its fjords clean. And his sandpiper, the broad-billed one, traced a shared ancestral path. Up the west coast of India, with pauses in Lebanon and Kuwait, brief stopovers in Iraq. Karl, naked in my childhood bed, charted a line with his finger across my belly, wet with our sweat, past my navel up to Kuwait, waiting, patiently, for the chance to enter Basra. His bird flew the geography of my genes. When he was inside me, and his blue eyes darkened to black, I remembered, with gratitude, what it felt like to love.

August 2013

This morning I'm telling Karl. I promised Karim last night. Karl considers life through the graceful idiom of birds. I don't know what his reaction to my case will be, and the uncertainty scares me. He's been trying to convince me to come to Norway for years. "Just a visit," he says, "to see what you think." The invitation has remained an unfulfilled promise between us for so long, I've come to take it for granted.

"I'm relieved."

"You're relieved I'm being tried for blasphemy?"

"I thought you were seeing someone else. Blasphemy seems less of a catastrophe."

I burst out laughing.

"Don't laugh! You've been evasive over the phone. You ignore most of my texts, strategically answering only a few a day. What was I supposed to think? Blasphemy didn't come to mind. How serious is this?"

"My lawyer says they'll accept a carefully worded retraction. It might be dismissed in court at the start of the trial."

"You believe him?"

I pause. "I think so."

"How could you keep something like this from me, Sara?"

His question stuns me. My silence has been a betrayal. "I'm sorry, Karl. There's been a wall around this inside me. I just couldn't bring myself to share it. Then Maria died and that made things worse."

"I figured Maria's death might have had something to do with your radio silence. I wanted to give you space." His tone is kind, not hurt, not accusing. He forgives me, or maybe he doesn't believe there is anything to forgive. "I'll book my ticket tomorrow."

"I won't be able to be seen with you in court. I'm nervous enough about Karim being there. If they don't accept my retraction—" I remember my brother's terrified face and gag on my words. "Just come after. Please." I hear the fear in my voice.

"You'll come to me. It's enough what we've done. Enough." He doesn't wait for a response, and I am thankful for that. "I want you to call me every day, twice a day."

"I will."

"I miss you, my one."

Something, I think, has been decided.

Karim and I assess the future as if a conviction is out of the question. He will help me sell the Surra house, close up shop. I will secure Aasif a job with good people, if he wants it. Or maybe he'll choose to return to Uttar Pradesh. No amount of money can ever compensate thirty-six years away from home, but I will pay him what I can from the sale of the house.

Lola has already chosen Mr. Al-Baatin. Bebe Mitu comes with

me, wherever I end up. Karim and I discuss the possibility of my moving in with him and Jonathan in San Francisco for a while. Or maybe I'll head up to Norway first, to Karl. Either way, I will quit my job, and the thought of losing the identity I have culti-vated for two decades doesn't fill me with horror. Open skies. Life can begin at forty-two.

A few days after he arrives, I drive my brother around Ku-wait City. He's disgusted by the transformed skyline, the gaudy glass and Alucobond towers clawing ever higher into a polluted sky. They overshadow the few remaining mudbrick buildings left from Mama Lulwa's time. The garish buildings are imposters, Karim grumbles, inhuman in scale and use.

We head to Souk Al-Mubarakiya, which retains its essence despite recent renovations. Beyond the neatly planned sections selling dates, vegetables, meat, fish, cheap bukhour, and flashy textiles remains a warren of unorganized stalls. Bright enameled kettles hang from tin roofs; tiffins and thermoses of all shapes; pyramids of bright powder dyes; hats with fur ear flaps and army jackets from China; pastel plastic tubs and buckets. The sellers—Iranian, Indian, Pakistani—call out their wares, their chorus ris-ing to meet the white-eared bulbuls, who take the men's cries for responses to their songs.

"All this, Sara," my brother says, sounding uncharacter-istically moved. I don't need to ask what he means. We wander through the old souk side by side.

The morning before the trial, we visit the cemetery together, dates of death in hand so we can try to locate them. I bring five razqi blossoms to place on each of their graves. We start with Ma-ria, easiest to find. Karim sits beside her headstone and cries. We locate Mama Yasmine and, with the help of the groundskeeper, Mama Lulwa. At last we find our parents, buried far away from each other, our mother beside strangers, our father beside Uncle Hisham. Someone had placed etched headstones on their graves, which is a relief. But already the names have been partially eroded by dust storms. In time they will disappear altogether.

We don't exchange a word. We don't need to. We both know this is goodbye.

2 0 0 6 – 2 0 1 2

In the summer of 2006, Israel obliterated Lebanon. Mama Yasmine harbored untold sorrow over it. Her brother, Yousef, and his wife had moved back to Lebanon at the end of the civil war, which coincided with the end of the invasion of Kuwait. They figured if they had to be in a country in need of rebuilding, it might as well be the place of their birth. Mama Yasmine had had a complicated relationship with her brother, blaming his recklessness, in part, for her decision to marry Baba Marwan, her dubious savior. But with the passage of time, she had forgiven him. And she had never stopped feeling responsible for him. After Baba Marwan died in 1978, Yousef and his wife moved back in with Mama Yasmine. Mama Yeliz, who died in 1989, had never moved out.

When Yousef left, Mama Yasmine's daughters asked her to move in with them, but she refused. She did a crossword puzzle as she drank her Turkish coffee every morning. Friends stopped by for chai al-dhaha. She listened to the radio all afternoon, even during her nap. Relatives would visit at dusk, keeping her company. She enjoyed her flower garden and ate delicious food prepared by her gardener, Siraj, who also happened to cook well.

She watched old Egyptian movies at night in bed while Julia, her Filipina maid of more than fifteen years, massaged her legs with Tiger Balm.

About a year after Israel's attack, Mama Yasmine announced her desire to visit Saida, the city she hadn't seen in over seven decades.

"Why now, Mama Yasmine?" I asked.

"To remember," she said.

"Remember what?"

She closed her eyes and swept one hand in the air. "All of it."

I think her sudden wish to go back had something to do with a doctor's visit. "It'll be protracted," the doctor had explained to me in a hallway of the Amiri Hospital as my grandmother put on her shoes in his office with the help of a nurse. "Two years. Maybe, if we're lucky, three. She's too old for chemo, and surgery is out of the question. We'll do what we can to alleviate pain and keep her home until the end."

"I'm not telling her," I said flatly. "If I do, she'll sense it. Her time will be wrecked."

The doctor didn't say anything, but he patted me on the back, gave me his cell-phone number, and told me not to hesitate to call him any time, day or night. "Your father was my professor. A good man, Allah yarhama. A great doctor. It's an honor to care for his mother."

I never told Mama Yasmine about her breast cancer diagnosis, but I suspect she knew. It was after that visit to the hospital that she began to recount to me the story of her life in earnest over my daily chai al-dhaha visits. She told it like a serial novel, ending each session with a cliffhanger. She was, in her soul, a writer. She was telling me her story, start to finish, because she hadn't fulfilled its promise and didn't want me to repeat her mistakes.

The chapter about Majid came last. "The love, as it turns out, ya Sara, of my life."

I accompanied Mama Yasmine to Saida. In the old city, we stayed at her sister-in-law's family home, the same part of Saida where her father's house used to be. Yousef, at eighty, and his wife, at eighty-four, had joined the ever-expanding circle of dead, but we were welcomed graciously by his wife's surviving family. We were given the best room in the house, with a divine view of the Mediterranean, the medieval Sea Castle, and the tiny island of Ziri. Mama Yasmine stood by the window, eyes wet, reciting lines from Abu Tammam: "'Your heart may follow its passion, / But love will always belong to the first lover. / However many homes you may live in, / Yearning will always be for the first home.'"

Her first home. Her first love. By then I had been told, many times over, the story of Saida and of Majid. Mama Yasmine had spent her life blotting out both, but there she was, compelled to wander down a path she had avoided for so long.

The people of the town remembered Mama Yasmine's father. We strolled down cobbled streets with a guide, Abu Tammam's words echoing in our minds, until we arrived at the unchanged door of my grandmother's childhood home. I asked if she wanted me to knock, but she shook her head. I wondered if she was thinking about Majid's face crying for her outside that door. She hadn't asked anyone about Majid or his family. If the people of the town remembered her father and his modest old house, they would surely have had news of Majid's prominent family, but Mama Yasmine didn't want to know.

During our last meal in Saida, my grandmother did inquire about Hikmet Bey. "He was kaimakam of the Ottomans in Saida, Jaffa, and Baqubah. My father worked for him. My mother, Yeliz Elmas, was the daughter of his cousin."

The oldest woman of the house, a matron at least one hundred years old, responded with the majesty of queens. "We remember Hikmet Bey but didn't know he was related to your mother, God rest her soul. He was a loyal man, loved Arabs more than his own kind. We heard nothing more about him after he disappeared in the twenties. Perhaps he went back to Istanbul, lived a long and prosperous life. We mustn't assume the worst."

But we all did.

The day before she died, in September 2010, Mama Yasmine held court. She was propped up against four pillows, a bedspread over her frail body, her defiant Chanel-red nails visible over the blanket. The light in the room was pinkish from the scarlet shawl thrown over the lampshade. Light bothered her eyes, so someone had used hair claws to seal her curtains, top to bottom.

Surrounded by her only remaining son, her daughters, and her grandchildren, Mama Yasmine described the colorful pansies she had planted in small clay pots and distributed around the verandas of the Basra palace. From pansies to the Pasha of Basra, dead before she married his son, to the missing Turkish bey, Mama Yasmine exuded her final energy. I knew all the stories, but I listened again, as attentively as the first time because I knew it was the last. After an hour, she leaned back against the pillows, inhaling rapidly. "I'll rest."

We took shifts in the room with her, sometimes massaging her legs. A burgundy web spread from her pretty toes up her calves, the mottling of death. When it was my turn, I crept under her covers and put my face close to hers. Her eyes were dull charcoal, no longer their extraordinary gray. I don't remember her blinking once. "I'm with you, Mama Yasmine," I whispered. "Don't be afraid."

Mama Yasmine died at dawn. With her died my mother and Mama Lulwa and my father and my uncle. When one dies, they all die again. When she heard about Mama Yasmine, Maria said, "I'm the last of the old ones left." I rubbed Maria's arm and said nothing because she was right.

The Arab Spring triggered a few demonstrations in Kuwait in 2011, calls for more political freedom and the rights of the stateless bidoun. It was a mixed bag of demonstrators, some sincere, some less so, shouting for democracy in order to pull the rug out from under it once they had it in their extremist clutches, or so it seemed to me. I didn't trust the alliances being forged in its name. Women's rights activists and Islamists don't make plausible bedfellows.

I'm not much of a joiner, but I went to a single demonstration under the Kuwait Towers. I was more curious than involved, and I thought of my mother's diverted passion for politics with guilt. The demonstrators, most of them men, left behind heaps of plastic bottles, figuring a Bangladeshi cleaning crew in yellow jumpsuits would clean up after them the next morning. I couldn't get behind that level of entitlement, not even in the name of freedom.

Still, the flourishing of an Arab Spring in other countries moved something long stalled in me—a sense that the crusty coating of religion and tradition could be sloughed off. Karim contended it would go to the dogs, as it always does here. I'm one degree more optimistic than my jaded brother because I see the event—aggregate of many disparate and singular events—from the perspective of the longue durée. A religious party may take over here, a dictator there, but the movement behind the demonstrations will persist in the bodies of those who lived it, and even those who witnessed it on television or Twitter. It will not be forgotten, and if it is forgotten in the short term, it will be picked up again at a later time, decades, maybe a century, into the future, like the stamps from Jerusalem I wrote about in my dissertation, abandoned evidence of a mingled past. On the other hand, remembered fragments could simply fall into oblivion. Hope is a broken legacy in this region, and some losses are irrecoverable. Karim, I fear, may be right.

4 August 2013

I awake from uneasy dreams, exhausted but eager for my trial to begin. One way or another, I want this limbo to be over. The request to dismiss altogether submitted by Mr. Al-Baatin to the public prosecution days after my arrest was denied early this morning. I try not to read it as an omen of the day ahead. "They're toying with us," Mr. Al-Baatin vents over the phone, "and we refuse to engage." I'm not sure we have a choice.

August is slow in Kuwait, furnace hot but unhurried, reminiscent of the forgotten days of deserted firjan and the songs of the bahaara reverberating along the coast. Before air conditioners and cars, relentless heat would impose decelerated movement, time for the mind to wander and reflect. Internet speed and the consumptive frenzy of indoor malls have superseded that calmer pace. Heat drives the majority of the population abroad, leaving behind a near-vacant country, ready to swallow up. It was no accident Saddam Hussein chose this time of year for his invasion twenty-three years ago, almost to the day.

The morning of my trial, Lola rubs herself against my calves, looking up at me as if she knows. I reach down and scratch behind her ears. I remind Aasif to feed her and Bebe Mitu. Who knows how long I'll be gone.

I wear a navy skirt and white silk blouse, the colors of my high school uniform. My concession to propriety is the long sleeves, which I button at the wrists. I keep the top open enough to reveal a gold-and-pearl necklace that belonged to Mama Lulwa looped twice around my neck. Mama Lulwa was given this necklace by her mother-in-law when she got engaged, almost ninety years ago. She was fifteen at the time. I wear a pair of my mother's high heels, a kick in the face of propriety. My nails are painted Mama Yasmine red. In my purse is Maria's sandalwood rosary. So many things borrowed, one thing blue.

"I wouldn't kill you," my brother says wryly as I sit across from him at breakfast.

"Thanks." He adds a generous glug of ilaichi milk and heaps of sugar to his tea, and I wonder how long it's been since he's had it this way. We sip in silence, waiting for Sana to pick us up.

I'm composed during the drive over. I'm not shaking and, apart from slight nausea, I don't feel unwell. I rehearse the retraction I've practiced a thousand times already. I try to forget the fact that every time I saw myself in the mirror repeating the words, my expression reflected contempt, not contrition.

We meet Mr. Al-Baatin at the Palace of Justice in the city. Because there is no exact precedent, Mr. Al-Baatin isn't sure how long the trial will take. Cases brought against journalists, writers, and owners of newspapers have ranged from a week to a year. But none of those cases were capital offenses. I suspect my trial will zip by, a sharp point to be made.

As we enter the courtroom, it's far more crowded than I

imagined it would be. Men with cameras line the back of the room. They ask to take my photo. I refuse, but they click anyway. I resist the urge to extend my elbows to prevent the wall of bodies from crushing me. "There are numerous cases on the docket," Mr. Al-Baatin explains, "not just yours." I recognize a few members of parliament and speculate whether they're witnesses for the prosecution in my case or merely curious observers. The empty seat behind the judge's bench gives pause. Whatever the man in that seat decides today will affect the trajectory of my life.

The air conditioner can't keep pace with the heat. The air is thick and muggy, and the throng of bodies releases an acrid stench that seems to intensify the more I breathe it in. An usher leads the four of us down to a row of chairs at the front, directly under the judge's bench. My case will be heard first. I sit back in the chair and wait for the process to begin.

Half an hour passes, then the bailiff calls out, "Court!" and the steady buzz in the courtroom falls silent. A few seconds later, we're instructed to rise as the judge enters. He wears a black robe, and his beard is long as a garden gnome's. The beard is unnerving. Karim squeezes my hand, and I'm not sure it's a good idea for us to be holding hands. Sana smiles at me and mouths, "It's okay." I suppose most of the judges in Kuwait at this point are bearded.

The judge is handed a portfolio and reads out a number, followed by my name. His accent is Egyptian. The authority in his tone conveys an indifferent omnipotence, and the horror it kindles in me is ancient, the kind that has been experienced by millions of humans standing against walls, in lines, at the edges of holes, falling to their knees. I feel the vibration of my father's last fear.

Mr. Al-Baatin stands up in response to the judge's question about my plea. "Not guilty," Mr. Al-Baatin booms, and then goes on to list the steps of my retraction. I'm suddenly baffled about how I can retract something if I'm pleading not guilty. What is it I'm retracting if I'm not guilty of having done anything wrong? What has become of my analytical brain that I could have over-looked the type of basic inconsistency I would have chided my first-year students for missing?

It's so humid, I think I see droplets suspended in the fetid air. I close my eyes. I hear Mr. Al-Baatin argue and the prosecutor respond. My case goes on without me.

I open my eyes at the sound of her name: Wassmiya Al-Mutlaaq. I twist around in my seat, looking for her. There are a number of women in niqab behind me; she could be any one of them. I try to catch their eyes, but none of them want to lock theirs with mine. I try to imagine her feeling guilty for what she's caused, this farce in the guise of a serious crime. But I think she must be overjoyed, collecting hasanaat from her God.

Wassmiya isn't being called up as a witness. She's introduced as the brave young student who made the recording. Mr. Al-Baatin attempts to convince the judge that the recording is inadmissible, but the judge is having none of it. Everyone is salivating to hear the recording. The judge picks at his cuticles as the lawyers argue, but after a few minutes, he strikes the bench with his hand three times and yells, "Enough! We'll hear the evidence, as planned!"

My voice on the recording is crystal clear. She must have been sitting right beside me that day. We hear the quote from Nietzsche, and then my own smug explanation. Mr. Al-Baatin attempts to distinguish between my words and Nietzsche's, but the judge, again, pounds his hand on the bench and orders the prosecution to continue.

I hear myself ask my students if they wanted to lead a squandered, decadent life, and I hear the unified sound of the girls shouting, "No!" I shiver despite the grinding heat. I've been enveloped in knee-knocking fear since the accusation, in layers of deadening apathy for far longer than that. But I hear the affirmation in that negation, one that I, like my mother, have long delayed acting on. A yes to creativity, a yes to life now, not in some future heaven, not in eternity. An affirmation of my earned capacity to think, despite every effort to stifle it. That "No!" may be damning, but it's so damn good.

I'm called to stand before the judge and made to swear on the Quran. My red nails on the book are a provocation I hope the judge notices. I'm asked if I made the statements on the recording. I answer yes, but that they were taken out of context. He hits the bench with the palm of his right hand and orders me to answer yes or no. I answer yes. The judge says that based on the statements made by me on the recording, I am guilty of blasphemy against Islam. He declares that my statements are in violation of the National Unity Law. They are also in violation of the amendment to Article 111 of the Penal Code of the State of Kuwait, dated the first of April 2013. A day of fools, I can't help but think.

According to that amendment, the judge states, I have the opportunity to recant my blasphemy before the court so that my case will be dismissed. "Sara Tarek Al-Ameed, do you recant your blasphemy before Allah and this court?"

The question is not phrased as Mr. Al-Baatin had indicated it would be. I'm flummoxed, my memorized response no longer appropriate. I hesitate and close my eyes again. I want to stab their faces—false as Alucobond towers—with Nietzsche: *This shop where they manufacture ideals seems to me to stink of lies. Resentment has found a new target.* I am that target. Maybe I deserve it, propping myself to one side for so long, silent witness to the fall. But maybe it was already too late. Before my family returned from St. Louis, perhaps even earlier than that, my mother noted the signs. Decisions were being made in the interest of power, not posterity. Justice had nothing to do with it, and foresight was blinded with sharpened spears tipped with oil.

The country belongs to the Wassmiyas now. It's their turn.

I open my eyes and take a deep breath. I see my brother's panicked face—my brother, whom my mother gave back to me because she knew in the end it would be just us. I see Sana's pleading eyes—my friend, whose existence will be the last confirmation that the world we once shared was real. They think I'm going to deviate from the script, put my life in jeopardy. I look at Mr. Al-Baatin, as out of place as I am in this alien arrangement of our desert town. I take another long breath and state: "I do."

"Case dismissed!" the judge shouts, and the room erupts in deafening sound and a violent flash of cameras. I step back, and my brother and Sana hold me as my legs give. I try to steady the rhythm of my breathing. A triumphant Mr. Al-Baatin leads us through the crowd.

I catch Wassmiya's eye on the way out. There's no space left in me to feel sorry for her. I'm led to an antechamber to sign a stack of worthless papers. I have no recollection of the drive home.

It takes less effort than I would have thought to dismantle the innards of our family home. Karim and I go through every item that belonged to our parents, and there isn't much we want to keep. As we place objects in boxes to give away, we realize that the vibrancy of our past doesn't exist in accumulated furniture or knickknacks or paintings. It exists in us. We save scattered photographs, medical articles published by our father, our mother's academic essays, elegant and bracing. I hold on to some of my grandfather's files on Kuwait, Mama Lulwa's pearl necklace, Maria's rosary, which her daughters have allowed me to keep. I tuck inside my heart a phantom copy of Mama Yasmine's lost diploma, award, and lover's note. As we pack up the books in Curiosity Bookshop to donate to our American school, I add my academic collection to the pile.

To proceed forward requires periodic turns back, even if those turns are denied, even if they hurt like hell. The past persists like a wound. If it isn't locked in place, it knocks around endlessly, without reprieve, as it did inside poor Mama Sheikha. That's what I've been doing these last eleven years: locking the past in place so that I can, again, savor its wonders. All I wanted then was to escape, but the escape I managed, like Nabil's, was haunted and incomplete. Only after a reckoning does it become possible to put ghosts to rest. It's as clear to me now as Norway's fjords.

But that's not what my country has done. There has been no gathering of shards, no consideration of what was in relation to what might have been. There was no reckoning with the invasion, nor with what preceded the invasion—the folly and squander of oil. No acknowledgment of errors, no attempt at course adjustment. A raucous, worldly port town no more. Hard work and humility mocked. Self-entitlement and stupidity celebrated. A past wiped out, not like a palimpsest—retaining traces, proof of better days—but like an Etch A Sketch—irrevocably, irredeemably gone.

If they knew my story, the women who made me, they wouldn't be disappointed. They would gather me into their generous arms, and then they would release me. I board a plane, three suitcases and an African gray parrot to my name. I leave them behind, their bones blended in barren sand. I take them with me, up to the top of the dazzling world. Together we fly, gregarious.

Author's Note

In 2013, the National Assembly of Kuwait, the elected parliament, passed an amendment to Article 111 of the country's Penal Code by a wide majority, making blasphemy a capital crime. The amir of Kuwait, who holds ultimate authority over the amendment of laws, rejected the National Assembly's decision. This work of fiction imagines otherwise.

The title of this book is taken from the following sentence in James Joyce's *A Portrait of the Artist as a Young Man*:

> *Then he was to go away for they were birds ever going and coming,*
> *building ever an unlasting home under the eaves of men's houses and ever*
> *leaving the homes they had built to wander.*

Nietzsche's quotations are from Francis Golffing's translation of *The Genealogy of Morals*, published by Anchor Books in 1956. The Rilke epigraph is from *Letters to a Young Poet*, translated by Charlie Louth and published by Penguin Books in 2011.

My depiction of seafaring life in old Kuwait is indebted to Alan Villiers's *Sons of Sinbad*; the carved bird wind vane with the feathered tail comes from his book. The following were also consulted: Mary Bruins Allison's *Doctor Mary in Arabia*; Farah Al-Nakib's *Kuwait Transformed: A History of Oil and Urban Life*; Fahad Ahmad Bishara's *A Sea of Debt: Law and Economic Life in the Western Indian Ocean, 1780–1950*; Abdul Sheriff's *Dhow Cultures of the Indian Ocean: Cosmopolitanism, Commerce and Islam*; Peter Sluglett's *Britain in Iraq: Contriving King and Country*; and Mike Pope and Stamatis Zogaris's edited volume, *Birds of Kuwait: A Comprehensive Visual Guide*. Any errors or inventions are my own.

Finally, a degree of creative license has been taken in the portrayal of some legal specifics.